The Taken

ALICE CLARK-PLATTS

PENGUIN BOOKS

PENGUIN BOOKS

UK | USA | Canada | Ireland | Australia

India | New Zealand | South Africa

Penguin Books is part of the Penguin Random House group of companies
whose addresses can be found at global.penguinrandomhouse.com

First published 2016

001

Set in 12.5/14.75pt Garamond MT Std

Typeset in India by Thomson Digital Pvt Ltd, Noida, Delhi

Printed in Great Britain by Clays Ltd, St Ives plc

A CIP catalogue record for this book is available from the British Library

ISBN:987-1-405-93592-0

www.greenpenguin.co.uk

Penguin Random House is committed to a
sustainable future for our business, our readers
and our planet. This book is made from Forest
Stewardship Council® certified paper.

PENGUIN BOOKS

The Taken

Alice Clark-Platts is a former human rights lawyer who has worked at the UN International Criminal Tribunal in connection with the Rwandan genocide and also on cases involving Winnie Mandela and the rapper Snoop Dogg. She studied at Durham University and is a graduate of the Curtis Brown creative writing course whose fiction has been shortlisted for prizes.

There was a young man of Dijon,
Who had only a little religion.
He said: 'As for me
I detest all the three,
The Father, the Son and the Pigeon.

Anon

PART ONE

. . . those promises which drew her across from
Asia to Hellas, setting sail at night, threading
the salt strait . . .

Euripides, 'Medea'

I

Tristan Snow switched on the lamp and eased himself out of bed, the scratching of the material of his pyjamas against the polyester sheets causing him to involuntarily shiver. The early light of the day lay quiet and undisturbed outside the boarding house. His mouth was thick with sleep.

Once upright, Tristan inhaled deeply through his nostrils and swallowed, centring himself. He came to standing and moved to the middle of the small room. Bending stiffly after a night in repose, he moved the prayer stool on to the damson-coloured rug at the end of the bed, noticing as he did so, that in several corners, clumps of its wool were gummed together with indiscernible dirt. Tristan concentrated on one particular patch in which something wriggled. He forced himself to watch as a louse emerged from the fibres. He continued to breathe steadily, lowering himself to bring his knees on to the worn and polished wood.

He remained there, his back as a mast on a ship, feet together behind him; his soles pink and bare. He pushed his hands together in the familiar pose, his index fingers in the shape of a steeple, as the words of the prayers rippled through his mind like a chattering stream. He fought to still the waters, to make each word count, trying to ignore the extraneous thoughts which fizzed resolutely on the periphery of his brain. His mouth was closed along with his eyes. The prayer began to work its magic.

A few moments later, Tristan started sharply at the clatter of something crashing into the window. Wings beat against the glass, causing him to open his eyes, a small furrow between his eyebrows. A bird of some kind – confused, perhaps, by the sudden noise of the railway tracks overhead.

He closed his eyes again. Breathed once more, finding his way back to that place where the clouds cleared and he was in that state of blissful, silent white. He remained there for some time, calm and still.

He didn't notice the door opening quietly behind him. Nor the shadow falling over him in the burgeoning light of the room. He failed even to register the blood trickling down his face as he fell forward on to the floor, so peaceful was his entry into eternity.

The dying red of the sun struck Erica Martin's face as she reached for a glass of retsina. Sam and she sat behind a stone balustrade, overlooking a verdant valley as the last strands of daylight weaved their way through the treetops. As the sky changed colour Martin removed her sunglasses and glanced to the right, where Sam was having to squint at his book.

'Shall we order?' she said. 'We've run out of wine.'

Sam looked up at her with a smile. 'Sure.' He shifted forward and gestured to the waiter who came over with a confident smile, the menu a familiar friend. Soon plates of stuffed olives, octopus salad, grilled sea bass and a basket of bread lay before them on the table. Martin watched

Sam as he tucked in, spooning food on to his plate, his brow unlined and tanned, the creases on his forehead smoothed out by the calm of the last few days. She found tears pricking at her eyes all of a sudden, a storm of something passing through her, wrenching her gut into a knot. With effort, she put her fork gently on to the white linen tablecloth and reached for her replenished wine glass. Without seeming to notice any of this, Sam put his hand on her free one.

'It'll be all right, you know. When we get back.'

Martin nodded, not understanding why she suddenly felt so at bay.

'Jim will be reasonable about us. He has to be.' Sam looked out at the vista as the last red streaks of the sun finally disappeared behind the distant hills. 'He left you, after all.'

Martin's stomach muscles clenched at that and, just as quickly, the sadness ebbed. She put down her glass and reached for her fork as candles were lit, popping into flame around like them like fireflies. 'And what about us?' she said, almost lightly, nearly as casual as a shrug.

Is there an 'us'? she thought, not daring to ask the question, pressing her lips together with a leaden pause.

He moved his eyes back to her and squeezed her hand. 'If that's what we want – what we decide – then of course there will be. No question.' He moved his glass to chink against hers. 'Here's to holidays,' he said, holding her gaze as he drank. 'Here's to the future.'

Martin waited a beat before tipping her glass back to his. '*Salut*,' she said, with a sad sort of a smile. 'To the future.'

2

Detective Inspector Erica Martin was already at her desk when the call came in that a body had been discovered at the Riverview boarding house. Snatching her keys from her desk, she made to exit the Major Crime Team office as soon as she heard the address from the uniformed police officer on the scene.

'Hold your horses, Martin,' DCI Sam Butterworth called after her, causing her to halt at the door.

'Jones is already on site with the Forensics Manager,' Martin protested, edging past the door jamb. 'It's my rap.'

Butterworth followed her through the door to stand in the corridor outside the main MCT office. 'Take it easy, Erica,' he said in a low voice. 'We're just back from holiday. Are you sure you want to dive straight back in? What with . . . everything else going on?'

Martin looked at him for a moment, her eyes bright and determined. 'This is what I do.'

Sam didn't reply, his shoulders stiff, arms folded.

'Honestly,' she repeated, 'it's what I need,' and she gave a small smile, her unspoken plea hanging in the air.

'Management meeting as soon as you're back, then,' Sam said, his shoulders drooping. 'And if it gets too much . . .'

'I'll shout.' Martin nodded swiftly, turning her back and pushing through the double doors that led to the stairwell out of the building.

The Riverview boarding house was under the Durham viaduct about twenty minutes' drive away from the MCT, which had moved to Chester-le-Street a year after Martin had joined it. Far from having a river view, the building sat halfway up the steep hill which led to Durham's railway station. It was old, from some indeterminable period, its walls dirty white, with musty bay windows wrapping around its front and a scrappy patch of garden leading on to the street.

Wearing a blue paper suit with white polythene bags over her shoes and two sets of latex gloves, Martin jogged up the stone steps to the front door, which had patches of peeling paint curling down it like faded party streamers. She acknowledged the constable standing there, who indicated that she should proceed immediately up the narrow staircase to an even thinner corridor; a few more uniformed officers were tucked in against the walls, a sombre guard of honour. The house was dark and sallow its palette dull. Martin walked alongside clammy brown wallpaper, feeling a sense of pendulous quiet pulsing softly. A blast of something would come, she could feel the certainty of it emanating from the walls.

Entering the bedroom at the end of the corridor, Martin ignored the others in the room. She approached the body with the weighted respect she gave to all the tasks connected with her profession. This was what she loved about her job, the pulling of the world on to a pinhead, grasping the fibres of life which swarmed in the air and rolling them into a ball, tumbling it along the ground to where a solitary spotlight shone; blocking everything else out apart from this moment, the now.

The man's body lay in that focus. Martin's eyes travelled over him keenly, from his head to his feet, which were splayed awkwardly out from the rest of his body. It looked as though he had been kneeling on a small stool, now overturned, and had been shunted forward by force, on to his face. She studied the back of his head, the bald patch at its crown but otherwise thick black hair, small scales of dandruff clinging to his scalp, remnants of life persisting.

Martin breathed out a small sigh before crouching down on her haunches. She let her gloved fingers move lightly over the collar of his dark blue pyjamas where blood had dried hard and stiff, the product of the dark spot on his skull below the baldness. There, the bone had been shattered, punched in like a splintered hole through a wooden door.

Martin swallowed. She could see the man's dead, still brain.

Detective Sergeant Emma Jones stood by the window of the small bedroom. Blue-flowered curtains were closed across them, thin as tissue paper, the morning sun putting her in shadow. 'Reverend Tristan Snow,' she said, folding her arms. 'He's well known. Got an MBE ... self-help guru and preacher. Works with kids. Have you heard of him?'

Martin gave a small shake of her head.

'His wife's downstairs,' Jones continued. 'They've been staying here for a week. He was found first thing this morning by his daughter. She's with the mother.'

'Have I missed Walsh?' Martin asked, not wanting to look at Jones yet. Her – *what was it, a fling?* – with DCI Sam Butterworth wasn't public knowledge yet, if it ever would be, and she wasn't yet prepared for the piss-taking she knew was inevitable from her team. If they dared.

Jones nodded, her voice normal. 'Yup. He said he'd see you at the post-mortem.'

'Morning, DI Martin.' Carl Partridge, the Forensics Manager, introduced himself from the other side of the room, where he stood with a camera. Martin turned to nod an acknowledgement to him. She'd worked with Partridge before and he was nice enough, albeit with a loud and often inappropriate laugh. Still, he was good at his job and Martin was pleased to see him here.

'We'll need blood spatter analysis,' Partridge said, and gestured towards the floor. 'On first look, seems likely he was kneeling on that stool.'

Martin said, 'He's not dressed. What time did the daughter find him?'

'Must've been just after 7 a.m.,' Jones answered. 'She came in to bring him a cup of tea. Says she found him like this. Didn't touch anything. Ran and got her mother. Called us.'

Martin peered forward at the crevasse in Snow's skull. 'Some whack,' she said. 'Wonder how many blows it took. Any obvious weapon?'

'Not that we've seen yet,' Partridge replied.

Martin stood up and shoved her hands in her pockets. 'How many people are staying here? Have we got a list, Jones?'

'One of the lads is on that now. Getting names. Landlady – a Mrs Quinn – says there were five people staying here last night. So six, all in, including her.'

'Any sign of a break-in?'

'Doesn't look like it. No windows smashed. Landlady says the doors were all locked from the inside this morning. She'd checked them last night before bed, around nine-thirty.'

'The guests have a key though, presumably?' Martin said. 'So that might not help us, timing-wise.' She scrutinized the body again. 'And his watch is still working, so no clue there. We'd better get them into the station while we wait for Walsh's report. Get their clothes, DNA, prints. How old's the daughter?'

'Eighteen,' Jones replied. 'Domestic, do you think?'

Martin looked around the room without answering. The air in the room was dense with the funk of stale blood and perspiration. She forced herself to breathe through it, to take in what she was seeing. A mahogany headboard was fixed to the top of the single bed, which she pointed towards. 'The wife wasn't sleeping with him, then?'

'Could mean they were scrapping?' Jones suggested.

Martin murmured to herself, continuing to look around the room. A dark-wood wardrobe loomed over the room from an alcove. A small desk sat under the window, a pointless blotting pad placed on its top, given the five or so biros which lay scattered across it. She walked around the body to the side of the bed, where books had been placed on a bedside table. The lamp was still on, its light negligible against the pale sunlight rinsing into the room. She picked up the top book, giving a quizzical exclamation.

'*Hostage to the Devil*?' Martin turned to show it to Jones, then looked again at the pile. '*The Devils of Loudun* by Huxley; Michael Pearl. The guy has some eclectic interests.'

'What's this under here?' Partridge asked from where he was crouched on the floor, looking under the bed. 'Can you see, DI Martin? It's more on your side.' Martin bent down, reaching into her jacket pocket to retrieve a pen. Stretching one arm under the bed, she managed to fish around and inch out the object.

'What the hell is that?' Jones asked.

Martin touched it with her pen, moving it around a little. Its dark grey wings were glossy but rigid, spread wide. The breast feathers gradually darkened up to the black of its head, from which a milky eye stared blankly at Martin.

'It's a dead bird,' she said. 'Some kind of carcass.' She looked up at Jones and Partridge, her mouth turned down, puzzled. 'It looks like a pigeon.'

'Why would a pigeon be under the bed?' Partridge asked. He walked across the room and pushed back the curtains to reveal the window, which was slightly ajar. 'Window's not open enough for it to have flown in. The gap's too small.'

Martin straightened to standing. 'Maybe it was put there for some reason? Or it flew in before the window was shut?'

Jones nodded and then frowned, observing Martin's stance, the clench of her jawline. 'Nice welcome back, Boss.'

Martin caught her eye and something passed between them, the merest whisper of comprehension and support. She smiled with a shrug. 'Ah well. All good things . . .' She touched the books on the bedside table briefly before heading out of the room.

Violet watched her mother. They sat opposite each other on the lumpy sofas in the 'best room', as the landlady of the boarding house had described it. There was nothing best about the room, Violet thought. Unless you considered it marginally more amenable than the rest of this scummy place. She and her mother had looked at her father in surprise when they'd turned up here a week ago. This was far below par, in comparison to the places they normally stayed.

'Talk to Fraser about it,' her father had muttered, lumbering up the front steps, leaving her and her mother to carry in the bags. They had walked into the dark entrance hall, the beady eyes of the landlady following them from the door all the way to the best room like a repugnant Mona Lisa – no smile whatsoever.

Sitting in the best room now, Violet studied her mother in the manner of an auctioneer looking anxiously at a Grecian vase about to topple from a pedestal. Would she move fast enough? In time to catch her mother when she tumbled? Sera was doing okay at the moment but it would only be a matter of time, Violet was sure of it. Soon, she would fall.

Violet heard a cough at the door and snapped her head round to establish the source of the noise. What looked like a policewoman was standing there. She had on a beige mackintosh with a white shirt and black trousers on underneath. Her red hair was drawn up, away from her face. Her eyes were green, cat-like. Violet sniffed surreptitiously. The woman smelt like authority. Like those ones at school. She was probably called Dorothy. Violet gave her best look of haughtiness and then turned back to her mother. Sera had also noticed the policewoman and shifted as if to stand.

'Please, don't get up,' the policewoman said, flattening her hands, palms down. Violet knew that gesture. It was submissive, designed to be used on approach with wild animals. *Don't trust her*, Violet thought.

Sera sank back down on to the sofa, her eyes wide like those of a discarded doll. As she did so, her foot caught a mug of undrunk tea on the floor. Its contents spilled all over the garishly patterned carpet. Violet stood up with a sigh and left to get a cloth from the landlady in the kitchen.

Eileen Quinn was standing pressed to the kitchen door, and got a mouthful of wood as Violet pushed it open to enter.

'Sorry,' she said without remorse, barging past the landlady to get to the sink.

Eileen swung round to follow her with her eyes, rubbing her face ruefully. 'I was just wondering . . .'

'What?' Violet asked. 'What were you wondering?'

'Well.' Eileen shrugged. 'What's going on? The police . . . Will they want to talk to me? Your poor father,' she shook her head in disbelief.

Violet leaned back against the kitchen counter, a J-cloth in her hand. She narrowed her eyes, studying the woman before her. Eileen Quinn was swollen from her ankles to her lips. Probably her toes too, although Violet couldn't see them, given as they were always encased in a pair of slippers. Gold hoops swung sturdily from Eileen's ear-lobes, and a gold cross nestled in the dip in her throat.

'My father is dead,' Violet said at last, watching Eileen grow increasingly uncomfortable at her scrutiny.

'Yes, dear. I know.'

'So I can't say I really give a fuck whether the police need to interview you or not,' Violet said. 'I've got more important things to worry about.' She swept past Eileen, through the open kitchen door and back down the hall to the best room. She halted just by the doorway, lean-ing forward to catch the conversation. It seemed weirdly quiet. At once, the policewoman appeared in front of her in the corridor.

'Ah, Violet,' she said, reaching for the cloth with a smile. 'Grateful if you and I could have a word.'

3

Martin gestured for Violet to come in and sit down next to her mother, noting Sera Snow's immediate grasp of her daughter's hand. Martin took the J-cloth and dropped it on the ground, tapping over the tea stain with her foot before sitting down herself on a hard-backed seat opposite them.

'I was just saying to your mum that I'd like you to come down to the station with us,' she said. 'We'll need to move your father soon, and it would be best if you weren't here then. Would that be okay?'

Sera glanced at Violet and she nodded.

Martin inclined her head towards Sera. 'We'd like you to make a formal identification of your husband once we've moved him.'

Violet looked confused. 'But I saw him. Upstairs. It's him all right.'

Martin paused, not wanting to reveal anything in front of Sera Snow about the position of the body, about the fact that he had been found lying face down. 'I'm sorry, but it has to be done.'

Violet shook her head. 'Well, my mother can't see him. She can't take that. I'll do it.'

Martin looked at Sera, who caught her eye briefly before staring down at her twisting hands and shrugging almost imperceptibly. 'If Violet wants to . . .' her voice trailed away.

Martin leaned back in her chair, puzzled by this capitulation by the mother. Something about Sera's voice sounded familiar, although she couldn't put her finger on it just then.

'The SOCO van is here, Ma'am,' Jones said, appearing at the door. 'We should probably get going.'

'There'll be press,' Sera said dully. 'They'll want to talk about it. My husband was revered, Inspector. We'll have to say something.' She looked defeated by the prospect.

'You leave that with us, Mrs Snow,' Martin said, standing up. 'After you.' She gestured to the doorway.

'What about our stuff?' Violet asked.

'You'll be able to come back later. But everything needs to be left as it was for the moment,' Jones explained. She looked down at her notes. 'Your sister is also staying here, Mrs Snow, so I believe?'

'Aunt Antonia stayed out last night. I'm not sure where,' Violet said.

Martin looked quickly at Jones. *Find out where.*

'Okay then, let's go.' Martin hung back to let mother and daughter leave the room first. Sera glanced up the stairs for a second, to where her husband lay, before she seemed to shudder and hesitate. 'Come on, Mum,' Violet said, hustling Sera out into the daylight, squinting after the gloom of the interior. 'Here, take my hand down the steps.'

Martin and Jones followed them out to the car waiting in the street. As they left, Martin looked back to the bay window of the room they had just left. A shadow flitted across it, marring for a moment the sunlight that poured on to the glass. Seeming to notice Martin's stare, Eileen Quinn moved quickly away from the window as a train rumbled overhead on the viaduct, its noise reminiscent of passing thunder.

Violet looked down at the waxy mask of her father, her fingers flexing a little as if to move to touch him, yet unable to bring herself to do so. The grooves in his face, running perpendicular to the hard line of his mouth, were static. No longer jiving and sparking, imbuing his face with a life that never seemed authentic – even when he was actually alive. It dawned on Violet that his hair was wrong; it was swept back from his head into a mane. It should flop irritatingly in front of his eyes. Those water-filled eyes. Water and fire. The fire that burned into her – and everyone else – day after day after day. Flicking the black curly hair back with a toss of his head, a smirk. That's how she would remember him. Not like this. Flat on a bed covered in a starched white sheet.

The policewoman was in the room – close but unobtrusive against the pale walls of the mortuary. Violet didn't look at her as she forced herself to touch the sheet. She could feel where the material rose, the mound of her father so silent and still. She had watched him when he slept on a few occasions. Even in slumber, he had seemed so vital. But now he was stone. Where had he gone? she wondered. To the kingdom he'd eulogized for so long? That pretend paradise – a dreamland of the fulfilment of childish hopes. To those golden and pearly gates, to his Father? Violet shivered. She could feel his eyes bore into her, blister at her through his lids, appalled at her blasphemy. No, it was impossible. He was dead.

'Violet?' Martin's voice punctured the silence.

'His gold cross is missing,' Violet said. 'He always wore it around his neck.'

'It may have been removed. I'll check,' Martin replied, a flash of alarm shooting through her, knowing as she spoke that nothing would have been taken from the body at this stage.

Violet slowly turned away from the body to appraise Martin. 'Well anyway,' she said coolly. 'This is Tristan Snow. My father.'

4

Afterwards, Martin drove Violet from the mortuary to Durham police station, where her mother was waiting for her in a bleak interview room off the main reception.

'I'm afraid that I'll need to interview you separately,' Martin explained.

'Procedure again?' Violet's question was curt.

'We need to find out about your father,' Martin answered levelly, the words of her mantra drumming in her head – *to find out how they live is to find out how they die.* She studied Violet, searching her face for chinks of light, for any kind of vulnerability, but the girl was as closed off as her mother. 'Let me do my job in the best way I know how, and then you can go. I realize this is extremely upsetting for you.'

Violet shook her head as if to say *you know nothing about us.*

'May I pray?' Sera spoke suddenly.

'I'm sorry?' Martin asked.

'I normally pray around this time of day,' Sera went on. 'If you could provide me with a space?'

'Yes, of course.' Martin recovered swiftly from the surprise. 'We have a prayer room here that you can use. Come, I'll show you.'

As they made their way towards the prayer room, Martin felt she towered above Sera Snow. The woman only came up to Martin's shoulder, despite wearing pumps with an inch on the heel. She had dressed for the August weather in a mid-calf linen skirt with a short-sleeved blouse, and shivered in the controlled temperature of the police station. She wore various chains and necklaces, which jangled as she walked. For such a mouse as she appeared, much of the jewellery was garish – amber and turquoise, a large silver medallion. Her grey hair was tied loosely in a bun at the nape of her neck.

Where were the tears? Martin wondered, as she led Sera down the corridor. Where were the signs of grief, of disbelief? Even of fear – if they thought a stranger had broken into the boarding house? Both Sera and her daughter seemed mute, although Violet had a simmering anger. Had they shut down in shock? Or was their reaction something more chilling; a considered response to a death that they themselves had had a hand in?

'It's here.' Martin stopped in front of a door in a small alcove. 'Take all the time you need.'

'Thank you,' Sera replied, putting her hand on Martin's arm before entering the room. 'He is always with me, you see.'

Martin inwardly shuddered at the touch and, nodding, moved away from the door, recognizing that Sera wasn't referring to her husband. The hand on her arm had been sanctimonious, patronizing; it had made Martin feel revulsion. And yet, simultaneously, a feeling of envy at the woman's faith, at once so powerful but equally so futile, came over Martin, and she felt her knees almost buckle with the strength of it. Spying the sanctuary of a Ladies' toilet a few doors down, she made her way there and braced herself at the sinks, looking at her reflection in the smeared mirror on the wall.

Her hands gripped the edge of the basin, her knuckles curved to the sky. She had to focus. Get on with things. A homicide. She had to lead them all. She screwed up her face. *Like the Pied bloody Piper.*

It had been nearly a year ago that her husband Jim had left. He'd packed up his bags and moved to Newcastle. Living on his own in one of the new apartments on the Quayside as if he were twenty years younger, as if he were back on the market. The anger she felt about it was disproportionate to the simultaneous feeling of release she had undergone. That he could leave so easily. Ask her for a divorce, as yet unsettled. Abandon the marriage, shake it off as if it had been little more than a dalliance. And despite everything she'd ever said about the pointlessness of the ceremony, the ridiculous tradition, she had actually married him. In a church. Not in some registry office or on some beach. She had loved him and so she had done it. They had stood in front of her family, who'd never thought anyone would take her, and promised themselves to each other until death.

Not just until five years down the track when it all got too hard.

Martin pushed the heels of her hands into her eye sockets. And then there was Sam. They'd only just started seeing each other, feeling their way around the outlines of this fledgling relationship. They were a right pair: her with her impending divorce; Sam with his reputation for being . . . God knows what. And then the small fact that he was her boss.

There had been a near miss. A late period, a few uncomfortable days touched with a glimmer of excitement before relief had come. Well, she'd laughed at Sam, she was used to blood in her job. He'd looked at her, appalled. Martin's cheeks flushed again now, to think of it.

He'd surprised her with a long weekend in Crete to forget about it, to move on. To make some decisions about what they were doing. But it all still seemed so unresolved.

What *were* they doing?

And all she could hear, over and over again, was that fucking cello. The music they'd played as she'd left the church on that October day in that white dress. It danced through her head, that music, the lower registers stabbing her in the gut, the shaft of the bow on the chords pulling on her, twisting her resolve into fairy dust, puffs of nothing, floating away into the air, leaving her with nothing but tears.

Fucking Bach.

Fuck.

Detective Constable Phil Tennant sat at his computer, a venti cappuccino next to his elbow on the desk. He typed in the name Tristan Snow and sat back, letting the results emerge, taking a gulp of his coffee as he waited. Absorbed in what he was reading, he didn't notice Jones sit down quietly on the chair next to him, spinning it around a little as she did so.

'What have you got?' Jones asked.

Tennant turned his head towards her and leaned backwards, scratching his chin. 'Tristan Snow. Reverend of the Deucalion Church in Blackpool. Tons about him on the web – has got his own website, you name it.' He frowned. 'I saw him once. On Richard and Judy or something. D'you remember?' He pushed back to the desk and scrolled down the screen. 'He was like their resident psychic. Used to talk to the dead, predict the future. Absolute codswallop,' Tennant pursed his lips. 'All very happy clappy. TV played down the religious aspect of course. But it says here blatantly', he gestured towards the screen, 'that he performs miracles.'

'Miracles?'

'Hmm. And exorcisms.' Tennant looked at Jones, saying nothing more. 'The church he ran, the Deucalion? It's known for the work it does with kids. Abandoned kids, kids with problems. He got the MBE for it, services to charity.'

'So . . . what's he doing here?'

'Came to Durham as part of his UK tour.' Tennant tapped his knee with a biro and drank more coffee.

'UK *tour*? Is he really that much of a celebrity nowadays?' Jones remarked. 'Wasn't he famous, like, fifteen years ago? Who's interested in him now? What does he even do?'

Tennant shrugged. 'All the rage, isn't it? Nostalgia for the eighties and nineties. And he does hypnotherapy, miracles, self-help books. Like that McKenna chap. All give you an easy way out. Save you grafting and trying to make something out of your life yourself. Bloke's got, like, a hundred thousand followers on Twitter, social media, whatever.'

'If that's the case, then why's he staying in that shitty B&B?' Jones observed.

Tennant clicked on another part of the screen. 'Fair point. He's sold out the Gala Theatre for two nights, booked in for three. He's been down south already. Heading up to Scotland next. He *was* doing that, anyway.' Tennant sighed a little, the philosophy of murder threatening to encroach on his thoughts.

Jones pushed her chair back. 'Come on Tennant, the boss is with the family. Let's show a little initiative. Head down to the theatre and see what's what.'

'Has she said anything to you?' Tennant asked, as he locked the computer screen and grabbed his jacket. 'About what's going on with her and Butterworth?'

'You must be joking,' Jones answered. 'None of our business, is it?'

'There she is: Saint Jones,' Tennant scoffed. 'Fights crime and leaves mundane gossip to the rest of us.'

'That's a big word for you, Phil,' Jones said. 'Been practising it at home, have you?'

Tennant shrugged. 'Opens her up to some piss-taking, is all.'

'From a pensioner like you?' Jones said. 'I'm sure she's terrified.'

'Aye. Call me romantic, Jones, I just like to know who fancies who . . .'

Jones cuffed him round the shoulder as they left the incident room. 'Everyone fancies you, Phil. Didn't you know?'

5

While Sera was praying, Martin headed back to the inter-view room where Violet waited. This room was brighter than the ones downstairs situated next to the holding cells. There was even a window. Once, the walls had been painted cream, although now various stains and patches of dirt provided a dismal mural.

'Apologies for the lack of air,' Martin said. 'A fan's on its way. The air-con has broken in here, for some reason.' She smiled ruefully, knowing that there would be no fan coming. The heat was intentional.

Violet looked cool, however, unbothered by the tem-perature. She took a seat opposite Martin, who could feel sweat dripping down her back and longed to take off her jacket. She resisted the impulse and switched on the tape recorder.

'You are absolutely entitled to a solicitor if you'd like, Violet. But I'm only taping this to help us both, so that we don't forget what you've said. Nobody's being arrested or charged with anything, at the moment.' She smiled at the girl, *at the moment* left floating in the air.

Violet, though, remained impassive.

'You're eighteen, is that correct?' Martin asked, making notes as she talked, and the girl assented. She was striking, with bobbed dark hair cut to her chin, a pale complexion and rosebud cheeks. She reminded Martin of a china doll she had been given once as a child. A cold face, hard to the touch, but that could shatter at the slightest impact. She remembered treating that doll so gently and carefully that, in the end, it was useless as a plaything. As rigid as it had seemed, in actuality it had been as delicate as a moth's wings.

'Have you left school then? Finished your A levels? Results are out soon, aren't they, I think?'

'I didn't do A levels.'

Martin waited.

'I need to look after my mum. In the church . . . she needs me. I'm going to carry on working for the church until . . .'

'Until what?' Martin prodded, after a beat.

'Until, you know, things are settled.'

Martin considered this. 'Until the end of your father's tour?' she prompted. *Make her my friend*, she thought. Since she had been separated from Sera, Violet seemed to have dropped her veneer a little. *Use it.*

'Yes, if you like,' Violet said, blithely.

What did that mean? Martin wondered. 'Tell me about this morning,' she asked gently, pulling Violet in. 'Tell me what happened.'

Violet took a breath. 'I woke up early. Too early. The room I'm in has these rubbish curtains. They don't hide the light. Although actually, I was awake already . . .' her voice trailed off.

'Your room is . . .?' Martin asked.

'Next door to Dad's. In between his and Mum's, on the same floor.'

'They don't share a room?'

Violet shrugged but said nothing more. She put her hands on the table and looked at her fingers as she continued. 'I lay there for a while but couldn't get back to sleep, so I got up in the end. I went downstairs to the kitchen. The landlady – Mrs Quinn? She sets out the breakfast things in there. So I made two cups of that rancid tea she gives us, for me and Dad, and took them upstairs.'

None for the mother, Martin observed.

'I left mine outside my door on the carpet and came back along the corridor to where Dad was sleeping.' Violet swallowed, and paused.

Martin said nothing.

'I knocked quietly, but there was no answer. I looked at my watch and saw that it was just seven. Dad, well, he likes to be woken up at the same time every day. He likes a routine.'

Martin noticed, finally, a reaction in the girl to the warmth of the room. A faint patina of sweat now lay on her forehead as she gave a thousand-yard stare to the back wall, clearly bringing to her mind the events of the morning.

'I opened the door,' Violet continued in a small voice. 'And there he was. Bent over in the middle of the floor.' She looked up at Martin. 'I dropped the tea on the ground and ran to get Mum. I mean I could tell. I could see . . .'

'I know this is hard, Violet.'

The girl moved her head from side to side, an animal in distress. 'It doesn't seem real. That he's gone. He was always . . . there, you know?'

'I'm sorry.' Martin inclined her head, waited a fraction. 'Did you hear anything odd last night? What time did you go to bed?'

'As soon as we got home from dinner. I said good night to Mum and Dad and read for a while in my room. I turned my light out about 11 p.m. I didn't hear anything.'

'And Antonia, your aunt? Did she have dinner with you?'

A shadow passed across Violet's face as she shook her head. 'No. I don't know where she was. Out somewhere else.'

Martin hesitated for a moment before continuing. 'What was it like?' she asked. 'Seeing your dad on TV? Watching him do those shows? I don't know,' she said, 'it must be odd having a parent in the public eye like that.'

Violet stared at Martin. 'Everyone loved him.'

Was there something there? Martin wondered. The merest suggestion of bitterness? 'Were you a believer? Did you believe in the things your father said and did?' Again, Martin waited, let the silence roam through the heat of the room.

After a moment, Violet exhaled impatiently. 'Look, Inspector Martin,' she said. 'Everything you need to see, you can find on the internet. Dad has a YouTube channel. You can see his website, the Deucalion Church. It's all there for you to see,' she repeated.

Martin weighed this statement up. Violet had dodged the question. What did she intend Martin to find on the internet? Violet was a child, she could tell, in spite of appearances. Her energy betrayed her, showing her not quite at the full maturity of adulthood where things could be fully hidden or battened down. She had tried, when they had met – she had attempted to be as indifferent as her mother – but she had dropped her guard. The act might be that of a child, Martin thought, but the ruthless reality was that she would not be considered one in the eyes of the law. 'I absolutely will, Violet. And how did you get on with your dad?' she asked lightly.

At once, the shutters came down. Martin could see Violet's eyes change as if she had closed them. One minute, they were soft, easily meeting hers. The next, the blank look was back, her lips together, hands in her lap. Martin had lost her.

'He was my father,' Violet answered, a brittle tone to her voice.

Martin cocked her head to one side. *Yes.*

Violet shrugged. 'What more do you want me to say?'

She could push her. Try to break behind the steel shutters, prod and tease information out about their relationship. But then she would make an enemy of her.

Martin called it.

'Okay, Violet. Thank you for talking to me. I'll speak to your mother once she's finished with her prayers. In the meantime, you're free to leave.'

Martin left the room, checking her watch. If Sera Snow was still praying or doing whatever it was she did, she had time to get an update from the team before she interviewed her. She would take a different approach with Sera: a wife in the same house where her husband had been murdered was a prime suspect.

She wouldn't try to make friends with Snow's wife as she'd done with Violet. Instinctively, Martin felt that

Sera was not a woman you'd befriend easily in any event. Something in her reigned cold and sharp. The thought flashed into Martin's head that this quality would be invaluable to a man so exposed to the world as Tristan Snow had been. But was that hardness what Sera had used to defend her husband against the spotlight? Or was it, in fact, what had driven her to kill him?

6

'If someone doesn't tell me what the fuck is going on, I swear to God, I'm going to have to crack some skulls!'

Despite the soundproofing required of a venue as large as the theatre auditorium, Jones and Tennant could hear the blistering voice coming from within as they stood outside the entrance doors to the stalls. The front-of-house staff had said that that Tristan Snow's business manager was on stage. The crew were in place; the choir were in their dressing rooms, waiting to start the technical rehearsal for tonight's service. But Snow hadn't arrived as scheduled, and Fraser Mackenzie was steadily working himself up into a rage.

Jones opened one of the doors at the top of the auditorium, and she and Tennant began to descend the long set of steps which led to the stage.

'I've been waiting here for over an hour. Nobody's answering my calls. I'm standing here like a fucking lemon. Where is he?!'

A soft murmuring from a speaker on the stage seemed to be trying to answer the inferno of words, to no avail. The angry man was centre-stage, whirling this way and that, as if looking for a target. The set-up for a band was behind him, the silver of the drum kit gleaming, defiantly silent. Choir stalls rose up on either side of the stage. They, too, were ghostly. The man was alone on the stage, bathed in the glare of a spotlight focused on him, his balding pate shiny with sweat.

'It's not fucking good enough . . .'

His voice halted as the shapes of Jones and Tennant appeared at the edge of the stage. He was a short, middle-aged man in an expensive-looking navy blue suit. His hair was cut close to his scalp in a semicircle – an attempt, Jones surmised, to disguise his hair loss. Although he'd stemmed the angry flow of words, the man's mouth remained fixed in a snarl, his lips curled in a sarcastic wave. His eyes were a pale blue, and appraised the figures of Jones and Tennant quickly. As the fact of their presence registered in his brain, the man took a visible breath.

'Shit . . .' he muttered to himself. He licked his lips and straightened. He turned to face them head on, hands in his pockets and shoulders squared. Jones was brought to mind of the image of a man facing a firing squad.

Jones showed him her identification. 'Would you like to come with us, Mr Mackenzie? Somewhere where we can sit down.'

'Whatever you've got to say, you can say it here,' Mackenzie said.

Jones paused before deciding. 'Okay then. I'm afraid we have some bad news. This morning, the body of a man was found in the Riverview boarding house.'

Mackenzie's nostrils flared, his eyes locked on Jones.

'It seems clear that the body is that of Reverend Tristan Snow,' Jones said, detecting some kind of odour from Mackenzie as he swayed a little on his feet. What was it? Fear?

'Body?' he muttered, out of one side of his mouth. 'He's dead?'

'Yes, I'm afraid so.' Jones hesitated. 'Are you all right, Mr Mackenzie? Would you like to sit down?'

Mackenzie moved his head to one side as if trying to shift the liquid of the knowledge to another part of his brain that could better understand. 'How? I mean,' he took his hands from his pockets and folded his arms, 'how did he die?'

'We're looking into that at the moment, Mr Mackenzie,' Tennant said. 'Right now, we're wanting to talk to anyone who might have seen Reverend Snow last night or this morning.' He paused. 'Can I ask where you were, Mr Mackenzie? At those times?'

Mackenzie shifted his sights on to Tennant and narrowed his eyes. 'Is this a formal interview, officer?'

'Nothing formal as yet, Sir,' Jones answered him, easily. 'Just making our enquiries. As you would expect.'

Mackenzie exhaled silently, his chest deflating underneath his crisp white shirt. The effort to bring himself under control was clear as the lights under which he stood. 'Sure, sure,' he said, giving a forced smile. 'Anything I can do to help, of course.' He tilted his head. 'How are the girls?'

Jones met his gaze impassively. 'I'm certain they'll be wanting to see you, Sir. Terrible thing for them, as you can imagine.'

Mackenzie released his arms from their locked position and seemed to relax somewhat.

'Have you had an injury of late, Sir?' Jones asked, suddenly identifying the aroma emanating from Mackenzie.

33

'Uh, yes, actually.' Mackenzie looked surprised. 'My shoulder. I hurt it playing squash. How do you know?'

'Recognize the smell,' Jones answered. 'Deep Heat. Remember it from my netball playing days.' She studied his face carefully. 'So, where were you last night, Mr Mackenzie?'

'I was here.' His face crumpled. 'I can't believe it. Tristan's dead?' He rubbed his hand over his head, sniffing, before looking up and coming to focus on his surroundings. 'Tonight. What are we going to do? We've got five hundred people with tickets.' His eyes darted from side to side as thoughts clanged into his head one after another.

'Mr Mackenzie,' Jones said, putting a hand on his arm, 'let's take a seat. Come on. It's obviously a shock for you.'

She led him down off the stage to the first row of seats in the black and red auditorium. Mackenzie sat next to Jones, concentrating on her. He ignored Tennant on his other side.

'You say you were here last night?' Jones asked, gently. 'What time did you leave the theatre?'

'Um, about 1 a.m., I'd say. Tonight's the first night, and we only had the get-in yesterday. Had to wait for some folk singers to get their kit out before we could set up.' Mackenzie's face was the picture of disdain.

'And was Reverend Snow here with you until then, as well?'

Mackenzie shook his head. 'No. He had been here from about 7 p.m., but all he needed to do was go through his sermon and walk through his marks on the stage. You know,' he said, looking at Jones, 'to work out where to stand for the lighting cues.' He sighed. 'So he did all that, and everything was great. And then he went to go and get dinner with Sera and Violet. Although he'd been a bit sick earlier, so in the end I think they just went home. Must've been about ten that he left.'

'But other people were here with you until 1 a.m.?' Tennant asked.

Mackenzie didn't turn to face him. 'Do I have an alibi, do you mean?' His tone was scathing. 'Yes. Other people were here. The lighting techs, the band and most of the choir.'

'You went straight home after the rehearsal?'

'Yes, of course.'

'And you didn't check in on Reverend Snow this morning? What time did you get up and leave the boarding house?'

'No, I didn't see him. I don't know, I must have left just before 7 a.m.?'

'And you came directly here, to the theatre?'

'Yes, yes,' Mackenzie's eyes flitted from one place to another.

'Is the theatre open that early?' Jones asked. 'Brutal start for you, Sir, if you were in bed so late last night.'

'I'm used to it.' Mackenzie's voice was curt. 'The venue always gives me entry via the stage door so I can come and go as I please.' He gestured behind him. 'I've got my laptop set up backstage. I treat the theatre like my office when we're on tour. Need to sort out logistics of the next few locations when we're on the move like this.'

'Sure, of course,' Jones replied. 'And when did you arrive in Durham?'

'Three days ago. We got here on Friday. We're supposed to do shows for three nights and leave on Thursday morning.'

Jones leaned forward on her knees, looking out towards the stage. 'It was going to be a big show, was it? Tonight and the rest of the week?'

Mackenzie shrugged. 'He's had bigger, but yes. Five hundred people tonight. Same again tomorrow. Wednesday's quieter, but we were hopeful we'd drum up some business in the meantime. Tristan has a lot of followers in the north-east.' His face fell again. '*Had* a lot of followers, I mean . . .'

'And in the show, what happens?' Jones asked. 'Reverend Snow would give a sermon. Is that it?'

Mackenzie gave a withering smile. 'You've never been to a healing service, then?' Jones said nothing, her answer obvious. He stood up and stretched his arms above his head. 'Gah! I'm going to have to get busy and sort all this. Fuck!' Some of Mackenzie's old spirit seemed to have returned; he had colour in his cheeks again.

'What happens in the services?' Jones repeated, as she stood with him. 'Why do so many people want to come?'

Mackenzie gave a laugh. 'Why?' He opened his palms to the heavens. 'Why *wouldn't* anyone want to come? Miracles, Sergeant Jones. That's what would've happened in here. Miracles.' He turned to face her, to send her a bullet with the nub of the case written on it. 'Tristan would've performed miracles here. He would have healed the sick and raised the dead. Who *wouldn't* want to buy a ticket to see that?'

7

The air was humid and clammy: pregnant clouds hung ominously outside the incident room windows, obscuring the midday sun. Martin positioned herself on the desk, which faced the large, square table in the middle of the room, around which the team sat settling themselves, passing takeaway cups of coffee and assorted biscuits to each other.

This investigation into Snow's murder – Operation Malta – had been allocated the larger of the rooms at the MCT. It was bright, if the sun ever battled its way through the inclement north-east weather, and its pale cream walls were empty except for leftover globs of Blu-tack and edges of Sellotape, reminders of previous investigations, the ghosts of which rambled through the room. After the interview with Violet, Martin felt back in the fray, more focused. She took a breath and a sip of sweetened tea, and allowed herself to enjoy being back. This was what she did.

The room turned dark as a crack of thunder boomed. Strip lighting flickered into action as Martin's phone vibrated next to her mug. She lifted it up to look at the caller identity and, frowning, put it face down again on the desk. Behind her head was a whiteboard covered with a large Venn diagram of concentric circles. As she gathered her thoughts to address the quietening room, one word shone in her head; the last word she had written on the board.

Motive.

'Tristan Snow. Found in the Riverview B&B with the back of his head smashed in. In the absence of anything at the moment from the allocated pathologist Dr Walsh, I think it's safe to say this is a homicide.'

Martin pushed her hands underneath her thighs and looked around the room at her team. Jones, as always, eager like a fox prickling on her haunches at the front of the table. Tennant next to her, one leg crossed over the other, relaxed yet alert. The others were gathered like troops; silent soldiers on whom this burden lay. *Who killed Tristan Snow?*

'Snow called himself a reverend although the church he set up doesn't appear to be affiliated with any of the big boys, religion-wise,' Martin said. 'His church — the Deucalion — was founded about thirty years ago, in Blackpool. From what I can tell from the information available, he was fairly end-of-the-pier when he started, performing shows down on the front and around other seaside resorts. Things stepped up a gear in the 1990s when his manager, a Fraser Mackenzie, got involved. Snow changed his act, became more of your Mystic Meg sort; seems to have cultivated a pretty lucrative career in the self-help vein.

'He was a TV personality for a while. Hung around as part of the light entertainment crowd it seems, the Barrymores . . . the Tarbucks. He's even written a book.' Martin held up a hardback book with Tristan's picture on the front. '*Pure as Snow*,' she said with a bemused air. 'Part autobiography, part self-help. What any of this has to do with religion is anyone's guess.

'The main line of enquiry', she continued, 'will obviously centre on those who were in the B&B the night before Snow was found, given there's no sign of forced entry.' Martin turned to the board behind her and tapped one of the circles. 'Violet Snow,' she said, 'the victim's daughter. She discovered the body. She's a spiky little thing.' She paused, thinking. 'I'm not sure about her. And the mother, Sera, is hard to read.' She leaned against the table, folding her arms. 'If I'm honest, neither of them seem overly bereft.

'Then there's the manager, Mackenzie. We need to check out his timings. Likewise, we need details on Antonia Simpson – Sera Snow's sister – she was staying with them. And then there's the B&B landlady, Eileen Quinn.'

Martin looked at her team. 'We found a dead pigeon under Snow's bed. Clearly, we're waiting for forensics, but I want someone looking into things right off the bat, no pun intended. Did it just fly in through the window? The one in Snow's room was open a little, but the gap is too small in my opinion. It needs looking at to see if that's possible. If it *did* manage to come in of its own accord, before the window was shut, for example, is it just a coincidence that it flew into the room where a murder was about to or had already taken place?' Martin narrowed her eyes. 'I'm not a massive fan of coincidences, so why did it decide to wind up dead in Snow's room? Was it, in fact, put there deliberately – or had it flown in days before and Eileen Quinn is just shoddy at her spring-cleaning? Walsh is good, but I'm not sure he can work out the time of death of a pigeon.

'The SOCOs are obviously still at the crime scene, but in the meantime, if you dig up anything of use, don't be shy. What's the symbolism of a dead pigeon, if any?'

'It's the church,' Tennant interrupted, with a start.

Martin looked at him. 'What is?'

'The symbol of the church. The Deucalion . . .' Tennant's tongue tripped over the word. He pushed a piece of paper towards Martin. 'Look. It's on their website, all of their stuff.'

Martin grabbed the paper and stared at it. At the top of the page was a circle with a blue bird inside, the name of the church curving around its wings. 'Is that a pigeon?' she asked.

'It could be,' Jones put in. 'Deucalion . . . we looked it up.' She glanced at Tennant. 'He's Noah. Another name for Noah. He had the Ark. Sent the dove or the pigeon, or whatever, to find land.' She swallowed, gathering her thoughts. 'The church was massively popular. Was known for helping kids. He was . . . Snow, I mean. Kids who were abandoned, had nowhere else to go. People loved it, loved him. Which explains why they'd managed to sell out most of three consecutive nights of shows at the Gala. And, um . . .'

'What?' Martin asked.

'Well.' Jones shrugged. 'Looks like Snow wasn't only into healing at his shows. He used to do, you know, miracles and things.'

Martin lifted her chin, her eyebrows drawn together.

'Exorcisms of the Devil,' Jones carried on, uncomfortably aware of her boss's growing antipathy. 'He'd do it at the shows. Films of it are on the net. And – on his website – you can buy videos of how to do a bit of DIY.'

'DIY?' Martin repeated.

'That's where it got dodgy.' Jones's voice changed, her cheery features darkening. 'How to train your child. How to remove the Devil from children.'

Martin bit her lip. 'This is online? You can view it?' She thought back to Violet Snow's assertion that everything could be seen, that nothing was hidden.

Jones nodded. 'We've already accessed the church's Twitter feed, other social media. His *fans* – if you want to call them that – are all devastated. Conspiracy theories abound already. They're calling for a statement from the church.' She grimaced. 'Want to hold some kind of simultaneous candlelit ceremony here and in Blackpool.'

Martin frowned as a few hard drops of rain began to rap against the window and a telephone rang on a desk near Tennant. 'Sera Snow said the press would be interested. Given Snow was some kind of celeb, we'll need to make a statement on that as well as the homicide. Violet Snow mentioned a YouTube channel, too, so that's obviously an area where we need to put our foot on the ball. See what Snow was up to in the church that might have caused an issue with anyone. And what was their family life like? Violet seems pretty anti her father. Why? I'm going to interview Sera Snow shortly, so we'll get more information then, hopefully. Particularly what she was up to last night, and whether she bashed him over the head.'

Martin paused. 'Have we managed to track down the sister? Antonia?'

'Yup,' Tennant answered, putting back the receiver. 'She rolled back to the B&B this morning after you'd left – when the SOCO team were still there. Looked much the worse for wear. Pissed up, you know. She's sobering up at the new hotel with the rest of the family apart from Sera, who's ready for you now, Boss.'

'Also, can someone check whether Snow was wearing a cross when he was moved to the mortuary? Violet Snow says it's missing. If he wasn't wearing it when he was shifted, where is it? And if he was, for God's sake, someone find it,' Martin said, raising her voice over the increasing battery of rain outside. 'Jones, you come with me to interview Mrs Snow before I head to the hotel and see Antonia. Then we need to chase up Walsh's pathology report and coordinate the statements of Mackenzie and Eileen Quinn.'

'Will do.'

'That's it then, folks. Can't say I've heard of him, but if Tristan Snow was as popular as everyone's saying, the media will be all over us. Professionalism, diligence and respect as always, please.'

Martin eyed a dustbin in the corridor and tossed her empty cup into it as her team filed out. And then she remembered the message she'd received on her phone at the beginning of the briefing and her stomach sank. Despite the rush of the past few hours, it seemed she was still destined to deal with the present – and the fact that her soon-to-be-ex-husband wanted to take her out for dinner, and he had no idea that she was seeing somebody else.

8

'Mrs Snow, can I ask for your full name?'

Martin sat opposite Sera in an interview room with Jones to one side of her, taking notes. The space was windowless, down in the bowels of Durham police station. Brown, sound-proofing carpet tiles lined the walls, the low chipboard ceiling adding to the claustrophobia Martin always felt when she was in there. She often wondered how it would feel to be sat on that bucket seat if you were guilty of a serious crime. How could you maintain a poker face throughout the dance you would do with the police officers, not knowing for sure how much they knew, how much they were bluffing?

'Seraphina Abigail Snow,' Sera answered evenly. She sat serene, her eyes wide and fixed on Martin. She reminded Martin of illustrations she'd seen of the witch in the fairy tale Hansel and Gretel, with her hooked nose, long bony fingers creeping out of a gingerbread house. What would she look like, Martin considered, if her jewellery were removed and she was devoid of the colours that glinted from her, gave her that eccentric air, that aura of being someone important, someone of note? What would she be, if the blues and greens and silvers disappeared to nothing? Just an old woman with a wispy knotted bun.

Before Martin could continue, Sera whispered something, as if to herself, which Martin didn't catch.

'I'm sorry?'

'I said he was fearless. He had no fear. Tristan was a man with no limits.'

Why had she said that, apropos of nothing? Martin studied her face. It was peaky; it had a nervous energy about it. As Sera moved her head, Martin noticed the yellowish-green of a fading bruise on her temple. She filed the memory of it for later.

'You liked that about him?' Martin asked, using her familiar instinct to find the right question.

Sera hesitated before speaking. 'I lived with it,' she answered, finally.

Martin waited, but nothing else came. She shifted in her seat, turning to the task, mentally running through her interview prep. 'We'd like you take us through the events of last night please, Mrs Snow, so we can establish what happened at the boarding house in the last twenty-four hours.'

Sera sucked in a breath and made a soft mewling sound, her eyes closing in despair. 'I just want this over with. Life seems . . . It seems in a stutter at the moment.'

Martin knew what she meant. A murder smashed into lives in a way that meant everything stopped; the moment seemed stuck on repeat, until the questions were answered and justice was fought and won for the victim. Then life could once again continue its bumpy journey, with the murderer locked up safely behind bars. But something about the statement didn't ring true. Sera Snow seemed too composed, too smooth. 'I understand, Mrs Snow. This must be very hard.'

Martin paused for a beat, waiting for the momentum in the room to shift: that elusive swing in the rhythm of things when her questions could mutate from easy and comfortable to precise and acute. 'Tell me what happened yesterday, Sera, if you will. The daytime, evening and then this morning.'

'Yesterday, we were all at the theatre rehearsing. Nothing more. It had gone well. We'd had some lunch. Prayed. We carried on late into the evening. Tristan felt sick though. He'd not been right all day.'

'Sick?' Martin asked. 'In what way?'

Sera shrugged. 'He wouldn't eat at lunchtime, and normally he's a big eater. Likes to take out the crew at least once before the run of the show begins. They enjoy it. He tells stories, anecdotes, buys everyone a drink.'

Martin could imagine. The emperor and his entourage, sitting around him, fawning over his tales of the D-list celebs he'd met in the past.

'But this time he was, well, sick. He couldn't eat, as I say. He managed to get through the rehearsal, but we must have left about nine-thirty or ten, and Tristan headed straight to bed once we got back to the boarding house.'

'You don't share a bedroom with your husband?' Martin asked.

'Tristan would have told you, that's the secret to a happy marriage.' Sera blushed a little at the attempt at a joke, snatching a glance at Jones. It felt uncomfortable, leaden in the airless room.

'So, after you said goodnight, did you see Tristan again that evening?' Martin asked, moving on.

Sera shook her head. 'No. I went to bed, too, and read for a while. I must have turned my light off about eleven.'

'And Violet?'

'She was in bed, too. The house was dark.' Sera looked down at that, circling her thumbs on her lap.

Martin studied Sera, thinking back to her earlier interview with Violet. The daughter resembled her father more, Martin considered. Her face was rounder, more symmetrical. She didn't have the sharp edges of her mother. Circles and triangles, she thought suddenly. People's faces could always be split into those two shapes. Their personalities, too, on the whole. 'She's your only child?'

'Yes . . .' Sera appeared to hesitate.

Martin looked at her enquiringly.

'We . . . uh, we had two boys. Twins,' Sera said quietly. 'They died over twenty years ago.'

'I'm sorry,' Martin said, storing the information. 'And this morning? What happened when you woke up?'

Sera closed her eyes briefly. 'Violet woke me. She rushed into my room, crying, saying that Daddy was dead. So I ran to see,' she said, her voice rising. 'I tried to get in but Violet shut the door, she wouldn't let me past. She was sobbing, saying it was too late. That we had to call the police.'

Martin pressed her lips together, thinking. The beat of the interview had slowed. She felt Jones breathing calmly beside her. Sera was silent; the blank look on her face had returned.

Martin shifted gear. 'Perhaps you could tell me a little about yourself. Where are you from originally?'

Sera raised her eyes. 'Actually, I'm from near here. I was born in Peterlee.'

Martin knew it. It was a town some ten miles away from Durham. That was what had sounded familiar to Martin when Sera spoke. The accent had flattened and become indistinct over time, but the lilt of the north-east remained present in her voice.

'My father was also a pastor,' Sera continued. 'In my twenties, we moved to Blackpool.'

'And that's where you met your husband?'

'It was a Tuesday afternoon. That day I entered the church and met Tristan. I've stayed there ever since.'

'When were you married?'

'We've been married for thirty years.'

Martin sat back in her chair as Jones's hand hovered above her notes. 'So, tell me about the Deucalion Church. It's hugely popular, so it would seem?'

Sera nodded.

'Particularly with children?'

'Well, we welcome everyone at Deucalion, young and old. But there are many children, Inspector, who need somewhere to call their home. Where their own homes have . . . failed them. We offer them that at the church.'

'And you came to Durham on some kind of tour?' Martin asked, glancing down at her lap. 'Why does your sister Antonia come with you?' She noticed something dark flit across Sera's face at that; a cold, hollow spasm.

'She's part of the church's family. She's a great support to me and Tristan. Always has been. And there's also Fraser, Tristan's best friend. We've known him for years. He's part of the family, too.'

'Ah yes, Mr Mackenzie,' Martin said, looking down at her notes. 'Was he at the boarding house with you, when you went to bed?'

'No, he must have come in later,' Sera answered. 'He had to stay at the theatre and finish up.'

Martin threw a look at Jones, who gave a brief nod, confirming that that was what Fraser had said.

'And so, after you turned out the light, you slept until you were woken up by Violet? Is that right, Mrs Snow?' Something rippled over the woman's face then, catching Martin's attention, causing her to lean forward, feeling the cadence of the interview change at last. 'What was it, Sera?' she asked, her tone triggering Jones to look up from her note taking. 'Did you wake up earlier than that? Did you hear something?'

'Ah, well, I don't know. I can't be sure.' Sera paused, her eyes half-closed, remembering. She shook her head a little, as if distilling the memory. 'Maybe, yes. A noise.'

'What kind of noise? A door? Someone's voice?'

'No. Not that. More . . . a fluttering. Deep down, in the dream . . .' Sera's eyes were completely closed, her lips moving as if in prayer. 'A fluttering of wings. Wings against something.' She opened her eyes fully, as if startled by the memory. 'Yes,' she said with certainty. 'It was the beating of wings against glass.'

9

Antonia hadn't reached it yet, but sobriety beckoned to her over the next hill. She still felt braver than normal, a kamikaze nugget of gold glittered in her stomach; her eyes had a wildness behind wet, blackened lashes. Her skin felt thick and itchy, caked on, like the make-up she had plastered herself with last night.

Last night. God, how long ago that seemed. Before this news. Before life without Tristan in it. Memories – no, she couldn't even call them that. Flashes of recall, still photographs of rolling events; that's how the fragments of last night appeared to her now. The rosy glow of the booze sinking down into her at first. The . . . the *happiness* of it. That was the good bit. Always. The good bit was always the start.

Then the bar or wherever would grow dark, like a blanket you wanted to crawl under. It would be nice in there to begin with. The lights pockmarking the walls, picking out bits of life you chose to look at. Not those bits that slammed into your face when you were least expecting them. It gave you *control*. That's what drinking did. Because even if at the end of the night you ended up flat on your back, with your legs in the air with everyone seeing your cunt while you screamed at them to just *fuck off* . . . Well, at least you were the one that had got you

49

there. You couldn't blame it on anyone else. You had done it. You weren't a victim.

The shower water mixed with soap de-clumped the mascara; the conditioner untangled the bird's nest of hair at the back of her scalp; the black coffee led her into the house next door to sobriety; the iced water quenched the daytime thirst. Breathing in the smell of jojoba and coconut, Antonia could pretend it hadn't happened. Just another hotel. Another show tonight. Same old uniform. Jeans on, boots zipped, concealer under the eyes. Just like nothing had ever happened.

She stood at the window, looking down on the pavement below. Rain drifted across the cityscape through holes in the sky, an archetypal summer storm. Thunder blared, making Antonia jump as a knock came at the door. She turned to face it. Say what you like about her. While it was easier to pretend, in the end, she always did face up to things.

In the hotel room next door, where she had returned after the interview with Martin, Sera was on the bed in semi-darkness, the pale yellow curtains drawn against the continuing clash of the storm outside. Dreamily, she heard Martin's knock on Antonia's door as she lay on top of the covers, fully clothed, drifting down into deep yet disturbed sleep. As she sank into unconsciousness, she moved her head from side to side, sweat pricking at her upper lip.

In the dream, she was in the room at the top of Rapunzel's tower. High walls, cream-covered cement, stretching up to a curved ceiling, ridged with time. The window was barred. She smiled at that.

Of course.

Rapunzel, Rapunzel, let down your hair.

He had sometimes whispered this as he pushed into her from behind. Her hair wrapped around his wrist, the ends of it split and rough like horsehair. As he rode her.

She sat up in the cell, sharply. Butting her head against the glass pane of memories, splintering it until the images exploded into shards raining down on to the bed. She noticed that her right hand clawed at the woollen blanket.

In another sudden and relentless movement, as if the earlier memory were now flattened on the road, mulched detritus under the heft of life's momentum, two uniformed men banged the door of the cell open. The harsh light in the corridor outside mingled with the insistent light of the cell, turning them into one and the same, an all-consuming whiteness. To her left, a door she had never noticed revealed itself. As it gaped open, she saw beyond it the masked man; the hangman she had dreamt of. But the reality was different. He did not have Tristan's face. His features were hidden under the cloth of his disguise; only his eyes glittered blackly from within.

But after all her dreams about him, he was not actually her focus. When she had imagined it, she had thought of staring into those eyes, seducing them, a conversation of pleas and bargains, communicated solely through her own blue gaze. As it was, she could only fix on the gnarly hewn-bramble beige of the rope, curled round, foetus-like: the circle of death.

There she would swing. Tied up with string.

If this was what it meant to be a single woman in middle age in the twenty-first century, then you could stick it, Martin thought. She studied Antonia Simpson, standing by the window in her cowboy boots, her dyed blonde hair curled to her shoulders, Dolly Parton eyelashes glancing off her cheekbones as she blinked vacantly back. Her breasts were fulsome, straining at her buttoned-down shirt, her teeth pearly white. Radiating around her, in an aromatic halo, was the unmistakeably sweet smell of stale booze, overlaid with a musky perfume, but there all the same.

Martin had a flash-forward; an image of herself in twenty years' time; alone and childless, putting more and more make-up on to hide the lines, the flabby folds of skin under the chin. *No*, she thought. *God, no.*

Rain clattered against the window, the daylight now officially became dusk, as slate-grey clouds swirled creatively behind Antonia's head. The Travelodge where the Family Liaison Officer had brought the family after their necessary departure from the Riverview B&B was typically plastic; primary-coloured swirls and zigzags splashed on to soft furnishings in an attempt to inject some personality into the mundane.

'How the mighty have fallen.' Antonia gestured at the marmalade-coloured bedspread and the white electric kettle with the tiny plug hanging down on the bedside table. She had the same remnants of the north-east in her accent as her sister, Martin noticed. Antonia moved to turn the light on over the bed. When it finally burst into life after a desolate hum, the room remained gloomy; a lone pinprick of a spotlight shining on the left-hand pillow.

Martin moved a chair out from behind a piece of furniture that could have been a table, a desk or a television stand, she couldn't tell. She sat and indicated that Antonia should do likewise. Antonia perched on the bottom of the double bed, legs tucked together like a prim bird on a narrow branch.

'Why are you seeing me here and not at the police station?' Antonia asked.

She was bright, then, Martin thought. A spark pulsed in the air and Martin felt suddenly sure that Antonia would reveal something. Brassy, leathery, tart with a heart, cliché . . . a cliché hiding . . . what? A cliché designed to conceal. Was that Antonia? The storm seemed to reach inside the room then; a flare of lightning, illuminating Antonia's face for a second, revealing the shadows under the make-up, the darkness of her eyes. In that moment, Martin saw that she was a drowning woman. Antonia's mouth twitched involuntarily for a second on one side. Yes, something would emerge from this.

'You will need to make a statement. But I wanted to see you first in more comfortable surroundings. I gather you were unwell earlier, at the B&B?'

Antonia's eyes flashed before she reined her expression in. 'I had too much to drink yesterday. Felt a bit worse for wear this morning.'

'Where were you?'

'Last night? Some pub in town, I don't remember the name. And then – up a hill?' She wrinkled her nose. 'A biker bar? There was a pool table.'

It sounded like the Angel, Martin thought. A dive popular with rough guys on the outskirts who rode into the city on Harleys and generally caused trouble. Someone would need to check it out. Antonia would have stood out a mile in a place like that.

'Were you with anyone else, with friends?'

'Just lil 'ol me,' Antonia said, smiling, her white teeth dazzling from behind pink, mother-of-pearl lips.

'Where did you sleep?' *Time to crack on*, Martin thought.

Antonia crossed her legs and inspected one of her nails. 'I made a friend.'

'Does your friend have a name and address?'

Her eyes lingered on her cuticles. 'Sadly, no.' She looked up at Martin then, and gave a small laugh. 'Friends come and go, though, don't you think?'

'What time did you get to the bar, and what time did you leave it?' Martin asked with a patience she didn't feel, itching to get uniformed officers round to question the bar staff with Antonia's photograph.

'I just can't remember,' Antonia said, smiling sadly at Martin. Her shirtsleeve dropped back, revealing an almond-shaped bruise on her wrist; purple round the edges, yellowish in the middle. *Old contusion*, Martin thought. Much like the one she had seen on Sera in her interview earlier. Why does everyone in this family seem to have bruises? Antonia carefully pulled the sleeve down, avoiding looking at Martin.

'So you would have left the theatre after Tristan Snow finished rehearsing. You didn't go to dinner with him and his family?'

Antonia's eyes narrowed at that. 'His *family* . . . sure.'

'Did you go to dinner?'

'No, I didn't.'

'You went straight to the bar you mentioned? Or you went to other places first? Look, Ms Simpson, it's pretty simple. I just need an account of your whereabouts from when you left the theatre, around . . .?'

'Seven p.m. Maybe?'

'Right. 7 p.m. until 7 a.m. Twelve hours. That's all.'

Antonia bent her head, squeezing her eyes shut. 'I left the theatre . . . walked into that square in the middle of the city? There's a pub in the middle of it. Some kind of tavern?'

The Market Tavern, Martin surmised, adding the name to the list of places to check.

'That was where I met this guy. He's some local journalist, I think. Wanted to talk about Tristan, once he found out I'm his sister-in-law. They always do.' She gave a low laugh. 'We had a few drinks then he suggested walking up a hill to another bar he knew. That was the biker place. We stayed there the rest of the night. Drinking, talking . . .'

'What time did you leave? Can you remember?'

Antonia shook her head. 'I can't. Tequila, you know?' She gave another little laugh. 'Anyway, we left and ended up at his place. Wasn't far from there from what I recall. We sat downstairs, drank some more . . .' she sighed. 'To be honest, I think I just crashed out on the sofa. He tried it on. Of course. Then he put on *Easy Rider*. I couldn't concentrate on it, you know? Bloody Dennis Hopper. Can't understand a word he says. He gave me a spliff . . .' Her eyes widened as a thought occurred to her. 'He had an Irish name . . . something Keagan? Logan? Anyway . . . two drags on that and I was out for the count. Woke up, he was gone.' She shrugged. 'Found my way back to the B&B. When I got there –' she waved her hand at Martin '– I heard the news.'

'Keagan? Logan? Is that his first name or surname?'

'I don't know, Inspector,' Antonia replied, wearily.

'So the upshot is – if we can't find this man – that no one can . . .'

'No one can verify my whereabouts, that's true,' she cut in. 'But I didn't kill the preacher.' She snorted another laugh. 'Sounds like a Dusty Springfield song!'

Martin didn't smile. 'Indeed.'

Antonia's face straightened. 'Seriously. I didn't. Much as I would have liked the bastard dead. Sadly, I wasn't the one to have the honour.' The curse sounded odd coming from her lips. Dolly gone bad.

'You didn't get on with your brother-in-law?'

'That's an understatement.' Antonia stood abruptly and went to the window, looking out and down on to the street. 'We tolerated each other for Sera's sake. And Violet's.' Her voice trailed away.

'But?'

'But . . . people aren't what they appear sometimes. The man was a pig. A big fat pig.' She traced her finger down the condensation gathering on the inside of the window, her reflection mirroring her actions in the spattered pane of glass. 'He deserved to die. And I'm a Christian woman.

Listen to me!' Irony dripped from her in company with the droplets on the window.

'Tell me about him,' Martin said. 'Why was he a pig? What did he do? From everything I've read so far, he seemed very respected.' She breathed in, hooking the fly on the line. Would Antonia bite?

Antonia looked at Martin in pity. 'Oh, that's a shame.'

'What is?'

'I thought you would be intelligent.'

Martin waited. *Too obvious.* 'People aren't what they appear sometimes,' she said at last.

Antonia raised an eyebrow. Taking a breath, she seemed to take a decision. 'If you really want to know, Tristan was a mix. He could be very charming, very comforting, a great host. A man always ready to top up your glass, sit you down, focus on you, listen to you. That's how he drew them in. The people who came. His voice, when he was on it. You could listen to him for hours. He would describe the world in colours that seemed . . . he gave you hope. And yet, at the same time . . . he stole it.' Antonia's voice dropped and she muttered something Martin couldn't hear.

'What was that?'

She turned to face Martin with a grim smile. 'I said he stole hope. Hope is a cheap date, Inspector Martin.'

Martin swallowed. *Here it comes: the reveal.* Antonia had let something in her go, thoughts were hurtling through her, racing past stop signs.

'He would lead you to a place where you would think you could achieve something, where you believed that you were actually worth something, not what you told yourself you actually were every day. He made you believe that you were good, that you could be whatever you wanted.' She hesitated, tears in her eyes as the last dregs of the comfort of the alcohol finally seeped away. 'He would tease you until you believed him, until you would relax, just a little bit. You would start to think it was true. Then, just when life was opening up and you would start to think that you weren't so bad, he'd remind you that it was all bullshit.' Tears began to fall down Antonia's cheeks, soaking into the denim of her shirt, turning the material dark blue.

'How would he do it?' Martin asked.

Antonia lifted her hair up off the back of her neck and rested her head on the glass, closing her eyes. 'In the cruellest way possible,' she said. 'He would belittle you.'

'Snow was an abuser, I'd say,' Martin said to Sam in his office. 'Mental – maybe physical – wife and her sister have some bruising. If so, though, they're being quiet as church mice about it.'

'Alibis?'

'Nope. Wife was in bed asleep, as was daughter. And the sister was out on the lash in a bar and then in some random bloke's living room who we're going to struggle to find based on the little she's told us.'

'Is she lying?'

'Possibly . . .' Martin sighed, looking at Sam, who had his head bent to the desk. 'Uh, I've heard from Jim. He wants to have dinner.'

Sam lifted his eyes and stared silently at her for a moment before picking up a paperclip from his desk and passing it to and fro between the fingers of his right hand, as if playing a game. 'Who with?'

'Dealing with emotions as sport on the merry-go-round, I see?' Martin's tone was bitter.

'Don't quote Hardy at me, Martin.' Sam exhaled loudly, tossing the paperclip to one side. 'Jesus.' He stood up, pushing his chair back, his hands in his pockets. 'What's the problem? Go and have dinner with him. He's the one who left, Erica. I don't see this as an issue.'

Why don't you care? Martin thought, hating herself as she did so. *Because isn't that the issue: that he was the one who left?*

'What is it?' he asked. 'Do you *want* there to be a problem?'

'I don't want to have dinner with him. Or anyone, quite honestly. I've got enough going on.'

'This is what I warned you . . .' Sam said.

'Don't "I told you so" me,' Martin snapped. 'I just want to be able to do my job without a whole bunch of other shit.'

'So do it,' Sam replied, a frustrated edge to his tone. 'Ignore Jim and get on with it. Come on, Erica. This is . . . I don't know what it is. It's like I've done something wrong. Like you're wanting something from me. What is it?'

Martin started to roll her eyes but managed to control the impulse. What was she, fifteen? This wasn't like her. She was pathetic. 'I need more from Violet, the daughter, is my feeling,' she said, her voice hard. 'None of them have decent alibis, but all of them have some kind of motive, I'm sensing.'

Sam gave up, sat back heavily in his seat and picked up his pen. 'Sure. Do what you need.'

'Walsh is being slow. I'll have to chase him after the press conference. The post-mortem's booked for then. But I mean, how long does it take to determine that someone was hit on the head?'

'Right.'

She waited, but nothing more came.

'Okay then, thanks,' she said as she left the room, closing the door behind her. She stood for a minute, breathing in and out quietly. Why was she behaving like this? She was pushing Sam away and that familiar cavern was opening up inside of her, pulling her down. She screwed her eyes shut and sent a bargaining chip up, past the plasterboard of the ceiling, into space and whatever resided there. *Take it away, God or whoever. Take these feelings away and let me do my job. And I swear, I'll do whatever you want. Please.*

Eileen Quinn watched them from her bedroom window, where she had scurried after she had been let back into the B&B. Five policemen with black rain jackets over their uniforms, polythene bags over their shoes, pacing methodically in a steady line over the lawn in the garden. The storm had cleared and only a light drizzle remained, spitting down the backs of their collars, their bent heads sleek like seals, eyes trained on every blade of grass.

Idiots, Eileen thought, witheringly. She moved her head in contempt, feeling the reassuring click of her earrings as they swung. She bit her lip, fingering the cross around her neck. *Ah well. Soon it would all come to pass.* But then she remembered the letter. She needed them out of here before they found it.

She was just deciding to go and make tea for them all when a knock came at the door.

'Mrs Quinn?'

It was the youngest one. He seemed to be about fifteen. Good-looking if you liked sticky-out ears and a weak chin. He was a beanpole; he had to bend his head under the door frame. This place was a dump really, Eileen sighed to herself. The ceilings were sinking along with the profits.

'Wonder if I could have a word?' the policeman persisted, pretending that Eileen wasn't giving him the stink-eye. She lifted her chin. She came from better stock than this, after all. Her great-grandmother, Anastasia, had been on the *Titanic*. Second class, too. She herself had been on the London stage. She had been Eliante at The Latchmere. Ah, those days . . . How had she ended up here?

'I'll make us tea,' she said, drawing herself up with something akin to a regal manner. Fielding swallowed. He had sampled Mrs Quinn's rust-coloured liquid earlier. Three chocolate biscuits later and he still couldn't get the acrid dairy taste out of his mouth.

Fifteen minutes later and they were sat at the kitchen table, china mugs in hand, a packet of chocolate Hobnobs standing sentry between them.

Eileen brushed crumbs off her ample lap. 'Where's the main woman? What's her name? Sounds like a man?'

'DI Martin, you mean?' Fielding answered. 'Oh. She might interview you later, but . . .'

'Got to see if I'm worth her time, have you?'

'Uh, no. Not like that.' Fielding reddened. He reached for the tea to displace his awkwardness, rueing the decision as the flavour of curdled roof tiles hit his taste buds. He smiled, nodding, grabbing a biscuit, cramming it into his mouth to override the sensation.

'Nice, them, aren't they?' Eileen nodded at the packet. 'Had them on sale at Lidl.' She put her head on one side and decided to give the young chap the benefit of the doubt. 'I suppose you'll be wanting to know my whereabouts.' She gave a small tut. 'Before you kicked me out of here this morning, of course. I couldn't believe I was barred from my own home. Deary me.'

Fielding coughed a little so as to better swallow the mush in his mouth. 'Sorry about that, Mrs Quinn. But obviously we needed to search Riverview thoroughly before anyone could be let back in.'

'What're you looking for in the garden, then?'

Fielding felt this interview slipping away from him. He seemed to be answering more questions than he asked. 'Nothing, uh, now then, Mrs Quinn.' Fielding sat up straighter in his chair. *Focus.* 'Can you tell me about your movements last night, please?'

'Certainly.' Eileen folded her hands on the table. 'I ate my tea at just gone six. Nice bit of gammon. Then I had a cuppa watching that Schofield man on that quiz show. I do like him, you know.' She stared off into the distance as if reminiscing about a long-ago romance.

'And then?' Fielding prompted. 'What time did you turn in?'

'About nine-thirty it must have been. I watched half that silly thing about the servants but couldn't be bothered with it, if I'm honest. So I toddled up to bed. Lights out.'

Fielding looked at her carefully. Had there been a tell, then? A glint in her eye as she rocked back in her seat, hand to her throat? They would need to check the TV schedule, although of course anyone could look it up, pretending to have watched things they had never seen.

'Do you lock the front door when you retire, Mrs Quinn?'

Eileen nodded approvingly. She liked the word *retire*. It was apt for someone of her stature. 'I do,' she answered primly. 'My guests all have a key. They can let themselves in when they *retire* themselves.'

'Do you have any sort of curfew?'

'Midnight.' She gave a silly sort of smile and another shake of her earrings. 'The witching hour, no less.'

'But you'd have no way of checking who'd returned and who hadn't, I suppose?'

'I'm up every morning at 5 a.m.' Eileen looked at Fielding sternly. 'I can't be waiting up all night for every Tom, Dick and Harry to come in, can I? I've got to cook breakfast at the crack of dawn.'

'So you would have heard Violet Snow come down this morning at seven, then?'

'What's that?' Eileen narrowed her eyes.

'Violet came down at seven to make her and her dad a cup of tea. Did you see her then?'

'Uh, no. I must have popped upstairs to get something.'

'What time would that have been?'

'Well, I don't really know.' Eileen began to look flustered. 'I don't wear a watch.'

Fielding leaned forward, his voice friendly. 'I understand, Mrs Quinn. But we need to establish what was going on in this house last night and this morning. Are you saying you didn't see Violet this morning?'

'No. No I didn't.'

'Did you see anyone else? If you were up at five . . .'

'Well, it may have been more like six *this* morning. Sometimes my alarm goes on the blink . . .'

'Right. But when you came downstairs from your bedroom at the top of the house, you didn't see anyone on the floors below? Is that right, Mrs Quinn? This is important.'

Eileen weighed it up. She wanted this whippersnapper to go. She could see the letter in her mind's eye in the drawer in the kitchen sideboard. It seemed to glow from behind the wood, burning like hot coals. She hadn't had a chance to move it – all these idiots snooping everywhere since the sun had been up. Whatever happened, it mustn't be found. She made a decision based on what would get this policeman out of here in the quickest possible time.

'I did see someone, yes.'

Fielding sat up. 'Where, Mrs Quinn?'

'On the corridor on the floor below me. I was just coming downstairs. I was in my slippers so I probably didn't make much noise.' Eileen rubbed her swollen toes absent-mindedly, thinking back to what she had seen.

'That was this morning?' Fielding asked urgently.

Eileen nodded. 'It was a man. He was dressed in jeans and that, but – I just thought it was odd at the time . . .'

'What was odd?'

'I don't know, something about him. He looked . . . *odd*.' Eileen looked at Fielding. They said nothing.

'And did you recognize the man?' Fielding asked at last.

Eileen nodded again. She paused, her theatrical training lending her a moment of suspense. Fielding raised his eyebrows.

'It was that manager. Mackenzie, I think his name is.' Eileen sat back in her chair, turning her fat thumbs around and about each other. 'Yes. Fraser Mackenzie. It was definitely him I saw.'

Martin put her head around the door of the incident room. 'Jones. Coming with me to the press conference? I've got an hour before I have to be at the post-mortem with Walsh.'

Jones got to her feet. 'Sure thing. By the way,' she said, raising an envelope into the air. 'This was dropped in at the front desk an hour ago.'

Martin frowned, coming into the room and taking the letter. She took some gloves from her pocket and put them on before ripping it open and scanning its contents, pursing her lips. 'Hmm,' she said at last.

'What is it?'

'Did you see who dropped this off?'

'Nope. Was just handed in to the desk sergeant. We can check CCTV if you want.'

Martin glanced down again at the paper in her hands before holding it up for Jones to see. It was a black and white photocopy of a photograph. Judging by the double denim and permed hair, Jones guessed it had been taken sometime in or around the eighties. A man and a woman stood together in an embrace. He had his arms around her waist. The woman's face was blurry and indistinct but she was looking up at him with such an expression of adoration that it made Jones smile. The couple were standing in front of a backlit theatre, on a grimy pavement. One of the woman's legs was kicked up behind her. They looked on the cusp of something; they were celebrating.

'Is that . . .?' Jones asked.

Martin nodded. 'Tristan Snow? Looks like it.'

'But who's that with him?'

'It's a good question,' Martin said, taking back the photo and popping it into an evidence bag. 'But a better question is why someone dropped this in here without leaving their name. And more to the point,' Martin continued, turning to leave, 'how is it relevant to Tristan Snow's murder?'

'This is going to be brief,' Martin said to the gathered journalists. 'But given that Reverend Snow is well known to the media and the public, we want to try and get across some accurate information.

'The Reverend Tristan Snow was, this morning, found dead at the Riverview bed and breakfast, where he and his family had been staying for the past three nights.'

'Circumstances of death, DI Martin? Murder, was it?'

That was Sean Egan. Martin threw him a bullet-shaped glance. He had form with Martin – having knowingly consorted with the murderer of a student a year or so back, purely *in the interests of getting the truth across*, of course. Martin had taken him down a peg or two then, to put it mildly. But he continued to bounce up again and again, an irritant made of India rubber.

As she heard him speak, though, something ticked in her brain, something just out of reach. What was it?

'Obviously, we will not be revealing anything about the manner in which Reverend Snow died, at this early stage,' Martin said patiently. No sweets for the Egan child. 'We are still in the process of dealing with Reverend Snow's relatives and focusing on establishing a formal cause of death.'

'But you can say that it was in suspicious circumstances. Surely . . .' Egan continued.

Martin cut him off. 'We *would* ask that anyone who was in the vicinity of Riverview in the early hours of this morning come forward and identify themselves. But this is purely a formality to eliminate people from our enquiries.' Martin stood up. 'If there's nothing else . . .'

'And the ceremony celebrating Tristan's life . . .' Egan persisted. 'They're calling it a vigil. Will that be taking place?'

'We are not aware of any official plans for a vigil, Mr Egan. If any of Tristan Snow's supporters wish to express their grief, they will of course be welcome. We would emphasize, however, that this should be done in an orderly and lawful fashion.'

Martin smiled briefly at the room before walking briskly out. 'Thank you, all.'

'Ultimate cause of death was a massive haemorrhage due to shards of parietal bone entering the brain. As you will have noted at the scene and during the PM, the skull was shattered by a forceful blow of an instrument of some kind. Something with a sharpened edge would have made it easier, I suspect.' Dr Brian Walsh passed a file over his desk to where Martin and Jones sat, opposite. 'Have you found the murder weapon yet?'

'No,' Martin acknowledged. 'We're looking, though. Partridge and the SOCOs are still at the boarding house.' She bit her lip. 'Time of death?'

Walsh raised his famously thick eyebrows and took a swig from a mug of tea. He was a small man with greying fair hair and glacial green eyes. Behind his head a skeletal diagram dangled eerily from the wall. Martin hated Walsh's office. It was overheated and stuffy, and the shelves that ran along the top of the room were filled with murky jars containing unidentifiable liquids and objects. Martin was convinced these were body parts, extracted under duress.

'Hard to be entirely precise. The window was open a little as you know, which made the room cold. There was a fair amount of fluid – saliva and vomit – which had come from the victim's mouth on to the carpet. I'd suggest this meant he was alive for a while before he lost consciousness.' Walsh pushed his chair back and crossed his legs. 'You'll see in my report that rigor had only just begun. I'd say anywhere from around 3 a.m. until he was found.'

'Fairly big time window,' Martin said.

'Sorry about that. But that's the truth of it.'

The words seemed to spin and float into the air in front of Martin. *The truth of it.* What was it that had fluttered into her head at the press conference? What was it that was bothering her?

'Martin?' Walsh was saying. 'Did you hear me?'

Martin focused on the room, shaking her head a little. 'Sorry. What did you say?'

'I was saying that I had one of my team have a look at the pigeon you sent in with the body,' Walsh's tone was neutral, but his gaze was filled with disappointment, as if Martin had been sent to him for school detention. 'A pigeon,' he went on, giving a slight shake of his head. 'Can't say I've been sent one of those before.'

'And?' Martin said, ignoring the reproach. 'Anything of interest?'

'Well, that would depend on your perspective, wouldn't it?' Walsh answered, his head on one side. 'But putting aside any anthropomorphism, the cause of the bird's death was, in my humble opinion – as a mere pathologist, you understand, and not as a veterinary surgeon – due to a broken neck.'

'Anthropo . . . what?' Jones put in.

'Presumably the pigeon couldn't fly with a broken neck, so it was either killed inside the room or was brought into the room already dead?' Martin asked.

'Indeed,' Walsh said, directed to Martin. 'The attribution of human characteristics to animals,' he said to Jones, his eyes twinkling a little. 'Another thing,' he said, leaning forward across his desk and picking up a piece of paper. 'We also ran a toxicology scan. Standard in a homicide, as you know.'

Martin inclined her head. 'Did it reveal anything?'

'Snow had extremely high levels of solanine present in his bloodstream.'

'Solanine?'

Walsh made a wry face. 'Commonly known as deadly nightshade. It's found in green potato tubers.'

Martin sat forward. 'What?'

Walsh shrugged. 'There it is. Eat too many green potato sprouts and you'll get sick.'

'Can it cause death?' Jones asked.

'Enough of it can. Snow had approximately 165 milligrams in his system; that's sufficient to cause toxicity. If he'd carried on ingesting it at that rate, eventually it would've been fatal.'

'Ingesting it?' Martin said. 'What are you saying? His wife wasn't cooking his chips properly?'

Walsh allowed a quick smile. 'Dissolve the potato sprouts. Filter and solidify them, turn them into a powder. Put it into his Horlicks. Enough of it, he'd suffer nausea, gastroenteritis, hallucinations. Finally, his lungs would have shut down.'

The room was silent.

'Obviously his death was caused by the haemorrhage in his brain,' the pathologist said.

'But that just sealed the deal,' Jones said quietly. 'Because unless he was on a gastro adventure of his own . . .'

'Someone had already been trying to poison him.' Martin finished for her.

THE DURHAM CHRONICLE ONLINE
MONDAY 8 AUGUST, 2016
TRISTAN SNOW: TV MIRACLE MAKER
FOUND DEAD

Reverend Tristan Snow MBE has been found dead in the city of Durham while on his sell-out MIRACLES tour across the British Isles. The Reverend was 69 years old.

The former presenter, most famous for his appearances as resident psychic and self-dubbed 'miracle maker' on *This Morning* and *Good Morning Britain*, has been found dead at a local bed and breakfast in the city of Durham.

Police are treating his death as suspicious, although no further information regarding the circumstances has been released at this time.

Tonight, tributes to the veteran presenter came in from the world of showbusiness, with tweets illustrating the high regard in which Reverend Snow was held. Radio presenter Jed Hamilton said that Reverend Snow, who was given the MBE in 2012 for his services to charity, worked 'tirelessly' to raise funds for various causes, including caring for the abandoned children he often took in at the Deucalion Church in Blackpool where he was Reverend. 'He was a very animated character,' Mr Hamilton told the BBC. 'But most of all, I remember him as just a powerful presence, a larger than life character. As he was in front of his followers, so he was offstage.'

The Reverend was often dubbed '. . . a proper British eccentric' and a close friend of his has been quoted as saying he was 'a man so unique a character, so extraordinary a personality that you could not have made him up'.

A close friend added that Snow 'didn't know his parents and so the charity work he did became his family. It wasn't just for the publicity. He was capable of acts of great kindness. You didn't really ever get to know "the man" because he was a showman . . . and like so many showmen, that's their main thing in life and he did it exceptionally.'

The Deucalion Church made a statement this morning, saying: 'It is with deep sadness that we can announce that our brother and friend Tristan Snow MBE was found deceased this morning. Everyone who knew Tristan is in shock and we are doing everything we can to assist police with their enquiries. While we thank the people who have offered their condolences, for the moment, we would ask that our privacy be respected.'

A memorial and book of condolence to Reverend Snow has been set up in the foyer of the Palace Theatre in Blackpool.

Snow leaves behind a wife, Seraphina (60) and a daughter Violet (18).

Did you know Tristan Snow? Do have any information concerning his death? Get in touch with your stories to Sean Egan via email at segan@durhamchronicle.co.uk or @seganjourno on Twitter.

13

'So Mackenzie takes fifteen per cent of Snow's earnings?' Jones asked, back from the pathologist, as she picked at a box of sushi on the desk.

'Yep,' Tennant answered, his burger stinking out the room from on top of his desk. 'Fifteen per cent of everything. Tours, DVDs, books, personal appearances.' He looked over at her lunch with a shudder. 'I don't know how you can eat that crap.'

Jones ignored him. 'Must be doing quite well, then. Not much of an incentive for murder, is it? Like killing the Golden Goose.'

'Except it's not so much golden as wasting away and the carcass about to be put into the soup.' Tennant popped a can of Coke and took a slurp. 'Snow and Mackenzie formed a company about ten years ago. They're both registered as directors.' He sniffed. 'But the company's in the shit. Hence them all staying at that crappy B&B. Hence Mackenzie's stress levels at getting tickets sold for the gig.'

'Why's it in the shit, though? They have actually flogged tickets. The conference centre was practically sold out.'

'Well, I'm no forensic accountant,' Tennant said, leaning back in his chair.

Jones raised an eyebrow.

'But my thought is Fraser Mackenzie had his hand in the till.' Tennant tapped the papers on his desk. 'So to speak.

He set up a partnership in the Cayman Islands just over two years ago with an entertainment company. They would invest money in *creative enterprises*,' he said, making the sign for inverted commas, before taking a large bite of his burger. Jones wrinkled her nose as grease dripped down his chin. 'But Snow wasn't involved in that,' Tennant continued, through his chomping, eventually wiping his mouth with a napkin. 'Profits are all registered to yet another company. And who's the registered director of that?'

'Fraser Mackenzie,' Jones said.

Tennant nodded. 'Correct.'

Fielding put his head around the door. 'DS Jones? Wondered if I could have a word?'

'What is it? Come on in, don't be shy.'

He walked into the room nervously, biting his lip.

'What is it, Eddie?' Jones asked, kindly; Tennant rolled his eyes as she moved to face Fielding. 'How did the interview go with Eileen Quinn?'

'She's a funny old bat,' Fielding answered.

'Yep, seems that way,' Jones said, turning back to tap on her keyboard. 'And?'

'Thing is, she was asleep all night, so she says. So no alibi there . . .'

'What's new . . .?' Jones said, almost to herself.

'But, well, she says that she was up early on the morning of the murder. That she saw something . . .'

Jones stopped typing and again turned to face Fielding. 'What did she see?'

'Fraser Mackenzie, the manager. Says she saw him walking down the corridor. She said he looked . . .' Fielding's Adam's apple bobbed with excitement. 'You know, *odd*.'

Jones sat back in her seat and flipped a glance at Tennant, tapping a chewed-up biro against her mouth.

Tennant shook his head with a tut. 'Old bint says Colonel Mustard looked odd on his way to the loo. Hang on a sec, I might tell them to hold the front page,' he muttered, before turning his back pointedly on Fielding. 'Nice try, Junior.'

'What time was this?' Jones asked, scowling at Tennant.

'She wasn't sure. Around 6 a.m. I'd say. She claims to be up from five, but if she's anything like my nan, she'll be slow getting her slippers on. In any case, five or six, it's still . . .' he looked down at his notes. 'What came over the radio, from the pathologist?'

'Yep,' Jones concurred. 'It's within the time frame for the murder.'

Martin parked her car outside the Travelodge for the second time that day. She looked at the glass edifice through the driver's window, considering what she would say when she entered. The day was once again muggy, insipid steam rising from the pavements after the downpour of the storm. The car interior was silent; she had nudged the radio off to think as she drove. People wandered around inside the hotel, lounging at the reception, walking past the vases of plastic flowers decorating the lobby. They were lilies, Martin noticed. Flowers of death.

Thoughts smudged and smeared in her brain, popping up randomly, uncharacteristically erratic. She breathed, envying her imagined simplicity of the lives of the people in the hotel reception; a ridiculous notion, she conceded. They were probably all as messed up as she was. *And* having to stay in a Travelodge. Her stomach growled and the image floated into her mind, idly, of fish and chips with lots of vinegar. With ketchup. Martin rubbed her hand over her face and sighed. She looked at herself in the rear-view mirror, thought about putting on some lipstick before dismissing the idea and opening the car door to jog across the street.

Sera Snow was already sitting in the little hotel bar adjacent to the lobby when Martin walked in. She could see Sera's petite figure, her grey head bent to the table. She appeared to have her eyes closed which she opened as Martin sat down opposite her.

Martin ordered a sparkling water for herself and an orange juice for Sera. Then she slid the copy of the photograph over the table.

'Who is this, Sera?'

Sera pulled the photograph to her, past the glass that a waitress had put in front of her. She bent her head to look closer and then briefly shut her eyes.

'That's my sister, Antonia.'

Martin scratched her wrist and thought for a moment. 'Did you bring this photograph to the police station? Drop it in anonymously?'

Sera smiled, meeting Martin's eyes. 'No, I didn't.'

'Do you know who did?'

'No.'

Martin leaned forward and pulled the photo back towards her, looked down at it. 'Why do you think someone would want me to see this?'

Sera said nothing. She took a sip of her juice, placing the glass back carefully on the table.

'They look happy, don't they? Tristan and Antonia. Do you know where they are? Where the photo was taken?'

Sera narrowed her eyes and rubbed her lips together. 'What is it you're hoping to wheedle out of me, Inspector Martin?'

'It's not a question of wheedling anything, Mrs Snow. Murder is a very serious thing. The worst crime there is. So . . .'

'Really?' Sera interjected. 'You think murder's the worst crime?'

Martin didn't respond.

'What about disloyalty? What about abuse? What about theft?' Sera's head moved from side to side, her fingers counting as she spoke. 'What about violence? And betrayal?' She stopped still, her hands in the air like stone birds caught in flight. 'What about the destruction of someone's soul?' She almost laughed, her face flushing with drama.

Martin waited for more but nothing came. 'What is the worst crime then, Sera?' she asked. 'What do you think?'

Sera pinched her mouth tight. She lowered her gaze to the table. Martin felt the minutes pass. Sera had retreated.

'Well,' Martin continued, deciding suddenly to push it anyway, to press down on the bruise. 'To solve your husband's murder, I'll need to ask difficult questions, uncover things that perhaps you don't want found out. That's what murder is, Mrs Snow. It's a stripping of a whitewash. It exposes those hidden things that have been festering away for years.'

Sera took a breath and exhaled softly. 'Yes,' she said at last. 'I realize that.' She pushed her glass towards the centre of the table and seemed to decide something. 'The photograph was taken in Blackpool. It must have been just after we were married. Tristan had been building up the parish, going out into the community. People were starting to love him. They saw something in him.' She gave a smile filled with secrets. 'He gave them what they wanted.'

'He had charisma?'

'Yes, he did. But it was more than that. It was a . . . a light around him. He seemed . . . *golden*. Everyone wanted to be around him. The children. Everyone.' Sera lifted her head and stared hard at Martin. 'Even my sister.' She turned to gaze out of the lobby windows and pushed some strands of hair off her forehead. Traffic noise filtered in and a group of young women – a hen do, Martin surmised – exploded the occasional laugh as they looked at something on a mobile phone. Sera appeared not to notice any of this. She was looking far away, back in time, Martin thought. She was in a dream.

'Your husband and your sister . . .?' Martin asked, trying to draw her back to the present.

Sera nodded, resigned. She tapped methodically at the photo. 'It had started before this. This was Tristan's first big show. We filled the theatre. I knew it was going on, of course.' She gave a sardonic laugh. 'They made me take the bloody photo.'

Martin studied Sera's face. How appalling for this woman to have watched her own sister make a successful play for her husband. Appalling enough for murder? 'So if this was just after you were married, this would have been . . .?'

Sera shrugged. 'About 1986, I suppose? Something like that.'

'And what did you do about it? What did you feel about it?'

Sera looked at Martin blankly.

'If it was me,' Martin explained, 'I'd have been livid. Furious with them both. It's such a betrayal . . .'

Her words hung in the air until Sera gave a slow smile. 'I didn't murder my husband, Inspector Martin.'

Martin put her chin on her hand. 'Did you consider leaving him?'

'Leave him?' Sera tossed her head, her large aquamarine earrings rattling against her neck. 'No, I never considered leaving him.'

'Why not? Most women would . . .'

A cloud passed across the older woman's face. She pushed her glass of orange juice a couple of millimetres away from her towards the edge of the table. 'You can't leave Tristan,' she whispered, almost to herself.

'He wouldn't have let you go, do you mean?'

'Don't you understand?' Sera sighed and looked at Martin as if talking to a child. 'If you can't understand, then I'm afraid this case will be beyond you.'

'I can understand a woman who's hurt, who's been betrayed. Who holds it in, year after year, until one day she snaps. Takes revenge on a man who has caused her nothing but agony. Is that it? Is that what I need to know?'

Sera stood up, her eyes flashed once, turned black, before she settled herself into blandness once more. 'No. It's not. You need to know about families, Detective. And the loyalty women have to their men.' She bent down to put her face close to Martin's. 'Watch,' she whispered. As she moved away, her hand caught her glass on the edge of table and swept it off, on to the floor. Martin looked on bewildered as Sera walked out of the hotel lobby, leaving pieces of glass and amber droplets of juice scattered in her wake.

14

There were always yellow bulbs glowing above the proscenium arch at the Grand. Do you remember? I thought of them as sunlit orbs; the golden ball that the princess drops down the well before she meets the frog. The curtains remained red velvet throughout the years. All those years that he performed there.

Tristan would often be late, waiting — up in his dressing room — preparing himself. He'd send me and Violet down in advance, to sit in the auditorium. We were his consorts. When we'd enter, a whisper would scuttle through the crowd, heads turning as we took our seats. The pride I felt then soaked through me. Often that made up for everything: the pride. Even the women with red lipstick and the trays of confectionery hanging down from them like window boxes would notice. When Tristan was ready to come on, they would leave the auditorium, walking silently backwards like a programme rewound in slow motion. I would give Violet fruit gums to try to help her stay awake as she leaned, eyes drowsy, against the prickly brushed material of her seat. In those days, she still had school in the morning.

Did you love Blackpool like I always did? Walking along the front to the Grand Theatre, that sense of anticipation. The smell of the vinegar from the nearby fish and chip shops would sting your nostrils. In the summer, the air was warm, dusky; the red and white stripes of the beach vendors' awnings turning pinkish in the fading light. The streets would be busy with people heading to dinner or to shows, or down to the seafront to watch the illuminations pierce the encroaching dark.

Inside the theatre, when the crowd became so restless it seemed as though they might stampede, Tristan would finally appear. He would stand on his tiptoes, his arms outstretched. Behind him, our Lord glittered on the cross and the organ would play melodies as Tristan spoke – pop songs, other songs of the time. Remember how tall Tristan was? As he spoke, he reached upwards, towering over everyone seated before him, as if he were trying to knock the top of his head on the very clouds that darted below heaven.

Everything he said, we believed. 'People say we're weird, don't they?' he told us. 'I bet they do. Your neighbours and friends. Perhaps even members of your own family?' He would wait, his fingers pressed together under his chin, swaying forward, as if he could hear our thoughts. 'I'm right, aren't I? They say we're weirdos; Bible-bashers; geeks . . . losers. I know . . .' He'd rock back on his heels, his face covered in empathy. Then he would shake his head, his black hair falling across his brow, his face crinkled in under-standing. He would drop his voice to a whisper. 'But I'm going to tell you a secret.' The hush that came then – well, it was something. It felt historic – that this was a moment.

I knew his speeches by heart. Still do. Tristan would lean further forward, his voice low but powerful. 'We are the chosen ones. We are the chosen ones.'

He would clap his hands, satisfaction on his face. 'How about that? Eh?' A laugh would burst from him. 'So the joke's on them, ladies and gentlemen! When they drop down into that abyss and their skin is flayed by the fires of hell, who will be laughing then? Who will be calling whom losers?'

Even now, as I write his words, they buoy me, make me whole.

'All of you! All of you here. And your children! Bring your children to this place. Train them up in the way they should go. It's so important, ladies and gentlemen. To show your children the love that I am showing you. The love that I want to show your children. Bring them here. To us. To Deucalion.'

When the speech was over, he would sink to his knees, a rag doll robbed of energy. His palms would be flat on the stage before him, his head bowed. We would all stand transfixed, where we had been cheering and clapping. We could see, we could tell, that this was a man who could heal, a man of God. The organ would be silent. We all held our gaze on the man crumpled low on the stage.

My husband.

Smoke would drift into amorphous ribbons, undulating across the stage, thinning into narrow lines, parallel across Tristan's body. He would do this thing – where he would stare unseeing into the dark of the auditorium but every member of the audience felt his eyes on them alone. His palms would be outstretched, skin so white his hands looked swathed in magician's gloves. Pink light would surround his body, a slippery hue that danced around the black core of his shape.

Finally, when the smoke had evaporated, trails reducing to nothing, Tristan would become meticulous. Soft. The audience would shift forward on their seats, lips parted, tongues curled. It was as if a pause button had been pressed. We were statues.

Lifeless.

'Come to me. Come and feel my love.' Tristan would beckon to us all in the dark. 'Come, please. Come and feel my love.'

Then all of us would walk up, on to the stage to receive Tristan's blessing, his healing. I felt such love for him as his eyes remained closed through it all, his mouth moving rapidly, offering up the words he knew better than his own soul. His hands would reach and stroke and caress their outstretched limbs, their knotted, gnarly veins, their bunions, their crepey necks. Even the young ones came forward with their calluses, their jumpers with baby snot on the shoulders, their empty pockets.

The filing past would end, and that was when the clapping would begin. It would rise, gentle like a wave until it crashed as a tsunami on to the stage; until nobody could hear themselves think.

And that was when the next beautiful thing would happen. Do you remember? It was so spontaneous, and yet it happened every time he spoke. The people who had been healed by Tristan wanted to thank him; they wanted to love him. They would push their notes and their cheques and their credit cards – their thank-you cards – into the buckets dotted around. They knew they wanted to keep this miracle going. That through their generosity, Tristan could continue his mission.

Our mission.

After the show was even better. Violet and I would walk out of the theatre and round to the stage door. Most nights there would be people milling there, waiting to see Tristan and ask for his autograph. He loved that side of things, and I did, too. We would stroll through the throng as if we were aristocrats in a summer garden in Paris, everyone's eyes on us.

Inside, it was less glamorous than it appeared to an outsider. Isn't that always the case? That was where Trevor, the antiquated doorman, sat with his three-bar electric heater on, the heater which was never turned off even in the midst of a blazing summer. Through the door and up into the maze of corridors in the bowels of the theatre.

It didn't take long to climb the three flights of stairs to Tristan's dressing room on the top floor. Tristan would be sitting in his chair opposite the mirror, sweat pouring off his forehead, black curls stuck to his temples, reminiscent of a 1940s film star.

I used to love to watch him.

Sometimes — only sometimes — I would observe as a coldness passed through him, mercury in his veins. He would become like marble and it would bring tears to my eyes. Because I knew that coldness, I had witnessed it before. That ice would be his undoing, I dared myself to think when I watched him fail in this way.

Then, something in me would pity him. But, remember, it was a pity to be flung over the cliff face and into the churning seas. For what is pity towards a being that has no heart? It is as meaningless as the smoky vapours that hovered in the air above the stage, long after our act had packed up and moved on to the next town.

15

'So it's her, right? Crazy turquoise necklace lady?' Jones asked, back in the incident room. 'Snow's wife?' She looked at her boss intently. Martin stared out of the window.

'Boss?' Jones persisted. 'It must be, right? She finds out about the affair between her husband and her sister and, boom, she snaps and puts a golf club in his head.'

Martin spun her chair slowly to look at Jones. 'Think about it. When was the photo taken? Of Tristan and Antonia?'

'Um, 1986 I think you said.'

'Hardly a boom and a snap is it – waiting thirty years to bump him off? And where's the golf club?'

'Well . . .'

'And what about Mackenzie? You told me what Fielding said – that he'd been seen prowling around early doors for some reason. And you and Tennant found a financial motive for him. He's looking like the most likely suspect at the moment, despite this stuff about the affair with Antonia.' Martin's tone was dogged, unrelenting. 'And we've got no forensics back from the boarding house yet? Nothing to substantiate this poisoning idea?'

Jones shook her head. 'The SOCOs took some cups and utensils for testing; the results haven't come back yet.'

Martin put her hands behind her head and stared off into space again.

'He smelled of Deep Heat too, you know,' Jones said absent-mindedly. 'Said he'd injured his shoulder. By the way, I checked with the SOCOs and the mortuary. Tristan Snow didn't have his cross on when his body was found. We didn't find it in among his belongings either. So either he lost it himself, or . . .'

'Someone's taken it,' Martin muttered, her eyes closed.

'Are you all right, Boss?' Jones asked tentatively, after a few minutes of silence.

Martin snapped her eyes open. 'Why'd you ask?'

'I don't know. You just seem um, a bit . . .'

'Distracted, disconnected?' Martin shot back.

'No, uh . . .' Jones said, her voice low. 'Don't worry about it. Sorry.'

Martin glanced at her before rubbing a hand over her face. 'No, I'm sorry, Jones. I'm just . . . things are a bit up in the air at the moment, that's all. What with the case, and . . .'

'I know, Boss.' Jones leaned back and looked at her watch. She stood up and grabbed her jacket off the back of the chair. 'Come on.'

'What?'

'I've been meaning to tell you for ages. We're going to a party.'

Martin looked at Jones as she drove out of the city in the early evening light. Their windows down, a soft breeze ruffled Jones's ponytail as she tapped her fingers in time to some generic song on the radio. Martin liked Jones's ponytail. It gave her an enthusiasm, a bounce, as she walked beside her through the cases they'd worked on together. Something in Martin envied Jones that bounce. She looked up at the sky reddening from the sunset and rued, yet again, the melancholy that seemed to seep from her in an all-consuming haze these days.

Jones wasn't talking as she drove and Martin was grateful. She flicked back through the messages on her phone. The one from Jim remained unanswered because she didn't know what to say. Sam had seemed about as bothered at her meeting her husband for dinner as if she'd said she was going to eat a Pot Noodle for lunch. If that were the case, why was she bothering with him? Why was she concerning herself with either of them? Jim, who'd barely spoken to her since he'd left their house a year ago. And Sam, who was probably going to get his conquest and move on like he'd done with countless others she'd heard about through the years she'd known him.

And the point was, that she should be angry with them both. But she wasn't. She just felt so desperately *sad* about it all.

'Here we are,' Jones announced, as they turned into a small estate. 'The metropolis that is Low Fell.' She pulled over and they got out, the slams of the car doors seeming to echo in the quiet streets. 'No one plays out any more,' Jones observed. 'Estate used to be full of kids when I was a nipper. Now everyone's too worried about paedos.'

Jones walked up a pathway to a bright blue door. Martin could hear music playing from inside. It sounded like Roy

Orbison. Jones opened the unlocked door and ushered Martin in ahead of her.

'Helloooo?'

'Ah, here you are!' A blonde woman appeared through the kitchen door. 'Get yourself inside. Come on. We've been waiting.'

'Thanks, Mam. This is Detective Inspector Martin,' Jones said, subtly pushing Martin towards the open door, through which the sounds of voices carried down the hall.

'Erica,' Martin countered, hearing the stiffness in her voice. Why was she here? She should be back at the station in the incident room, figuring out this delicate spider's web that had twisted its way around the Snows. What had Sera meant by walking out of the hotel lobby so dramatically? She would stay here half an hour tops, and then head back and check out Tristan Snow's YouTube channel herself. She would get Sera and Violet back in for a formal interview. She would . . .

'Wine?' Jones asked, pushing a plastic cup into her hand.

'Ah, yeah. Okay.' She sipped at it, the liquid sharp on her tongue. Her eyes focused on the room; people were bundled into the kitchen and spilling out into the garden. A barbecue smoked from outside, the smell of sausages and fried onions in the air.

'This is Rob,' Jones said, pulling a lanky, smiling man up to Martin. She looked up at him proudly. 'My fiancé.'

'Your . . .?' Martin said in surprise. 'I'm sorry, Jones. I hadn't realized.'

'Not to worry,' Jones said cheerfully. 'Happened when you were away. I wanted you to come tonight. Despite the case. Wanted you to come and meet us. See where I'm from, you know.'

Martin looked at her sergeant, her earnest grin, her hand wrapped in her lover's. She felt a sudden stab of jealousy followed just as quickly by a hot flush of shame. A sense of panic that time was slipping away from her. That she'd sorted out nothing. That everything was shit and always would be.

'Congratulations,' she said, holding out her hand to shake Rob's. She wondered if she should move to give Jones a celebratory kiss on the cheek, but bailed on it at the last minute, ending up patting her on the shoulder as if she were the Mayor or something. Seriously, she had to get out of there.

'Emma's told us a great deal about you.' Martin turned to see a man in his sixties approaching – Jones's dad perhaps? 'Raves about it, working with you, she does.'

Martin coughed. 'Ah well, we're uh, very lucky to have DS Jones on our team, of course.' She nodded as if to reinforce the point. 'She's a great asset to her colleagues.' The words came to her like a television script. She gulped down some more wine, longing for the burn of relaxation it would bring.

'We're very proud of her.'

'Dad . . .' Jones demurred.

'Well, we are. When a member of your family does well, you want to shout about it, don't you? Boast a bit.' He chucked his daughter under the chin. 'And now you're getting married, as well.' He shook his head, the mysteries of life enveloping him for a moment; that he should be so lucky. He beamed at Martin. 'Your parents must be very proud, too.'

'Uh, yes. They are,' Martin said vaguely. It occurred to her that she didn't actually have any evidence of this. The desire for it strained and pulled within her like a dog on a lead, sniffing out clues and pointers. But she had nothing to show for it. Her police badge. And her sad face in the mirror, she supposed. She shivered a little as her mobile buzzed in her bag.

'Excuse me,' she said, turning away to take the call.

'Looks like Partridge and his lads have got the murder weapon,' Tennant said, with no introduction.

'What is it?'

'It's some kind of statue.'

'What kind?'

'You need to see it really.'

'Where was it?'

'Well, that's the thing . . .'

'What?' Martin asked. 'What's the thing?'

'It was found in a public bin outside the B&B. It's why it's taken a while to find. It was wrapped in a garment.'

Martin waited, tapping her fingers impatiently on her hip.

'A nightdress, I think. Some kind of dress, anyway. And that's the thing,' he repeated.

'Spit it out, Tennant. Jesus, this is painful.'

'The dress has got bloodstains on it. We've swabbed them. It's Snow's blood.'

'Who does the nightdress belong to?'

'DNA found on it matches that of the daughter.'

'Tristan's daughter, Violet?'

'Yes,' Tennant said unequivocally. 'The dress wrapped round what looks like the murder weapon – from the DNA we've found – appears to be Violet Snow's.'

16

It was a metal cross, a foot or so high. The figure of
Christ was spread-eagled in its middle, in his usual fashion; his head lolling to one side, his arms stretched as if
to eternity on either side of him. Above his head and
around his body were the metallic, curling words of a
prayer. Martin held the plastic bag that contained the
cross up to the light in the incident room. Tennant sat
on the desk in front of her. One of the fluorescent lights
above them flickered on and off, plunging them into
darkness sporadically.

'Can someone get that fixed or just turn it off?' Martin
said irritably. 'It's like a bloody horror film in here.' She
felt the cross through the plastic as Jones flipped off the
main switch and turned on the smaller desk lights. At
once, the room became close, intimate, puddles of yellow light framing their faces. 'The bottom of it juts into a
point,' Martin said. 'It's sharp.'

'Reckon that's what caused the skull fracture,' Tennant
said.

Martin bit her lip, thinking, rubbing the edge of the
cross with her thumb. 'Not initially,' she said. 'You could
use it to thump him over the head first, knock him out.
But you'd struggle to stick this into bone, on the off.
Would be like trying to skewer a nail through wood without a hammer.'

They looked at the cross, considering this. The bottom of it was stained.

'Snow's blood?' Jones asked.

Tennant nodded, easing himself off the desk and stretching his back. 'Seemed likely, all things considered.'

Martin frowned at his sarcasm, turning her attention to the nightdress, also sealed inside a plastic bag. She smoothed out the top of it, examining the brown stains smeared across the embroidery on the neckline. 'That's an arrest. She'll need to be brought in.' She glanced at her watch. 'Even though it's late. I want a wire put in their hotel room, too. Okay?'

Jones nodded her assent.

Martin looked again at the bag with the cross inside.

'The cross itself. Is there anything distinctive about it? Why did you call it a statue on the phone?'

Tennant folded his arms, looking pleased with himself. 'Well, it's interesting.' He gestured towards it. 'See the writing on it?'

Martin nodded.

'I'm a good Catholic boy, me. That there's the prayer of St Anthony of Padua.' Tennant pointed it out on the cross, as Martin and Jones peered closer.

'What does it say?' Martin asked. 'You can hardly read it here, the writing's so small.'

'Behold the cross of the Lord,' Tennant intoned, without looking at the inscription. 'Fly you powers of darkness. The lion of the tribe Judah has conquered, Hallelujah.' He sat back, grinning.

Martin looked at him. 'Well, before we break out the champagne, Tennant, at you solving the case . . . perhaps you'd like to tell us what that means?'

'I remember it from Sunday School. Me mam always made me go. You know how it is, the story of St Anthony's brief.' He looked over at them with emphasis. 'There was this woman in Portugal. Hundreds of years ago, like. And she got possessed by the Devil, who made her think she should go and drown herself in the river.'

'And?'

'And, on her way to do it, she goes inside this church to have a pray and ask God for his help. So, she's at the altar praying and she falls asleep. Later, she wakes up and remembers this vision she had while she was sleeping. It was St Anthony come to her in a dream. And she looks down, and there's a letter in her hand.'

'And what's in the letter?'

'It's the brief of St Anthony. It's that prayer,' Tennant said, pointing at the cross.

Martin looked again at the tarnished silver metal. It was heavy in her hand. It could have smashed Snow's skull, it was true. 'And what does it mean, the prayer? It just helps you when you're in need?'

'Not quite,' Tennant answered, patiently. 'The woman was possessed, right? This prayer here, they say – well – it's used to get rid of the Devil.'

'It's . . .' Jones interrupted.

'It's an exorcism cross,' Martin finished for them.

'Correct,' Tennant said. 'Priests use the brief of St Anthony when they're conducting exorcisms. When they're ridding the body of evil spirits.'

At that, the strip lights in the room flickered on for a second and then off again. They looked at each other, startled. Martin gave a short laugh.

'Shit, what was that?' Tennant asked, his eyes searching the room.

'Come on Jones, let's head over and pick Violet up. We can settle her in and then interview her first thing,' Martin said, walking over to the wall and hitting it with the flat of her hand. Lights flared one by one across the room, a dazzling expressway of fluorescence, illuminating Jones and Tennant as if they'd been caught at a crime scene.

'I don't believe in ghosts,' Martin said, before turning and leaving the room.

'What is it, Boss?' Jones asked, as they crossed the car park to Martin's car to drive to the Travelodge to arrest Violet. 'You look bothered.'

Martin shook her head, perturbed. 'It's a bit too good to be true, isn't it? Violet's nightdress covered in her father's blood, wrapped round the murder weapon. She's not an idiot. Why would she do it?'

'Didn't think it would be found?'

'Or she's being set up.'

Jones flipped a glance at Martin. She seemed unwilling to accept that the girl might be responsible.

'If you had whacked your dad over the head, what would you do with the thing you'd done it with? If you were an eighteen-year-old girl? Scared of being caught? In shock at what you'd done?'

'Panic and shove it in a dustbin?'

'Outside? And then come back inside and coolly go and make some tea and call the police?' Martin asked, unlocking her car. 'I don't know . . .'

'So it doesn't fit?' Jones said.

'No, it's not necessarily that. It's just there's . . . It feels like there's something missing.' Martin pulled out of the car park and headed towards the roundabout by the central shopping centre. 'The Market Tavern,' she muttered, noticing the pub as they drove around past the Market Square.

'What's that, Boss?'

'That's where Antonia Simpson started her pub crawl on the night of the murder. The Market Tavern.'

'Where the journos hang out, you mean?' Jones asked.

Martin touched the brake with her foot involuntarily, and the car slowed suddenly. 'Say that again, Jones . . .'

'What? About the journos? That's their local. The Market Tavern.'

Martin gave a cold laugh, frowning as she turned the steering wheel. 'No way. It can't be. Fucking Keagan? Un-fucking-believable . . .'

'What is? What are you on about, Boss?'

Martin shot Jones a look in the dark of the car interior, street lights zooming over their faces. 'Antonia says the bloke she met that night was Irish. In the Market Tavern. Had a name like Keagan.' She paused. 'Ring any bells? Where the journalists hang out? I *knew* something was bugging me at that press conference. That little shit is everywhere . . .'

Jones continued to look nonplussed.

'Sean Egan, Jones. That deeply annoying journalist. I bet you a million pounds that that's who Antonia was shagging the night Snow was murdered.'

17

A sudden shaft of sunlight, hosting a thousand dust motes, sprinkled through the lace curtains at that window, do you remember that window? I had that kidney-shaped dressing-table with the pink satin cloth which fell from the top to the floor. That day, in particular, it was hot as a furnace sitting there in the shadow of the sun. The folds of the material rested on my knees like a blanket, hiding my dress.

I had the comb you had given me — something borrowed. It was cream plastic with satin roses stitched into the side. Once it was tucked behind my ear, they'd only be able to see the flowers.

Then you came in. Suddenly you were leaning in, pushing your face next to mine, beneath the curlicues around the mirror. You pursed your lips and made a kissing sound with your blonde hair waved around your head and down, on to your bare shoulders. Your dress was incredible. I was impressed, despite myself. It was turquoise and strapless and stretched across your chest, shimmering with undertones of gold and peach, pulling down into a fishtail.

You looked like a mermaid.

I didn't even resent how good you looked. Something had been taking place in me of late. Thoughts pinpricked in my head like soap bubbles, bursting into nothing before they could make any impact other than a negligible wet stain, so pathetic it was meaningless.

I did think it was odd, though, when you touched my shoulders. So rare. So tender. 'Well,' you said to me, before hesitating. 'Today's the day.'

I could hear the rush of the sea outside the window, could picture the sucking of pebbles under the foam, water stretching over them and the sand until it retreated again and again, back into the depths, to another part of the universe – over on the other side.

'Sera? You look like you've seen a ghost. What is it?'

Your voice pulled me back into the room and my fingers quivered over my stomach. That small bulge which had hardened in the last few days. The tiny fluttering inside, the heartbeat, the insistent tapping of life.

'Nothing. I'm fine.' I smiled at you. 'Couldn't be happier, sweetie.' I looked around the apricot-hued bedroom, the sun's insistence at the window. And then I was confused again. Wasn't this room west facing? I couldn't understand such bright sunlight so early. I asked you what the time was and you told me that it wasn't the morning. It was three o'clock and we had only an hour to get to the registry office.

I looked at you. My sister. Your reflection in the glass. How could time have passed so quickly?

I had slept all day, you said, managing a smile. No sneer, for once, this time.

'Come on,' you said, with a forced joie de vivre. 'Let's go down and have a drink before Dad arrives in the taxi. Drink to your last minutes of freedom?'

I felt sick suddenly. Everything around me seemed at once a pink or an orange. Apart from my dress, of course, which was still white. But, as we went downstairs for a Malibu and Coke, I couldn't help it. I saw a chorus of waves lapping at my feet. And the water was pink with blood.

Later that night, I lay in another room as moonlight washed over my naked stomach. Tristan stirred next to me, his arm flung across my hips, heavy on my bones. I twisted the ring on my finger slowly round. Was this the happiest day of my life? That heartbeat again, tapping away inside. I turned to look at Tristan, his eyes closed, fast in sleep, a lock of hair sprung free across his forehead, breathing through his nose in a regular rhythm. His breath matched the sounds of the sea. In and out. In and out. Here, he was mine. Here, we belonged together. And the tapping inside me was part of us, part of that in and out, the movement of the moon tides.

Earlier in the day, in the hotel ballroom, underneath the streamers and the pale blue cut-outs of carriages and twinkling fairy lights, I'd also watched him. A whisky glass in his hand, holding court at a large round table. He was telling a story to his acolytes, their grins fixed on their faces, salivating at the thought of the laugh which they knew would eventually come, panting with joy at how they all slotted in together, fitted in as one. What's a collective noun for a bunch of sycophants? I had wondered. A sap? Again, the thought bubbled up and burst on the fringes of my brain, barely leaving a mark.

This wasn't like me. Or was it?

Tristan reached his punchline and the crowd duly laughed, meeting each other's eyes with relief, mirth spilling out of them, pooling on the floor in a puddle. He turned to look at me and raise his glass in my honour.

My honour.

His friends rolled on their feet as one towards me, their glasses stretched up to the ceiling. I bowed my head well enough. The queen in her place.

But as Tristan put his drink to his mouth, I saw his eyes snap for the briefest second to someone else. His pupils dilated, his nostrils flared. He guffawed a laugh at something pointless. I knew before I looked, although I forced myself to prove it. I followed the direction of Tristan's glance and there you were.

My sister.

Standing at the pillar, your head back, mouth wide, pink lips wet and open; the blue-gold fishtail spread around your feet. Venus on a fish slab. You flicked your golden hair off your shoulder and lowered your eyelashes, hiding me from your peripheral vision.

Tap, tap. Back in the moonlit dark, I felt that heartbeat thud again inside me, the waves swooshing outside. This was my ace to play. Once Tristan knew about the tap, once he found out about the baby, he would be mine entirely. The ring, the tap. Then you could laugh as loud as you liked, could swing into as many rooms as you wanted with your perfume and high heels and your clever, clever remarks.

But I know the value of peace. I suffer not a woman to teach, nor to usurp authority over the man, but to be in silence.

I would say nothing. Tristan was tied to me now. I twisted the ring back round and closed my eyes.

The sound of the waves washed over me and into sleep.

18

Martin let herself into her house long after midnight. Violet Snow had been arrested and was in a cell beneath Durham police station. She had come with them quietly, calmly. It had been Sera who had wailed, who had stamped in frustration. She who had screamed threats of lawyers and suing for damages. But Violet had said nothing, aside from giving the answers to the questions she was asked by the custody sergeant. She had quailed only once, when the door to the cell had opened and she had seen where she would sleep: the white cell with its rounded walls and steel toilet bowl; its hard, unyielding bed. But she had swallowed and entered like a lamb, sitting on the bed with her eyes closed, her hands in her lap, barely registering when they had closed and locked the door on her.

Martin had gone back upstairs to prepare for the next morning's interview and then had watched seemingly endless videos on YouTube of exorcisms, miracle healings, and of Tristan Snow himself, working a crowd up into something of a frenzy. On the whole, the participants in his services or healings were merely emotional, longing for something beyond them. But, on one occasion, a clip had shown the congregation dancing and yelling wildly. Before it looked like it was getting too out of control, however, the tape had suddenly stopped.

Martin noticed that this clip didn't come from the official Deucalion Church website. This had been uploaded by someone anonymously, someone who had just turned up and managed to secretly film what was going on.

Snow professed to enable the lame to walk; he made a deaf woman hear, a blind man see. All pretty much end-of-the-pier stuff; things that Martin could have pulled apart in an instant if she'd have had five minutes with one of these people. If she'd been able to show them that the healing of a supposed arthritic crippled leg was merely a tugging down of a shoe to give the illusion of the leg lengthening; that the cure for deafness was achieved by carefully choosing from the audience someone with impaired hearing as opposed to complete silence – they would react to loud clicks and bangs. And many healings of the spirit were merely to do with the manipulation of hope. Something it seemed that Tristan Snow was expert in.

The exorcisms were trickier to debunk, other than to dismiss them as pure nonsense. But it was hard to reconcile the sight of an adult flailing wildly, being calmed by the words Snow uttered. Why would anyone agree to take part in this spectacle? Did they honestly believe that they were possessed by the Devil?

Martin wondered if videos existed of child exorcisms; the ones on YouTube only involved adults. She suspected, if there were any, that they wouldn't be publicized – that would have been a red flag to social services. But the articles on his website, the books he self-published on Amazon, were all filled with methods of 'training up' children; turning them to the ways of the Lord.

This side to Snow's *ministry*, or whatever you wanted to call it, had only developed after he had left his job on morning television. It seemed unlikely that even producers of anodyne TV shows would approve of this kind of hocus pocus.

Martin pondered as she sipped at her coffee, long gone cold, on the reasons people had for coming to Snow, for succumbing to his spiel. True, he was a charismatic speaker. He had a certain kudos from his media career. But were these people so stupid as to think that just because the guy had been on TV, he had a direct chat-line with their God? That through his hands and nothing more, he could actually beat modern medicine at its own game? That he could defeat death? Were these people so hopeless, so downtrodden, that they had resorted to magic to get them through their lives? That living entirely reliant on fantasy made up for some deeper chasm within them, something they didn't or couldn't admit, even to themselves?

Martin switched off the computer eventually. She couldn't bring herself to watch any more. She looked at her phone, where Sam had texted to say he would head to her place after work. She'd given him her spare key just before he'd asked her to Crete. It felt weird, looking at his text. It reminded her of Jim. And also spurred a feeling in her, one she wasn't certain of . . . that someone was in her space again. Part of her felt good about it, a settling into comfort, a zone of content. But another part of her kicked against it.

And she hated that part of her.

He was sitting in the dark when she got back, watching a murmuring chat show, an empty whisky glass lolling in his hand. He looked up as Martin came into the lounge.

'Top-up?' she asked, moving over to the shelf where she kept the bottles of spirits and retrieving the Talisker.

'Sure.'

'What are you watching?'

Sam ignored the question. 'Partridge and the SOCOs did well to find that cross. You've brought the girl in?'

Martin sighed and sat down in the armchair next to Sam's. The TV continued to throw light on their faces, occasional laughter puncturing the silence. 'She was meek and mild as could be.'

'Good.'

'I've got to be up at six. We'll interview her first thing.'

Martin looked over at Sam. She wanted to ask him, lay it all out on the line. Was there any point to this, or were they just going to turn out like her and Jim, sat in a darkened room with a TV on that neither of them watched? Instead, she relied on her old friend booze and took a long drink.

'How are we doing, Erica?' he asked, scrutinizing her. 'How are you?'

'Fine. Right as rain. Why?'

'You're closing off from me.' He sighed. 'I know you. Remember when we first met?'

Martin thought back to that time in Newcastle over ten years ago – when she was in uniform and he was, again, her boss.

'Remember?' Sam persisted. 'When I asked you out? We were in The Windmill. It was a Thursday.'

'You remember the day?'

Sam didn't answer.

'I said no to you,' Martin replied, her head on one side.

'Yep. You didn't want to know.'

'You were my boss . . .'

'I'm still your boss.'

'You had a reputation. Everyone fancied you.' Martin looked at him. 'Ah, don't get too up yourself,' she said, smiling. 'But they did. I didn't want to be one of many.'

Sam got to his feet and switched off the television. They were now in darkness, the glow of the street lamps spilling into the room.

'You had that same look then,' Sam said softly at Martin's back. He touched her hair, resting his hand on the top of her head and then her shoulder. She reached up and put her hand on his. 'Closed off and far away. Not letting yourself have something that you really want.'

She hesitated a second before saying, 'When we thought . . . before Crete . . . when we thought I might be . . .'

'Pregnant?'

Martin nodded. 'What . . . would you have wanted it?' Her breath caught in her mouth, her heart beating loud under her shirt.

'I don't know,' Sam said gently. 'Honestly, it would have been a big thing to happen so soon. With things so up in the air.'

Martin exhaled quietly, her glass hanging from her hand.

'But that's not to say things wouldn't change,' Sam said, coming round to kneel in front of her. 'I mean, you said you were relieved. I thought . . . Things are such early days, Erica. You're just out of a relationship. We don't even live together,' he gave a little laugh.

'I know,' Martin acknowledged.

'Let's just see how things go? Get things settled with Jim. Get the divorce finalized. Take things slowly,' he said rubbing her hand with his thumb.

'Right,' Martin said.

'Don't close down. You know? Don't shut off from me. Please, Erica. We can have anything you want. I promise.'

'And what do I want?' Martin asked, thinking as she did that she didn't believe him. Not really.

'Did you text Jim back?'

'What do I want, Sam?'

He got to his feet and moved to the doorway, stood silhouetted in the light from the hallway. 'I don't know, Erica,' he said, as he turned to go up the stairs. 'Just come to bed.'

Martin heard his footsteps overhead in her bedroom as she finished her drink and poured another. And another, as she sat alone in the dark while he slept.

19

Violet's arms were bare. She wore a white shift dress which hung limply from her thin shoulders. Her black hair cut into her cheekbones, emphasizing her smallness some-how, her cap of hair encasing her, holding her taut. Martin sat opposite with Jones next to her. Violet's solicitor was inert in a corner, a Starbucks cup on the floor beside him, a notebook on his lap. The tape spools whirled, the air-conditioning hummed.

'You had it fixed then?' Violet shivered a little, jutting her chin towards the wall where the air-con vents blew their recycled oxygen.

'Are you too cold?'

Violet shook her head. Her hands rested on her lap. Her face was calm in repose, eyes down, mouth closed. A Piero della Francesca, Martin thought; Mary at the birth of Jesus. Martin pushed the plastic bag containing the exorcism cross over the table towards her.

'Do you recognize this, Violet? I'm showing Violet Exhibit D3,' Martin said, for the benefit of the tape.

Violet put her head to one side. 'It's my father's,' she answered, cool as the room in which she sat.

Martin considered her lack of reaction, her watchful-ness. Either she was a bloody brilliant actress or she had no idea of the significance of the cross. 'He would use it to pray with?' she asked, fishing.

Violet appraised her for a moment, weighing something up. 'Yes, he would use it for prayer,' she answered eventually.

There's the lie, Martin thought. She shifted on her chair. She needed to get a purchase on this. She focused on the girl. Everything else: Sam; her divorce; all of it, dissipated into the air of the interview room. She saw only Violet. Her black eyes a meditation. Through them she would find Tristan's killer.

'For prayer, Violet? Or something else?'

Violet shrugged. 'Often my dad did things I didn't know about.'

Martin frowned. That sounded as if Violet were leading them to something. She thought back to the original interview. *It's all there for you to see*, Violet had said, referring to Snow's YouTube channel. Was there more to it than that? Martin leaned back in her chair, picked up a pen which lay before her on the desk and started tapping her knee with it.

Violet's eyes moved down to the pen. She gave a brief smile. 'Do you attend church, Inspector?' The question came out of the blue.

Martin gave a look of surprise. 'I did as a kid. Not now.'

'Why not?'

Martin took a breath. If this was what it took, she would answer. 'Not sure if I believe. Not in need of it so much.'

'Not sure . . . not so much,' the girl parroted, her eyes wide. 'Doesn't sound like you're certain about your relationship with God.'

Martin gave an easy shrug. 'It's not something I think about,' she said, tapping her pen again. 'What about you?' she asked lightly. 'Do you believe?'

Violet leaned forward, putting her elbows on the table. She rubbed the corner of one eye and looked disarmingly at Martin. 'I should do, right? The way I've been brought up. I've had it shoved down my throat twenty-four seven . . . The truth is, I used to. My father would tell me that the Devil was inside me. He was inside all of us. That the only way we could be clean was to seek forgiveness.' She paused for a moment. 'The thing was, though,' she said, leaning back in her chair, 'you could only get that forgiveness through him.'

'And you didn't like that? Having to go through him?'

'No. I didn't. It demeans it. Makes it more about him than you. Or God.'

'So would you say you've lost your faith?'

'One day . . . it just left me, you know?' Violet gestured at her midriff. 'Once it was there, heavy inside, like a weight. And then, it just went.' She clicked her fingers. 'Like that. That was a good day. I was light as air,' she smiled. She was outwardly calm but there was an unyielding euphoria about her; a glass veneer that shone with hostility. Martin had the feeling that were she to put any pressure on it at all, it would splinter into a million pieces.

Martin knew where she wanted this interview to end up; she started the journey. She nudged the cross nearer to Violet. 'The reason we brought you here last night, why you're under arrest, is that this cross was found in a dust-bin outside the Riverview boarding house.'

Violet moved her eyes to the bag and back again to Martin. 'And?'

Martin pulled out the other plastic bag, the one containing the nightdress. 'I'm now showing Violet Exhibit

D4,' she said, moving it across the table. 'Do you recognize this, Violet?'

She waited as the girl stared at the bag. 'It's my nightdress, I think. Why have you got it?'

'Do you remember the last time you saw this nightdress?'

'Uh . . .' Violet flung a look to her solicitor.

'Inspector Martin,' he said, with a jaded weariness. 'You didn't inform me that you would be showing my client this.'

'I'm informing you now,' Martin replied. 'When did you last see this nightdress, Violet?'

'You don't have to answer, Miss Snow.'

Martin examined Violet's face. Her confusion appeared to be genuine.

'I don't know. What are those stains on it?'

Martin said nothing.

Violet flushed. 'Uh, it was in my drawer I think. I left it there when I unpacked. I wasn't wearing that one to sleep in.'

'You're sure about that? You didn't see it yesterday morning? When you went into your father's room?'

Violet shook her head. 'Why would I take my nightdress into Dad's room? I was holding the tea. There's no reason . . .'

'So, if I were to tell you, Violet, that this nightdress – Exhibit D4 – was found wrapped around the cross that you've seen – in the dustbin – you couldn't offer an explanation for that?'

'What – no! Of course I couldn't. That's . . . why would you think that? Why would I be able to?'

'You didn't enter your father's room, with the cross in your hand? Smash it into his skull, and then carefully wrap it up in the nightie? Run outside and throw it away before coming back in to wake your mother up? Tell her that you'd found your father dead?'

'God, no!' Violet exclaimed, her eyes darting to different points in the room, desperately trying to think of a response. 'Someone must have stolen it,' she said, looking at Jones quickly, pulling her in. 'You know, put it round the cross to get me into trouble.'

'Who would want to do that, Violet?' Jones asked.

'I don't know . . . Because someone wants to make out it was me who killed him?' Violet had turned white, a sickly colour. 'But it wasn't! I can't think. You're frightening me. Look, I had issues with my father. You can see that. But plenty of other people didn't like him, too.'

'Who didn't like your father, Violet?' Martin asked, pushing on.

The girl began to cry. Martin watched the tears drop. She was just a child, after all.

'Loads of people. Antonia for a start . . . Fraser. You must see that,' she looked up at Martin, rubbed her hand across her wet cheeks. 'Everyone in that place, in the B&B, hated him.'

'Your mother?'

'No. Not her . . . other people. People from back home. He did things . . . he hurt people. You must see. I've told you . . . on YouTube. It's all there. What he did . . .' Violet dissolved into sobs, her hands over her face.

'Talk to me then,' Martin said, her face unreadable. 'If you know something about another person, you have to tell me. And you have to do it now, because things aren't looking good for you, Violet. Not good at all, I'm afraid.'

Violet swallowed, her eyes wide, as she stepped on to the bridge of no return. 'Mercy. Her name is Mercy Fletcher. It all started with her. Years ago. If she hadn't come along ... She was my friend. And then ...' she stared at Martin, with waterwheel eyes. 'And that was when it all went wrong.'

'Talk to me, Violet,' Martin asked gently. 'Tell me what happened.'

You didn't come.

You cried off, saying you had things to do back at the church. I knew it was a lie. I think — now — it was because you'd already worked out what was going on. That you couldn't bear to face it. As always, I was the idiot. The one that turned to face the storm and bore the brunt of the weather.

There we were, in Margate. Another show, another theatre. Violet was shivering at the shoreline. Her lips blue and her arms wrapped around her thin frame. The sea was the colour of an Orkney seal, slick and lively.

Mercy was there — yelling at her from the water, her head bobbing amidst the springing waves. 'It's not so bad once you're in! Your body sort of goes numb. You can't feel yourself. It's really nice!'

We — her father and I — sat in deckchairs, up the beach, covered in a blanket, a Thermos flask at our feet. Fraser was, of course, sensibly back at the hotel.

'Go on with you, Violet! Don't be so pathetic!' I remember Tristan calling.

I could tell, just from the sight of Violet's rigid back, that she didn't want to go in. She was jumping up and down on the spot. I could feel her thoughts. *I always knew my daughter. Who in their right mind wants to go swimming in the North Sea in December?* The sand was like mud beneath our feet, the sky bearded with clouds, pushing down on us, giving me a headache.

Violet went for it! She ran in, the icy water must have grasped at her heart as she plunged through the surf. I trembled at the thought of it.

'Told you!' I heard Mercy shout, a typically sloppy grin on her face. I glanced to my left where Tristan sat forward, his elbows on his knees, peering at them both through the greyness.

'It's horrible,' Violet called to us, with chattering teeth. 'Can we get out now?'

'Lame,' Mercy yelled, before making a porpoise dive under an approaching wave, her bottom raised in the air for a second, before flattening out under the water. She emerged, murmuring something I couldn't hear, pushing wet strings of hair from her eyes.

I got up and waved at them to come in. It was too cold. I didn't want Violet to get ill. Seagulls squawked above us, wheeling down to where Tristan had tossed the remains of his chips. I looked along at the bleak curve of the beach, which led to a promontory stretching out into the sea, its clock tower marking the hours and minutes we would have to stay in that town, with this atmosphere.

Where were you, Antonia? Having your nails done? Going to one of those bars you liked so much with the cocktails filled with ice which glittered like diamonds?

At first, Violet and Mercy had been excited about the trip. They were only ten years old, after all. They'd gabbled in the car about eating rock, scoffing fish and chips, spending money on arcade games, drinking Fanta through a straw. Like home, like Blackpool, they chattered, but somehow better because they were on holiday. They called each other sisters. *Makes you laugh that, doesn't it, Antonia?*

Sisters.

They raced up the beach, dripping wet. Their skin was blue, shuddering and goose-bumped from the cold. I handed Violet a towel and she rubbed it hard over her skin, bringing it back to life.

This bit will be hard, Antonia, if you didn't know already. Then again, I think you did. You certainly knew some of it later, if not all of it. I wouldn't have seen it myself if a bird hadn't suddenly dived down to the empty polystyrene chip tray Tristan had dumped by his deckchair. I turned to see what the ruckus was, as the bird screeched loudly before flapping off with the tray in his beak. As I swung round, I saw him wrapping a towel around Mercy. And as he did, in a move so deft that later, I almost had to convince myself I hadn't invented it, he rubbed his right hand between Mercy's legs, his thumb slipping under the crotch of her swimming costume. Mercy turned away and Tristan looked right at me, his eyes sapphire-blue against the grey sky behind.

'All right, sweetheart?' He smiled at Violet. 'Time we got back and got nice and dry.' He looked at his watch. 'Show's starting in a few hours.'

I'm sure Violet saw. But she said nothing, picking up her bundle of clothes and walking mechanically away from the surf up to the cluster of buildings that lined the seafront. I was stuck. Was I shocked? I don't know any more. But I focused on putting one foot in front of the other and soon I reached the top of the beach. Mercy's cheeks glowed red, but perhaps that was from the cold water.

That was Margate, Antonia.

That was what you missed.

20

'Mercy Fletcher is a childhood friend of Violet's who she says was abused by Snow,' Martin said to the team, pushing a sandwich away untouched on the desk in the incident room. 'Violet says she doesn't think Mercy moved away from Blackpool, so someone needs to work with Lancashire MIT and see about tracking her down.' She stared at them all in turn. 'There were loads of kids at the Deucalion Church, weren't there? It was known for taking them in. Was it only Mercy he was abusing? Are there more of them? It's possible this is going to spark a whole new investigation, and God help us if the press find out at this stage.

'I'll speak to Lancashire today. Get them prepped on a coordination.' Martin shrugged. 'But in terms of Snow's murder, are we saying that there's yet another suspect? Someone who hasn't even been placed in Durham? Violet's implicated by the nightdress, Mackenzie's got no alibi. And if Mercy is involved, we're still facing the problem of where she is in the city – if she's here at all – or how she got into the B&B given it was locked up all night.'

'What about Violet? She's saying that Snow was an abuser,' Jones pointed out. 'What about her? Did he abuse his own daughter? It must be a possibility, right? Violet said she and Mercy were only ten years old on that trip to Margate.'

'She said not in the interview and . . . I don't know, I believe her. She seems so strong, if I'm honest,' Martin answered, with her eyes closed, remembering the girl's response. 'She doesn't strike me as a typical victim of abuse and, even if she's lying, what can we do about it? He's dead, isn't he?'

'But if she was being abused, it gives her more of a motive, doesn't it? To kill him. So it's an incentive for her to keep quiet about it,' Jones remarked.

'True. But the statement about abuse is problematic in itself, isn't it? I mean, it's coming from Violet, who's in a tricky situation at present. Arguably, she's telling us this to take the heat off her.' Martin rubbed her hand across her face. 'It was Snow's blood and hair on the cross, but there were no fingerprints on it. Blood spatter analysis shows he was definitely kneeling, so it looks as though he was deep in prayer when he was hit. Apart from that night-dress, nothing's come up on any of the clothes we took for analysis from the people in the B&B. I mean . . . let's say Violet's not the killer . . .'

Jones raised her eyebrows.

'Whoever did it must have had to change their clothes after the murder. They would have been covered in blood.'

'Hence the bloodstains on the nightdress,' Jones said. 'There's no DNA on it apart from Violet's.'

Martin looked hard at the team. The fight with Sam last night had deprived her of sleep and the result was dark circles under her eyes, her skin pale. 'Yep, she's our major suspect. But I want to get Mackenzie in and look him in the face. And Sera's still very much in the frame, with a huge motive.'

'Although if she murdered him, why would she want to pin it on her daughter? Why would she have planted the nightdress?'

'I agree. Still, if you look at the nightdress on its own, it's fairly circumstantial. There's none of Violet's DNA on Tristan or the murder weapon.'

'She was there. She found him,' Jones said, exasperated. 'She's telling us about Mercy to shift the blame on to someone else.'

'We can keep her in for another twelve hours but I think we'll struggle with just this evidence with the Crown Prosecution Service. It's not enough, particularly with all the other potentials. I don't want to jump to a solution just because it seems the most obvious. Whoever killed Snow wants us to do that, is my feeling.'

'Not that the simplest explanation is usually the right one?' Jones asked.

Martin gave her a swift smile. 'Occam's Razor, eh Jones? Well, perhaps. But right now, I think we should bail Violet and see where we get to with our other enquiries. Let's get Mackenzie in for an interview, for starters. Antonia's so-called alibi needs confirming.' Martin's mouth tightened. '*I'll* follow that one up. And let's track down Mercy Fletcher as soon as we can. Regarding Sera and Violet, we've put in a wire at the Travelodge, so that might yield something.'

Jones bit her lip. Why was Martin so unwilling to see Violet as the perpetrator? Martin, sensing Jones's disapproval, felt a surge of energy. She jumped down from the desk and prowled the incident room, her eyes narrowed, hurling glances at the team, willing a victim to present themselves.

'Um, excuse me Ma'am . . .' Fielding flushed red in the face as he spoke, and all eyes in the room focused on him. Martin seemed like an Amazon at the front, her red hair coming loose from its bun, green eyes piercing Kryptonite. This was his first posting with the Major Crime Team, and being wet behind the ears wasn't the half of it. Fielding faltered.

Martin saw him dig his nails into his palm. He was a baby, she thought. She took a breath. 'What is it, Fielding?' she asked. 'If you've got a feeling about something or think something's relevant, say it. This room is where we can say things to each other. Even if it sounds stupid.'

'Mrs Quinn,' he said. 'I said so earlier to Sergeant Jones. There's something about her that's a bit . . .' he searched for the word. 'Strange?'

'In what way?'

'Well, we had tea together but she kept looking at her sideboard. Like she was fixated on it. It was a tic. She could barely look me in the eye.'

Tennant came into the room then, a baguette in his hand, crumbs on his tie.

'Nice of you to turn up,' Martin said.

'Sorry, Boss.'

'Is that it?' Martin directed to Fielding.

'Kind of,' he answered. 'I just felt like . . . like she was hiding something.'

'Eileen Quinn?' Tennant asked.

Martin nodded, her eyes flicking down to the baguette, disapproval marking her face. 'What about it?'

Tennant grinned. 'Mrs Quinn's got a bit of form. Spate of shoplifting about ten years ago. Nothing much. Make-up. A blouse.'

Martin raised her eyebrows. *And?*

'So she's on the system, like.'

'This is like pulling teeth, Tennant. Can you spit it out, whatever it is?'

'So I checked the CCTV of the front reception when that photo got delivered here – the one of Snow and his bit on the side. Nothing. Person had a hat on or something, got their back to the screen so you can't make out anything. So I sent the envelope off to the lab. And got a fingerprint on it. Ran it through and what do you know?'

'Eileen Quinn?'

'Eileen Quinn,' Tennant said, taking a bite of the baguette as a dollop of mayonnaise landed squarely on his lapel.

21

Fraser Mackenzie was waiting for Martin by the front desk of the police station as she was leaving to head to the Riverview boarding house.

'Ah, Mr Mackenzie, good,' Martin said. 'You've beaten me to it. I was going to come and find you today.'

Mackenzie stood with a frown. 'I need to know when we can leave Durham. I need to get back to the church, to my office. Sort out the mess we're in.'

'I understand,' Martin answered. 'Perhaps you'd like to come with me now, to somewhere more private?'

They walked through the swing doors behind the desk to a small interview room along the corridor.

'How's Violet?' Mackenzie asked. 'Is she still here after you nabbed her in the middle of the night?'

'She's been bailed. I believe she's gone back to the hotel.'

'Are you thinking she's to blame for Tristan's death?' he asked.

Martin watched him sit in the chair opposite her, interested in his choice of phrase. He made it sound like Tristan had been hit with a car, not had his skull bashed in. 'Ah,' she replied with a smile, 'I'm sure Violet can fill you in if you want to know the details.' Martin sat back in her chair and crossed her legs. 'So, when did you start working with Reverend Snow?'

'Uh, I think it must have been the early nineties? I'd lost my job in London. Well, I was, uh . . .' he shifted in his seat. 'I was in a bit of a bad way. I knew Tristan from when we were teenagers. He'd lived up in Edinburgh for a short while; we went to school together, played in the school band. When he moved away, we used to write, you know? Stupid boy stuff. But we were pals. So when I needed a job, Tristan offered to have me come up to Blackpool. Work with him at the church.'

'Are you a religious man, Mr Mackenzie?' Martin asked.

'Not especially,' Mackenzie folded his arms. 'But a job's a job, and Tristan certainly knew how to put on a show. That's more my line. Entertainment, you know. So, as I said outside, when can I leave? When can we get back to business?'

'That's going to be difficult, isn't it?' Martin said, looking up, an easy expression on her face. 'Now that the cash cow's been killed?'

'That's a punchy thing to say.'

Martin smiled at him, meeting like with like. 'I'm a punchy sort of person,' she said.

Mackenzie gave an angry cough. 'The church still exists. It has a large congregation. The outpouring of grief has been extraordinary. I've got journalists wanting interviews, we've got this vigil tonight and then I need to head back. We need to handle the fall-out. Work out a strategy.'

'Indeed,' Martin said. She looked down at the papers in front of her, then glanced up to find Mackenzie's sights on her, an expression of pure steel. She smiled again. 'You and the Reverend were directors of the company formed out of the Deucalion Church, is that right?'

'I still am.'

'Is the church a registered charity?'

'No.'

'So when people donate money to Deucalion, they're giving it . . . for what?'

'To help with its upkeep. To help run it.'

'Including your salary?'

'Of course.'

'You don't find that to be, shall we say, somewhat unethical?'

'No I don't, Inspector Martin. What's your point?'

'Well, let's say when I go to church, I'm looking for some spiritual guidance, a little help in life.' Martin sat forward in earnest. 'I probably get that from my time there. I feel enlivened, emboldened by what I've seen. I feel really *grateful*. So I want to give something back. What can I give? I think to myself. Well, I can give my time. Help out at the coffee mornings. Work in the shop. And . . .'

Mackenzie continued to look calmly at her, his eyes hard under the bright fluorescent ceiling lights.

'. . . perhaps a bit of cash? Perhaps I could sign up for a little . . . monthly Direct Debit?' Martin tapped the papers. 'Like we've got here. Church membership: one hundred pounds. Church maintenance fee to be paid monthly, direct into the church bank account: amounts ranging from fifty pounds to five hundred pounds. Special festivals and celebrations, perhaps a little light *exorcism* – fee to be arranged on request.' Martin put her hands behind her neck, an expression of disdain floating across her face. 'But nowhere does it say, in the information on the church website, that the money collected will not, in fact, go to the maintenance of the church. Nor will it actually help to run it, won't be used to upkeep the building, no roof repairs. No. That money goes straight to you and, before his untimely death, Reverend Snow.'

'Yes. And we pay for everything. We support all the staff. Contrary to your derogatory remarks, we *do* maintain the building. We fund the tours. The church is a *business*, Inspector Martin. It's run like a business. You're naive if you think we're using the money to make jam to sell at the Christmas fair.'

'But there's no transparency. You're using the idea of miracles – of hope – to trick people into giving them their money. Poor people. The people with the biggest need for hope and the least wherewithal to fund it.'

'I find this conversation extremely offensive.' Mackenzie made as if to stand up.

'Sit down, Mr Mackenzie.' It was Martin's turn to fold her arms. 'Have you heard of a company called Winterbourne?'

Mackenzie lowered himself back gently on to his chair. His eyes flickered, shifting to the table for a second before meeting Martin's again. He sighed loudly. 'Yes. Yes, I have.'

'Tell me about it.'

'As I'm sure you know, Winterbourne is a partnership that I've invested in. They fund creative enterprise in various places.'

'With the idea of making a profit from those enterprises that you would eventually see the benefit of somewhere?'

'Yes.'

'And where would the profits go, once you had received them?'

'They were apportioned to a company called Digby Limited.'

'Of which you are a director?'

'Yes.'

'Along with Reverend Snow?'

Mackenzie's face was bland. 'No. Tristan wasn't a director of Digby.'

Martin raised her eyebrows, feigning surprise. She looked again at her papers. 'But, hang on. It says here that you were both directors of the Deucalion Church Company?'

'That's right.'

'But then you set up another company – Digby – to receive the profits from the partnership with Winterbourne?'

'Yes.'

'And did Reverend Snow know about Digby?'

'I don't believe so, no. I don't know,' he said wearily.

'But you were funding the Winterbourne partnership with monies realized from . . .?'

'Deucalion,' Mackenzie said, quietly.

Martin grinned out of the blue. 'Why's it called Digby, out of interest?'

Mackenzie rubbed the back of his neck with his hand. 'Digby was my dog when I was a boy. A collie.' He looked at Martin with a grudging respect. 'He ran off after I'd had him three years. I searched everywhere for him. Was distraught. Spent hours roaming the streets, calling out for him.' Mackenzie's eyebrow lifted in irony at this idea of himself, so vulnerable, when now he was so guarded.

'And did you find him?'

'I did. He was living with another little boy about four streets away. The boy had been feeding him, caring for him.' Mackenzie chewed his lip. 'In the end, the dog preferred the other boy to me.' He glanced at Martin. 'How did you know? I mean, why I'd called the company after the dog?'

'I didn't.' Martin paused. 'But I was thinking . . . I thought that if I was going to betray my childhood friend, one who'd cared for me when I needed it most . . . Well, I'd want some reminder of why I was doing it.'

'Which was?'

'A time when you yourself had most been betrayed. When you learnt to protect yourself.' Martin shrugged. 'It was just a hunch. Sometimes they pay off, sometimes they don't . . .' She tailed off, bending her head again to the papers. 'So, Digby gets the siphoned-off profits from Winterbourne. But then,' she looked up. 'Judging by the state of the church's accounts these days, I'm imagining Winterbourne started losing money.'

Mackenzie sighed again and leaned forward. 'Look, I'm going to level with you. You've clearly done your homework. Let's not drag this out any longer. Even if Winterbourne made a loss, I could offset that loss against any tax revenue. So it was a win–win. But then HMRC got the measure of it. Shut it down. Demanded the back taxes.'

'How much?'

'Three mill.'

Martin gave a low whistle. 'Did Tristan know?'

Mackenzie nodded. 'We spoke about it just before coming up here. He wasn't best pleased, shall we say.'

'So the church is broke. Hence the less than top-notch accommodation, the desperate need to sell out the conference centre? How did Tristan take it? Hearing about this?'

Mackenzie was silent, grim.

'He wanted you gone, didn't he? He told you to pack up and get out after the Durham shows.' It was a statement, not a question. 'Where were you going at six in the morning on the day of Reverend Snow's murder?' Martin asked sharply.

Mackenzie's head whipped up. 'What do you mean?'

'You were seen walking along the hallway of the boarding house. Where were you going?'

Mackenzie's face turned ashen. 'Would you believe me if I said I was just going to make some tea?'

Martin put her head on one side.

'The truth is just as shaky,' Mackenzie said.

'Try me.'

'I went for a walk. I'd got in late but I couldn't sleep. I'd slept to begin with but woke up about 5 a.m. I always do this when I'm stressed. Go off to sleep okay but then wake up in the middle of the night, and then that's it. So I just gave up. Thought I'd get some fresh air, wander around. Clear my head.'

'Did anyone see you on your walk?'

Mackenzie gave a laugh. 'The milkman?' He shook his head sadly. 'Nah. Afraid not.'

'You know what this means, don't you?' Martin said gently.

'I've got no alibi.'

Martin nodded her head. 'And you've also got a motive.'

22

I had cooked for hours. As usual it was left to me while you cavorted like a show pony in the arena of Tristan. We gathered all together and I brought the leg of lamb to the table, steam wafting from it, potatoes crowning its glory. There we were. Such a happy family. Violet between Tristan and you; then Fraser and, once you were all sitting, finally I took a seat at the end of the table.

Tristan sharpened the carving knife, slicing the pink meat thinly, placing it delicately on plates. What did you think of Fraser? Did you like him? I thought he orbited Tristan like a planet, occasionally bumping into us asteroids — the others who moved around him. When we came together like this, there could be sparks, could be explosions. I knew, and I think you did as well, that it was better alone, in the dark of the void. Where everything was silent and still.

We angled ourselves towards Tristan, our spindly antenna fingers pointed in his direction, trembling, poised, in the air. The mood was shaped by him, by which side of the moon he chose to appear on.

'Lord, we thank you for this food. May it strengthen and refresh our bodies. We ask you to nourish our souls with your heavenly grace, in the name of Jesus Christ our Lord.' Tristan would always say grace, would give a brief nod at the rejoinder of Amen, and we would raise our forks as one to start eating.

That meal in particular I remember. Do you, Antonia? It comes to mind because of what happened during and what happened after . . . oh, you'll remember. Let's see, shall we?

'How many people are expected tonight, Fraser?' Tristan had asked. 'A lot I would think, given we had to change venues to the leisure centre?'

'Aye. Word spreads on nights like this.'

'Could you pass the peas, please?' Violet asked. She looked lovely that late afternoon. Her skin peachy and soft, like a fawn. Nevertheless, she was ignored.

I remember the relief when Tristan gave a satisfied sigh, glancing down at his fork. He beamed at us all. I felt the collective slowing of heartbeats pulsing softly around the table. Slowly, slowly, careful now, I thought.

Tristan smacked his lips. 'Sera, you've outdone yourself again. The perfect bite. Just the right amount of lamb, a little bit of potato, some gravy. Perfect.'

I looked at him, across the carcass of the lamb leg. A trickle of blood pooled under its rump, mixing slyly with the potato juices, turning red to brown.

'We won't be filming it, though. Not tonight,' Fraser had said, lifting a small glass of red wine. 'Better to keep off the radar.'

'Really? I suppose so . . .' Tristan sounded uncertain.

I couldn't help myself. To this day, I don't know why. A devil in me, perhaps. 'She's too young.'

Tristan's look was like an arrow.

'Right. Whatever. It's a private affair, this one,' Fraser said, his eyes shifting to his plate, a bead of sweat appearing on his brow.

'If the press got wind of it, it would be a disaster,' Tristan said, his eyes still on me. You said nothing, if you remember? Not even when Violet asked you again to pass her the vegetables.

'Will her parents be there?' Fraser said, to cut through the silence. His voice already bore the stain of fear.

Tristan removed a piece of gristle from his mouth and placed it carefully on the side of his plate. Something about the movement angered me. Such an uncommon emotion for me to feel, I almost didn't know what to do with it. And so I spoke again. 'Her mother is a church member. Her father passed.'

'Maybe that's why she's close to Violet? She needs a proper family.' You said something at last, smiling at Tristan as you chewed. You were deliberately provocative. You knew what Mercy was to the church.

'Her mum's never around,' Violet chipped in. 'Works at the arcade on the change counter. Penny Lane, we call her,' she giggled.

I breathed softly as the sound of stainless steel on china tapped relentlessly into the room.

Tristan shifted his eyes to Violet. 'Come here,' he said.

Oh Violet. She looked so confused.

'Lean in, bring your face to mine.'

She put her fork on her plate and moved forward, pushing her nose in towards her father's. He brought his head down to within a whisker of hers. There was silence. I closed my eyes. Like you, I was at once a coward, my hands immobile on the table either side of my plate.

Opening my eyes, I saw Tristan breathe in deeply. Then he grimaced, leaning back in his chair. He waved his hand in front of his face, a look of absolute disgust on his features.

'Violet, your breath smells like shit.'

The words spun across the table with the smash of a juggernaut into a pram. Violet crumpled, pulling her lips taut. Her eyes glistened with tears. I moved my hand at last, pushing it across the tablecloth towards my daughter.

'Don't,' Tristan ordered. 'Little teases must be taught not to use potty mouths on others.'

I could see Fraser smirking at the end of the table, his lips wet with gravy.

'It was hardly potty-mouthed . . .' you interjected, before a look from Tristan silenced you. As usual. But you did try to defend her. I'll give you that.

'Enough, now,' he said. 'Violet, run upstairs and get changed.'

Violet scraped her chair back and fled from the room, tears spilling down her cheeks as soon as she had her back to us.

'Clear the table, Sera,' Tristan said to me, and I stood to do his bidding. His face was flushed with pleasure. 'Now it's time to deal with another little tease.'

We stood, blank-faced, watching her. We were dressed in white, all of us. The pock-marked moon was huge and impassive, doming visibly beyond the leisure centre windows. Light was low, candles spitting wax and flame on to the parquet floor. Mercy stood in the middle of us, her hair loose on her shoulders, blonde, straight and true. Her fingers spread against her thighs, pointing star-shaped towards the shadows moving towards her on the floor. We came softly, moved with determination, our eyes fixed on a spot deep within her. She didn't understand it then, what it was that we saw.

Violet was with us, dressed in white alongside me, with red eyes, sobs still lurking in her chest. She walked stiffly at first, separate from those who walked with Tristan, but I caught her eye and at my look, she melded in. At that moment, she did not see Mercy, she was blind to her. She saw only the pentagram, the limes and the flowers placed at each of its points, chalk and mud scored into the floor. And her father at the head of it. His eyes closed.

The whispers came like dry leaves, skittering through the room, its high ceilings alive with the candlelight and shadows morphing into beasts.

'Release the spirit. Release the spirit . . .'

We edged in closer. You and Fraser, you edged in too with the circle. You held his hand. Even our father was there. He'd come back to the church after . . . well, you know what happened. He was trying desperately to appease Tristan. And me. It didn't work.

I watched as Mercy dug her fingers into her legs as our shapes loomed over and around. I ended up so close to her, I could smell Mercy's body odour mixed with the perfume she always wore. Something far beneath clicked in my brain then, I must admit. Did it you? That Mercy would have dabbed perfume on to her wrists and neck before leaving the house. That she had groomed herself for tonight. That there was a world outside of this moment that still existed, cold and fresh with the smell of early bonfires and beyond the exit doors. That there had been a 'before'.

The thought occurred to me that I could stop this. That I could take her hand and pull her out; away from the encroaching white figures.

Tristan seemed to have stretched and lengthened to a magnificent height, leering down, his hands reaching for Mercy.

'Release the spirit. Release the spirit . . .'

It could have been an olfactory freedom. I smelt Mercy's fear. I was different from the others, at least. I was different from you. I saw the girl's toes curling hard into the floor, the dampness of her white gown, the faint path of urine trickling down her legs.

I didn't stop it. I continued to watch.

Tristan moved behind Mercy. He reached up and placed his hand, strong on her forehead. With one sharp movement, he pulled her flat, backwards to him. Her eyes slowly closed.

Tristan knelt next to Mercy. He held his hands above her. 'Behold the cross of the Lord, flee bands of enemies.' He reached down and *picked up the silver cross which hung around his neck. 'The lion of the tribe of Judah. The offspring of David hath conquered.'*

'Release the spirit. Release the spirit . . .' The insistent murmurs were hot in the air.

Tristan reached up to the heavens as Mercy began to shudder on the floor. Her eyes rolled back, the whites showing; viscous orbs. Tristan picked up her head and murmured into it, urgent now. Mercy's legs kicked and flailed. Tristan pressed down on her, pushing her into the ground. Mercy bucked and reared.

'Release the spirit. Release the spirit . . .'

Our whispers were unrelenting. I saw you, crouching low on your haunches like a dog, still moving inwards. We were indiscernible from each other, a wall of white and flame. Flecks of spit flew from our mouths on to Mercy's rocking body. We were pushed and squeezed together; it was hard to breathe. There we were: trapped in the heat of the candles and Mercy's writhing and my dark-faced husband staring into the black as a challenge.

Mercy heaved up, her mouth slashed down, a curl on her lips. She inhaled deeply through her mouth and swallowed, bringing her chin to her chest. She looked at us, hard and glassy. She licked her lips.

Then I caught a glimpse of Violet's face. Don't, I thought. Please, don't, Violet.

'Where is my crown?' Mercy whispered, hoarse. She whipped her head back to look at Tristan. Leaning forward, she clambered on to her knees and brought herself to standing. Her hair was mussed now, wild. 'Where is my crown?' she repeated.

'Deliverance in Jesus's name,' Tristan said softly, also standing. 'Cunning serpent. May you be snatched away and driven from the house of God. The Most High God commands you to be gone.'

He pushed her on her shoulder. She snapped back, her hands clawing at the air. 'Kneel,' she rasped. 'Kneel before me.'

Tristan removed the cross from his neck and held it up to Mercy's face. She licked her lips again, spittle droplets collecting on her chin.

'Deliverance in Jesus's name.'

'Release the spirit. Release the spirit . . .'

Mercy jerked forward as if to leap at Tristan. He pushed the cross into her face, striking her cheek. She cried out. Violet let out an involuntary moan, undetected by everyone apart from me. Please, I thought again. Please keep back, keep safe, Violet.

'Release the spirit. Release the spirit . . .'

'Deliverance in Jesus's name!' Tristan roared, his cross in the air. 'You will kneel to HIM!'

Mercy screamed as, at once, the candlelight was extinguished and the room was plunged into darkness. There was a rumbling, a scrabbling, feet clambered over me, fingers dug into my arms. I lost sight of Violet.

And then the lights came on.

Mercy lay still in the middle of the pentagram, breathing calmly, her eyes closed. She looked as if she were sleeping peacefully, the only sign of what had transpired a red welt on her cheekbone. I got to my feet with the rest of them. We were silent, looking as one to Tristan. He slowly raised his arms. 'Hallelujah,' he said. 'Praise be to God.'

There was a heat throughout that room. A boil of wildness. We felt it in our cheeks, the top of our heads, our loins.

Only Violet was pale.

Tristan gently touched Mercy on the shoulder and her eyes opened. He brought her to her feet and we cheered them. Even me! Even I cheered, Antonia – as you did. Arm in arm, they moved to leave the circle. I watched them exit the room as if they were bride and groom.

As I followed them, I met Violet's eyes. Such hatred she had. I had never before seen such hatred on another's face.

23

Jonah Simpson sat at the small drop-leaf desk in his sitting room. The room was no bigger than his kitchen but he liked to eat in there properly, albeit at a makeshift table. His breakfast was meagre: a boiled egg, a sprinkled puddle of salt. He sipped from a glass of hot water and lemon. Before he ate, he said grace and then cut the egg systematically into tiny squares. He would press a square into the salt before placing it carefully in his mouth; his eyes closed, chewing deliberately.

He was a tall man, bone thin; a frame that could have taken much more than the substance of him. His long face was elongated further by a grey beard. He had a protruding white mole on one cheekbone, which often prompted uneasy stares. He ignored them.

When he had finished his egg, Jonah stood and took the plate and his glass into the kitchen where he washed them up immediately, turning them upside down on the draining board to dry. He paused for a moment at the sink. It was a fine morning. The sun dripped through the net curtains at the window over the sink, dappling the counter top. He turned to look at the crucifix on the wall and breathed in deeply; the words of a prayer spinning in and among him, turning the wheels within him, calming him.

He returned to the sitting room and sat in his one armchair in the tiny bay window, which looked directly on to the street. He prevented nosy parkers from peering in by hanging yet more nets. It gave the room a dusky feel, as if it were perpetual afternoon. Next to the electric fireplace, in the corner where a television might have stood, a lectern faced a mirror the height of Jonah himself, bolted on to the wall. He opened the newspaper and sat in quiet reverie for a few moments. The house was silent, dust motes drifting quietly down through the shaft of sun at the window, which persisted despite the nets. Finding it hard to read in the light, eventually Jonah stood to close the curtains. It was then, as Jonah settled himself again, that he saw the article.

White heat flashed through his veins. He swallowed roughly and grasped the arms of the armchair to steady himself. He snatched up the paper to stare at it; his eyes were deceiving him, surely? But no. There was no mistaking it.

Tristan Snow was dead, the article said so. Somebody . . . a journalist, Egan someone . . . they had set it all out. He had been found two days ago, dead in Durham. Jonah's already pale face blanched to an unhealthy white; his throat felt dry.

He needed to think what was best to do. Suddenly, with a silent explosion, the world had changed. He needed to figure it out. He needed to calm himself down.

He walked over to the lectern and slowly unbuttoned his shirt. His eyes met his reflection in the mirror as his stretched skin was revealed over jutting ribs. He removed the belt, biting his lip as metal studs were released from where they stabbed into his waist. Dried blood had congealed there, but Jonah failed to notice it. He felt only the difference in sensation from the constant pain he experienced from the rivets on the belt, now being eased. Release was yet another interesting thing, he thought, as his stare burned into the mirror.

He brought to mind the verse that had kept him company for all of these years. He had been out in the cold, in the wilderness, while Tristan frolicked with his daughters, in his rightful place. *In due time, their foot will slip. For the day of their calamity is near. And the impending things are hastening upon them.*

Jonah returned to his seat, the belt hanging from his hand. He sank down as if he were undone, his mouth open, eyes glazed. He could taste it in his mouth, the whisky he was desperate to drink. But he wouldn't. He wouldn't be undone – yet again – by that family.

He forced a prayer from his mind. Prayers were useless now. Only one idea could possibly replace, for him, the loss of Tristan Snow.

And it wasn't God.

It was revenge.

24

Antonia curled her toes on the sheepskin rug. The sound of breathy pan-pipes weaved around her and she closed her eyes in anticipation of the relaxation that was to come. Eventually, the white-jacketed, bland-faced therapist directed her to a corridor where the scent of frangipani danced across her nostrils. She was led to a softly lit room where she undressed and lay on a raised bed, a towel brought up to her chin.

She wiggled her fingers on her stomach, enjoying her nakedness, enjoying the sensation of the brushed cotton on her skin, the cool of the air-conditioning, the flicker of an expensive candle in an alcove. The therapist returned but said nothing. This place was costly enough that those who worked here knew not to chat; knew not to disturb the clients' peace, for which they paid handsomely, with chatter about holidays or nights out.

Antonia closed her eyes again, breathing gently, allowing her brain to soften to mush. She deflected any thoughts of Tristan or Sera; anything related to the murder. Soon enough, she would have to go back to that hell-hole of a Travelodge and see them all again. Their faces pinched and pale and suspicious. Here, she could forget all of it. Forget the truths that scorched her brain when she was upright. And sober. Here, she existed only in a state of pan-piped, fragranced relaxation. It was heaven.

The therapist swept her face gently with cotton pads and began to paint a mask on to Antonia's face. It felt cool, tingling over her skin, renewing it. The therapist wrapped a towel around Antonia's hair before massaging an oil of some kind into her naked shoulders, skimming the tops of her breasts with her fingers, delicately trained in the art of what was appropriate. Her hands applied pressure to Antonia's forehead as she sank into an exhausted doze. Somewhere in her subconscious, she heard the door of the therapy room open and close. She slept.

In her dream, she was holding a baby. She rocked it gently, against her breast, looking down on to its rosebud lips, its dark and knowing eyes. The love she felt for the baby, in her dream, was all-consuming. Its body was vanilla sponge and filled with cream, a puff of a body. She wanted to eat it, to have its love drop into her being like a well of sunlight. *Please don't leave me*, Antonia thought in her dream. *Please don't leave me.*

The mask was being wiped off her face now in slow, gentle, circular motions. The therapist stroked her fingers across Antonia's cheeks as she emerged slowly from sleep into consciousness. The frangipani still whispered to her; the music still lulled. The therapist began to apply another solution to her face. Broad strokes, coating her cheeks and her forehead, her nose and underneath her eyes. She placed a warm flannel over Antonia's eyes and over her mouth, leaving only her nose exposed, so as to breathe.

Again, the therapist seemed to Antonia, in her sleepy state, to retreat, to leave the room.

And that was when the burning started.

The solution seemed to stick to her skin; crampons of fire which dug viciously into her pores, spiking down with branded irons. Antonia's hands began to scrabble, ripping off the flannels on her face, moaning. She couldn't breathe, chemicals gagging the back of her throat. Her eyes began to stream as she cried out, blindly throwing herself off the bed, trying to find the door, the way out. She reached the door and tugged at it, barely able to see. The aroma of flowers was now assaulted by something more pungent, a medicinal smell. Antonia screamed as she flung herself, naked, into the corridor. Another therapist emerged hurriedly from a room further down; the noise an aberration in the calm. She saw Antonia, wild, her hands to her face.

'Let me help you,' the therapist said to her, bewildered. 'Let me see your face.'

Antonia removed her hands, all the while crying and sobbing and stamping her feet with the agony of it. 'Get the mask off,' she begged. 'Please! Take it off!'

Once her hands were removed, the therapist could see that removing the mask would prove difficult. For there was, in fact, no mask. Antonia's skin was disintegrating, blistered and covered with pus. Her face was shrivelling, red and angry; her eyelids now swollen beyond recognition; searing sores rivering up her face and into her hairline.

'We need an ambulance!' the therapist yelled, her training in calm abandoned at the horrific sight before her.

Her voice became hoarse as fumes curled into her throat, too. 'Call 999 now!'

Antonia sank to her knees at that; praying to her God that she would black out. What had happened to her? What had happened to her face?

'Hydrochloric acid,' Martin said in the incident room. 'Someone came in, pretending to be carrying on with the facial, and carefully applied hydrochloric acid to Antonia's face. She's in intensive care. Second-degree burns. Her sight may be compromised.'

Jones looked at Martin in disbelief. 'Hydrochloric acid?' she said. 'Where can you get that from?'

'Any builder's merchant. It's used in industrial cleaning,' Martin answered. 'Really vicious.' She shook her head. 'She might need plastic surgery. The spa's a write-off, too. Designated a hazardous area. It'll need to be closed down for a while to be decontaminated.'

'Who would do something like that? Who would even come up with that idea?'

'Someone with a bunch of screws loose. Someone who hated Antonia. Or someone who wanted to keep her quiet,' Martin said. 'We'll need to find out where the Snows were at the time Antonia was at the salon. And a team will be needed ASAP for that investigation on its own. I'll talk to DCI Butterworth about it.' She looked over at Jones, wondering if her voice betrayed her feelings about Sam.

'Got it,' Jones replied, seemingly unaware.

Martin stood up and walked over to the whiteboard, where Tristan Snow's face continued to stare at them all in seeming defiance. The spider's web of lines still travelled from his photo to the edges of the board, leading to faces of his family, to endless question marks.

'It's getting hard to see the wood for the trees,' Martin said. 'All of them spinning around Tristan like satellites.' She tapped the board and sat back on the desk in front of it, her eyes searching the board for answers. 'Sera mentioned the importance of families. I wondered about that. A lot of revenge-seeking here – Sera, Antonia and Violet.'

'And Mercy,' Jones said, warming to the task.

'Yes. Mercy. If she's even called Mercy any more.' Martin shrugged. 'Lancashire don't have any info on her. No record that we can see. The last we can find is her at a local secondary school – a Saint Joseph's. Left at sixteen with no qualifications. And then nothing.'

'She'll turn up,' Jones said, positive as always. 'Revenge . . . revenge for what?' she asked, feeding Martin her next line. They did this dance, the two of them. Martin using Jones as a soundboard, as the reflection of her assembling thoughts.

'Revenge for Tristan's behaviour. His affairs. His betrayal. His abuse?' Martin sighed, standing up and stretching her arms above her head. 'And what about the pigeon? What do we know about pigeons?'

'Hmm,' Jones replied, flipping through her notes. 'Well, as we know, it's the symbol of the church. A bird is, anyway. The bird that sought land after the flood that wiped out mankind. Deucalion was the hero that brought in the new era, the new age of mankind . . .'

'In other words, Tristan Snow . . .' Martin said, her tone wry.

'Well, yes, I suppose. It says here,' Jones read down the page, 'that the flood wiped out the Bronze Age and brought in the Heroic Age . . . according to Hesiod?' She looked up with a question on her face. 'But then . . . pigeons come from the same family as doves – although, while doves are linked with ideas of peace, pigeons are the black sheep of the family, the naughty cousin. Dirty yet determined.'

'Rats of the sky, my mam always called them,' Martin said.

'Yeah. Well, they're also thought to represent the home, the house.'

Martin narrowed her eyes. 'Really?'

'Yep. So, although we don't know yet whether the pigeon died there or was placed there deliberately – probably the latter given the broken neck – if it was the latter . . .'

'It might be a message of some sort,' Martin said. 'Interesting.' She hopped off the desk and moved to the door. 'I'm going to head to Snow's vigil, or whatever you want to call it, show my face to the press. Did you see the headlines this morning? Painting him like some kind of saint, wanting to give him a posthumous OBE or some such rubbish,' she sighed.

'Are you going to talk to Sean Egan?' Jones asked.

'Ugh. Yes. Tomorrow, after I've put on a protective, hygienic suit.' Martin walked to the door. 'Are you coming?'

Jones had turned back to her computer and mumbled distractedly. 'Yep, I'll meet you up there. Just want to finish off something first.'

Martin left the station via the front entrance and turned left to walk up to the Market Square. The summer evening was still light, and she wondered how effective any candles would be against the pale sky. As she walked the short distance up Saddler Street, she saw that in fact, it wouldn't be the candles that would make the impression – more the volume of people who were making their way into the centre of the city.

Martin stopped briefly and made a quick call back to the station on her phone. Tristan Snow had booked out nearly three full nights at the Gala Theatre – roughly five hundred people a night. If they were all going to come into the Market Square tonight to pay their respects, Uniform would need reinforcements for crowd control. As she began walking again, she had difficulty edging into the outskirts of the square through the throng. A make-shift stage had been set up in the middle of the square, around Raphael Monti's copper-plated – call it green and mouldy – statue of the Marquis of Londonderry sitting atop a great beast of a horse.

The statue always made Martin smile, not least because of the size of the Marquis's Hussar's hat and phallic sword at his side. But also because of the legend that Monti had declared proudly, at the unveiling of the statue, that there were no imperfections in the work. A blind beggar had, at that moment, toddled up and felt inside the horse's mouth. He announced with glee to the surrounding masses that Monti had forgotten to give the horse a tongue. Poor old Monti, Martin would think as she passed it. The arrogance of men. It was the epitome of being hoisted on your own phallic petard. And a salutary lesson that nothing was ever perfect.

Martin managed to find a spot next to the ATM machine at the entrance to the square, and looked again at her watch. The vigil was late in starting. Next to her, a middle-aged woman in a purple skirt and short-sleeved cream blouse stood crumpling a tissue in her hand.

'I just can't believe it,' she said to Martin.

'What's that?'

'I can't believe he's dead,' the woman said, raising her voice over the sound of the crowd. 'He was such a good man.'

Martin nodded and smiled at the woman, thinking as she did, that this was the first person she'd met, since investigating Tristan Snow's death, who had shown genuine grief at his passing.

'When my Ronnie died, I came to see the Reverend at one of his shows. Would have been about five years ago now.' The woman turned her body towards Martin, although her gaze sought out the stage in the middle of the square. 'He was amazing. He *healed* me.' She dabbed at her eyes with the tissue and shook her head. 'Because of him, I meditate every day. And,' she said, finally turning to look at Martin, her eyes wide and shining zealot-like, 'my diabetes has completely disappeared!'

'Because of Tristan Snow?' Martin struggled to keep the sarcasm out of her voice.

'Say what you like,' the woman said, challenging Martin with her stare. 'But I believe it. Tristan Snow cured me.' She moved her head to take in the stage once again, where Fraser Mackenzie had jumped up and was holding his

146

hands out to the crowd. 'And now he's gone,' she sniffed, edging away, giving Martin a nasty look.

A text buzzed on Martin's phone and she tapped out a reply to Jones, telling her where she was. With relief she saw some extra uniformed police arrive. It would be a hard task trying to disassemble this bear pit in the square without incident.

Mackenzie began to speak, thanking everyone for coming. Martin barely listened. She was busy keeping her eyes on Sera and Violet, who sat on chairs on the stage, their heads bowed; the embodiment of familial grief. Had they been to visit Antonia at the hospital already? Martin wondered. Flashes from the press photographers sparked up at the front of the crowd. Martin shoved her hands into her pockets as Jones joined her.

'It's just downright weird,' she whispered to her sergeant. 'What did they see in him? Look at her,' Martin jerked her head towards the woman who had been talking to her. 'She looks normal, doesn't she? But she's a complete fruit loop. Reckons Snow cured her of diabetes.'

Jones shook her head. 'I don't know, Boss. Gives them a sense of joining in, I suppose. Reminds me of girls screaming over the Bay City Rollers.'

Martin looked over at her. 'How old are you, Jones? Seriously. We've got to work on more up-to-date pop music references with you. Bay City Rollers . . .' she muttered. 'The thing I can't work out,' she continued, as Mackenzie's speech roused the crowd noise to ever-greater volume, 'is why the mother and daughter sit there like saints or something? I mean, what have they got to do with it? Sure, Snow was a healer, a soothsayer, whatever.

But why are *they* revered? They don't do anything except sit there, saying nothing..'

Something was shoved into Martin's hand, and she glanced down at it. It was a bucket, filled with coins and notes. On the side was written *Collection for the Snow Family*. Martin gave a short laugh. 'Ha, of course. Good opportunity.' She looked up at the stage to where Mackenzie was swaying with his hands folded in front of him in a prayer position. He happened to look over at the same time and caught her eye. Martin inclined her head in a small bow, the bucket in her hand. *Bravo*, she appeared to be saying to him, *bravo*.

25

The morning after the vigil, Sean Egan sat in the Market Tavern, halfway through a pint of Guinness, his iPhone on the bar top before him. His hand shook as he scrolled through his emails. He was pissed off with himself. He'd left the Market Square in good time last night. Had been heading to his bike when his phone had buzzed. He'd slapped the visor down on his helmet, promised himself he wouldn't answer it. As he straddled the bike though, the voice came to him: he could just go for one. One wouldn't hurt. He'd meet Danny, have a jar and then head home for . . . for whatever he had in the fridge. Maybe he'd get a kebab en route, thinking about it.

At 3 a.m., when he'd finally let himself into his ground-floor one-bedroom flat, he'd collapsed on the sofa. Hadn't eaten. And woke up there five hours later, feeling like shit and knowing he must have ridden home because there was his bike outside on the street, winking at him as he squinted into the morning light.

Now the day was bright again and the only way he'd get through the next few hours was with a couple of pints. And the longer he deluded himself that he wasn't an alcoholic, the harder he would fall when the realization finally dawned. He wasn't an idiot, Egan. He knew in his soul that he was a sharp and clever lad who had it in him to change the world – to write stories that would change the world. But the booze always called to him; that deep, dark hole that was so nice to fall into. That let you forget everything; how much of a failure you were.

There were too many like him; that was the problem, he thought, as he ordered another. Too many of the living dead who reached to him with their bony fingers, offering him the booze; telling him that it would all be fine. That he was just like them. That he could just have one.

Antonia whatshername. She was like that. They'd met here a few nights ago. He couldn't believe his luck when she'd turned up in the pub. He'd chatted her up in the hopes of getting some gossip about Tristan Snow . . . *MBE* – as she'd kept saying – clearly dropping the name to get yet more drinks in her. So she'd ended up at his, but ultimately he couldn't bring himself to shag her. She'd had nothing useful to say and had wound up snoring on his sofa.

And then it had transpired that Snow had been killed *that very night*.

Egan rubbed his hand over his two-day-old beard. Since then, he'd heard Antonia had been attacked, was in the hospital. He might pay her a little visit, come to think of it – see if he could get anything out of her about the murder. Given she had had acid thrown in her face, he wouldn't want to be seeing her for any other reason, that was for sure. He might be desperate, but a shag with a Freddy Krueger lookalike was not something he was up for.

Tristan Snow's death was an interesting prospect. Bumped off by his wife, most likely, after she'd found out about the affairs and the teenage girls. It was an open secret that Snow liked them young. He recruited them from stage doors, teasing them with free tickets and invites to parties. Egan had been digging, found a few noteworthy contacts. Something that Inspector Martin might be keen to know, if he could be bothered to tell her. He'd seen her last night, wafting round the vigil like a bad smell.

He took another swig of his pint. God, his next crap was going to be like chocolate sauce at this rate. His stomach cramped as it was. He hadn't eaten for a day or so now. He would need to get something before heading to the office. There were only so many days he could pull this shit off before he'd starting getting the fish-eye from McClaggan. Then he'd do a few days' detox; make a big show of drinking smoothies at his desk, going for a run at lunchtime. So far, it had always worked. Until the detox ended with the wagon derailing outside The Marlowe, or The Court, or The Three Swans, or . . .

A new email arrived in Egan's inbox and he looked at it idly, debating whether he could fit yet one more pint in. He was about to press delete without reading it, not recognizing the sender. But something stopped him. He read on:

To: segan@durhamchronicle.co.uk
From: pastorsimpson@hotmail.com
Subject: Information regarding the Deucalion Church

Dear Mr Egan,

I do apologize for contacting you out of the blue. But I may have some information about the Deucalion Church which you might find useful. I am a pastor myself – although unfortunately without a flock at present.

I knew Tristan Snow intimately. In fact, his wife is my daughter. I admit to being very shocked at the news of his death. I wonder if we could speak at a time convenient to you?

With God's blessings,
Jonah Simpson

Egan bit his lip and read through the email again. Without even looking at his watch, he gestured to the barman. There was definitely time for another one now.

26

Martin looked with suspicion at the cup of tea that Eileen Quinn slid across the table towards her. She nodded her thanks, however, and leaned back on the kitchen chair, a smile on her face. The kitchen was stiflingly hot, the windows closed, the heat of the summer pressing against the glass.

It was a small room with a low ceiling, lined with cupboards and a counter sticky with food stains and jellified sauce splashes. Martin and Eileen sat at the kitchen table in the centre of the room – Eileen looking for all the world as if she had recently been crowned the domestic goddess of the year. Pots and pans hung from hooks behind her head and a bouquet of dried rosemary dangling from a shelf crisped up even further in the dry, unrelenting heat.

As Martin talked to her, explained what they needed from her, she saw that Fielding had been right. Eileen's eyes moved constantly to the cream, chipped sideboard that lined the back wall of the kitchen. The smeared glass of its cupboards revealed shapes of mugs and plates stacked higgledy-piggledy inside; its surface was littered with piles of papers; straw baskets with the detritus of vegetables sticking to their sides; a set of knitting needles with lavender mohair wool attached; some sheet music; a sewing basket; a china cat. What was it that Eileen Quinn was so desperate to check? What was it that she didn't want Martin to see?

'So, you explained to DC Fielding that you saw Mr Mackenzie walking along the hallway upstairs on or around 6 a.m. on the morning of Reverend Snow's murder?'

'Yes, that's right.' Eileen squeezed her eyes shut as if the film of that morning could be viewed behind her lids. 'It was definitely him I saw. But I can't tell you anything else.' She looked at Martin innocuously. 'Nothing at all.'

'Thank you, Mrs Quinn. That's very helpful. Now,' Martin said dryly. She leaned forward to fold her hands on the table, feeling the surface dirt on her hands, ignoring the instinctive shudder within. 'Just a couple of questions about you, if I may. About your life here. At Riverview?'

Eileen darted a look to the sideboard at that, her face turning pale. She gave a little laugh. 'What about me? Nothing to tell, so there isn't.'

'Have you always lived in Durham?'

Eileen swallowed, her hand scrabbling at her neck. 'No, not always. I came here with my late husband at the beginning of the 1990s.' She sighed. 'He came into some money. We bought Riverview. It seemed a good idea at the time.'

'Where had you lived beforehand?' Martin asked, her eyes warm, her body language open.

Eileen sniffed regally. 'I was on the stage. Repertory theatre. I did it for twenty years.'

'You must have travelled around a fair bit, then? Different theatres, different venues?' Martin hesitated. 'I'm wondering whether you ever performed in Blackpool?'

Eileen's eyes met Martin's, and she noticed their colour all of a sudden; they were a vivid blue. She would have been pretty in her day, Martin thought. Her eyes moved lower, spotting the chain around the older woman's neck. A feeling prickled at the back of Martin's neck. 'That's a pretty necklace,' she observed. 'May I see it?'

Eileen flushed, brought a hand up to her neck, covering the string of gold. 'No!' she said, flustered. 'I mean, why do you want to?'

'No reason,' Martin answered, dragging her eyes away from it. 'So . . . Blackpool. Did you ever perform there?'

'I might have done,' Eileen managed to quell her anxiety. Her hand dropped, exposing the tiny cross in her cleavage. 'I can't really remember. Why do you ask?'

Martin reached into her bag underneath the table and pulled out the copy of the photo. She pushed it across the table towards Eileen, who looked at it briefly before glancing back at Martin. 'You haven't touched your tea yet, dear. It's going to go cold.'

'Do you recognize that photo, Mrs Quinn?'

'Can't say I do, no. Who is it?' She peered down at it. 'Although. Is that Reverend Snow in it? With the lady?'

Martin folded her arms. 'You know that's Tristan Snow, Mrs Quinn.'

'I do, do I?' Eileen gave a short smile. 'And how do I know that, pray tell?'

'Because you delivered this photograph to Durham police station yesterday morning. You put it in an envelope and left it there, anonymously, for my attention.'

Eileen licked her lips quickly, her tongue darting in and out of her mouth. 'No, I didn't.' But her voice shook and beads of sweat dotted her hairline. The room seemed ever more musty and close.

'We have your fingerprints on it,' Martin said gently. 'I'm afraid it's incontrovertible.'

'It's what?'

'We know it was you, Mrs Quinn.' Martin paused. 'But the question is, why would you want me to see that photo? And more to the point, how did you come to have it in the first place?'

Eileen pushed her chair back as if she wanted to flee. Her hands shook and fluttered again at her neck. She looked over to the sideboard.

'What is it, Eileen?' Martin pointed to it. 'What's over there that's so concerning you?' she asked. 'Tell me. Whatever it is, we can sort it out.'

Eileen shook her head emphatically. 'No. Get out. You have to leave.'

'I can't leave like this, Eileen, I'm afraid. There are a lot of unanswered questions which I need your help with.'

Tears began to fall down Eileen's face. 'Please. Just trust me. I haven't done anything wrong. It's all been a mistake. It's not my fault.'

'What's not your fault? Talk to me, Mrs Quinn. Come on now. Let's calm down. Have a biscuit and talk this thing through. Is it about the cross? Around your neck? If you took it from Reverend Snow, we can sort it out. I'd rather you just said,' Martin reached over the table to touch her hand and the landlady reared back as if she'd been scalded.

'No! I said, no.' Quinn stood up, her lips quivering. 'I must ask you to leave this house now. If you want

156

anything else you'll have to arrest me.' She wiped her face and stared coldly at Martin. 'I mean it.'

'I can do it,' Martin said, standing herself. 'But I don't want to. It doesn't have to be like this. If anything emerges from this conversation that proves to be important later, it won't look very good.'

'Please leave,' Eileen whispered. 'Now.'

'All right, Mrs Quinn,' Martin said, picking up her bag. 'Have it your way.'

27

Martin drove up to the University Hospital straight after leaving Riverview, thinking about Eileen Quinn. The woman was strung out, worn out. It had rubbed uncomfortably against something in Martin, made her anxious. *All the lonely people* . . . Quinn, Antonia. All these women who ended up on their own with nothing except booze or cats for company. She should have stayed put, forced Quinn to say more. To explain why she had dropped that photograph off anonymously, confess to stealing Snow's cross, if indeed she had. But Martin had wanted to get out of that house with its hot, cramped ceilings and rooms, patterns of desperation crawling up its walls. She had wanted to flee.

Now she forced herself to think it through rationally. The delivery of the photograph was a malicious act, it must be. The only reason for doing it seemed to be that Quinn wanted them to know about Tristan's affair with Antonia. And the very fact of her having it in her possession in the first place must mean that she had known Snow in Blackpool, whatever she said now. Maybe she was an old girlfriend of Snow's? But why she had stolen the cross? Because the way Quinn had reacted to Martin trying to look at it made Martin certain it was his. She caught her own reflection in the rear-view mirror as she indicated to turn off the main road. A sharp crease bit down the middle of her brow; crow's feet lined her eyes. She pressed her lips together and with effort pushed those observations out of her brain, focusing on the case. What was in Quinn's sideboard? The property had been thoroughly searched after the murder, whether Mrs Quinn realized it or not, and nothing of any relevance to the killing had been discovered. So what was it she was so afraid of?

It was another heartbreaker of a summer's day. The vivid blue of the sky remained unmarred by wisps of cloud, and the honey scent of the golden Lady's Bedstraw washed in through the car window as Martin turned her thoughts to what she had read last night. She had finished Tristan Snow's autobiography in a couple of hours. There wasn't much to it. Snow, according to himself, was the greatest thing to have hit the British Isles since the potato. He had a deep connection with the spiritual world; he was a genius at reading people's innermost emotions. He was, quite frankly, a pretty top-notch human. So far so pointless.

The most interesting thing about the book was that he barely mentioned his family. There was no information about his background, his parents. A few tall tales about his childhood, but nothing that hinted at the marvellous person he would grow up to be. There was barely any mention of his wife, and nothing of his children. Of Violet. Or their twins, who Sera Snow had said had died. There was something strange about that omission, Martin felt.

She knew Jones suspected Violet and thought Sera was just plain old crazy. Was it no coincidence that a woman, despite suffering the loss of her husband, seemed to engender no sympathy from anyone, other than the syco- phants who had lined the Market Square the other night? What would they think, if they knew about the allegations Violet had made about Mercy Fletcher? And why was Sera so unreachable? It was frustrating. Martin wanted to sink her teeth into her: feel either terrible pity for her, or a hard suspicion that she was responsible for her husband's death. And yet, she felt nothing. Sera was the personifica- tion of closed off.

Martin shivered a little as a gust of cool air drifted into the car, thinking about them all, how Antonia had lived with Sera and Tristan. This trip was a punt – coming up to the hospital. Nothing had emerged from the investigation into the attack on Antonia as yet. The spa had no CCTV, and none of its employees had noticed anyone strange on the premises. The doors to the treatment rooms were always closed when clients were inside, so it would be easy for the perpetrator to check that no one was around before entering or emerging from a particular room. Antonia had now been released from intensive care, but she was still very ill. The ward sister would put up a fight before allowing Martin to speak to her, she was sure of it. She regretted not bringing Jones, who was much better at softening up war-weary doctors and nurses.

'She's far too ill to see anyone,' the sister said predict- ably, as Martin explained the reason for her visit.

'I realize that. But this is a murder inquiry. And now also an investigation into what happened to Ms Simpson at the beauty spa. I just need to see her very briefly. Just to ask her a couple of questions.'

'I can't allow it. Maybe in a day or so. I've already had journalists sniffing around. The poor woman needs to rest.'

Bloody Egan again . . . Martin thought. 'I'm not a journalist, though,' she said. 'I'm a police officer. I'm trying to help Ms Simpson.' She looked down at the floor briefly before lifting her eyes back to the sister. 'Look, not even for a minute? Not even if I offered a guided tour of the station as a raffle prize? You know, for the hospital fund?'

The sister laughed. 'You're joking, right?'

'Sadly not. I've really only got my wit to get me through this work,' Martin smiled. 'I know you're doing your job. But so am I. And whoever did this to Antonia Simpson needs to be found and stopped before they hurt someone else. You know?'

The ward sister looked at Martin.

'Just five minutes?'

'Go on then, but I'm timing you.'

Martin entered the room quietly. Antonia lay on her back, her head and face wrapped in white bandages. Her eyes were closed, their lids red raw and swollen. A machine beeped regularly by her side. Martin approached the bed.

'Antonia? Can you hear me?' She saw the woman's eyelids flutter but remain closed. 'It's Detective Inspector Martin here. Erica. How are you?'

The machine beeped a longer sound. Martin turned to look at the green zigzags zooming across the screen.

'Antonia,' she whispered. 'Do you know who did this to you? Did you see who it was?'

Martin could see her breathing, but otherwise Antonia seemed cast in stone, her hands lifeless on the bed next to her. Martin shook her head. It was useless. Antonia was too ill. It could be days before she was ready to answer questions. The door opened behind her and the sister came in.

'Come on, Inspector. That's enough. She's very sick, pet.'

'Yes, I can see.' Martin turned back to look at the motionless form. 'Thanks anyway. Will you let me know? If she makes a rapid recovery? It's really important we speak to her.'

'You don't know who did it yet, then?'

'No. Not yet.' Martin straightened to leave. 'But we will.'

'Come on, then.'

As Martin pushed away from the bed she was suddenly grabbed by Antonia, who held Martin's hand down on the bedclothes in a vice-like grip.

'Antonia?' Martin said, shocked. 'Are you okay? What's wrong?'

The machine started to buzz and beep as if panicked. The sister leaned forward quickly and pushed a button on the wall.

'What's going on?' Martin asked, her hand still in Antonia's grasp.

'She's gone into respiratory arrest. You'll have to leave. Now.'

Releasing her hand with an effort, Martin stepped back as the door was flung open and bodies in dark blue scrubs began to fill the room, barking orders as they moved into positions around the bed. Martin flattened herself against the wall as they worked, watching the almost silent activity with utter respect.

As the paddles were applied to Antonia's chest and electricity jolted her body, Martin stared. Antonia's head was flung to one side by the violence of what was being done to her. All at once, her eyes flapped open. It may have been due to the physical effects on her body, but, later, Martin would swear that the look in Antonia's eyes had been something very clear. She had stared at Martin, her eyes wide and fearful, as if she were desperately begging for her help.

'I was with Mum, here in the hotel,' Violet said, her eyes lowered, fixed on the froth on her mocha latte in the Travelodge coffee shop.

Jones moved her gaze to Sera, who was equally subdued. 'Mrs Snow?'

'Yes, I told the other one earlier . . . the man?'

'DC Tennant?'

'Yes. I told him,' Sera said. 'Violet came back from her interview with the inspector and we stayed in our room. Violet was so very tired after all of that. So we watched television and both of us had a nap before we went to the vigil . . . for, for Tristan.' She wiped her eyes and looked at Jones reproachfully. 'I mean, when is this going to end? This harassment? Haven't we been through enough? What have we done, Sergeant Jones? What can you prove?' She shook her head. 'To take my daughter into the police station like a . . . a criminal. And then to only let her out *on bail*? So it's not even over, it's still hanging over us. It's too much.' She rubbed her thumb over the turquoise stone in her necklace rhythmically, her breath trembling from her in little gasps.

'Your sister has been severely injured,' Jones answered. 'She's been in intensive care. We just need to establish where you were when that attack took place.'

'You think I did that too, don't you?' Violet burst out, her cheeks red. 'For fuck's sake!'

Sera put a hand on Violet's, shushing her softly.

Jones shook her head. 'We're just making enquiries, Violet. No one's being accused of anything.' She looked across the lobby to where Mackenzie stood at the reception desk, glowering at her. 'Well, I think that's it then. You've made it clear that you were here in the hotel when Antonia was getting acid painted on her face.' She stood up as Sera lifted her coffee cup to her lips. 'You've been most helpful,' she said as she left them both.

Jones walked across the hotel lobby, feeling three pairs of eyes on her back, then exited the hotel and crossed over the road to her car.

She loved me more than anyone. Did you know that? Every night, every single night no matter what, I would sit at the end of Violet's bed. She'd be tucked under covers, her face freshly washed. We'd talk about her day, what had happened at school. Her night light would be on – she always wanted one – the room would be tranquil, minty-breathed, prepared for sleep.

'I love you, Mum,' she'd say to me, drowsy-eyed, her fawn's legs curled beneath the duvet, still at last.

I would stroke her hair, watch her tumble into sleep. Just our breath, the whisper of our breath the only sound.

After . . . what had happened at the leisure centre – with Mercy, you know. Once, she asked me about it. Only once. She asked me if we were normal.

Can you imagine?

I sit here now, with my view over the lawn and I think – what is normal? Was it what happened after Mum left? Was it that silence that we endured? Or was it later on? When I was the brave one, and you were the little sister who followed me?

Years after and I still dream of the boys. They gallop on horses, wild and woolly over the West Pennines. They are always older in my dreams. Tall, with sapphire eyes and glossy blue-black hair. They canter across the heather, the sun at their back. But then a hedge rears up in their path, zooming into view as if in a video game. The horses buck. And I lunge into wakefulness, my mouth circled in anguish.

You followed me when I was sixteen and you followed me later. After the boys had gone. All those secrets. All the things we shared.

You drank. I stopped speaking. These were the different ways we coped.

But then Violet came.

She asked me once, if we had any secrets, and I shook my head. She closed her eyes, her head heavy on the pillow, reassured. 'No secrets between us,' she said.

'No, baby,' I answered. 'Never ever.'

PART TWO

weigh the blood you take upon you . . .

Euripides, 'Medea'

28

'Hell is empty, and all the devils are here.'

'What did you say, love?' Sera asked from where she was lying on the bed in their hotel room, a book face down in her lap.

Violet sighed. 'Nothing. Just remembering something.' She turned away from the window through which she could see night draping lethargically across the city, lights beginning to twinkle across it. It was an apparently benign landscape, although Violet felt the devils circling above it, beating their wings. She was out of that police cell, thank God. But still they came, the police. Sergeant Jones earlier, the other ones before that. She couldn't shake the claustrophobia away: the white walls pressing down on top of her, pushing her down into the dank and musty earth.

She was on bail, they had told her. She shook her head, pushing her face into the glass, trying to catch her breath through it. Was it a crime to have the thoughts she had? Could they read her mind? Because if they could, she was going away for a long time.

'Can you shut the curtains?' Sera asked. 'Make it cosier?'

'I like them open. I want to see the sky.' Violet answered, leaning back against the window. 'When can we leave this bloody place anyway? It's almost as bad as being in prison.'

Sera met her daughter's eyes but said nothing.

'Eh?' Violet persisted. 'When is this nightmare going to be over?'

Sera swung her legs round into a sitting position. She patted the bedspread next to her. 'Come here, darling. Come and sit down.'

'I don't want to sit down.' Something in Violet was taut, stretching over a chasm of fear. What was happening to this family? Her father was dead. She shuddered to remember the image of his head encrusted with blood. Her aunt was in the hospital . . . Fraser was in their face as much as ever, his breath rank with garlic. It made her want to heave. And her mother . . . mother was mute, as usual. She had refused to allow them to visit Antonia – which Violet thought was stupid. It made them look even more suspicious.

And now, she just sat with her hands folded, smiling to herself, singing the songs they had sung in the church when Violet was a girl. When she had learnt about greed and sin and lust and longing and how the Devil would reach down into her throat and grab all of those things which lurked inside her, and yank them out on a bloody string. Whatever she had said to Inspector Martin, she still lived in terror of that, the Devil coming dark and hooded in the middle of the night.

Sometimes, her bedroom door would open in the darkness when her night light's timer had switched itself off. A sliver of light would arc across the carpet through the gap. Violet would lie still as a statue, hardly daring to breathe, her eyes tight shut. She would hear the Devil's breath; loud and uninhibited. She could feel him watching her, his bug eyes travelling over her shape under the covers. *Please*, she would whisper in her head, *please, oh Lord, protect me. I trust in you, my Lord. Our Father who lives in Heaven, hallowed be thy name; deliver me from evil.* She would say the prayer repeatedly, until the words fell into each other and she couldn't find any meaning in them. Then, she would hear the door gently close.

And he would be gone.

'Well, what *do* you want?' Sera asked, breaking into her thoughts.

Violet strode to the telephone on the desk by the door. 'Hello, room service? I'd like a double gin and tonic please. Room 114. Thank you.' She put down the receiver and glared at her mother, her eyebrows raised.

Sera bent her head to study her hands.

'Aren't you going to say anything?'

'What do you want me to say? You can have a drink if you like.'

'Ugh!' Violet tore her hands through her hair. She pulled up suddenly as a thought struck her. 'Where's Dad's cross? The gold one he always wore?'

Sera stared at her. 'I don't know.'

'You don't know?'

'No.'

'He wasn't wearing it in the morgue. Did they give it back to you?'

'No. I don't think so . . .' Sera moved her head a little. 'I can't remember.' She lifted her head to meet Violet's gaze, her irises yellow like a cat's, in the dark of the room, with only reflections of the city lights illuminating her face. 'What are you insinuating?' she asked.

'Did you kill him?'

Sera was silent.

'I mean, I don't blame you if you did. But, if it was you, why did you stick that cross in my nightdress, smear blood on it? Dad's blood!' Her eyes shone with tears. 'Did you do that? Because, if you did, I have to leave you now. I can't stay here any more. I can't live this life. You'll get on all right without me.'

'Of course I didn't kill him. How could you say such a thing?' Sera said quietly.

Violet waved her arms at her mother. 'This is what drives me insane. You! You're always so *reasonable* about everything. When do you ever get angry? When? I've never seen it.'

'Why do you want me to be angry?'

'You sound like a fucking shrink.'

'Just calm down, Violet.'

'Saying that is the surest way to wind someone up, don't you know that?' Violet perched on the side of the desk. 'You weren't even angry when . . .' She held up a finger to her mouth.

Sera said nothing, a vein twitched in her temple.

'Don't you want to know when?' Violet threw at her, her voice hitting a screech. Sera looked at the door. 'Worried someone will hear, are you? That's always the main priority, isn't it? Keeping everything under wraps. Making sure no one knows our family's little secrets?'

'We don't have any secrets, Violet. You know everything,' Sera said. 'Everyone does.'

Violet spoke quickly, agitated. 'You have got to be kidding me. Seriously? If that's true, then why have I been having a nervous breakdown inside – ever since Dad died – worried about protecting us from the police? Even though I've fucked that up, obviously, given I'm on fucking bail!'

Sera stood slowly and faced her daughter. Her hair hung either side of her face in the dusky gloom. Something passed across her eyes – a pitiful look – but underneath it, just spiking through, was a point of hatred. 'Tell me what you mean.'

'What do you think, Mum? What do you think happened to Antonia?' Violet sank on to the bed, exhausted. 'You must have known. The way you spoke to that policewoman.'

Sera seemed to sink in relaxation, her shoulders dropped, and she smiled. She moved to sit next to her daughter and took her hand. She brought it up to her lips, kissing it, closing her eyes. 'Oh, my darling girl, I was hoping you'd tell me,' she said.

'I *hate* her,' Violet spat. 'For everything she's done to you.'

Sera shook her head. 'She loves you. And me. She just doesn't know how to show it.'

'I don't know how you let her get away with it. All those years. With Dad. It makes me *sick*.'

'She's my sister.'

'She couldn't give a shit about you! All she cared about was getting one over on you. Like she was his fucking queen or something . . .' Violet looked at her mother. 'When we came here . . . you know, I'd already planned it. I wanted to hurt her and then I was going to leave.'

'Leave?' Sera asked, a vague tremor discernible in her voice. 'What do you mean, leave?'

A knock came at the door and Violet stood to open it. She took the glass and the bottle, signing the chit before drinking greedily. 'God, that's better,' she said, coming back to her mother.

'Leave, Violet?' Sera said, a knife-edge sharpening in her voice. 'What do you mean by that?' She got up herself and moved in front of the hotel room door, her arms folded. 'Tell me what you meant just now. When you thought I should have been angry.'

'Jesus, Mum! Mercy? Remember her? All of that,' Violet shuddered. 'All of what was going on back then.'

For a moment, Sera was frozen, her pounding heart the only sound in her ears. 'What do you think I should have done about it?' she forced herself to say.

'Um, I don't know? Called the police, perhaps?'

'You were never hurt.' Sera's face was rigid.

'Sure,' Violet looked sorrowfully at the ice cubes revealed in her finished drink. 'What have we been doing, Mum? All these years? Why have we put up with it? Isn't it time to put an end to it? I can't do it any more.' She glanced over at Sera, who was motionless, lit up by the city lights easing in through the window.

'What could I have done? Answer me. Where would we have gone? We would have been destroyed. No money, nowhere to go . . .'

Violet ignored her, woozy from the alcohol. 'You never bloody well speak, Mum.'

'I've never defended him,' Sera said.

'You didn't defend me either.'

They looked at each other as the low hum of traffic carried on outside the window, sounds of life shuttling past beyond the door.

'What did you want, Violet?' Sera asked at last, her eyes fixed on her daughter's. 'More fights? More shouts and violence and sadness?'

'No, of course not,' Violet answered. 'But now he's gone. It just seems – all of it – so pointless. Why are we here? Why did we come here?'

Sera bent her head.

'Was it you? Did you want us here? Was this all a plan?'

'No. You've got it wrong.' Sera wobbled on her feet, her head rolled a little, her eyes glazed.

'Mum? Look . . . let's . . . are you okay?' Violet crossed the room and went to hold her mother's shoulder.

Sera shook her hand off, staring coldly into her daughter's face. 'You're talking rubbish,' she spat. Her face had changed, the momentary blankness had drained away, leaving fury in its place.

'What?' Violet asked, suddenly uncertain. 'What's wrong? You look . . . different.'

Beyond Violet's head, Sera could see a satellite moving across the sky, its red and gold lights marking a trail, observation on the move. It would see everything eventually. Soon, nothing would be unknown. Sera moved to the phone, the realization coming to her of what she had to do.

She spoke in a low voice, ordering another gin and tonic. Then she replaced the receiver and looked at Violet.

'Mum . . .?' Violet's voice had changed. Something in Sera was frightening her. She was cold, standing in the shadows. Violet was grateful for the lights outside the window. The room felt too dark, oppressive. 'Please, Mum. Tell me . . . what's wrong? Talk to me.'

But once again, Sera retreated into silence.

29

Jim Lacey sat at the back of the Indian restaurant, his hands cradling a huge bottle of Kingfisher beer.

'Either your hands have suddenly got tiny or that is the largest beer bottle I've ever seen,' Martin said as she sat down opposite him. He had his back to the wall, leaving her to sit facing away from the door — her most hated position, as he well knew.

'It was all they had,' he shrugged. 'Long day. Could do with a drink.'

Martin gestured to the waiter and ordered a Coke. 'Me too. But I'll be up at five. I'm in the middle of a murder.'

'When are you not, Erica?' Jim sighed, and pushed his bottle away. A few seconds passed. 'Let's not do this. I don't want to.'

Martin nodded. 'All right.' She called back the waiter. 'Can I have another glass? And . . .?' She looked over at Jim, who acknowledged the implied question with a smile. 'And chicken tikka, yellow dhal, garlic naan — times two please.'

She poured some of Jim's beer into the glass that was brought to her and drained half of it in one gulp. 'How are you?' she asked.

'Oh, you know. Ticking on.'

When did it get like this? Martin wondered. Other than knowing what Jim would want to eat in an Indian restaurant, most of the time she felt she didn't know him at all any more.

'You look good,' he said. 'You've got some colour in your cheeks. Have you been away?'

'Crete. Long weekend.' Martin's face flushed with the beer and what she knew was coming.

Jim looked surprised. 'That's unlike you,' he said. 'Managed to tear yourself away from the bad and the ugly of Durham?'

Martin chewed her lip as the waiter put a bowl of poppadoms on the table in front of them. She took another gulp of beer. 'Yep,' she said. 'Anyway, how's the new flat?'

'All right. Small. Empty.'

'You can come and take anything you want, I've told you. The spare bed. Saucepans. Whatever.'

'I don't need saucepans, Erica. I've got a bed. But . . .' He suddenly looked tentative, staring down into his glass before clearing his throat. 'What I've been thinking about lately, is that what I haven't got . . . in my flat, is . . .'

Don't say it, Martin thought. *Please don't say it.*

'. . . you,' he finished. 'You know? I just think . . .' He reached his hands out across the table. 'Maybe we shouldn't sign the papers. Maybe we're making a mistake.'

The laugh came out of Martin's mouth before she could stop it. 'Mistake? Jim . . . a mistake is buying a pair of trousers in the wrong size. It's booking a flight on the wrong date. It's not going a year barely talking to me and seeing a solicitor and getting papers drawn up to put into court to actually ask a judge to declare your marriage over!' She shook her head, her eyes blazing.

A mistake?

178

Jim drank some beer and moved the condiments dish around. 'Tom-ay-to, tom-ah-to,' he said at last.

'No,' Martin said firmly. 'It's not how you look at it, how you say it. Whatever word you use. It *isn't* a mistake. It wasn't one and it isn't. We decided. We thought about it and we agreed. We agreed that it was what was best. For us both.'

'We haven't really spoken, though, have we? We've just let it go on and . . . now it's just sort of happening.'

'You know how to contact me Jim,' Martin said. 'You know where I live. You just haven't been bothered. Living the life of Riley in Newcastle . . .'

'Then why does it feel like shit?' Jim interrupted, before waiting a beat. 'You feel it, too. I can tell.'

'I *don't*.' Martin tucked her hair behind her ears angrily. 'Don't be so fucking arrogant! I mean, yes, I feel sad about it. You know, like it's something I failed. And I miss you. You were my friend. I loved you . . .'

'Loved?'

'Yes. Past tense. Now . . .' she stopped.

Jim looked at her. 'Now, what?'

Martin glanced down at her left hand, at her third finger, where there was no longer a faint tan line caused by her wedding band. 'I'm seeing someone else,' she said. 'Someone from work.'

Jim leaned back in his chair, saying nothing, as the waiter returned yet again with plates and cutlery and the sizzling tikka plates.

'Thanks, that's great,' Martin said as she gazed at it all, her stomach so sick that she knew she couldn't eat a bite of it. How could he say this now, after all this time? Right now? In the middle of everything, when she was tired and stressed and . . . a *mistake*?

'Who is it?'

'Does it matter?'

He shut his eyes briefly. 'I suppose not.'

She frowned at him. 'And you're telling me you've been in bed by 8 p.m. every night, are you? In that fancy flat of yours overlooking the water? No girls coming back from The Boat, down on the Shore?'

Jim rubbed a thumb over his mouth before answering. 'Who do you think I am, Erica?'

She said nothing.

'Really? You think that's what I'm doing? When I left . . .' He exhaled, looking round the restaurant, the strained notes of the sitar his backing track. 'I thought it was for the best. I just . . . I thought you weren't *invested* in us any more. And I wanted to get back to work. To focus on that, not always be worrying how I was messing things up with you.'

'You make it sound so reasonable. Really . . . But it wasn't like that.' Tears crept into Martin's eyes. 'You were so cold and then you just said divorce, like it was the only option. I shut down. I didn't have time to argue. Do you have any idea what I see? What I do?' She shook her head in exasperation. 'It's like you expect me to be a certain way, like a certain kind of woman. And I *can't*.' A tear fell down Martin's cheek as she sank back into her chair. 'I just can't.' She lifted her head as Jim stood up. 'Don't . . . don't go,' she said.

'If that's what you think, then I have to. I'm not going to persuade you,' he replied, getting out his wallet and putting some money down. 'You think what you want and you'll do it whatever I say.'

'No,' she shook her head. 'That's how it was . . . how you made it.'

'Then it looks like we don't know each other at all,' Jim said sadly, as he moved out from the table. He touched Martin briefly on the shoulder. 'See you, Erica.'

And that was the trouble, Martin thought, as she poured the rest of the bottle of beer into her glass. The trouble was that deep down inside her sat a dark and dangerous fear.

A fear that, of everyone, Jim Lacey was actually the one who understood her best.

Martin threw her bag on the sofa and walked into the kitchen to get a drink to rid her mouth of the taste of the beer. As water splashed into the glass, the sound of the doorbell broke into the thrum of her thoughts. Carrying the glass, she opened the door to find Sean Egan standing on her doorstep, a bike helmet in his hand, the smell of booze on his breath.

Martin cocked her head to one side. 'Don't recall giving you my address, Egan.'

'Ah, you've forgotten. It was on the back of the envelope with your Christmas card last year.' He threw her a raffish smile, holding out a bottle of Talisker. 'I promise I'll get a cab home.'

'I've been putting off coming to see you, as it happens.' Martin's voice was cold. She glanced back along the hallway, debating whether to let him in or not. 'Suppose you've saved me the joys of hunting you down in all the pubs.'

'Intriguing,' Egan said. 'Shall I come in, then?'

Martin raised her eyebrows. 'I'm sure I'll live to regret it,' she said, leaving the door open for him to follow.

'Nice place. Redecorating, are you?'

Martin didn't respond as she considered the tall, awkward figure of Egan coming into her space. As she led him into the sitting room, she saw it as he must view it and felt suddenly and unaccountably embarrassed. When Jim had left, she had wanted to peel away any vestige of him in the little house they shared. One solitary weekend, after admittedly too much whisky, she had ripped the carpets up, angrily rolling them back into the corners to reveal the grey and splintered floorboards underneath. Since then, she'd never had the time to rent the sander needed to renovate the floor, and the only rug she owned – bought long ago, on a random trip to Turkey – wasn't big enough to hide the paint splashes and bent nails that adorned it. The walls were clean and freshly painted a chalky white, but they were bare apart from a large silver-framed film poster of *It's a Wonderful Life* above the empty fireplace. The whole place looked like a student flat; a shrine to minimalism and loneliness.

Hating that Egan was seeing all of this, nosing into her life and space, tart words tasted good on her tongue but she swallowed them with effort, keener to establish what information he thought he was going to give her. And then she'd sit back and see if, as she suspected, he had been with Antonia Simpson on the night of the murder. She turned on the only side light before heading back into the kitchen to get two glass tumblers filled with ice.

Something needed to break soon. They couldn't hold the Snows indefinitely in Durham. Violet was on bail but she would apply to have her conditions moved to Blackpool; pretty soon, they would insist on going home.

She gave Egan a glass, who grimaced before tipping his ice into a lone pot plant next to his armchair.

'Make yourself at home,' Martin observed.

'Thanks.' He poured himself a good measure of whisky before passing Martin the bottle. 'So, young, free and single now, is it?'

'Yeah, that's it,' Martin replied. 'None of your business, of course.'

Egan gave her a wink. 'I've got you all alone, then?'

Martin narrowed her eyes, ignoring him. 'What is it you want to tell me?'

Egan wiped a hand over his mouth and took another swig of his drink. 'I spoke to someone today that knows quite a lot about Tristan Snow. A good deal, in fact.'

Martin shrugged. 'And?'

'And he says some things that I would think you'd be very interested in. Things about what the good Rev and his mates liked to get up to in their spare time.'

Martin considered this nugget, wondered how to play it. 'What kind of things are we talking about?'

'Things that a man of the cloth shouldn't be doing, that's for sure.' Egan patted his nose with a finger. 'If you know what I mean. And also,' he reached into his rucksack and brought out a DVD case. 'He's sent me a film of one of Snow's sermons. Which is disturbing, to say the least.'

Martin eyed the DVD before taking a drink and sitting back in her chair. 'Yes, I would find that interesting,' she said eventually. 'But before I get overexcited and start charging round blowing up balloons for the end-of-case party, I'd want to know a few things.'

Egan tipped his glass to her.

'The main thing I'd want to know is, what's in it for you? Because,' she said, leaning forward and topping up her glass, 'I'm pretty sure that you haven't come to see me tonight in the hope of getting a *Crimewatch* sticker.'

'Sure, sure,' Egan replied. 'But it's an easy ask. I just want exclusivity.'

Martin frowned. 'On something that no one knows about yet except for you? I don't buy it.'

Egan exhaled loudly. 'Listen, last time we got together over a murder, I went about it in the wrong way. I can see that now. I pissed you off. And ended up with egg all over my face. So,' he grinned, 'call me a sentimental old fool, but I thought this time, I'd do it properly. Be upfront. And then you and I can help each other out. Work together instead of against each other. How about that?'

'I don't believe you, Egan,' Martin paused. 'I know you, you little shit. There's something you're not telling me.'

'Well, how about I tell you who this source is? Then you can decide if my offer's a good one?'

Martin opened her palms. *Go ahead.*

'Jonah Simpson, his name is. Whole buffet of sandwiches short of a picnic. *But,*' he said, wagging his finger, 'he has known Snow for the last twenty years, in Blackpool.'

'Simpson . . .' Martin half-whispered, her nerves tingling all of a sudden.

'Ring any bells?' Egan grinned, nodding. 'Father of Antonia Simpson and . . .'

'Sera Snow,' Martin finished for him. She definitely wanted to speak to him, although there was no way she would let Egan know how important this information was.

'He remembers some interesting things, does old Jonah. He's a man of the cloth himself. Worked with Snow at that Deucalion place. Then there was some falling out – I haven't got to the bottom of it yet – and they became mortal enemies.'

'So no reason for him to try and stitch Snow up, then,' Martin said wryly. 'Even though he's dead.'

'Well, I suppose. But I believe him. He seems proper shaken up about Snow's death. You know, like the only reason he had to live was to hate him. And now Snow's not around, he doesn't know what to do with himself. And the things he says tally with what's on YouTube. You've seen all that, obviously?'

'Exorcisms, miracles,' Martin said. 'Anyone can see it.' Again, the words of Violet came to her, that *everything was there for all to see.*

'Yeah. So the dude was into some weird shit, right? But Jonah reckons there was other stuff going on. Stuff with kids. One kid in particular, in fact. A friend of his granddaughter's.'

Martin's skin prickled, knowing what Egan was about to say. 'He can identify her?'

'Says she was called Mercy. Remembers it because – in his words – it's such a beautiful name.'

Mercy. There she was again.

Martin leaned back in her chair and took a long drink of Talisker, regarding Egan.

'What?' he asked.

'There's something more. Something you're not telling me.'

Egan gave a short laugh and ran his hand over his head. 'All right,' he said, sheepish. 'Busted.'

Martin waited, her glass on her knee.

'A girl's come forward,' Egan sighed. 'Says Snow put his hand up her skirt, back in the day, when he was performing in Blackpool. She went backstage to meet him, went into his dressing room. He tried it on and she fled.'

'And?'

'We're running it on the front page tomorrow. I'm just giving you fair warning, Martin. It'll cause issues.'

Martin sat forward, her hackles raised. 'Why, Egan? Why will it cause issues?'

'Because it relates to the Mercy thing.' Egan put his glass carefully down on the floorboards next to his chair. 'Because she was only thirteen when she says that it happened.'

Martin tilted her glass, looking at the amber liquid as it slid towards the rim. Perhaps this was the chink of light. Perhaps this was where things began to open up. 'What's on this DVD, then?'

Egan laughed. 'Movie night with the inspector? There's an offer . . .' He pushed the case over the floor with his foot towards Martin. 'Go ahead.'

Martin picked it up and looked at the case. It was blank, innocuous. She threw Egan a glance. 'You're saying this is of Tristan Snow?'

He nodded.

'You sure it's not something else. *Easy Rider* perhaps?' Martin allowed herself a brief smile as Egan's face turned blank, before realization dawned.

'Where were you, Egan? The night Tristan Snow was killed?'

Egan recovered, rubbing the stubble on his chin, a glint in his eye. 'Things that bad, Martin? Surely you've got better hopes than pinning it on me?'

'It was Sunday night, as you know. In the Market Tavern, your second home. Then on to the Angel. Made a little friend for yourself. Took her back to yours. Ever the romantic, put on *Easy Rider*. I won't mention the spliff . . .' Martin paused. 'No? Not biting?' She settled back in her chair, pulling a knee to her chest. 'Come on, Egan. When were you going to let me know you'd got the alibi for Snow's sister-in-law?'

'Ah, now. Where'd be the fun in that?'

'What time did you leave each other?'

'About 8 a.m., I'd say,' he replied, with a wink.

'You're disgusting,' Martin said, scowling.

'Aye.'

'You'll need to make a statement.' She sighed, getting to her feet and walking over to the television with the DVD. Pressing play, she stood in the middle of the room, arms folded, watching the static, before the blurred heads of a congregation sharpened and the figure of Tristan was revealed on a small platform at the front of a hall.

Martin had to admit that Tristan was magnetic. Tall, with dark curls which would spring down over his forehead as he jumped about the stage; he burst with energy. Sparks seemed to shoot from his fingertips as he swept his audience into his arms with magnanimous gestures, enveloping them with the certainty of his words. He smiled and moved with rapture and the crowd swayed in tune with his dance. They stood in front of him: some with their palms upturned towards the heavens; some with one hand in the air, their eyes half-lidded, drowsy with admiration. Beneath the music of Tristan's words, the crowd hummed and nodded, a backing track of pure assent.

Martin watched, caught between scorn and disbelief. She had seen only a few minutes, barely listening to what Tristan was saying, when she stepped forward, sharp as a tack. She was barely aware of Egan any more – the video was old and the images were hardly crystalline, but Martin suddenly saw what was obvious – what he'd been alluding to when he'd given her the video.

The majority of the congregation were children.

Martin hadn't noticed it when the film had started as the camera had panned over the backs of heads. But now it moved behind Tristan, homing in on the faces looking up at him. Some of the children were teenagers, but others were as young as four or five. Behind them stood the adults, but it was clear, as Martin began to listen hard to what Tristan was saying, that this was a sermon for the young.

He held a stuffed toy in his hand as he prowled in front of them, speaking rapidly, musically, in a rhythm to which they could sway along.

'Sin comes at you in a delicious way,' he said. 'The Devil preys on the young. He knows that you are vulnerable. He knows where you are weak. He comes in the guise of something nice, that you want to pet.' He held up the stuffed animal. 'At first you think, oh it's harmless, I'll just think that dirty thought, or say that swear word. But then, just when you're least expecting it – BAM!' He clapped his hands together, dropping the toy. He bent in close to them and the children began to move closer, mushrooming into one organism. From a discrete helper, Tristan grabbed a huge toy tiger. 'Then you've got a tiger by the tail . . .' He began to swing it round and round, whirling it in front of the children, who huddled in even nearer, cheeks flushed, their eyes fixed on the reeling tiger.

'You can't see where he is or where he's going . . . now, now, now, you're not in control. NOW . . .' Tristan pushed the tiger menacingly into the faces at the front, making them rear back in shock. 'Now, you've got the Devil inside of you.' He dropped his voice. 'I know that some of you have two sides to you, yes I do.' Tristan crouched down in the middle of a circle of children. 'I know. I can see you. You play a clever game, right here in this room. You pretend to be good Christians, to love the Lord and Jesus Christ. You pretend to be good children.' He beckoned to them to lean in further. 'But I know you're a bunch of phoneys,' he whispered. 'You're a whole bunch of fakers.'

Martin held her breath as she watched some of the little kids in the front of the circle begin to cry.

'That's right,' Tristan said. 'You need to get yourselves clean. You need to make yourselves whole. Because, *right now* . . .' He paused, getting to his feet. 'You phoneys are *going to hell!'* He rocked on his feet with his hands in the air. 'Give me the water, please. Let these children become clean. Let them confess their phoney ways. Give me your hands, children.'

A bottle of water was handed to Tristan and he began to pour it over the hands of the children who held them out willingly to him.

'Wash it away. Wash it clean, boys and girls. You are dirty, with your thoughts and your deeds. Wash yourselves clean. That's right.'

The children moved forward in small groups to put their hands underneath the water. Many were wailing with their hands in the air, sobbing; their eyes red with pain. Martin could hear some of them crying apologies as they rubbed their hands underneath the water. At the back of the room, their parents – presumably – nodded happily, watching the weeping of the children.

As Martin stared disbelieving at the screen, the camera swept past Violet. She must have been about ten, her hair in a high ponytail. She stood, her eyes raised to the ceiling, palms outstretched. She had no tears on her face but, as the film came to an end, and Martin reached to switch it off, the detective realized that her own cheeks were wet and her heart was pounding with an acute and desperate pity for those children.

30

They bring me tea here, which is nice. About the only thing that is. The view and the tea. And the paper and pencils.

They sharpen the pencils for us themselves. Worried the points will get too sharp and we'll slit a vein open with them, I imagine.

The day we left our home, were you sad Antonia? I wasn't sad. Not in the slightest. I never wanted to think about it again. About the dirty white house we'd left behind, stubbed into the ground like a half-smoked cigarette butt, its view over the concrete bridge obscured by the ever-present rain. I jabbed my nails into my arms as I walked, hugging myself as if making a vow. That would be the one lesson I took from our mother. I would block it all out for eternity.

Remember how we spent hours on our beds? Me more than you. You were always off, standing by the bridge, chatting up the boys on the estate. But I could lie for ages in that room, listening to the walls, hearing the words imprisoned within them; those unsaid sentences and paragraphs which bubbled underneath the wallpaper, crawling up and around the struts of the house like giant stag beetles, phrases jutting from their horns.

I could put my head on one side and hear the rattle of their whispers behind the plaster spread thickly over the walls. It muffled the sounds of the unspoken words, secreted them in my imagination.

The words were never uttered though, were they? They remained captive in the walls, rotting into the mulch of a thousand beetle carcasses.

We never spoke about it. How Mum had left us. We never knew why, nobody ever explained. Everything was conjecture wrapped in a pretty bow of silence. Did you feel anything about it, anyway? Any feelings we had, I think, were expressed only in our sighs, the whites of our knuckles curled round the china handle of a mug of tea. Maybe one day — the words behind the walls whispered — one day, it would change. Maybe the net curtains on our pinched and mean-spirited house would be lifted and sunlight would spring through the hallway and into the rooms, lighting up the truth for everyone to see.

One day she was there, tucking us into bed. The next — she was gone. A vanishing act! At once, the house clanged with the sound of nothing. Even Dad — he was an approximation of a father, I suppose. He was as silent as the grave. A saying I've always wondered about. Because graves can speak, did you know that?

Believe me. I'm an expert.

Anyway, Dad said nothing. He just sank into disappointment, leaning against the note on the fridge as if it could replace his backbone for the rest of his life. He carried on going to the church though, didn't he? God forbid anything prevented him from that. I sometimes wonder whether, if he'd ever lifted his eyes away from the altar and looked at our mother, she might not have left.

When I think that, though, I laugh to myself. Because look who I married! Talk about history repeating itself.

The day we moved, I stood in Mum and Dad's room, looking at her things. They were exactly as she'd left them, even the black and gold case of her lipstick covered in dust. I thought about her face. She had that expression, do you remember? That wounded but unbroken face of a martyr. I realized then that she hadn't ever wanted things to get better. She loved the drama too much, didn't she? I remember when they fought, her lips would rise with a tick of enjoyment, and again afterwards, with the endless cups of tea and the mascara-smeared faces. What did you think about that? I was disgusted by it.

So then we were gone. Blown out of the front door on the back of a resettlement from the church. Dad took it like a drowning man reaching out for a life belt. I stood at the threshold of our house that very last time, and after all those years of whispering to me, the words that had festered in the walls tore their way out of the wallpaper with their spindly legs. They followed me out, Antonia, dancing across the doorsteps at my ankles, trying to clamber up my thighs and into my heart. But I didn't let them; I shut them out. I vowed then that I would never speak of our mother, and I took it into my heart that I would never see her again.

Even if she crawled, begging to me, on her hands and knees.

Blackpool was a grey cake iced with neon. Do you remember that old gypsy song Mum used to sing before bed? That's what we were now, raggle-taggle gypsy-ohs. Only once I cried for what we'd lost. There on the promenade on our first day in Blackpool. I cried for our mum. And for our dad. And for what we were going to do with ourselves in this new place where we knew no one.

I walked along. It was raining, of course. My tears blurred the ground and the rain-leached chalk of the pavement paintings. Before I knew it, I'd crashed into a tin billboard, which stood like a taunt outside a tiny, run-down theatre.

'DO YOU NEED A MIRACLE?'

I looked up at the heavens. A cosmic joke, right?

I went inside.

A man was standing on a dais by a makeshift bar as I entered. The gloom made it hard to see but his shoulders were broad, and his eyes were kind.

'Done in by the rain, were you?'

I shrugged, my hands hidden in large pockets.

'You look like a drowned mouse,' he said. He stretched his arm towards me. 'Come . . .'

I stepped up to join him on the stage and felt as if I had stepped into a force field. From one second to the next, it was as if I had left everything behind.

'Would you like something to make you warm?' he asked.

I found myself holding a steaming mug of tea; the sugar biting on my tongue, relaxing my tense jaw. I was too afraid to look directly at him in the beginning. But I could sense him above me, bending down, the heat of him enveloping me.

As the first clap of thunder snapped, breaking the storm, I knew that I had come to the right place.

'This is my church,' he said, as he took my hand in his.

We had escaped. And our escape led me to my love.

To Tristan.

31

Martin was running fast, her lungs screaming with the effort. She ran along a narrow corridor where the brown carpet zigzagged into infinity. The walls were encroaching; she had to use her hands to propel herself along them, her palms damp and clammy with sweat. At the end of the corridor, light from a window cut like a scythe on to the dark floor and she saw she was racing towards a life-size cardboard cut-out of a photograph. She slowed herself, breathing hard.

The photo looked like one of those carnival cut-outs they have at the end of the pier, where a head is stuck through for a photo atop a fat woman's body in a red striped bathing costume. But here, the faces remained uncut. And the figures were her and Jim. She was in his arms, one leg kicked back gaily, a look of love on her face so pure it made her sob. She leaned in closer, her fingers outstretched, wanting to go back, be in the photograph again, just for a second.

With a start, she realized her mistake.

The man in the image wasn't Jim. It was Tristan Snow and his arms around her were iron and the smile on her face was contorted, fixed in place. Martin snapped back her hand and then she heard someone calling her name.

Mercy.

She knew it was her, in her bones she knew it. Mercy kept shouting for her, screaming for Martin's help. But Martin was stuck, trapped in Snow's arms, and she couldn't break free of them . . .

The noise of the phone crashed into the dark of Martin's comatose sleep, bringing her to its surface without apology. She flung herself over to the other side of the bed, her mouth dry with the taste of stale whisky, her hand scrabbling on the bedside table to stop the ringing.

'Hello?' she mumbled, pushing herself up on to her elbows.

'Detective Inspector Martin?'

'Who is this?'

'It's DC Allen. I'm calling from the surveillance team on the mother and daughter at the Travelodge.'

Martin sat up immediately, calming her thoughts from the rattle of the abrupt awakening. 'What's happened? What's the time?'

'It's just gone 1 a.m., Ma'am. They had an argument a few hours ago. Nothing major, just a barney. It went quiet so we left it, thinking they were asleep. But . . .'

Martin switched on the light next to her bed, swinging her legs round, wide awake now. She eyed her clothes bunched on the floor, her head pounding. *Bloody Egan*, she thought, ignoring her own culpability in her hangover. 'But what, Allen? They're still there, right?' She gave a short laugh.

'They're not, Ma'am. Their room is empty. We've checked CCTV at all entrances and exits to the hotel and they've been seen getting into a car.'

'Can you track them in the car?'

'We've got footage of it leaving, as I said. We've traced it on the PNC to a hire car company.'

'Is there a wire on it?'

'We were instructed to put a wire in their room, Ma'am. Which we did. If we had been instructed to put an officer outside their door, we would have done that. I'm afraid we didn't know to put a wire on a car that we had not been informed the suspect had in the first place.'

'All right Allen. Stop with the attitude,' Martin said, pulling on her trousers with the phone balanced under her chin. 'So we've lost them?'

'I'm afraid that's the case, Ma'am.'

Martin looked at her reflection in the mirror on the wall opposite her bed, her pupils dilating, her lips dry.

Where have you gone, Sera? What have you done?

Martin stared at the empty hotel room. It was in semi-darkness, the lights of the night-time city sprawling across the vacant bedlinen. 'What is the point of surveillance? Tell me that.' She hit the wall with her hand. '*Shit!*'

'Where is she?' a voice said from the hotel room doorway.

Martin whirled round to find Mackenzie standing there. His face was crumpled from sleep, although he was dressed.

'Christ, Mackenzie, what are you doing here?'

'Couldn't sleep,' he shrugged. 'I told you before, I'm an insomniac. Went for a wander and saw Sera's door was open. Where is she?' he said again.

Martin whirled back to the empty room. 'I don't know. Not here.'

197

'And Violet?' Mackenzie's voice was tense.

'She's gone too. As you can see.'

Mackenzie licked his lips as Martin strode to the window, looking down on to the street. She turned back to him in the murk of the unoccupied room. 'What? What is it?'

'This isn't good. I'm worried,' he answered.

'Why are you worried?' Martin queried. 'I mean . . . worried for who?'

'I'm concerned that she's taken her,' he said. 'Sera, I mean. Taken Violet.'

Martin stared at Mackenzie. 'I don't understand. You think Violet's been taken against her will?'

'They're gone, aren't they? Both of them. Nothing else makes sense. Look at what happened to Antonia.'

'What are you saying? Do you know something about the attack on Antonia? Was it Sera?'

'I don't know, exactly. But I'm worried for Violet.' Mackenzie was breathing rapidly, the noise of it stuffy through his nose. In the dim light of the room, Martin suddenly saw how unattractive he was. His mouth hung open a little, pasty folds of dry skin around his neck. His eyes were concerned, but they had the look of someone with another agenda. Under the worry, a crocodile lurked.

'What do you think has happened, Mr Mackenzie?' Martin asked.

Mackenzie was silent for a moment, as if gathering his thoughts.

'Mackenzie? What is it?'

'It's happened before,' he said, reluctantly. 'Going off.'

'Who?'

'Seraphina. She ran off a number of years ago.'

'And, what?'

'When she came back . . . well. She'd not been in a good state. She'd . . .' his voice dropped low. '*Done* things.'

'What do you mean? What things? What are you talking about, man?'

'Look, I'm concerned about Violet. About the wee girl. Alone with Sera in this state. Last time . . .' his voice trailed away, his lips trembling.

'Spit it out, Mackenzie. You've got my full attention.'

Mackenzie lifted his head to meet Martin's gaze. The room was quiet, the whirr of a far-off helicopter the only sound. 'Don't you understand?' he said. 'This is what I'm trying to tell you. Seraphina is dangerous. She is a very dangerous woman.'

32

Do you remember? How they used to come in, out of the rain? Shaking their umbrellas, wiping droplets of water from their brows? Blessed are the meek, I used to think, watching them file along the wooden benches. They would never change their positions in the congregation, would they? They were too afraid — of someone challenging them, asking them to move out of their seat. They were all so frightened. Fearful of life.

Dad was there, serving with Tristan. It was easy, wasn't it, once I'd met my husband, for you all to follow me. The Deucalion was so much better for us. And for Dad. Tristan was like a son to him.

Do you remember how they would wait in the small room behind the altar; bowed heads, a last minute of silence before Tristan would stride into the foreground, emerging like a Bethlehem star on to his stage?

The night Dad had to leave the church. I can see it so clearly. It must have been Christmas because there were poinsettias. I was at the front. I don't remember where you were. Probably having it off with the choirmaster.

I'm joking.

But that night. It was important, wasn't it? It was when Tristan finally showed his metal. He finally became the true master of the church. Of us all.

I helped him, of course.

I remember singing that hymn I always liked. We sang as one, Jesus shining a light, filling the land with his hope and glory. At least, I tried to sing it. I moved my lips, but often in those days my voice would vanish. Just for a few moments. Looking back, I think I understand now why it happened. I don't think you ever learnt this lesson; you would carry on talking right until the end of the tequila bottle.

But I . . . I controlled myself. I knew what Tristan needed. I knew my place. On the rare occasion I would speak my own mind, trouble always arrived on his chariot. So it seemed as though that effort — to shut my words in — meant I lost the right to choose. I would only talk at his beckoning. I had become his.

That night, the choir emerged as always, from the door to the left of the altar, singing along with the congregation. Tristan and Dad were the last to appear, stern and serious looks on their faces: the work of God is no laughing matter, after all.

It was the eighth month of my pregnancy and the babies were kicking me. I was uncomfortable. I hadn't wanted to come. Tristan had insisted. Later on, I understood why.

I considered both men as they stood side by side. So different in so many ways. Tristan's sense of purpose went deeper than Dad's. His was an underground cavern dripping with a thousand stalactites of seemingly neverending resource.

Things took place as normal. Dad moved behind the altar to break the loaf of bread. He held it aloft and tore it from the middle, crumbs dripping down on to the white tablecloth that covered the altar. Then he filled up the clay mugs with wine. People began to process up to him, to receive the spirit, the body of Christ.

Then I saw that Tristan had moved to the lectern. This was unusual. Dad had provided the sacrament; he should give the sermon. But then Tristan began.

'Faithful are the wounds of a friend.' His voice was low; the candlelight danced behind him, reinforcing his stillness. 'St Paul tells us in Corinthians about the power of truth. *The truth we know about ourselves. And ...*' He paused. '*... the truth we know about each other. Here, in this room.*'

The babies inside me stopped their squirming as if they knew what was about to happen. I realized then. He was going to do it. He was going to bring down our father before the congregation.

'The truth is hard. It is a wall of rock that looms over us sometimes. It bears down on us, overshadowing our lives. It takes over our lives, prevents us from living like good Christians. But yet, how much easier to live like that ... like that,' Tristan continued, 'than to climb that wall of rock, to overcome it and put it in its place.'

Remember how he spoke that night? He needed no notes; the words flowed out of him in a gush, a waterfall of power and belief, sweeping us all along by his force, by his conviction. He spoke of Paul again, his voice rising to the ceiling, his arms bringing us in closer, teaching us, loving us, if only we would do as he said: he spoke of the Pauline conversion which meant that nothing else mattered; nothing except our relationship with God. And with the church, of course. He smiled at us. *The truth hurts ... Godly sorrow brings repentance that leads to salvation and no regret ... And again: faithful are the wounds of a friend.*

Now – ha! Now, the cold night was forgotten, now the room was hot with faith. Tristan was magnificent, Antonia. You must have thought so, too: his hair falling down across his brow, his eyes burning into ours; he seemed to soar above us. The love in the room was palpable.

Except – it's true – for the cold, dark corner where our father sat. He was steeped in a dank pool, slick with the oily sheen of rainbow-coloured rage. He sat on his hands. I wondered: would he fight back?

'Remember,' Tristan said, 'remember the awful time when witches were burnt at the stake, when Senator McCarthy accused innocent people of being traitors to their country?' He put his hands to his chest and nodded his head. 'We are not like that. No. But —' and here he crooked a finger '— we have a duty to our church to set forth before us all a carpet of truth. A tapestry of words that we can release into the open. So that nothing will be hidden from us again. So that our church can move forward with dignity, and in a spirit of love, knowing that nothing is more sacred than forgiveness.' I remember him leaping down from the lectern and pacing across the dais. 'Let us begin. Come forward.'

I realized, then, what he meant for me to do.

He smiled at me. 'Come forward, little hen. Take my hand. Come and stand with me before our children.'

I was nervous, my mouth suddenly dry, my belly tight and awkward.

'Now tell us, little hen. My Seraphina. You begin us. We will take our lead from you, our mother. What do we need to know? What is there hiding like Lucifer, like a rat in the shadows here tonight?'

I closed my eyes. What he was asking me . . . he was asking me to denounce my father. And I was to do it here, in front of everything I held most dear.

You remember that, don't you?

While you hid in the back, lounging on your own inadequacy, I did it.

I stepped forward, taking my place alongside my husband.

'I know things about Brother Jonah,' I said. 'I remain true to God's name. I will tell of them now.'

And then I began to speak.

33

Violet knew something was wrong.

Several things occurred to her at the same time. From sleep, her senses had become suddenly bombarded with sensation. A metallic taste: thick lips, heavy eyes and . . . pain? Was that what it was? Pain in her stomach, at her right temple. And then again, was it actually sleep that she had emerged from? She felt she was still sucked half into it, groggy and stupid. That wasn't normal, was it?

She thought she had better sit up. But that was strange, too. As her stomach muscles contracted into the movement, something held her back. She tried again and the same thing happened. That was when she realized she wasn't just in the dark of her bedroom in the early morning. The blackness was pitch: a coal black heavy on her face.

That was when she realized that she couldn't move her hands.

That was when she realized she was blindfolded.

'Talk to me.' Martin gestured to the bed in the hotel room for Mackenzie to sit. She'd turned the lights on in the room, and the electric hum combined with the drab colours of the carpet and walls gave her the feeling of being back in the nightmare she'd just had, one from which she would never wake up.

Mackenzie sat heavily, his mouth petulant.

'We don't have much time. If you're as worried about Violet as you say you are, you need to get busy telling me what's going on.' As Martin spoke, her brain was crashing around, sorting out thoughts and ideas that hurtled through it like a shower of meteors. They'd done background checks on the Snow family. None of them had criminal records, their slates were clean. Not even so much as a parking ticket.

'But did you check her medical records?' Mackenzie asked, as if reading Martin's mind.

Martin looked at him, waiting.

'It was a long time ago, right? Tristan and Seraphina . . . they – well, they were going through a bad patch.'

'What kind of bad patch?'

'Tristan was . . . well, let's just say he wasn't always the most faithful of husbands.' Mackenzie exhaled loudly. 'He had a lot of attention, you know? Especially after he was on TV. Women, honestly, they – they threw *themselves* at him. And then there was the congregation, they all fawned on him. When he stood up there, he was kind of . . .' he gave an almost proud smile '. . . well, *powerful*.'

'And?'

'And so, he enjoyed it. Took a little present now and again.'

'He was sleeping with these women,' Martin confirmed, an edge to her voice.

'Said it was for the pressure. That he had to be strong for them all. If that meant getting a bit of release, with a bit of a . . . well, so be it.'

'And Sera knew about it, obviously . . .'

'Would've been hard not to. Especially in the early days, we were a small community. We lived on top of each other. So to speak.'

Martin listened, her pulse racing. She wanted to be out on the search for Sera. Sitting here, waiting for Mackenzie to slowly spill facts was, for her, like torture. 'Tell me,' she said, burying her impatience. 'Tell me what you mean. Why is Sera dangerous?'

Mackenzie met her gaze, leaning his elbows on his knees. Something about the ease of his pose unsettled Martin. A truck rattled by outside, a reminder of the world beyond this place where time seemed to be standing still.

'What?' Martin barked, frustration pulsing through her.

'Look, I don't know, Inspector. A lot of things happened in the past. Sera was crazy for a while. Mad with jealousy. She turned against everyone. She was like, I don't know, like fury personified.'

Weird choice of word, Martin thought, but chose not to remark on it. 'But why do you say she's dangerous?'

Mackenzie stood up, his hands curled into fists in his pockets. 'Nothing was ever proved. I'm not accusing anyone of anything.'

'Mackenzie, what are you talking about?' Martin got to her feet as well, impatience etched on her face. 'Have you got anything to tell me, or are you just wasting my time?'

'The twins, Inspector Martin. Look back and see what happened to Sera and Tristan's boys. Now just find her, though. Find her before anyone else gets hurt.'

34

THE DURHAM CHRONICLE ONLINE
THURSDAY 11 AUGUST, 2016
REVEREND TRISTAN SNOW ACCUSED
OF SEXUAL ABUSE

It emerged today that Tristan Snow MBE has been accused of sexually abusing underage teenage girls by a fellow pastor at the Deucalion Church in Blackpool, where Snow worked throughout his career.

Snow was never charged with any abuse offences during his lifetime.

Jonah Simpson, who worked as a preacher with Snow, has claimed that several of the vulnerable children who were supervised by the church were subjected to abuse by the Reverend while in his care.

'He was a sort of Godlike figure,' Simpson said. 'Everybody knew of the good that Tristan did and what he did for children. But these children were powerless.'

Tristan Snow, who appeared on television shows such as *This Morning* and as a recurring celebrity guest on various game shows, was found dead in suspicious circumstances last Monday.

An alleged victim of the abuse, Nina Forster – who was thirteen at the time – said she had been molested in Snow's dressing room after one of his popular shows on the Blackpool promenade in the 1990s.

'I knew the moment I was asked to join him in his dressing room, I knew what was expected of me. Because I was having this wonderful time, and I was expected to pay for it. And that's what I did.

'I now know it was wrong and I can still get very angry about it, but nobody believed me then, so I don't expect anybody to believe me now, if I'm honest.'

Durham police who are investigating Snow's death have said they will be looking into the allegations, and are working together with Lancashire police in conjunction with these claims.

For more on this story, see pages 3, 4, 5, 6 and 7.

Have you suffered any abuse at the hands of Tristan Snow? Were you a member of the Deucalion Church? If so, get in contact with Sean Egan via email at segan@durhamchronicle. co.uk or @seganjourno on Twitter.

DC Fielding looked up at the boarding house from across the street as a train rumbled over the viaduct above. He glanced at his watch, checking that he still had time to kill before he was due at Martin's morning briefing. He shuffled his feet and thought about the best way forward. His stomach gurgled with hunger. He should be in the café with a bacon sarnie, not standing here without any kind of clear plan.

This was what his ma had only just last night yelled at him for. His lack of direction. *Jesus wept*, she had cried, raising her hands to the ceiling in a typically dramatic pose. The photo of John Paul II gazed beatifically down at them both from above the mantelpiece. His ma had yet to accept his passing, refusing to adjust to Pope Benedict XVI, let alone the latest pontiff who, his ma was apt to whisper in an appalled tone, agreed with *The Gays*, as she called them. Homosexuals, drug addicts, prostitutes and single parents were always capitalized in his ma's house. Fielding sighed. Her beef these days was his single status. He knew she worried he was himself one of The Gays. When was he going to give her the grandchildren *she deserved*, she would cry. As if there were some kind of guarantee possible, a thirty-year warranty the likes of which you got from Argos – except they handed it to you with your first-born at the hospital, and a few decades later you'd be fully entitled to expect a grandchild. He was *incapable of making a decision*, she would say to him. He should be getting down on one knee to Kelly, or Rachel, or Sarah or whoever it was he'd been seen chatting to in the Royal Oak last weekend.

So absorbed was Fielding in his recollections of this haranguing, that he failed to notice the Riverview front door open.

'You coming in then, or standing there all day?' Eileen Quinn yelled at him, standing in her slippers.

Fielding jerked his head up and gave her a grin.

'Cup of tea, do you?' She sniffed, before turning back into the hallway.

Nodding ruefully, Fielding went across the street and up the steps into the house.

*

Eileen Quinn poured the tea. 'My father was a policeman,' she said, skewering Fielding with a territorial look.

'Is that right?'

'So I know about you chaps.' She sat down heavily, opposite him, taking a digestive from the packet. 'Know what makes you tick.'

'Thank you, Mrs Quinn,' Fielding said, turning the mug of tea around on the table, putting off the inevitable moment when he would have to drink it.

Eileen drank her own, her eyes fixed on Fielding. 'You came back,' she said.

Fielding nodded, his mouth pursed in consideration. 'My guv told me you'd been iffy with her. Hadn't wanted to tell her what's going on.'

Eileen took a breath. She narrowed her eyes.

'But,' Fielding continued, 'I thought that you and me got on.' He smiled at her. 'So . . .'

'You thought I might tell you?'

'Something like that.' Fielding forced himself to take a sip from the mug. 'Will you?' he asked with difficulty, as he swallowed the foul-tasting liquid.

Eileen sighed. Her eyes moved once again to the sideboard. She studied the boy in front of her. *So young*. He barely looked old enough to drive. Could she trust him?

Fielding reached for a biscuit and took a bite, crumbs leaping from his mouth as he spoke. 'Did you know Reverend Snow? Before they came here?'

Eileen looked down at her fingernails and considered this question. Of course, this was what they wanted to know – she had given them the photograph, after all. She had led them to her. She wasn't an *imbecile*. She knew what she was doing. Remembering those times: how she and Tristan had met all those years ago. How they had fumbled with each other backstage; hot and breathless, cheeks flushed with desire, grabbing at zips and buttons while out front, on the stage, the audience sat silently in the dark, watching people pretend to live when all along, life was rumbling along with passionate intensity behind the curtains.

'I did,' she said eventually.

'Why did you bring the photo to the station, Mrs Quinn? You wanted us to know something. What was it?'

'He was a liar,' she said with bile. 'He turned up here, same as he'd always been. I couldn't believe it when I opened the door to them. He didn't recognize me, of course. Walked straight past me in the hall as if I wasn't there.' She darted a look at Fielding, a smudge of embarrassment on her face. 'Just because I'm old, and fat, and . . . useless these days,' she said. 'It doesn't mean I don't have feelings. That I'm not the same person I used to be, deep down.'

'I know, Mrs Quinn,' Fielding said, patting her gnarly hand. 'I understand.'

'*She* knew, of course. She remembered everything.'

'Mrs Snow?'

Eileen glared at him. 'She treated me like Salome, for heaven's sake. As if it all hadn't happened a million years ago.' She sniffed. 'When he was . . . when he was dead, I wanted it known. How he had treated me. What kind of man he was. I deserved more than that, but he didn't care.' She looked up, almost bewildered, at Fielding. 'He just didn't care.'

'How did you get the photograph?'

Eileen pursed her lips. 'I stole it. Years ago. Back when we were in the theatre. He had it on his wall in his dressing room. Can you believe that?' She stared at Fielding. 'A picture of him with his own wife's sister! One evening, after he'd ended it, I took it. I don't know why, really. I wanted something of him. Something . . .' she paused. 'Something that I could use to hurt him. Later on. When he wasn't expecting it.'

They sat in silence for a few moments, Fielding digesting these revelations along with the tea.

'But . . .' Eileen continued. 'All that's not going to help you.' She nodded towards the sideboard. 'What's important is . . . well, it's in there.' Her voice shook all of a sudden, fear flashing across her face. 'That's what . . .' She faltered.

Fielding swallowed the remainder of his biscuit with an effort, unable to drink more tea to wash it down. He leaned forward over the table towards the landlady. 'What is it, Mrs Quinn?' His eyes were kind, crinkling at the edges. 'You can tell me. Let me help you.'

Eileen watched him before deciding. He reminded her of her nephew, Roger.

'You can trust me,' Fielding nudged. 'What is it you're so afraid of?'

35

Violet tried to produce some saliva in her arid mouth. She moved her lips from side to side, feeling them stretch and crack for lack of moisture. Her tongue was heavy and furred. It was no good: she was the fucking Gobi Desert.

She must have fallen into unconsciousness again at some point. When she came to, the blindfold had been removed. Gradually, her eyes had adjusted to the darkness and she could see she was in a kind of cellar. She was on a hard concrete floor and the ceiling was rough plaster covered in cobwebs. Her feet were tied tightly to each other and she jolted as something hairy brushed against her big toe. Her shoes must have been taken off. Her hands were also tied, uncomfortably, behind her back so she felt as if she were rocking on them, her shoulders pinching together. The pain of that had worn away to a numbness so that she could no longer feel her arms. That, and the weight of the darkness, gave her the curious feeling of being suspended in space; she was only a head, bobbing in the black. Albeit a head that throbbed with the intermittent ache of the effects of a crash into her skull.

How had this happened? The last thing she could remember was going down in the lift with her mother to the hotel bar. After their row, Sera had ordered her another gin and tonic and then said they should move downstairs.

By then, Violet had felt unsteady and suggestible. Sera had shaken off her silence and become warm. Violet loved her mother when she was like that. She had wanted to bury her head in her lap and have her stroke her hair. The gin sank like a stone in her stomach and she floated down after it. The lift doors had closed and then . . . nothing.

Where was she? What could have happened? Who had tied her up in this way, hit her over the head? And what was wrong with her insides? They griped and raged like an angry cobra leaving her sick and then winded in turn. Violet tried again to work her tongue against the inside of her cheek in order to create some liquid, something to swallow to quench the dreadful thirst, calm the nausea.

A vision of a huge papier-mâché head came into her sights, from her favourite film as a child: the image of Oz, green and vaporous and huge. Her head was Oz's head. She was the great and powerful Oz. She had to get home, there's no place like home. The ruby slippers. She had worn them one Christmas. Had she been five or six? The heels were like blocks underneath the soles, so wide she could actually walk in them. The red glitter of the shoes so rough to touch, but so sparkly. She had tapped her way across the kitchen floor, her hands reaching up to the skylight, a moment of candy-striped happiness.

Then her father had lifted his head from his armchair and seen it. Happiness in any form, innocence at its zenith, would only be tolerated under his command. She saw the panic ooze from him like hot tar spread across a new road. It would be stamped out, this moment of delight; made to succumb to his say-so. But not outright. Even at five, she knew this.

Christmas night, when she was supposed to be asleep, she had woken up for some reason, and crept downstairs. She had watched Tristan as he carefully placed the ruby slippers into the fire in the sitting room. He had sat alone in his armchair and Violet had sat at her station midway up the stairs. Whether he had known she was there, she didn't know; he never turned to face her. They sat together but apart, until the slippers were burnt and the fire was cold.

She was the great and powerful Oz, she murmured, as the relief of unconsciousness fell over her again. She was the head of Oz that had the answers. She would let them all go home. There's no place like home. She nearly drifted off into oblivion, begged for it as a means of relieving her thirst. But a chink of light startled her, causing her eyes to widen.

Violet watched as somewhere above her, somewhere in the darkness that swirled around her, a door began to open.

36

Now we're getting to it, aren't we?

Getting closer to the nub of things.

The day when everything changed — and, in a way, the day that probably led to what happened to Mercy and the others . . . you certainly remember that.

Do you recall, sweet sister?

You had a delightful bruise on your cheek. Delivered with a kiss from my husband the night before. I thought it interesting that nobody noticed in church. They didn't ask you about it, anyway. Maybe they had some sympathy for me, the downtrodden wife. Maybe getting a few slaps and punches from Tristan was seen as a decent punishment.

I know what he used to say when he did it to me. He would have tears in his eyes. He used to cry that I just didn't love him enough.

You see?

It's beautiful in its own way.

We were packing up the teas and coffees as everyone filed out after morning service. You stood by the great steaming urn as I threw the plastic cups into the bin. I ignored you as I did much of the time. I bet you thought my face was flat, didn't you? Fatfish, Flatfish, you used to call me when we were children. I wasn't fat. And neither is my face anything that you can describe. It's just my face. And if you could be bothered to try to see beneath it, maybe you'd find out some things.

Anyway.

I saw you watching Tristan at the door, shaking hands with the congregation, his well-wishers, his donors. Fraser was there, too, of course, never far away was Fraser. You almost looked admiring as you stared at him. Tristan was as I knew him constantly to be; a smiling Houdini, always in control of the escape. I saw when he'd greeted you that morning, kissed both cheeks, his lips grazing the cut under your eye as if it were his, as if he owned it.

The men moved out of sight into the hall porch, their voices fading to a murmur. The twins continued to play in the hall, a shriek and a thudding of shoes the intermittent reminders of their game. I put down my cups, stood still, taking you in.

'Just get it over with, Sera,' you huffed a sigh, oozing bravado. 'You can see I've had my punishment. What more do you want to dole out? A lecture too?'

I said nothing.

'I know it's wrong. But . . .' You began to twist the top of a paper packet of granulated sugar around and around. 'But, it's just the way it is.' What you did next made me laugh as you lowered her voice, checking your eyes at the door, desperate for Tristan not to see this little tête-à-tête. 'This is the deal. You give him something . . . And I give him something else,' you said, putting the sugar into the crate filled with tea and coffee supplies. 'It's not normal, perhaps, but it's the way it works in this family.'

That word, normal, again!

'This family?' I asked, genuinely confused. *To me, a family is rooted in loyalty. As soon as you whored yourself with my husband, you destroyed our family.*

You nodded but couldn't meet my eyes. 'Yes.'

'What is this family?' I asked you, quietly.

'You, me, Tristan and . . . the boys.'

Oh, that was cruel!

I was speechless. I became stiff, as if all the words in the world had been sent away. As if all the laughter was gone. You knew you'd made a mistake. You drew back, your hand still clutching the sugar.

'Family,' I said again. I felt as if I were floating. 'What is it like, do you think – to be in a family?' I asked.

You looked at me, bewildered. 'It's like this. We're in a family. It's like this.'

'Like living?'

'Yes.'

'And breathing?'

'Yes,' you answered, your voice frustrated.

'Like eating when you're hungry, or swimming into a patch of warm water in a cold lake?'

'I don't know what you're talking about, Sera,' you said, picking up the crate.

'Wait . . .' I said. 'Let me show you.' I came to stand next to you, on your side of the table. 'How can you know whether any of it is worth it?'

'Any of it is worth what?'

'All of it. The marriage. The sex. The children . . .'

'I don't know. You just do, I suppose. You have good days and bad days.'

'That's what you think, is it? That it's so mundane that you can just shake it off when things feel bad? That you can just toss it away, push it under the carpet – don't worry – things will get better?'

'Well, yes. I mean. What else can you do?'

The boys were still screeching around the hall, I could see the dark of their shapes scuttling around, running faster and faster. But it was only background noise. My eyes blazed into yours, asking you to understand. And then I felt your pity for me, sharp as a knife.

'We're on the same team, you and me,' you said with conviction. 'We're in this together.'

'Things won't get better,' I said, as if you hadn't spoken. 'Because you end up watching it all taken away from you. By death. Or,' I enunciated my words very carefully, so that you could understand, 'by your own sister. Which feels like this . . .'

I moved my hand underneath the tap of the silver urn. 'Better to feel it and exist, though,' I said, turning the tap on, sending boiling water gushing on to my skin.

'Sera, stop!' you cried, trying to dash my arm away. You hopped back as water splashed up on to your legs from where it was hitting the floor in a stream. I wasn't as afraid as you. I closed my eyes and let the water turn my hand red and raw.

'Turn it off. Please God! What are you doing?'

'It's like this, my sister,' I said to you. 'Better to teach yourself how to experience pain than have it forced upon you.'

'What's going on?' Tristan suddenly appeared at the doorway, his eyes moving from our faces to my outstretched, dripping hand.

Well, I knew we were for it now. I quickly flipped the tap.

'Nothing,' I answered. 'Just tidying away.'

You refused to meet Tristan's eyes and stared at the floor. The twins had pulled up short and sat cross-legged, quiet as mice.

'Sera,' Tristan said, softly. 'Show me your hand, please.'

I extended my arm to him and showed him how little white blisters had begun to pop across my skin.

Tristan frowned. 'Are you hurt? How did this happen?'

I shrugged. 'It was an accident.'

We looked at each other, the three of us, for a long minute.

'See that you bandage it properly,' Tristan said finally. 'We don't want it getting infected.'

I nodded, gathering the boys with my good hand. And then I turned to leave. I felt both of your gazes bolting down upon my shoulders as I went. Such turmoil inside, a dervish of hatred and longing and fear. The wind rushed through the open door, scattering umber leaves across my path. I walked into the sunlight and then I was gone.

37

'Mum?'

The figure was silhouetted at the top of the stairs leading down to the cellar. Whoever it was remained silent.

'Mum, is that you?'

The figure began to walk slowly down towards Violet.

'What's going on?' Violet jerked her head towards the light. 'Why am I tied up like this? It hurts. Mum?'

The figure knelt next to Violet. She couldn't see their face, it was so dark. But as a hand was put to Violet's forehead, her daughter could smell the scent of her mother, as familiar to her as breathing.

'Mum?' she whispered. 'Why am I here? Why have you hurt me? Was it you? Please . . .' Violet began to cry, rasping breath punctured by dry sobs. 'Mummy . . .'

'Ssh,' Sera whispered, stroking her face. 'Ssh, baby. Mummy's here.'

Martin splashed water on her face in the Ladies', her brain racing ahead of her in too high a gear. Her phone beeped. They'd traced the car Sera had left in with Violet to a hire company on the outskirts of Durham, and the search was ongoing. They would find them soon . . . *God willing*, Martin thought, as she stared at her reflection.

What was Mackenzie talking about when he'd mentioned the twins? Had Sera harmed them? Martin had pushed him for details, for *anything*, but he'd stormed off, refusing to say more. What was he getting at? They'd checked Sera's records in Lancashire and there'd been nothing. Fielding would need to go across to Blackpool and collect Jonah Simpson for questioning. While he was there, he could chivvy along the Major Investigation Team, see if anything about the twins' death was relevant.

She looked down again at the *Durham Chronicle* she'd put on the edge of the sink. Sean Egan had told her the truth; his article blared from the front page. The accusations against Snow, and an interview with Nina Forster, the girl who claimed the Reverend had abused her when she was thirteen. She was thirty-four now, with a bosom as pendulous as her earrings.

Mercy . . . and now Nina. Was he a paedophile? Were they facing an investigation that could create the need for an inquiry, an investigation into why children were allowed to be supervised in a church that was covering up their abuse? Or was Nina Forster just searching for her moment in the sun, her own little piece of celebrity?

This case was like a festering sore, scabbed over – but did she have the edge of it now? Could she peep beneath its crust? If what Mackenzie alleged was true, was it as they'd suspected from the beginning, that Sera was the killer? But Mackenzie had his own reasons for wanting to set someone else up for the murder. Why was he always wandering round hotels late at night? Was he just pushing them to Sera to misdirect, to trick them?

Violet and her mother seemed as thick as thieves. Had they plotted Tristan's murder together, perhaps? But that still didn't answer the question of Violet's nightdress, and why it had been found around the murder weapon. And yet, if they weren't responsible for the killing, why had they run? If Sera were dangerous, would Violet go with her mother willingly, unless she was herself involved? Or was she crouching in her shadow, afraid? What was it that lurked in Sera's background, that would open up a fissure? Enable Martin to squeeze her way inside her brain and see if she were culpable?

Martin left the bathroom and went back to her desk, looking despairingly at the mound of paperwork that surrounded her keyboard. Her mouth was dry and her hangover suddenly announced itself, postponed by the adrenalin of the discovery of Sera's disappearance. Her phone beeped and she glanced down at the text. She closed her eyes.

She'd managed to push last night's dinner with Jim far out of her mind with the whisky drunk with Egan. But now he'd texted. He would be filing the divorce papers this week. The news settled in her stomach like lead.

She would block it, she thought. Send it packing from her head. She would do what she always did when things got hard.

She would work.

She took a drink from the mug on her desk and grimaced at the cold coffee, remembering instead what she'd seen last night on the DVD. It burned inside her. All those children in that church, so vulnerable to adult monsters.

She swung her chair around and stared at the rooftops that fanned out from her window. She watched as a pigeon flew to a nearby building and hopped a few steps, pecking at the ground, jerking its head back and forth.

Pigeons, she thought, pushing her chair back and leaving the office and the heap of papers on her desk.

As she headed downstairs, she bumped into Fielding striding along, buzzing from the last hour of his time. He had done it, his first piece of detective work in a murder case. He had discovered the truth of the mystery of Mrs Quinn's sideboard, and he had got it off his own bat, on his own initiative and with – dare he say it? – a little bit of charm and good looks. He swung into the reception area, heading for the lockers.

It was going to be a good day.

'Ah, Fielding,' Martin said, as she saw him open the door to the locker room. 'Just the bloke.'

'Guv?'

'I need you to get on a train to Blackpool. Sera and Violet Snow have gone AWOL and everyone's tied up with looking for them. So you've got to collect a Jonah Simpson from the Lancashire Major Investigation Team. And while you're there, you can chase up on Mercy Fletcher's whereabouts, because they're being about as fast as drying paint in coming up with any info for us.'

'Eh?' Fielding stepped back into the corridor, his brain computing all of this information, and looked at his boss in bewilderment. 'Who's Jonah Simpson?'

'Sera Snow's dad. He's a priest as well, and he might be able to shed more light on what was happening with Mercy. I think that's the key to finding out whether we can eliminate Violet or charge her. Go to the MIT first and then pick him up. If anything comes from the meet there, let me know straight away. Got it?'

'Okay,' Fielding said, his triumph diminishing somewhat. Mentally, he said goodbye to the lunch in the Oak, where he had already imagined the round of drinks he'd have been bought in celebration.

'You all right Fielding? You look confused.'

'Yes,' he answered, straightening his shoulders. 'It's just . . . I went to see Eileen Quinn this morning. You know, the landlady at Riverview? And –' a smile broke out on his face '– I found out what's in the sideboard.'

Martin raised her eyebrows.

'The *North East Digest*,' Fielding said.

'The magazine?'

'Yeah. She got a load of letters from the *North East Digest*. Saying they were going to take her to court.' Fielding was almost jogging on the spot in his eagerness to relay the information. 'She'd never ordered it, see? A subscription to the . . .'

'. . . *North East Digest*.'

'No. So she was befuddled. And upset. Thought they really would do it. She got scared that she'd forgotten she'd ordered it. Or that someone else had done it for her maliciously, like. They're like that down her street, she says. Spying and playing tricks on each other.'

Martin looked as baffled as Fielding's description of Quinn.

'I know . . .' Fielding went on. 'So she just stuffed all the demands in a drawer in the sideboard. There were about thirty of them. Saying if she didn't pay up – I think it was about six hundred quid all in – she'd be in front of a magistrate.'

'So why were they doing it? The *Digest*?'

'Oh, they do it all the time. About three of me mam's sisters have had the same thing. They just scare old ladies into paying up money. It's a scam basically. You just need to call them and tell them to shove off. But old Mrs Quinn fell for it. Then when Snow was murdered, and we turned up, she was terrified we'd find out and cart her off to prison.'

'Why did she send us the photo? Why has she got it?'

'Turns out she was having an affair with Snow, way back in the day. Says he treated her like Salome.' Fielding frowned. 'Whoever she is . . . She hated him. He'd dumped her when he got bored.'

'Yet another motive,' Martin observed.

'Maybe . . . but then why send the photo to draw attention to herself, unless . . .'

'What?'

'I think she did it deliberately to bring us to her. I think she wanted the company.'

Martin leaned back on the wall in the corridor and put her head on one side. 'Really?'

Fielding nodded. 'Yeah. She's had that photo for years. Stole it when she was in Blackpool. Kept it to remind her of the days when she was young. You know, when life was a bit better.'

'Even though she isn't in it? The photo?'

'He is though . . . Tristan Snow.' Fielding shrugged. 'She's just a lonely old woman, I think. Kept a souvenir of a time when she was young, when she had romance in her life.'

'And the cross, Fielding? Did you notice the cross?'

Fielding blanched. *What cross?*

Martin sighed internally. 'Draft up an arrest warrant, Fielding.'

'For what, Boss? I told you . . . It's just a red herring. The sideboard . . .'

'No, no,' Martin snapped. 'The sideboard is irrelevant. We searched the whole place, remember? Come on Fielding, keep up.' She hesitated before taking a breath, remembering his inexperience. 'Around her neck, Fielding. Did you see it?'

'See what, Guv?' Fielding felt like crying.

'Tristan Snow's cross. The one that's missing.' Martin looked down the corridor, her mind already on the next thing. 'Eileen Quinn is wearing Snow's cross.'

38

Nina Forster's voice was acerbic but no-nonsense. Hearing her down the phone, Jones was relieved by it; reassured that the plaintive, whinging pitch described by Sean Egan in his article was nothing but a fabrication of tabloid hyperbole. Nina sounded less screechy and money grabbing than weary and fed up.

'They were opening up a memorial book, at the Palace Theatre in Blackpool,' she explained. 'A journalist was there, outside. He put me in touch with your man in Durham, that Sean Egan. I went to have a look because I couldn't believe it. Couldn't believe people still thought he was a good bloke.'

'Why couldn't you believe it?' Jones asked, scribbling a note of this conversation as they talked.

'He's disgusting,' Nina muttered. 'He was vile. Back then . . .' She sighed. 'But what's the point of dragging it all up now? I said that to Egan. But he told me there might be others. That someone should be held accountable.'

'It's certainly a possibility,' Jones answered. 'So, would you mind, Nina? Telling me what happened? Often what's in the press is less than accurate.'

'All right.' Nina sounded tired. 'I mean, it was like twenty years ago now. I went with my mam. She was the one who wanted to see him really. I wasn't that bothered. But I went 'cos, you know, I was thirteen. I did what I was told.'

'What kind of show was it?' Jones said. 'What did Tristan Snow do?'

'He did all this self-healing stuff. You know, like David Copperfield but . . . like, better. He'd just got on the telly and said he could change your life. Stop you eating so much, stop smoking . . . My mam was a bit overweight at the time.' Nina paused. 'She's lost three stone since going on Atkins, though.'

Jones coughed. 'And . . .?'

'Ah, well. We went backstage afterwards. Mam wanted his autograph. We stood outside. I remember it as a really cold day. I was freezing. We were waiting, a whole bunch of us. The stage door opened and one of his bodyguards or his manager or something came out. He said Tristan would be a few minutes. And then he looked at me, and just sort of beckoned. Mam and I followed him in. We didn't really get a chance to think about it. We were just in, all of a sudden, and up the stairs to his dressing room.'

'And then what?' Jones said, quietly.

'He was ever so friendly. Of course.' Nina's voice was tinged with bile. 'He was sat in front of the mirror. All these flowers and cards around. And he was drinking wine. He offered us some.'

'He offered you wine?'

'Yeah. Mam said no. She wasn't *that* into him.'

Jones couldn't tell if Nina meant her mother wouldn't let her daughter drink wine because she was underage, or that she wouldn't drink alcohol if Elvis himself had offered it to her.

'But then the manager, or whoever he was, started talking to her, sort of pulled her over to one side, away from Tristan.'

'Was there anyone else in the room?'

'Yeah, a few people. I don't know who they were. It was crowded. Stuffy.'

'And then?'

'I wound up standing near where he was at the mirror. He talked to me, looking at me in the reflection.' She sniffed, but it was a hard sniff, Jones thought. Nina wasn't crying. 'He asked me how old I was. Where did I go to school? I didn't really know what to do. I was embarrassed. Then . . . then he said I was really pretty, and that was when I felt his hand.'

'Where was his hand?' Jones asked.

'I was wearing a skirt and he put his hand on the back of my thigh, underneath it. And then he put it into my knickers.'

Jones was silent.

'He didn't say anything, just stared at me in the mirror,' Nina said.

'Did you speak? Tell him to get off? Move away?'

'I was shocked! I didn't know what to do. He was an adult. My mam was right there. I was . . . I just didn't know what to do.'

'I understand, Nina. I'm sorry, it must have been horrible for you.'

'Then his manager came over and said it was time to go, thanks very much. Before we knew it, we were bundled outside,' Nina said. 'My mam didn't even get his autograph in the end.'

'Did you talk to her about what happened?'

There was another pause. 'Years later. We had a fight. She said I was distant, closed off. That I'd never loved her. I couldn't answer her. It was such an awful thing to hear, for her to say. So the only thing I could do, was tell her.'

'You told her, because – well, what she was saying to you, you think it was caused by what happened to you with Tristan Snow?'

Nina laughed; a rasping, bitter noise. 'What do you think? Told how pretty you are and then assaulted. Makes you hate yourself, doesn't it? That being pretty's all you're good for. That you can only be touched by people who are evil. That I should have stopped him. Why didn't I, eh? How could I forget that? Course it had an impact. A massive one.'

'And you never wanted to bring charges?'

'What was the point? Everyone loved him. There was no proof.'

'You never heard of this happening to anyone else?'

'Who knows? But men like that, they don't do it just the once, do they? Not when they've got that power.'

Jones hesitated, thinking it through. 'And so, why, Nina? Why did you go to the theatre where the condolence book was?'

The woman laughed again, the laugh of a person who has known abject failure but has survived. 'Because I wanted to be sure he was dead. I wanted to see that Tristan Snow would burn in hell.'

39

Fielding studied Jonah Simpson as they bumped along cross-country in the train. The old man was hooked over, his head curling on to his chest as if he couldn't bear his face to be seen. His hair hung down in hanks either side of his head, but Fielding had noticed the wart on his cheek despite this. He had a stillness that was faintly unnerving. As he sat opposite him, Fielding found himself checking on a fairly regular basis that the priest was still breathing. Jonah had said little from the moment Fielding had knocked on his front door until now, when he merely stared out of the window, refusing Fielding's sporadic offers of tea or biscuits.

Giving a mental shrug, Fielding thought back to his earlier meeting with the Major Incident Team in Blackpool, where he had looked in vain for Mercy Fletcher. He had managed to find her last known address, and before meeting Jonah Simpson he'd gone there, walked down the street filled with terraced houses, televisions shrieking from lace-curtained windows in the middle of the day. He'd stood outside a grimy green front door and knocked, but nobody had answered. Then he'd tried the neighbours who, after looking at him as if he were the Devil himself when they'd seen his police identification, had said they'd never heard of Mercy Fletcher and then slammed the door in his face. He didn't have time to find out more before he had to head back to the MIT office. There, no further information regarding Sera Snow was to be found either. She had no criminal record and there was nothing about her on their files. In contrast to the triumph he'd felt this morning, he now felt an abject failure. *So stupid*, he thought, picturing that gold cross around Mrs Quinn's neck: Eileen for nicking it and him for not noticing. Why hadn't he spotted it, put two and two together? He'd looked like an idiot in front of the boss . . .

Even so, he couldn't shake the feeling that Eileen Quinn was just an old woman, torturing herself with shadows in corners. It didn't seem possible that she had anything to do with Tristan Snow's death. The cross was a souvenir she'd stolen, along with the photograph. Fielding was sure of it.

He sank back in his seat, feeling suddenly cold.

Jonah glanced over at him. 'You all right, boy?'

'What? Er, yes, fine thanks.'

'You've gone a nasty shade of green.'

Fielding now felt burning hot. His head seemed to loom above his body, his mouth was loose: it felt as if it were moving from side to side, out of control. He could taste something familiar on his tongue. He lurched to his feet, placing his hands on the train table to right himself.

A goblin reared in his stomach, climbing the walls of his oesophagus with muddy feet. Fielding pushed his way out of his seat, racing unsteadily up the aisle of the train carriage. Just in time, he made it to the toilets, before the contents of his stomach splattered all over the Trans-Pennine express lavatory with the force of a bullet from a gun.

Fielding was not to leave the toilet for an hour and a half, until he made himself stagger out as the train pulled in to Durham station. Stumbling out on to the platform, he saw Jonah Simpson calmly waiting for him.

'Got a bug, have you?'

Fielding brought his lips together, limply moving towards the station exit. 'The tea,' he mumbled as he went. 'The old woman's bloody tea . . .'

40

Martin looked out from her office window, down on to the police station car park. Beyond it, she could see the modern buildings of Durham lining the curve of the River Wear. Behind her, the medieval jigsaw of the Cathedral seemed to weigh against the city, creaking on to the cobblestones of The Bailey, leaning against its university colleges and overshadowing the students trip-trapping along. The beauty of the Cathedral and the historical buildings of the city never managed to make Martin forget the decay they represented: the transience of life, as the waters of the river lapped over and over again at its banks. As those venerable buildings hardened with age, so sprouts of new life, of the new generation, pushed their heads up through the earth. Martin leaned her head against the window, condensation wetting her hairline. Sometimes, everything seemed just a little bit too complicated.

She sat back at her desk, thinking about Fielding's call from Blackpool and the seeming impossibility of finding Mercy Fletcher. She still couldn't shake that dream about her, and now it seemed that getting hold of her was like looking for the proverbial needle in the haystack. And nothing more had been revealed about Sera Snow and her twins. If Mackenzie's insinuation was right – that she'd had some involvement in their death – wouldn't there be evidence of it?

A few taps on her keyboard later and Martin had brought up the local paper based in Blackpool. Looking through the archives for any reference to the Snows, she trawled for a while through countless mentions of Tristan opening various clubs and attending association dinners. He'd advertised a preventative hair-loss product. Martin wrinkled her nose, looking at his grinning face holding up the bottle. There was nothing more until she went back further, searching for any articles on the Snows in the 1980s.

And that was where she found it.

THE BLACKPOOL DAILY
FATALITY ON A583: TWO-YEAR-OLD TWINS DEAD

23rd January 1988

Tragedy struck the town of Blackpool yesterday when two-year-old twin brothers Peter and Michael Snow were hit by a lorry on the A583 leading out of Blackpool towards Preston. Both boys were killed on impact.

Eyewitnesses say that the boys appeared to run out into the middle of the road in front of a truck. The driver of the vehicle, Graham Steele (43), was also killed.

As it happened, Sarah Snow (32), the twins' mother, was left helpless on the side of the dual carriageway as she watched them run in front of the lorry, witnesses say. She has been transferred to the Victoria Hospital for assessment although she suffered no injuries.

Popular self-help guru and local healer, Tristan Snow (41), was said to be too devastated to comment.

The family have asked for privacy at this time.

Martin read the article rapidly, images shunting into her brain as she scanned down the page. Pictures of those boys, running out into the road, turning back to their mother who stood powerless on the verge, then the slamming of the truck, the scream of the brakes. But after what Mackenzie had said . . . was that the truth? Had Sera stood by in agony or had she pushed . . .? Had she . . .?

'Murder suspect on the run with the victim's daughter,' Sam's voice said from the doorway, making Martin jump. 'Unfortunate headline.'

Martin felt a clutch of nerves in her stomach at the sight of him. 'If they've printed that, they've seriously run away with themselves. It's Violet who's been bailed anyway, not her mother,' she said.

'Right, well. Bit of a fuck-up at the hotel, so I hear.'

'That's an understatement,' Martin replied, getting to her feet and snatching up her bag.

'If that is the headline, we'll be talking about a review team.'

'This isn't helpful, Sam,' Martin snapped. 'I'm on my eighth coffee of the day and I'm en route to talk to the troops. You coming?'

'Look,' he said, unexpectedly catching her hand and holding it in his. 'I'm sorry about the other night. I really am. I know you're under pressure, and . . .'

'And?' Martin asked, her eyes softening.

'And I don't want to add to it. I just . . .' He moved his hand in between the two of them. 'I just think we should take it slowly.'

'He's putting in the divorce papers tomorrow.'

Sam nodded. 'You're sad?'

Tears sprang to Martin's eyes and she wiped them away quickly, embarrassed. 'Yes . . . no. I mean . . . a bit, I suppose.'

'You'll be all right Erica,' Sam said, looking at her intently. 'You can't be perfect at everything, you know.'

She gave a half-laugh. 'I'm not perfect at anything, I don't think.'

He reached up to touch her cheek. 'Just don't push me away,' he said.

Martin looked at him for a long minute. 'I'll try,' she said at last.

'So Mercy has disappeared, it seems,' Jones said, settling herself back at the table in the incident room.

'Yep,' Martin replied wearily. 'But maybe the priest Jonah Simpson will know more about her. I mean, why did he contact Egan in the first place? Does he know anything about Mercy? Was there systematic abuse going on at the church? Jones, I know you spoke to Nina Forster about her claim that she was assaulted by Tristan in his dressing room in 1995.' She breathed out before addressing the rest of the team, filling them in.

'From what Nina says, Snow is looking like your basic paedophile. Means the papers will be digging like ferrets – looking for other girls. It's pretty bloody imperative we get hold of Mercy. Not only to get more background on what was going on when she was around, but also to secure her alibi for the time of Snow's death. Clearly, though,' Martin said, rubbing a hand across her face and catching a glimpse of Sam watching her from the doorway, 'our main priority is to find the AWOL Sera and Violet. What does the hotel say?'

Tennant spoke up, looking down at his notes. 'No one saw them leave. Receptionist reckons they must have taken the staff lift at the end of their corridor which goes down to the basement car park. They'd parked the car there. Surveillance were expecting any movement to be on foot.' Martin glared at Tennant, who shrugged. 'It's a cock-up, Boss. But the flying squad's out searching. It won't be long until we find them.'

'Let's hope that's the case,' Martin barked, stealing another glance at Sam. 'So, Mackenzie warned me at the hotel that Sera was – I quote – *dangerous*. And I just found this.' She passed out copies of the *Blackpool Daily* page. 'An article describing how Sera and Tristan's twin boys died in an RTA nearly thirty years ago. Note the name change. She was called Sarah back then. Not Seraphina. Why is that, I wonder?'

Jones and Tennant waited without speaking.

'I don't know,' Martin admitted. 'I don't know if it means she's responsible for their deaths, although that seems to be what Mackenzie's implying. And if she is, does that mean she's *taken* Violet rather than the girl going with her mother voluntarily?'

'They could just be scarpering, Boss?' Jones put in. 'Either one of them could've killed Snow, so now they're legging it.'

'That's true,' Martin acknowledged. 'The whole lot of them. They act almost like a *hive*. It's like they don't do anything separately, off their own bat. They were in his thrall – Snow's. And now he's gone, they're spinning.' Martin paused, thinking. 'Who is he, eh? Tristan Snow? I always say it: if you find out how someone lived, you'll find out how they died. So . . . who was he? How did he live?'

'He was a bully,' Jones answered.

'A religious nut-job,' Tennant added. 'And a paedophile, looks like.'

'I read his autobiography,' Martin said, with a sigh. 'It says nothing. Yes, he was those things, but he was more than that. He was someone who had a persona. Didn't he?' Martin gazed round the room. 'He wasn't what he appeared to be. To the world, he was righteous, moral; upstanding. But in reality he was committing assaults, having affairs, and, by the looks of the bruises on Sera and Antonia, well versed in a dash of domestic violence. But he took those children in, didn't he? And his followers – the people that watched him on telly, that came to his services, asked him to heal them – they thought he was the dog's bollocks, didn't they?'

'Even his wife and daughter,' Jones said.

'His wife, yes. Violet, I'm not so sure,' Martin replied.

Jones sighed.

'What is it, Jones? Why the despairing face?'

'Why are you so adamant that Violet isn't anything to do with this, Boss? I mean . . .' Jones swallowed, aware of the eyes of the room falling on her flushed cheeks. 'She's the only link we have to the murder weapon. She had motive . . . She was being psychologically mistreated by her father – look at the DVD you showed us. She knew about his affairs. Maybe she knew about the sexual abuse? She obviously knew something about Mercy. Maybe she was protecting her mother?'

'And the pigeon? Why would she – why would anyone, for that matter? – plant a pigeon carcass under the bed?' Martin asked, pushing her on.

'We still don't know for sure it didn't just fly in of its own accord,' Tennant said.

'It couldn't have flown in that gap. It was too small, the bird's neck was broken,' Jones continued, thinking out loud. 'The pigeon was a symbol of the church. Deucalion was Noah, right? He sent the pigeon to find land to save them all. Snow thought he was Deucalion, or Noah, saving everyone, so . . . whoever killed Snow sent a pigeon to kill Deucalion . . .'

Martin looked approvingly at Jones.

'. . . it's a symbol of all that was wrong in their home, their family. Violet could have left it there to make a point.'

'Killed it, brought it into the B&B and stuffed it under the bed, without managing to leave a scrap of DNA on it?' Martin asked, testing the theory.

Jones shrugged.

'Where would Violet have got the pigeon from?'

'I don't know, Boss. Where would anyone get a pigeon?' Jones gave an apologetic smile.

Martin waited a beat. 'I take your point on all of that. I do,' she said, shoving her hands in her pockets. She glanced at the door but Sam had gone. 'And that's why she's on bail. Why she's skipped bail,' she grimaced a little.

'But there are still loads of unanswered questions. And now with Sera missing, and this idea of the twins . . .' Martin shook her head. 'I just know it's important. I want to know how that pigeon got in that room,' she said as she leaned over the desk to answer a ringing phone. 'Hello? Yes . . .' She looked at Jones. 'Yep, got it,' she said, before putting down the phone. 'Jonah Simpson is downstairs. Come on, Jones. Let's go.'

Violet drank greedily from the water in the glass. Her mother watched her from a chair in the corner of the cellar, her head on one side.

'Thanks,' Violet said. 'I was so thirsty.' She looked around: at her feet stuck out in front, still tied up with a length of rope. 'What's going on? Why I am here . . . like this?'

'Ssh,' her mother answered. She looked towards the cellar door. 'I don't want him to hear you. He thinks you're out of it, asleep.'

'Who's he?'

Sera didn't respond. She moved her hands over the knees of her crossed legs. She looked prim: a librarian at a book sales conference.

'What's going on, Mum?'

Sera shook her head. 'I can't tell you now. You just have to trust me. He's going to help us.'

'Who *is* he?'

'You don't know him. He's a member of the flock. He's going to try and get us away from here. Far away.'

Violet tried to sit up further, wincing as she moved her head.

'It hurts.' She looked at her mother. 'Who did this? Why am I tied up?'

'Violet, I can't tell you now. I had to get you here.'

'But if he's going to help us, why am I tied up?'

'Because if they find us, we need an excuse – why we've left the hotel.'

'So we'll blame him?' Violet's voice rose a little in her confusion.

'Ssh! I don't want him to hear,' her mother repeated.

'But why would he agree to hide us and then risk being accused of kidnapping us? It doesn't make sense.' Violet began to slide her feet along on the ground. 'I don't like it. I want you to untie me.'

'I can't Violet. Please. Just trust me.'

'No, I won't. I can't breathe. It's horrible down here. Why have I been tied up like this? I don't like it. Let me go!'

'Stop shouting! Do you want to ruin the whole thing?'

'What thing?'

'I'm trying to do what's best for us both. *Please!* Please just be quiet.'

'I don't understand.'

'If you don't quieten down, I'll go. Then you'll be left alone here again, in the dark.'

'No, don't do that. Why would you do that?'

'Shut up. I can hear something.' Sera paused, listening. Above them, a sound stabbed into the silence. 'It's him! He's come back.' She stood up and brushed her skirt, as if ridding herself of the cobwebs and dirt of the cellar. Violet looked at her, bewildered, from her prone position on the floor.

'This is insane. Where are you going?'

'I'll be back soon. Just keep your trap shut.'

'Mum, please don't go. My head hurts.'

Sera's shadow passed across the light at the top of the cellar stairs.

'Mum – Mummy . . .'

Sera didn't look back as she shut the cellar door behind her, leaving Violet once again in the pitch black.

42

It was an effort for Martin to disguise the uneasiness she felt as she looked at the elongated form of Jonah Simpson. His mouth was downturned; his chin seemed to stretch to his chest, giving his facial expression a sombre and mournful quality. He smelt stale, with that tang of the unwashed and a faint metallic aroma of blood. Martin had the feeling as she looked at him that he was hanging by a hook in an abattoir of his own destruction; he eked out his existence as a cipher, more ghost than man.

To focus, Martin looked down at the papers in front of her. 'Mr Simpson . . . may I call you Jonah?'

'Mr Simpson is fine.' The priest's mouth was tight as she came into the interview room, appraising her fully from toe to head. He had not deigned even to acknowledge Jones. When he reached Martin's eyes with his own, however, he had sat up straighter, as if recognizing that she were the person to whom he needed to communicate his role in this whole affair, as if he were somehow desperate to impress upon her his status.

Martin shrugged. She didn't care what he thought about her, good or bad. 'Why did you get in touch with Sean Egan at the *Durham Chronicle*, Mr Simpson? Obviously, we've read the article, but I wonder – why did you go to him first? Why not come straight to the police with these allegations?'

'*In due time, their foot will slip. For the day of their calamity is near. And the impending things are hastening upon them . . .*' Jonah said, his eyes closing briefly. 'When I read that Tristan Snow had died . . .' He brought a tentative hand up to his face and touched the wart on his cheek, swallowing deeply. 'When I . . . when I heard about Tristan's death. It was as if a great weight had been lifted from on top of me. A weight I've had for many years.' He nodded, his hands moving down to his lap. 'I'll admit it, I'm glad he's dead, Inspector.'

'Yes,' Martin said, zeroing in on him with her stare. 'And I want to ask you about that. But I'd like you to answer the question. Why go to the press first and not the police?'

'I told the journalist this . . .' He wagged his finger at her. 'The man was, well – not to put too fine a point on it – he was a monster.'

Martin waited.

'All right, then,' he said, and gave a short laugh. 'Because I didn't know . . . I didn't know who else to tell, as a matter of fact. My daughter . . .'

'Seraphina . . .'

'Sarah,' he rebutted, sharp. 'She was christened Sarah.'

Martin inclined her head.

'She and I haven't been in touch since I left the church. We don't speak . . .' His eyes closed for a moment. 'But once he was dead, I saw the tributes. Heard the eulogies . . . and I couldn't . . .' He straightened in his seat. 'I couldn't sit by and say nothing.'

'A monster . . .' Martin parroted the priest, ruffling through her papers ostentatiously, although she knew exactly what it was she wanted to ask. 'You mentioned a girl called Mercy to Mr Egan. What can you tell me about her?'

'Mercy was a victim of his, just as we all were.'

Martin leaned forward, her hands on the desk. 'What kind of victim?'

Jonah licked his lips. 'I think it was sexual. We all thought it. Although no one ever said it.'

'Did Mercy ever bring charges?'

The priest laughed. 'No, no, Detective Martin. Charges? Her mother was . . . absent. Who else was there?'

'You? Other members of the church? Your daughters?'

He remained silent, shaking his head.

'The church . . .' Martin said. 'Were other members of the church involved in this abuse?'

'I'm not aware. If there were, I was not aware of it,' he replied, a look of disgust creeping across his face.

'Was Violet abused by her father?' Martin asked.

'No,' Jonah sounded certain. 'He loved Violet. He wouldn't have hurt her. He was vile, Inspector, but perhaps not that vile.'

Martin glanced over at Jones, thinking through what Simpson was saying. Egan had said that Tristan Snow and Simpson had fallen out about ten years prior to Violet even being born. Was the priest just maliciously shit-stirring, Martin wondered, in accusing Snow of abuse? Was this the revenge of an old man for something that Tristan had done to him long ago? They had to tread carefully here. If the abuse had been systemic within the church, involving such a well-known figure, the ramifications were huge.

'You must realize, Mr Simpson, that this is a very serious accusation. You're alleging that children were being abused by Reverend Snow while they were in his care. If what you say is true, how many children were affected? Was it just Mercy, or were others involved?'

'I don't know, I can't be sure. But I'm certain there were more,' he said.

'Was the church the kind of place where behaviour of this kind would have been tolerated? Ignored?'

'No. We were a normal, loving church,' Jonah answered, his back rigid. 'We held services to worship, marriages, funerals, sermons, Sunday School . . .'

'Sunday School?' Martin cut in. 'Lots of children attended that, did they?'

'Children came from all over the area. It was popular, yes. Parents too hungover, too disinterested to bother. We taught them, Bible lessons and the like. The children did arts and crafts, played in the loft.'

Martin considered this, doodling a picture on her pad of a barn with children inside it. 'Would the children have special sermons? Just for them?'

Jonah lifted his eyes to the heavens.

'What is it, Mr Simpson?'

He ran a hand over his face. 'There were occasions . . .'

Martin waited. When he spoke, his voice was so quiet that Martin and Jones had to crane forward to hear him. 'We would have ceremonies. In the church. We had one with Mercy. A kind of communion, if you like. To welcome her into the community.'

Martin's mind was racing. There was so much to ask. Each layer of this case revealed yet more secrets, untruths, misrepresentations. 'This ceremony . . .' she asked. 'Was it private? Or were the congregation involved?'

'We were all there.'

'And what happened at it?'

'We said prayers. We asked for forgiveness. We banished evil spirits.'

'Banished? As in an exorcism?'

Jonah searched the ceiling with his eyes. 'It's a label.'

'Well, was it? Was Mercy subject to a child exorcism? Was she considered to be possessed?'

Jonah shifted in his seat, his chin still down on his chest, his shoulders hunched. He reminded Martin of a wide-feathered vulture. 'It's easy for those who don't understand to try and put things into boxes,' he said. 'You say the words *child exorcism* and a certain image is conveyed. A vision that society finds uncomfortable; that you both consider uneasy.' He waved his hand towards Martin and Jones. 'And yet, much of it was done with great love. With respect and care.'

'I'm sure,' Martin said, something inside her darkening, gearing up. 'So what happened to Mercy? After all of this took place? Where is she now?'

'I don't know, Inspector. Life went on. The church went on.'

'Did Mercy stay in Blackpool? Or did she leave, do you know?'

'I saw her once, not long ago. She was coming out of the corner shop near to me. She looked different.' He fluttered a hand across his head. 'Her hair was different. Shorter, I think. I called to her, across the street, but she didn't hear me perhaps. I went after her. To see, you know,

250

how she was. To tell her . . . that I regretted certain things. That maybe, I should have spoken up . . .' His voice trailed away, his hands twisting around themselves in neverending circles.

Martin said nothing, waiting for more.

'I reached out, took her by the arm, and then she looked at me.' Jonah pushed his teeth down on to his lower lip. 'She looked at me with such revulsion it made me breathless. "Mercy," I said to her, "Mercy, please." But she was so bitter, so shrivelled. "There is no Mercy for you," she said. All of her beauty was gone. It had all . . . been *taken*. "Mercy has gone. Don't ever call me that again," she said. And she was right,' Jonah rubbed stained and blemished fingers over his eyes, shuddering a little in his seat. 'She couldn't offer Mercy any more. She was tainted and she knew it. She was right.'

Martin shot a glance at Jonah. 'You're saying that she changed her name?' she asked, her heart beating faster, ignoring her disgust at what he was implying. 'Mercy changed her name?'

Jonah had covered his face with his hands.

'Mr Simpson? This is very important. Did Mercy Fletcher change her name after she left the Deucalion Church?'

He nodded reluctantly. 'I believe she did, yes.'

'Do you know what her new name is?'

'I did know . . . someone told me once. But I forget . . . it's gone from me I think . . . No I don't remember.'

Martin exhaled softly. There was still hope. Still hope that the address they had for Mercy was, in fact, correct, and her neighbours didn't know who Mercy Fletcher was because that wasn't her name any more. Martin paused for a moment, digesting this news, aware of the hum of traffic outside the room, of that heavy cadence that envelops an interview, the way its rhythms wrap their way around its participants. As if she were choreographing a dance, she changed tack.

'You've said you don't speak to your daughter, Mr Simpson,' she said. 'But how about your grandchildren? Do you know them?'

Jonah's shoulders visibly stiffened. 'Violet? Yes,' he answered.

'And the twins, Peter and Michael . . . they died before Violet was born, didn't they?'

'Sarah was pregnant with them when I left the church initially. When I returned, about three years later, they had sadly been killed.'

'You don't know anything about how they died?'

'I wasn't there.'

Martin shifted on her chair. Nothing to be gained from him about the boys' death, then. 'Do you know where your daughter is now?' she asked lightly, glancing down at her pad of paper.

Jonah's face turned beady. 'What do you mean? Is she missing?'

Martin bit the inside of her cheek. The priest's response was genuine. He didn't know where she was. 'When you first left the church,' she continued, ignoring his question, 'back before Violet was born. Why was that? You told Sean Egan . . .'

'I know what I told him,' Jonah interrupted. 'Tristan Snow was a difficult man. A treacherous man.'

'Treacherous?'

'He was not a true man of the cloth. He cared only for money and notoriety.'

'And you?' Martin put to him. 'Are you a true man of the cloth?'

His lips turned up slightly, moist; a look of pure cold blood. *'For everyone who exalts himself, will be humbled and everyone who humbles himself will be exalted,'* he said.

'I've never understood that quote,' Martin said, leaning backwards on her chair. 'I mean, all it seems to say is that the only reason for being pious and self-effacing is to get a whole load of credit for doing it. Kind of defeats the point, don't you think?'

Jonah said nothing, his eyes cast in stone upon her.

'Anyway,' Martin said. 'Whoever was the bees' knees in the church, it seems from what you've relayed to the press that a schism took place. I think you knew about the abuse. You knew that Tristan Snow was assaulting members of his church, of his congregation. I think you threatened to tell someone. And then, you were seen as a loose cannon.' She studied his face. 'I'm right, aren't I? I think you warned Snow. But . . .' Martin processed her thoughts as she spoke, '. . . what happened? What did he do to make you leave? To not say anything?'

Jonah's eyes closed, picturing the past. He was silent for a while before speaking. 'The night it happened, she stood there . . . Sarah. She stood there, in front of them all. She was calm, composed. I couldn't believe what she was doing. Tristan was behind her but . . . but, he said nothing. It was all her. Nourishing him, feeding his narcissism.' His head twisted back and forth as if trying to loosen a yoke, a thorny halter of memories. 'She said I was a drunk,' he hissed. 'That I liked young boys. Awful, dreadful things fell thudding from her mouth like clods of dirt.' His hands reached up from his lap towards the heavens, his face rumpled, closed shut in distress.

Martin's consideration of this emanated from her; it hung in the air above them, beating its wings. 'Was it true?' she asked.

'What does it matter?' he answered. 'It's benign now, isn't it?'

Martin thought fast, her understanding of him catching up with what he displayed. 'What she said . . . drinking; the boys. Those things were a cancer?'

'Yes,' Jonah spat. 'Cancerous things. None of them true. None of them.' His eyes were squeezed shut but a pearl of salt water escaped. He drew in a long breath. 'What could I do? Even if I denied it, no one would believe me. Once those things are uttered, they have a life . . . they *breed*. She was pregnant, she was his wife . . . she was unimpeachable.'

Martin waited in silence until at last, Jonah's eyes opened wide, sparking hot life, exposing his unending lack of peace.

'She was a horned snake, biting at my horse's heels. She brought me down. She was behind it all.' He shook his head as if still baffled by it. 'I thought once that she was Medusa, her serpents writhing from her head, to catch, to kill. But then . . .' he looked directly at Martin and she felt a sudden stab of pity for the old man, his fingers gnarly and rough, stretching out into nothing.

'Then, what?' she asked.

'But then I knew I was wrong. She was Medea. She betrayed me, her father. For *him*.'

Martin looked him. He was breathing heavily, his eyes rheumy and pale. 'So why come back, after you were cast out?' she asked. 'Why were you still hanging around the church when Mercy Fletcher came along?'

'Because there was nowhere else to go,' Jonah said, his voice tepid like stale water. He closed his eyes and lowered his chin to his chest.

Martin leaned back in her seat as a knock at the door came. Jones got up quickly and opened it, murmuring to the person outside. She came back inside, whispering into Martin's ear.

'They've tracked down the hire car, Boss. We need to go.'

Martin leaned over to turn off the recording equipment and stood to leave.

'Wait,' Jonah called out, his face calm, a smile floating across his lips. 'Inspector Martin,' he sang, holding them in the balance as Martin stopped by the door, her back to Jonah. 'I might remember. That name you wanted.'

'Mercy's name?' Martin said, turning back to him, a feeling of disgust stealing through her. The man was just here for attention. He didn't want to help. He just wanted to punish. To make other people suffer as he did.

'Yes. Ah . . .' He frowned, his eyes closed, put his head on one side. 'What was it? It's so hard to remember you see?'

'You can give the name to the desk sergeant when you go, Mr Simpson,' Martin said, her voice cut with rage. She wasn't going to indulge this manipulation. They had to get moving and find Sera and Violet.

'Vicky,' Jonah blurted, his attempt to keep Martin in his sights now clear as day. 'She took her middle name, Victoria. And then she married.'

'Her married name, Mr Simpson? Her full married name?'

He smiled again, glanced at Martin's white-knuckled grip on the door handle. 'It's important to you, is it Inspector?'

Martin said nothing. She would give him three more seconds.

'Sneddon,' Jonah exhaled eventually with undisguised glee at having kept them in his thrall, however briefly. 'Her name is now Vicky Sneddon.'

43

Martin parked her car opposite the squat building that grandly entitled itself the Prince Bishop Assembly Rooms. The police back-up cars waited for their pickings like sleek and silent panthers a short distance up the road.

The building was barely the size of a grocer's shop, its front garden twisted with ivy and the grey fluffed-up heads of dying dandelions.

'There's the hire car,' Martin said, as she pushed open the gate. Jones glanced at it before looking down at an old stone tortoise sitting inside the garden, seeming to stare up at her with its sleepy eyes. They pushed their way through the weeds up the path to a door panelled with grimy glass set in the beige pebbledash of the walls. To the right of the building, a garden tap dripped incessantly on to a patch of newer concrete splatted higgledy-piggledy among the path stones.

Unable to find a bell, Martin rapped on the glass. Waiting a few seconds for an answer that didn't come, Martin signalled to Jones to take the left-hand side while she moved around to the right of the building. The greenery was fiercer there. A bramble caught in Martin's shirt as she tried to sidle between the wall of the building and a fence marking the boundary. Noticing a window, she stood on tiptoe to try to see into the gloom.

The hall was empty. Cans and flyers littered the ground, a toilet bowl lay randomly in the middle of the floor, but there was no one inside. Martin frowned. She looked around some more. At the back corner of the building, there seemed to be a hole in the ground. She moved forward awkwardly through the brush. As she neared the back, she realized that the hall was actually on two levels and that it had some kind of cellar. Martin stumbled over a pipe that emerged ghoulishly, unbidden from the earth. She steadied herself, grasping for the wall of the building. Crouching down, she could see that the space she'd thought of as a hole was actually a well leading into the basement. It had stone steps, now broken away from the wall, which had once led down to a door. The door and its accompanying window were boarded up.

Martin hesitated, anticipation popping inside her, that familiar buzz of adrenalin that she felt when she was on the right trail. Something told her to turn down her radio, to approach in silence. Making up her mind in an instant, Martin jumped gently down into the hole.

Violet had lain in the dark for too long. Her breathless heartbreak at her mother leaving her alone had, in the cramped and airless space she lay in, gradually hardened into something more recognizable as sheer bloody anger. Thoughts that she normally kicked out of her head and never acknowledged came thick and fast here in this dense soup of blackness.

She loved her mother with all of her being; she had been unwittingly shunted in her loyalties to her by the narcissistic bullying of her father. She could never understand why her mother had stayed with Tristan. Ever since Margate and Mercy and what had happened afterwards, Violet had fostered a hatred of her father that was now so much a part of her, she couldn't remember herself without it. His touch repelled her. His eyes, his voice, the way he broke the sacrament. When she tasted wine, she wanted to be sick.

Her faith in God had splintered at the same time as she realized that her father was evil. That splintering had eventually ripped wide open, a jagged tear that left her on one side of love, and God on another. God had nothing to do with her. He had nothing to do with Tristan, come to think about it. He was as insubstantial as the papier-mâché Oz head she had dreamt about all those hours ago.

A phantom.

Violet had bided her time. Now she was eighteen, she could leave. But the love for her mother held her captive; she had to stay to protect her. That love. Violet moved her head from side to side on the concrete floor in frustration. And now her mother had bloody well gone, abandoning her to this . . . prison. It was . . . unbelievable.

At least she could be grateful that Sera had untied her hands before she left. Violet managed to elbow her way up to a sitting position, but her stomach cramped so violently all of a sudden that she was almost thrown back on the floor. She lay there, breathing, waiting for the cramps to pass. She needed to lean against something to give her some purchase; see if she could untie her ankles.

When the cramping seemed to have abated for a few minutes, Violet slowly made herself roll across the ground. She could barely see anything in the dark, but with effort she managed to shove herself alongside one of the cellar walls. She leaned against it, breathing heavily. Her stomach twisted again as she bent down towards her ankles, the pain sending sparks into her vision, making her feel dizzy. The knot was too tight. She couldn't undo it. She gave a small sob of frustration. Why was she here? Where had her mother gone? She thought about Sera, her quiet, unflinching eyes. The way her hands would stroke her back. Another sob shuttled up in her. No. She wouldn't cry. As much as she loved her mother, she had something of her father in her, after all.

Feeling around the ground with her hands, she felt something hard and metallic. It was a bracket of some sort. She found, again, the rope that bound her ankles. Her head continued to throb but she ignored it, rubbing the bracket against the rope fibres. *Slowly, slowly. Careful now.* It was going to take a long time. The bracket edge was dull and the rope was thick. *That's okay*, she thought. *I have time.*

It was then that she heard a noise smack into the black stillness of the cellar.

Someone was trying to get in.

44

Sera sat wearily in a patch of sunlight on the ground, some-where . . . she didn't know where any more. She had never felt so tired. Everything in her was draining away down some terrible plug hole. Since the boys . . . since then, she had built a fortress around her a mile thick, topped with blazing arrows drawn back, ready to fire should weakness threaten to suffocate her. But now . . . she couldn't even muster the energy to work out any kind of next step, any kind of plan.

It wasn't her fault. Any of this.

Everything had changed. As soon as Tristan was dead, she'd had to re-think it all, the perceptions she'd had. She knew what people thought about her, how they laughed at her behind her back: her eccentricities, her devotion to Tristan; the way she had been humiliated by him. But, in all of that, *she'd had him*. And so it didn't matter.

Now they were all caught up in a sandstorm, tossed by the wind of God's machinations. How she raged at God sometimes. How he had let her down. Even now – look! Sera almost wanted to laugh, thinking about how he toyed with her. Since Tristan had died, everything was shot. But it still wasn't over.

Violet knew about Mercy and the others. Sera thought she'd kept it from her, protected her. But yet again, she had failed. Just like last time, just like with the boys. Tristan would strip her of everything before he was done with her.

At the hotel, Violet had said she wanted to leave.

Sera looked at her feet pulled together in front of her, at the dust floating around them, caught in the light. Its delicacy seemed to mock her sudden heaviness, her inability to uproot herself, to get going and make everything work again. She couldn't block out the image of Violet's face in the cellar. The eyes of the girl, looking at her in such bewilderment. Tears began to fall down her cheeks, dropping in a steady rhythm on to the ground in time with her wretched breathing.

Violet could not be allowed to leave.

This was how it had started before. The mesh of emotion, netting her so tightly inside herself that she couldn't breathe. Back then, she had walked. The boys' hands in hers. She had walked fast, pushing on through, moving it all on – the hatred, and disappointment and bitter failure.

Now, though, she was stuck. Nailed down under the weight of her own inarticulacy. She had flung herself into the marriage with Tristan like a beached whale heading out into the escape of white water at last. But she had lost her bearings and grown tired. The only way she had been able to survive, had been to remain mute, bobbing in the shallows, sucking in air when she could. And so she had survived – tired and battered, but alive.

But now, it was happening all over again – again, she was helpless and turning back to the beach.

And this time, she was sure to meet her death.

*

The bricks of the building were chipped and scarred with age. A heavy board lay across the basement window, blocking any view of the interior. Martin moved to the door and ran her hands over its rough wood. She leaned her ear against it and listened. Something in her drummed insistently. The building looked abandoned, but she felt an energy coming from it . . . a hum of something. She turned back to look the door up and down, taking a breath before putting her shoulder to it.

She pushed her body weight firmly against the door. Nothing. She hefted again, but it wouldn't budge. She imagined Sean Egan's face, tried a further time and was rewarded by a splintering noise. Progress. She pushed again and again until a gap an inch wide appeared at the edge of the door. Now she could get her foot in and use it to jemmy the door open bit by bit.

Her mind blocked out everything else – Jones, the back-up team outside in the garden, everything – and she made slow but steady headway. Sweat dripped from her face as she continued to push, but she found she wanted to laugh. Why was she even doing this? She would just end up back at the station covered in dust and grime. But something was nagging at her, and she knew from experience that if she didn't listen to it, it would drive her round the bend until she'd scratched the itch.

Martin swung her shoulder heavily into the door once more.

This time, with a loud crack, the rotten wood gave way and the door swung wide open into a dark and musty space.

Martin's face tightened as she moved forward. For some reason, the image of her mother flashed briefly across her mind. She touched her radio for reassurance and then stepped into the room.

45

Jones skirted back along the wall of the Assembly Rooms before returning to the front garden. She had found nothing on the other side apart from more brambles and a revolting outdoor toilet cubicle, stained with God knows what and smelling to high heaven. The day was hot and a gloss of sweat shone on her forehead. Martin's name was on the tip of her tongue to call when she saw that her boss wasn't back in the garden, but something inside prevented her from making too much noise. Instead, she pulled her radio to her lips and softly called Martin's sign.

No answer.

Next she radioed the back-up team: 'Where's the boss? She was just here.'

'She hasn't said anything, Sarge.'

Jones went to the door and peered into the hall. Again, nothing.

She made her way around the side of the building where Martin had gone, edging through the brambles, flattening herself against the wall to avoid being scratched. 'One way to stop squatters,' she muttered, merely to break the piercing silence. Her breathing was soft and even.

Suddenly she heard a crack or a pop. She halted as if on a land mine.

'What was that?' her radio crackled, comfortingly.

'Nothing.' Her senses quivered, but there was indeed nothing to see.

'Sending someone in to join you,' came the reply.

Jones came to the basement and jumped down into the well where Martin had been. She moved to the doorway where the broken door leaned against the wall and poked her head through to look into the room. Flashing a Maglite, she saw nothing except an empty concrete floor and some old shelving.

'Where the hell is she, then?' Jones said into her radio. 'Back-up team requested. I can't find DI Martin.'

PART THREE

. . . The things we thought would happen do not happen; the unexpected God makes possible . . .

Euripides, 'Medea'

46

Martin lay groggy and semi-conscious. As the darkness lifted, she instinctively tried to sit up, but a weight kept her down. She struggled against it but it was too much for her.

'Shut up,' a voice muttered fiercely, the same person who pinned her to the ground, a hand over her mouth. 'Wait till they've gone.'

The voice – female? – and the bitter smell of ancient ammonia stung Martin into sudden alertness. Her eyes snapped open, taking in her surroundings – where was she? She appeared to be in a tiny outside toilet block, among the tangled vegetation of the garden. The pipes of the missing toilet jutted out from the wall above her head, dripping God knows what on to her. Her head was squashed up against the back of the block, her knees pushed into her chest by the bulk of her assailant on top of her.

Fear surged through her as she tried to lurch upwards, but her attacker kept her immobilized, leaning into her further, trapping her on the ground. Martin moved her head from side to side as much as she could, trying to inhale some oxygen from beneath the weight of the hand on her face. As she moved, a sharp pain told her that her nose was broken. She tried to reach for her radio but she was too tightly pinned, then heard a voice outside and felt a flush of relief; it sounded like Jones. Martin battled against the mass on top of her, but she couldn't get any purchase. She scrabbled in vain until the voice receded and finally disappeared. Martin let her head fall back on to the floor in frustration.

What was going on? She couldn't see who it was, holding her down. Martin tried to breathe, summon her training, her cool-under-pressure demeanour. But she was injured and vulnerable, and she had no real knowledge of her situation. It was a dangerous place to be, and she knew it.

The last thing she remembered was standing outside the door of the basement. What then? Tasting crusted blood on her upper lip, she surmised that she must have been smacked in the face by something hard. Her vision was blurry. *Shit.*

'Let me up,' she managed to mumble from under the hand, her voice cracked and her throat dry. 'Don't make this worse for yourself.' She tried to get a look at the person in the gloom of the cramped space, tried to get some moisture back on her tongue. 'False imprisonment. Wounding with intent. Assault of a police officer . . .' Her own voice sounded to Martin as if it were coming from someone else.

'Shut up, I mean it. They're still here.'

All around them, the quiet of the garden seemed to amplify, punctuated only by a rustle of the trees, the low call of a bird. Something about the voice above her was familiar, the shape of her assailant's head. 'Let me up,' Martin repeated, blinking, trying to get her eyes to work properly.

'You'll get hurt again. Please.'

It came to Martin then, like a break in the clouds. The voice belonged to an impassive face, brittle like china in its stillness and composure.

'Violet?' she said. 'Is that you?'

47

Fielding lay in a bed on the Shearer Ward of the University Hospital. The sun blazed through the window beside him but his eyes were closed to it. He didn't sleep, but the mental effort of asking the pain in his stomach to leave took all his strength. He could hear the groans of his ward companions as he lay there; the sighs and expulsions of elderly gentlemen reduced to flattened-out skin and bone on the worn, white sheets of the NHS.

The pain came every few minutes. They had given him an IV drip that pumped fluid into the crook of his arm, but the pain persisted. It stabbed at him with the malevolent gusto of a sugar-crazed toddler. Fielding had worked out its pattern now, he was on to it. He just had to pretend that he was on a journey through the mountains and troughs of this pain, and that soon the evil bacterium ripping through his gut would work its way out and be gone.

His mother had been in; he'd heard her sniffing and muttering to the nursing staff. But he'd kept his eyes firmly shut. The day was bad enough already.

He lay, counting his breaths. He could get four in before the pain stabbed again. He was on his second of that round when a shadow fell over his face.

'You've got a visitor, Eddie,' one of the more friendly nurses said, as if talking to a child. 'Here you go love, sit here. He's in quite a bit of pain, but he'll live.'

Fielding carried on breathing. His mother had undoubtedly sent his aunt or one of his cousins twice removed to check on him.

The visitor said nothing. He could hear the click of a handbag clasp and the rustle of a magazine. The pain knifed again, leaving him breathless. Then the blessed relief of it passing. He exhaled.

In the reprieve, he felt curiosity rise. Who was it in the chair at the end of his bed? He lifted an eyelid to see blurrily past his feet.

The alarm bell clanged at full volume in the nurses' station. They looked up hurriedly to see Fielding trying to struggle out of bed, tugging at the wires that ran into his arm.

'Get her out!' Fielding screamed. 'Get her away from me! Get her out of here!'

48

'I mean it, be quiet,' Violet said.

Martin heard the aggression but underneath, she also heard the fear, the raw panic of the girl.

'You have to stop this, Violet. You're in big trouble. Let me help you,' Martin said. 'You've broken your bail bond. You've wounded a police officer. This is – and I'm paraphrasing – a *shit* position to be in. This whole place is surrounded by police.'

'Shut *up!*' Violet began to cry quietly, tears rolling off the end of her nose. She seemed broken, her hard shell obliterated, revealing only a desperately sad and lonely little girl.

'What's this on your face?' Martin put her hand up to Violet's temple where there was a large, purple bump surrounded by a bruise.

'Leave me alone,' Violet spat, batting Martin's hand away. 'You don't know anything about me.' She turned and grabbed Martin's jacket. 'I've hit you once and I can do it again.'

'You don't know what you're saying, Violet,' Martin answered, her chin jutting uncomfortably towards the girl; Violet had her by the collar. 'Just let me go and let's get out of here. We can sort this all out. Come *on.*'

Violet didn't answer. Martin could see the intake of breath holding the sob at the top of the girl's throat, the attempt to keep it down causing a vein to stand out on her forehead.

'All I have to do is turn up my radio, just here,' Martin flicked her eyes towards the top pocket of her jacket. 'And you'll be in handcuffs. But if you come with me now – voluntarily – it will be better for you. Don't you see?'

Violet shook her head, her lips firmly together. She lifted up the metal bar and pushed it into Martin's face. 'I'd use this first,' she hissed. As she shifted to do this, for a second she relaxed her hold on Martin's legs. Martin bucked, kangaroo-kicking Violet, smashing her head into the concrete wall of the toilet. Martin leapt to her feet and grabbed Violet's hands, wrenching them behind her back. As she did so, the toilet door swung open, and Jones was standing there, her baton raised, eyes wide.

'What took you so long?' Martin gasped.

'Sorry, Boss,' Jones said, leaning down to release Violet from Martin's grip, handcuffs twirling in her grasp. 'Thought you were just spending a penny.'

Martin scowled at Jones, as she stood up. 'Come on, Violet. Let's get you to the station,' she said, taking in the swirl of blue lights flashing across the garden in the searing sunlight. She went to edge Violet past Jones, who didn't move.

'Come on, Jones. Out of the . . .' but Jones's mouth had slackened and something in her sergeant's eyes stopped Martin in her tracks. Cold fear slid down her spine as she realized what it was.

'Sorry, Boss,' Jones said. 'You always did tell me to watch my back.'

A thousand thoughts and images flew into Martin's head like a rustle of dirt-black crows. They settled into stillness, perching on telegraph wires in an apricot sky.

'It's time now, Violet. Come with me please.' A voice came from the door.

Martin craned her head around Jones, knowing who she would see as she did. The petite figure of Sera stood calmly behind her. A shaft of sunlight sought out the turquoise glass of her rings, making the stones glitter and throw their triangular lights on to the knife blade she held, which pointed into the side of Jones's neck.

'I think it's you that needs to get out of the way, Inspector Martin,' Sera said, steadily. 'Once you've let Violet go, of course.'

'Don't do this, Sera,' Martin warned. 'Leave the girl alone. She's just a kid.'

Sera dug the tip of her knife into Jones's skin, creating a tear-drop of blood, causing Jones to close her eyes. 'If you follow me, I'll kill her,' Sera said. 'Come on Violet. It's time to go home.'

Martin unlocked the handcuffs mechanically, her eyes fixed on Jones's. *Don't worry*, she seemed to be saying. *I've got you.* Jones nodded briefly, her jaw resolutely firm. Sera backed away, bringing Jones with her, Violet dragging Jones's other hand. They backed off the short distance down the garden to the gate, where the hire car was parked.

'Stand down!' Martin yelled at the officers there. 'She's got a knife!'

Sera pushed Jones into the front passenger seat of the car, her knife at the policewoman's chest as Violet jumped into the driver's seat. Sera moved to the back, the knife at Jones's throat as the car swerved off and down the road.

49

Martin flew like a hurricane into her car as uniformed police spilled out of several police vehicles that had skidded into place in front of the Assembly Rooms. 'She's got Jones!' she yelled as Tennant ran up to the driver's door.

'Boss, you need to wait,' he said, seeing the blood on Martin's face. 'You're injured.'

'I'm not leaving Jones. Either get in the car or shut my fucking door so I can drive.'

'Yep,' Tennant nodded, running around and getting into the car just as Martin skidded away from the pavement, talking into the radio as she did so.

'Looks like she's heading east. Get a chopper authorized.'

'What's she thinking?' Tennant said, his voice tight. 'Abducting a police officer . . .'

'I don't know,' Martin murmured, as the car sped through the Durham streets. Tennant, unnaturally for him, said nothing, waiting for the lead from Martin.

'Stupid, stupid, stupid . . .' Martin was muttering to herself. 'Should have bloody known.' She hit the steering wheel in frustration.

'Ah, it's not your fault, Boss. You know? How could you have known she'd get her kid to whack you over the head?'

'They should have been separated from the minute Snow's body was found. We put the child into a hotel room with a manipulator and a murderer.'

Tennant shook his head, emphatic. 'Sera's her mother. If anything, it seemed like a domestic violence case – self-defence against years of bullying. Why would we think Violet was in danger? She's eighteen, she's not a child.'

'Violet Snow is about as mature as mozzarella.' Martin looked in the rear-view mirror, checking that the blue lights were still behind her. 'I've been stupid, Tennant. And now I'm going to have to deal with the consequences.'

'Turn left, and then second right. Hurry . . .' Sera said, her eyes fixed on Jones in front of her as the car hurtled through the streets.

'Mum . . .'

'Go as fast as you can. Once we get out of the centre, we'll be okay. Here!' Sera blurted as Violet wrenched the steering wheel round. 'That's it. Careful now. Keep to the left fork and then go with the road. Are they behind us?'

'I don't know.' Violet checked the rear-view mirror. 'I don't think so.'

'Good. Just drive.' Sera squeezed Violet's shoulder. 'You're a good girl.'

Jones sat stock-still in the front seat next to Violet. The blade of the knife was still sharp in the skin of her neck. Her eyes moved rapidly, checking the route they were taking. Violet hadn't gone on to the dual carriageway that led out of Durham; she was heading fast on a smaller road, whipping through small hamlets on its outskirts. A grey and white chequerboard of pebbledashed miners' cottages flashed by, long abandoned, with boarded-up doors, flaked and rotten doorsteps. The occasional window had the white and red flag of St George stuffed into its crevices, but otherwise there was no sign of life. A hot and empty day, the streets as void as the unnaturally blue sky. Jones tried to catch sight of a signpost.

'Don't even think about touching your radio, Sergeant Jones,' Sera said, pushing the edge of the knife against her jawline. 'If they want to find us, they can come and get us.'

Jones was mute, her mind racing to discern their destination. She had no intention of touching her radio. Martin would find her.

The car carried on in silence for a few minutes.

'Mum . . .'

'I know, I know. You want to know what's going on.' Sera nodded from the back seat, propped forward between Violet and Jones. 'It's a bit of a mess.' She stared flatly out of the windscreen with a small smile. 'But I've got it now. I know exactly what I'm doing.'

Violet threw a glance back at Sera before looking again at the road. Her mother seemed keyed, alive like an electric fence. There was a wild, frenzied quality about her; she buzzed with an energy unfamiliar to Violet, making her feel as if she were dealing with a stranger. 'What's going on? I don't understand. What happened to the man?'

'The man?'

'The man that held us prisoner. The one in the basement? I hit that policewoman thinking she was him.' Violet shook her head in disbelief.

Sera glanced at Jones, who kept her breathing level, staring straight ahead at the tarmac of the road ahead of them. 'Don't pretend, sweetheart.'

'What do you mean? Who's pretending?'

Sera gave a soft laugh. 'You *know* I made him up, Violet.'

Violet swallowed, shocked. 'No I didn't! I don't understand.' She paused, thinking. 'So then . . .'

It had been her mother who had brought her to that basement. Her mother who had tied her up and drugged her.

Sera frowned, moving her gaze as houses gave way to countryside. 'I'm sorry about all of that. But I had to think fast. I had to get you away, out of that hotel.' She shivered in her seat, her face pale. The energy bouncing off her felt feverish in the small space of the car interior. 'I didn't want you to fight me, Violet. I knew you'd stay there quietly if I frightened you.'

'But you hurt me,' Violet said in a small voice. She felt sick: ideas and explanations bouncing uncontrolled inside her head. It didn't make any sense. If – and she still had no idea why this would be the case – her mother had wanted to escape with her, why hadn't she talked about it? Told her what was going on?

And now they were here, having kidnapped a policewoman.

'We had to move,' Sera said, as if reading Violet's mind. 'I had to keep you with me. And then you hit the Inspector, and dragged her off.'

'I thought she was the man you'd made up – who you'd said was holding me there! When I realized who she was . . . I panicked.' Violet threw a glance at Jones, whose expression was unreadable. 'And then I was trapped,' Violet said, bewildered. She eased her foot off the accelerator, thinking perhaps she could turn back and explain everything. Make everything better. 'But it was a mistake. I didn't mean to do it. We can explain . . . Take her back.'

'Assaulting a police officer? On the back of what you'd already done?' Sera smiled again. 'They would take you away, darling. I can't lose you like that. Not like I've lost everyone else.'

Violet bit her lip but said nothing. The fact of Jones sitting next to her became suddenly real. 'Shut up, Mum.'

'What you did,' Sera said. She leaned forward a little to whisper into Violet's ear. Imperceptibly, Jones moved to catch what she said. 'What you did to Antonia's face. I was so proud of you, Violet. So proud of your loyalty. You don't know how happy it made me.' She gave Violet an inscrutable smile. 'We'll always be together, won't we?'

Her expression became purposeful. 'We'll need to come off soon. We're nearly there.'

'Nearly where? Where are we going?'

Sera didn't answer but continued to stare out of the window, a peaceful expression on her face. 'It's always good to keep moving, Violet, in times of trouble. Don't ever forget that.' After a minute, she pointed. 'There. Just up there. Take a right into the estate.'

'Where are we?'

'Stop here,' Sera said. 'By that bridge, see?'

'What is it?' Violet asked. 'It looks like a spaceship.'

Sera rubbed one hand over her face, the other still holding the knife against Jones. Her hand trembled as she reached for the door handle.

'This is home, baby. We've come home.'

Violet turned, then, to look at her mother. Something in her face had altered, in the dull light of the approaching summer storm. An alchemy was taking place in Sera.

And, as she realized this, Violet was suddenly afraid.

50

Martin could hear the police helicopter churning the air above them as they drove. 'She said she was going home just now.' Driving fast out of Durham, she whipped her head to look at Tennant. 'Home . . . Do you remember, Tennant? From the interview notes? Her accent . . . she grew up in Peterlee. Look it up on the GPS. Are we going in that direction?'

'God, I think she'd planned this all along. Bringing them all here. Who knows what horrors lie in that woman's wake?' Martin shook her head, her eyes on the road. 'At first, it seemed all about Tristan Snow. But, I wonder . . .' her voice trailed away. 'She banished her own father. Stood up in front of a whole congregation and told terrible lies about him. Brought him down.'

'So he says, anyway,' Tennant answered, holding the GPS and typing instructions as the countryside flashed by.

'True.'

'Peterlee's not far from here, but where, Boss? Where will we find her? Peterlee's not big but . . . it's not small either,' he finished, somewhat lamely.

Martin gave a quick grimace of agreement. 'I don't know, but let's get there and we'll see.'

They lapsed into silence as the car sped onwards. Black clouds shifted without warning across the horizon as if transfigured by the passing helicopter blades. The scent of approaching rain floated in through Martin's open window, the air damp with expectation. *Jones . . . Jones, I'm coming. I'm sorry. Please don't hurt her, Sera. Please don't . . .* Sera's face flashed into Martin's head, the vision of her holding the knife to Jones's throat. She felt as if she couldn't breathe and wound down the window further. They were driving fast, past fields of rape flowers and the curdled aroma of the stacked-up silage bales rushed in along with that strange sense of the unrelenting nature of life despite things hanging in the balance; that portion of time that never seemed to move while you were in the midst of it, although everything around you continued unawares, as cruelly as normal.

Martin still couldn't shake that nightmare she'd had where Mercy had been screaming for help. But had it been Mercy calling out? Or was it really Jones? Had she foreseen this happening? Had she really let this happen? Let down the one person she depended on to always be there?

The crackle of Martin's radio suddenly jerked her into the present. She bent her head to listen, and murmured, 'Sunny Blunts.'

'What?' Tennant asked.

'Sera Simpson – as she was then – lived in Sunny Blunts. It's an estate in Peterlee. That's where she'll be heading, I'm sure of it. Well, at least, it's our only option.' One eye on the road, Martin spoke again into the radio. 'That's where we need to go.'

Tennant began to scroll down the screen on his iPhone, tapping on it, reading the information. 'It's a new town, it says here, is Peterlee. One of those built after the war. Bunch of collieries around it, in the day.'

Martin said nothing, thinking about Jones. Thinking about Sera being here with Antonia. Not so far from where Martin spent her formative years. 'Here we are,' she said, slowing down as the car reached the outskirts of the town. 'Peterlee. Where Sera and Antonia grew up.'

At the GPS's robotic instruction, Martin turned right into a housing estate and slowed to a snail's crawl. The helicopter still whirred above them, puttering in and out of the clouds. A few spots of rain began to hit hard on to the windscreen. The estate was neatly divided by roads and blocks of grass, bleached brown and hard by the summer. The houses were boxy, slotted in next to each other as closely as molars. Some were brick with pitched roofs but others appeared from another time, their first storeys elevated by square pillars. They had flat roofs and what looked like frontages of white and brown clapboard.

'Looks like a Butlin's holiday camp,' Tennant observed.

'God, it's run down,' Martin said. 'Bloody hell, what on earth is that?'

Ahead of them, over a patch of man-made lake, stood a dirty-white horizontal structure. It was thick and straight, stretching over the water like a pair of upturned, abstracted buffalo horns.

'It's a bridge, isn't it?' Tennant suggested.

The ends of the bridge stood upright like the struts of a hospital bed. In between them, the walkway across the water was half-hidden by a complicated jumble of worn-out and mildewed concrete blocks that seemed to slot together. Underneath, whatever lake had once existed had now disappeared to leave a dried-up quagmire, home to a three-wheeled shopping trolley and scattered debris from the surrounding houses.

'I guess so,' Martin said, surveying what lay before her. If this was where Sera Snow had grown up, it was a fairly miserable beginning. Rain began to spatter on their heads, causing her to wipe her brow as she read an information sign. 'The Apollo Pavilion, it's called,' she said in a low voice. 'Let's go for a walk on the moon, Tennant.'

They got out and moved towards the marshy puddle under the bridge. At once, Martin saw the silver hire car that Violet had driven, parked at an angle on the kerb.

'They're here,' Martin said.

Sera pushed Jones up the stairs and on to the bridge, the knife held tight to her back. Jones still had said nothing, her eyes fixed upwards, seeking out the whirr of a helicopter's blades in the rapidly darkening sky.

'Mum?' Violet called, them behind. 'Stop for a minute. Tell me what we're doing here.'

Sera waited, breathing hard, as Violet caught up with her. 'We lived in that house,' she said, jutting her chin towards a boxy terrace on the other side of the bridge. 'See that window? That was the bedroom that I shared with Antonia. That's where we lived – me and your aunt.'

'I think the police know where we are. I can hear a helicopter,' Violet exclaimed, looking up at the sky. 'We need to think about what we're doing. We're in trouble, Mum. We need to let her go, please?' She turned to face Jones, seeking reassurance from the policewoman as her voice trembled with confusion. 'We can explain everything. Can't we?'

'It's not too late, Sera,' Jones said, reaching out to her, her tone neutral. 'We can work it out.'

Sera didn't answer, continuing to talk to herself, a look of puzzlement on her face. 'It waits at the edges, Violet,' she said. 'It flutters there, you can't see it. But it's on the fringes of everything.'

'What is?' Violet asked, looking desperately over the concrete struts, expecting to see any minute the police cars and cavalry.

'It's not madness, Vivi,' Sera said. 'Don't believe that. I know exactly what I'm doing.'

Without warning, Sera spun and slashed the knife across Jones's upper arm. Jones cried out and bent over, her hand glued over the wound. At once, Sera's strong arms twisted Violet down and around. The girl wept as Sera pushed her down, kneeling with Violet's head in her lap. 'I just wanted her to stroke my hair. Like this, see? To love me like . . .'

'Mum!' Violet struggled in Sera's grip but her arms were iron and she held Violet fast. 'Stop it. You're hurting me.'

'Let the girl go, Sera,' Jones managed to yell. Her face had turned white and blood seeped through the fingers of the hand pressing into her arm, running rivulets down the sleeve of her jacket. She let go of the injury for a moment to grab her radio.

'Do that and I'll use this on her,' Sera said, her voice thick as treacle, her eyes fixed on her daughter.

'You don't want to do that, Sera. Not really,' Jones said, dropping her hand.

Sera began to cry throaty tears, her voice hoarse with emotion. 'I just want you all to stay with me. Is that so much to ask?'

Violet tried to turn around, to look her mother in the eye. 'Mum, it's me. Please.'

'But then, I got it, you see? With Peter and Michael, the boys. I understood. I saw how I could keep you.'

A rattle of thunder preceded the rain as tears ran down Violet's face. She heard the sound of approaching car engines. 'The twins? What did you understand? Mum? Tell me. I love you. Please don't hurt me, Mummy.'

'She went away. She left and never came back. And it was because of him. I know it. Once I remember . . .' Sera breathed in sharply, wiping her hand across her face. 'She'd made dinner. Like she did every single night. And he tasted it. And he had this . . . this *look* on his face. Like what he was eating was poison. He just stared at her. Never spoke. Just put his knife and fork down and left the room.'

Jones watched her carefully, weighing up the odds of grabbing her. But the knife was at Violet's throat and her left arm was useless. The rain had started to pelt, making it difficult to see; drops of water kept running into her eyes.

'We sat there. All of us. You can't understand it, if you weren't there. The weight of it. How . . . *vile* we felt. Always it was about him. The man of the house. We were nothing but subordinates to him – us *women*. He knew best about everything and if he wasn't pleased, it was as though we had so utterly failed. That we had failed him and ourselves. The way he'd looked at us before leaving us

288

all sitting there . . .' Her voice cracked. 'Such *disdain*. Like he could never love us again, if he ever had. And all for a pork chop!' A dot of spittle flew from her mouth and was subsumed by the rain.

'Then, after a while,' Sera wiped her mouth, 'my mother went after him. And when they came back down – *hours later* – we had just been waiting there, frozen. When they came back down, he'd painted a black eye on her with her make-up. It was purple and blue and came halfway down her face. He thought it was funny. That it could make us forget. And she just looked at us, like, she knew it was wrong, but what could she do? This is why she left. Because of *him*. But why didn't she take me with her? I would have gone. I would have run alongside her. But she didn't . . . she just went away.'

'Mum, I know. But you grew up, left all that behind. You met Dad. And had me. All of that's behind you now. You're a different person,' Violet said, her voice sweet like the opening violin of a concerto.

'Have I, Vivi? Have I left all that behind? Look at me. Look at what your father was. I meant to change, I really did. I *swore* I'd be different. But, in the end, wasn't I just the same? What you said in the hotel – you had the same thoughts about me that I had about my mother. And so you want to leave. And I can't bear it . . .'

'You can be different,' Jones said, faltering a little as her knees buckled. She sank down to the base of the bridge, the sudden downpour plastering her hair to her forehead. 'Let us help you.'

'You can't help me, Sergeant Jones,' Sera said sadly, raising her face to the heavens, letting the rain wash over her face. 'You can't keep Violet here with me. Only I can do that.'

She bent her head to her daughter. 'I'm sorry, my darling, I'm so sorry. But the only lesson I ever learnt from this place,' she said, as she carefully sliced into the flesh below Violet's chin, 'is that the only way to keep you, is to give you eternity.' The warmth of the blood flowed over Sera's fingers in rivers as she moved Violet lovingly to one side and got to her feet.

Martin and Tennant moved forward through the rain, scanning every inch of the grey surroundings for any signs of life. Two more police cars pulled in next to where they'd parked, and their occupants jumped out.

'Anything?' an officer asked.

Martin waved her hand to indicate that they should keep quiet. 'Seems that's the car she used,' she said. 'Fan out round the estate. She's pretty good at hiding, if the basement episode's anything to go by.' Martin touched her nose gingerly; it still pulsed with pain. 'I'm going to go up on the bridge.'

'I'll come with you,' Tennant said in a no-arguments tone, moving ahead of Martin.

They crossed the wet grass to the edge of the lake, which curved around and out of sight under the bridge, framed by another row of white and brown clapboard houses.

A crack of thunder bellowed as Martin pulled Tennant sharply back by his sleeve. 'Stand down,' she whispered fiercely into her radio. 'One suspect seen. Stand down but keep positions.'

Tennant flashed a look at Martin, who gestured with her chin down ahead of them in the direction of the ground. He turned back towards the bridge, straining his eyes through the rain bouncing off the concrete path before them. A lock of dark hair curled around the foot of a pillar guarding the stairs leading upwards. As Martin edged closer, she saw that the hair belonged to Violet. Signalling to Tennant to flank her, she moved forward, adjusting her eyes to the murky space underneath the stairwell.

It was then that the gash on Violet's neck became visible. Her eyes were open as she lay cold on the walkway, blood being washed away by the rain from the gaping wound in her throat, as fast as it could thickly ooze.

51

'She's dead,' Martin said, in a strangled voice. She felt light-headed as she stood from taking Violet's extinguished pulse, images of the girl flashing through her head: Violet sitting, spiky and brittle, in the boarding house, at the police station. She said nothing more, merely turned to the stairs to go up on the bridge.

'Boss, wait. You need back-up. She's armed,' Tennant called after her.

Martin didn't reply as she made her way up the stairs. Her heart pounded, adrenalin blistering through her, making her breath shallow. A plea ran through her head as she climbed – *please don't let Jones be dead*. None of this made any sense. Why had Sera done all of this? To cut the throat of her own child; it was vile.

Rain coursed down Martin's face, in place of the tears she would never cry for Violet. But she felt her death like a hole in her stomach. She felt the responsibility for it; she had been too slow. Madness was always capricious, yet she should have been wise to its prospect. And so, she was to blame.

The walkway over the bridge was narrow. Its walls edged in on Martin as she made her way across. The interior was pockmarked with nooks and corners.

'Sera,' Martin called, her voice battling against the pounding rain. 'Where is Sergeant Jones? Come out now. Let's put an end to this. Give me Jones.'

She carried on, shuffling forward in the racket of the heavenly drowning. She locked away the panic at Jones's whereabouts, her anger at Violet's death, and forced her voice to be calm and free from aggression. 'Come on, Sera. It's wet, and you must be tired. Let's sort this all out. Tell me what happened; let's try and work it out.'

Ahead, Martin's vision was blocked by a concrete strut that stuck out like a wall in the middle of the bridge. *Who designed this place?* Martin thought. It was like a hell on earth, a brazen middle finger at the poor sods who had to live here. A park? A community centre? No, a useless lump of concrete, ripe for drug addicts and rapists. Martin hitched her stab vest a little as she began to broach the wall.

'Jones, are you there? Are you injured?' Martin wiped her face free of the rain that spattered loudly on the bridge. She couldn't hear a thing.

'Sera, I'm going to come round this wall now, okay? So I want you to pass me your weapon. Put it on the floor and skid it across to me. The armed response team are here. Don't let's get anyone else killed.'

A blast of rain-soaked wind spat into Martin's face. She leaned into it, creeping forward. 'I'm coming now, Sera. Hand me the knife. It's over.'

Martin reached the edge of the wall and paused, leaning against it, taking a breath. She spun her head around at a sound, and saw Tennant and an armed officer approaching on the bridge. The officer with the gun came forward on silent feet, close to Martin by the corner of the wall.

As he did, a black-handled knife with a four-inch blade skidded across the wet concrete into their path, just beyond their reach, its blade taunting them through the rain. Martin felt perspiration itch under her jacket, the sound of rushing blood hammered in her ears.

'Is that everything, Sera?' Martin called out, her voice steady. 'Why don't you come out with your hands up just to make me happy, eh? Come on, now. Let's get out of this. Let's end this, Sera.'

With another blast of thunder, the police helicopter made a turn above them in the sky, the noise of its engines drowning out the sound of the rain. Martin took her opportunity and leapt for the knife. She moved to one side, her back against the concrete of the bridge. Kicking the knife towards the other officers, she whipped her head around the corner of the block.

'Officer down! We need the paramedics,' Martin shouted as soon as she saw Jones lying on the floor. She moved forward, pulling Sera's arms behind her and putting on handcuffs. 'Are you all right, Jones?'

Jones nodded, her eyes dim. 'Knife wound, Boss. Arm . . .'

Martin shoved Sera to Tennant so that she could kneel down next to Jones, her hand on her shoulder. 'You'll be all right, Jones. Surface wound, I reckon.' Martin turned away with worried eyes to the sky beyond the bridge. 'Where are those medics?'

Tennant began to lead Sera away as the green figures of the paramedics ran up to Jones. As Sera retreated, bound by the handcuffs, her head twisted round and she eyeballed Martin. Her look made Martin involuntarily recoil. She had never seen such cold hatred followed by the crumpling of features into complete despair. It was as if ties had been loosened behind Sera's head, those ribbons that had held her controlled and calm for all this time. But now her mask fell sodden and useless into a puddle on the ground, and she was revealed as she truly was — embittered and lonely, and utterly filled with rage.

52

The storm had disappeared, dragging the summer with it kicking and screaming. It left a day dripping with disappointment in its wake: pavements stained with water, anticlimactic clouds on the horizon.

Martin reached the hospital as soon as visiting hours would allow. She pushed gently into the room where Jones lay with her head against the pillow. Her eyes were closed, causing Martin to halt on the room's boundary, uncertain whether to go in. But Jones opened her eyes and smiled, moving her unbandaged arm to beckon Martin inside.

'How are you, Jones?' Martin asked quietly. She sat carefully on a chair next to the bed, snatching a look at Jones's arm, wrapped in white and placed carefully across her body.

'I'll be out soon. Might be a while before I get back to spin bowling, though,' Jones answered.

Martin nodded and a comfortable silence settled between them.

'She's in custody?' Jones asked after a while.

'Yep. Charged with Violet's murder. She won't get bail.'

Jones moved her head away from Martin and gazed out of the window. 'I'm sorry, Boss. I tried . . . but there was nothing I could do. I couldn't move.' Her mouth turned down in an expression of sadness.

'I know, Jones,' Martin said, patting the blanket on the bed as if she were patting Jones's hand. 'There's no one to blame apart from Sera herself.' Martin bit her lip, the reality of it punching her in the stomach. Violet was dead and she had failed to protect her.

'Will we get her for Snow's murder?' Jones asked, turning her head to look at Martin again.

'Tennant's prepping the interview for later,' Martin said. 'There's still no real evidence though, is there? I mean, the assumption is that, yes, she did it. But I still don't know why she planted the nightdress. We need a confession . . .' She shrugged, the words tailing off.

Jones stared down at her hands, then looked back up to meet Martin's gaze. 'I'm sorry, Boss,' she said again.

'What for?'

'I kept telling you that Violet was the one. You know, with the cross in her nightgown and everything. I didn't get why you didn't suspect her.'

Martin shook her head. 'This family isn't what it seems, Jones. It feels like we haven't even scratched the surface yet.'

'Yeah, I know,' Jones replied, 'because Sera talked a lot when we were on the bridge. Rambling. Like she was in a dream, about her mum and dad and . . .' She closed her eyes for a minute.

'Are you okay, Jones?' Martin asked.

'Yes. She mentioned the twins. I don't know. She didn't say more. She went off on one about wanting to keep them with her. That that was all she'd wanted, and now she knew how to do it . . .' Jones tailed off.

'I need to go back there,' Martin said. 'Work out where Sera came from. If you're all right, Jones . . .? Just get some sleep,' Martin said, getting up from the chair.

'Yes, okay. But what . . . where are you going?'

Martin touched Jones's shoulder gently, before withdrawing her hand. 'I'm going to find out about Sera. I'm going back to Peterlee.'

Martin drove through the streets of Peterlee, not really knowing what it was she was looking for. She drove in again to the Sunny Blunts estate and walked past the Apollo Pavilion and over to the house where Sera had grown up. The eyes of the house were dull, reflections from the windows shielding its secrets. She inhaled the wet air, taking in the grey of the skies and the threads of mists that hung low over the roofs. There was nothing here any more.

She got back into her car and carried on driving. On a whim, she pulled over as she saw the sign to the Peterlee cemetery. As she got out, she was surprised at the strength of the wind whipping up her hair before she realized that the cemetery sat right on the edge of the coast, facing the sea.

There it was, beyond the stern backs of the gravestones. It felt like a mirage after the greyness of the drive and the drag of the weather. The sea was bottle green, dipping and curling below clouds slung claustrophobically above, yet light seemed to shine beneath it, glowing warmly; white froth marking the tips of the waves. The salt stung Martin's nostrils and she breathed in deeply. It was beautiful.

As she walked between the graves, the cemetery shrugged off its austere appearance. For all of the plots, without exception, were decorated in a rainbow of flowers. Some flowers were paper or plastic, but many were fresh, placed carefully against well-considered headstones engraved with poems and photographs and football colours. Martin had never seen a graveyard like it.

She started at the back, moving slowly along the rows, reading the inscriptions. She took her time, thinking about the fates of these people, young and old. She moved on, gradually making her way to the front line, towards the sea. It was cold in the wind, and she pushed her hands into her pockets. Taking a break and straightening, gazing out to the horizon, she noticed a selection of graves set back a distance from the others. She wandered over, taking a band out of her pocket and pulling her hair into an untidy ponytail.

As she approached, Martin saw immediately that the solitary section was for children.

The graves were tiny: little angels' heads, open pages of the Bible, and teddy bears, all covered in a carpet of multi-coloured flowers.

> A flower lent not given . . .
> Sleep our beautiful angel . . .
> Born asleep, too special for the earth . . .

Martin pulled up short. She felt tight in her chest, something was pushing into her. She rubbed her heart, trying to breathe, to take in the sea air. She turned her back on the graves, tried to focus on the blue before her. The image came into her head of her laughing with Sam. The joke she'd made about the blood. How she always seemed to deny herself what it was she really wanted.

She shut her eyes tight and was confused to discover tears, wet on her cheeks. She let out a sound which felt like a laugh, but deeper, as if it came from the very core of her. She sank to the ground, and put her face in her hands and gave herself up to it. She was crying.

She sat there for a few minutes sobbing, her knees pulled up to her chest. At last, it passed. She wiped her face, then rubbed her hands on her trousers. She didn't have a tissue in her pocket and had left her bag in her car, so she tried to clean her nose as much as possible, conscious that mascara would be streaked down her face.

She pulled herself up to stand and breathed out loudly. She was aware of being totally alone, there in that cemetery. Nothing between her and the ocean, and at the back of her, the remnants of life. That was all that remained: statues and headstones and memories of people who had disappeared from the earth, who had turned to dust.

Life before her, and death behind.

Martin lifted her chin and turned back to the headstones. And straight away, she saw it:

Peter and Michael Snow
Remembering our angels
Taken too soon
3.3.1986–22.1.1988

Martin crouched down in front of it. The headstone was simple: white with a ribbon etched into the front above the epitaph. Martin shook her head, thoughts flying around it.

At the bottom of the stone was a small vase of flowers. Martin looked at them with a sudden jolt.

The flowers were violets. And they were fresh.

53

Martin paused with her hand on her office door. She couldn't bear to go in, to see her desk again – with its piles of paperwork, her computer blinking at her, the lack of pictures on the walls. It was all so depressing. She had to interview Sera soon but before she did, she needed to get her thoughts straight. It still confused her, why Sera would have wrapped the cross in Violet's nightdress if she had murdered Tristan. Why had she wanted to frame her own daughter?

She did an about turn and headed back down to where she had come from. Pushing open the doors from the main reception, Martin inhaled a gulp of the street air. It was damp from the recent downpour, puddles lay on the pavement, rainbows of oil slicks greasing their surfaces. She drank in the air, relishing the remnants of drizzle on her face.

Tristan Snow. Narcissist. Married to Sera. Who, judging from Martin's interview with Jonah Simpson, had been brought up by another narcissistic man; a man filled with his own anger and resentments. Patterns in families, chains from which you could never break free. Victims of ego, seeking out yet more torture from even worse monsters. As such, the idea of the woman smashing her husband over the head with his own exorcism cross wasn't that unrealistic.

All well and logical. But would she want to set her own daughter up for it? Martin pressed the button at the pedestrian crossing and then ignored it, running over the road through the traffic, horns blaring as she went. That seemed improbable at best. And so was Jones right? Was it Violet who had taken her father's life? And still the other possibilities lurked. Mercy Fletcher, or Vicky Sneddon; Jonah Simpson; the seemingly countless people who had wanted Tristan Snow dead.

Martin took the fork up on to Elvet Bridge and marched on, into the Market Square. There was the Marquess of Londonderry again; still green, still looking down his copper nose at all who passed him. Martin headed in the direction of the river. She could think there. She ran down the steps at Framwellgate Bridge and was at once enveloped in the lush display of summer that the River Wear put on at that time of year. The trees lining the riverbank seemed to bend to meet her, settling her, making her feel at home. She tramped down the path, watching the mist from the recent rain gradually dispel over the water.

Sera Snow. A woman who lived in the constant shadow of death. Had she known about her husband's abuse? If she had, how had she lived with it? And how had her twin boys died? Had they really been hit by a lorry outside Blackpool, or was there yet another secret lurking there, something more horrific to imagine? This was a woman, after all, who had slit the throat of her teenage daughter. Martin couldn't shake the mental image she had of Violet lying on the pathway underneath that weird space-age bridge. Her doll's face frozen pale, the gaping gash of red underneath, and her dark hair framing her face for eternity.

What kind of woman did that?

Martin dodged out of the way of a lone runner on the riverbank and sank on to a convenient bench. She leaned forward over her knees, gazing at the wet earth, at the peaty orange of the strewn leaves. How was she going to start with Sera? Something tugged at Martin. Did she feel pity for this woman? Or was pity the only way she could get her brain to accept the terrible things the woman had done? Wasn't that what forgiveness was, in the end? Just a word for moving on, putting an event in its place after you'd stopped caring about it? But Martin did still care about it. She cared about it very much.

She closed her eyes and breathed in the scent of bark, the dank aroma of the swirling waters before her. Because if you still cared – if you still had that fire of all-consuming emotion – you could never forgive. It would be the same as having starved for a month and then depriving yourself of your favourite food.

Look at her motive, Martin thought. Look at why she's done what she's done. An idea flitted on the periphery of her consciousness, dancing on the edges, calling to her.

She thought about it, about forgiveness. She thought about the competing emotions she had felt when Jim had left her. The relief at the same time as the searing humili-ation. And then later the hurtful reality that maybe Sam didn't care about them us much as she did. What would Sera have thought, watching her husband with her sister? Could there be a more blistering betrayal?

And then it crept into her thoughts, slowly, line by line: the way in to Sera, the way to get her to speak. She was a Christian woman after all – whatever she'd said to Violet – and Martin remembered it from her own days at Sunday School, when she had stared out of those stained-glass windows, barely listening to what the vicar had said. There was one verse, one song, which had always stayed with her . . . what was it? Solomon something . . . *Set me . . . set me as a seal upon thine heart, as a seal upon thine arm.* But then how did it go? Something like, *love stronger than death* or *as death* and then . . . Martin turned away from the river and hurried back to the station. It had come to her in a rush:

For love is as strong as death; and jealousy is as cruel as the grave . . .

54

Sera was pale and drawn, her hands unmoving on her lap. She sat folded in on herself, shielding herself with invisible wings on the plastic chair behind the interview table.

She had been waiting for over an hour there at Martin's request. Martin wanted her exhausted, at the end of her tether after the episode on the bridge, in the hope that, finally, she might break her silence. Sera had signed the appropriate form in front of the duty custody officer, waiving her right to legal representation. Martin didn't like interviewing in the absence of a lawyer but there was nothing for it. That was the hand she'd been dealt.

Martin examined her subtly, feeling instinctively that Sera had used silence as protection for all these years. That something about what had happened in the marriage with Tristan, between her sister and her, meant she had become mute. *As cruel and silent as the grave.*

Martin missed the stolid presence of Jones next to her. Instead, Tennant sat beside her taking notes. She squared her shoulders. What would it take for Sera to speak? What was the key to unlocking her words? Tennant turned on the interview tape and Martin repeated the words of the caution.

'I think I know how this has all happened,' she began. 'And I think we can work it all out. I think I can help you, Sera.'

The woman said nothing, gazing down at her hands.

'I think you're someone to have pity for. I mean, Tristan Snow. What was it like being married to a man like that? A bully. An abuser. A paedophile . . .'

Sera's eyes dipped, her thumb rubbing the knuckles of her other hand.

'I think you protected your own children. To the detriment of yourself in all probability. Unfortunately, you let him have his way with everyone else, didn't you?' Martin paused. 'But I know that you were abused by this man.'

Sera's face was as motionless as granite.

'I think he had involved you all in some pretty appalling practices. And I think that, one day, you just snapped, you'd had enough.' Martin nodded, her eyes on Sera, her heart beating. It was like speaking to a statue. 'I can understand that, Sera. God, anyone could – right, Tennant?'

'That's right. Anyone could.'

'I can't imagine what life was like. Travelling around to do these shows. Tristan being treated like a god.' Something glimmered in Martin as she said those words . . . a tiny light in the black hole of this case. 'I bet he had loads of other women, didn't he? You'd think that, wouldn't you Tennant?'

'Yeah, I would. Definitely.'

Martin quietly moved back to her chair. She wasn't sure whether Sera had even noticed her. She took hold of the back of the chair and, without warning, lifted it up and smashed it hard on to the floor. Tennant did well not to react. His pen paused for a millisecond above his pad before continuing to write down what was being said.

'But I don't want to talk to you about Tristan. Fuck him,' Martin said. 'Who gives a *shit* if he's dead? Wanker like that, treating everyone like dirt, as if they're his slaves. Abusing children, subjecting them to exorcisms. Who acts like that and thinks he can get away with it, right? *Fuck him!*' Martin took a breath. 'No, I don't care who smashed his head in. Dickhead deserved it if you ask me. And maybe if that was how it had been left, we could all be heading home. We could have helped you, Sera – if you'd spoken to us, that is. Fixed up a nice little self-defence ploy with the CPS. Done a deal with the court.' Martin carried on, well aware that this was all untrue. But she wanted Sera to regret her actions, regret not speaking.

'But you didn't talk to us. And that was a big mistake, I'm afraid. Because what you did today has changed everything. I don't care about Tristan. The person I really care about,' Martin said, dropping her voice, moving to lean over the table, inches away from Sera's face, 'is your daughter. That's who I give a shit about. I care about what happened to Violet. And we're going to sit here and work out how that young girl ended up dead, if it takes us all night,' she hissed.

The walls of the room seemed to bend inwards unrelentingly . . . Martin's gaze was fixed on Sera, who still betrayed nothing.

Sera blinked and moved her head back, her eyes closed. A smile grew on her face. Martin watched as Sera breathed in deeply. She looked far from disturbed or upset; she looked like someone at the beginning of a yoga sequence.

She opened her eyes and met Martin's stare. 'You want me to speak?'

'I do.'

'You want me to regret the murder of my daughter? To cry and wail, and show you how sorry I am?'

Martin moved her head to one side, considering her response. 'I want you to tell me why you murdered your daughter,' she said at last, her words dropping on the floor of the room like hot stones.

Sera shook her head slowly from side to side, a desperate leer on her face; tears flooding her eyes. She gave the sound of a small sob. 'You don't know anything, Inspector Martin,' she said. 'Anything at all.'

'What don't I know, Sera?' Martin's voice had altered; it was softer, inviting. 'Tell me what it is.'

Sera bent her head before lifting it steadily to meet Martin's gaze. For some reason, the room seemed to darken almost imperceptibly before she spoke.

'She wasn't my daughter,' Sera said simply, at last, bringing her long hair around to twirl in her fingers.

'What did you say?' Martin asked, her mouth suddenly dry.

'Violet,' Sera replied quietly. 'Violet was not my daughter, Inspector Martin.'

55

I was at the kitchen table as usual. You were both opposite me – you and Tristan. You had been crying. The tears and flushed cheeks made you resemble our mother.

The day seemed very still and silent, as if a blanket had been thrown over its face. Birds chattered outside, a mug of tea sat in front of me. But real life was motionless.

I waited for you to tell me.

Tristan breathed through his nose heavily. He had put on weight, I noticed. I'd been feeding him well. I wanted him to eat to fill the void where the boys had been. It would never be made whole in me, of course. I'd always have it, black and empty, craving impossible peace in my stomach.

I thought grief would be different. I thought it would encompass me, that the memories I had of the boys would be laid out before me as if a luxurious carpet where I could lie down, running my hands over the fibres, feeling its caresses. Death brings a rush to the grieving, do you know? He enters your house and stirs up a cold wind. But then he flies, leaving you alone. And alive.

But with the boys . . . I was separated from the gift of grief. I was forbidden it; the walls of its city were closed to me. Instead, there was only empty silence.

Now here we were. Me on one side of the table; you on the other. Tristan's hand on your knee. Why hadn't you just ignored me? Got on with things and spared me the humiliation of this *little tableau? But of course he wouldn't spare me. He wanted to hurt me. And you – you had always wanted what I had, since we were children.*

'So you see,' Tristan said, breaking the moment. 'We don't have any choice, Seraphina. If the church find out about the baby, it'll be a disaster. I'm filming next month. It doesn't bear thinking about, if people . . . well, you know, if they suspect anything.'

I forced myself to glance at your belly before dragging my eyes away. I didn't need to see the emergence of the rounded dome, the hard swelling beneath your jumper. I think I touched my own stomach, feeling it flat and lifeless.

'We live here together anyway,' Tristan was saying. His voice was pleasant, rich in persuasion. 'What does it matter?'

'And the baby?' I asked. 'Will it matter to the baby?'

'I don't know,' Tristan answered. His eyes flickered. That was an inconvenient thought which would be better ignored, I could tell.

I studied you both. I was precise. 'If I agree to this, I want it.'

'No,' you said, understanding immediately what it was that I desired.

'What?' Tristan asked.

'The baby. The baby will be mine.'

'No,' you repeated. 'Never.'

'It will think I'm its mother. That's the only way.'

'Surely we can come to some . . . ?' Tristan countered.

'It's the only way,' I said again. 'Otherwise I won't agree. I won't do it.' I closed my mouth and turned my head to stare out at my garden.

'You bitch,' you cried. 'You absolute bitch. You have to take everything, don't you? Everything! I hate you.' You collapsed low in your chair like a child.

Tristan tried to soothe us with shushes. 'Come now, little hen,' he directed to me. 'We need to be reasonable. What's important is the church; what people think . . .'

'You can't be trusted with children,' you spat at me, your words hurled into the air, bouncing hard around the walls. I closed my eyes briefly, the image of my sons leaping into this very room flashing into my mind before I could stop it.

'You can't be trusted with husbands,' I threw back.

'Enough,' Tristan roared, getting to his feet, patience with us women lost. 'The pair of you disgust me. You disgust me.' He strode to the door and looked back at us. You were cowed, shrunken, at the table. I was placid, still focused on the garden.

'You will come to me after Mass tonight, each of you, with your reasons for your request. And I will decide. What I decide will be final.'

I began to laugh: quietly at first and then louder until you jumped up from the table and ran from the room, pushing past Tristan in the doorway. That was when I stopped laughing and stared at Tristan's back, rigid before me. 'And then what?' I asked. 'You'll cut the baby in half?'

Tristan turned slowly to face me. 'Be careful, Seraphina,' he said. 'Be very careful.'

'I gave up everything for you. My family, my home.'

'No,' he replied. 'You came to receive a better life. A life where you were valued and loved.'

I looked at him, tall and fat, in a green jumper with that unruly hair. 'This isn't love,' I said simply.

'And neither is envy,' Tristan answered. 'A good name is worth more than riches — a King Solomon quote, I believe.' He sneered a little. 'You will not destroy what I have made, Sera. You will not. I

would rather pour petrol over your body and set a match to you than have that happen.'

I turned once again to the window. My heart did hammer. But it was unseen by Tristan.

'You can have the baby,' Tristan said, after a moment, leaving the room to find you, your sobs gradually dying out in the hallway.

56

Martin tugged on her trainers and walked quickly out of the briefing room, ignoring the beep of incoming emails from her computer and the vibration of a text message arriving on her phone. They had halted the interview. Sera needed to sleep. They all did. Wanting to avoid seeing anyone, she chose the stairs over the lift, and pushed open the emergency exit door at the back of the station on to a cloud-free and starry Durham night.

She turned left out of the car park and headed up the hill, running past the Student Union and across Kingsgate Bridge. She had always liked this sparse concrete structure, which led from the brutal modernity of Dunelm House where students parried and politicked to the cobbled enclave of university colleges near the Cathedral. The moon was high and in the light of the street lamps she could see the river below her; hear the gentle slap of its waters on the banks.

The rain earlier on in the day had left its reminders, and Martin's feet were soon wet from the puddles. She ran fast, sprinting over the bridge and up to Palace Green, where she paused, breathing hard, hands on her knees, looking up at the spotlit shape of Durham Cathedral. She was in the university heartland here, nostalgic for an earlier case that had also tested her, brought her to the edge of her understanding of humanity and its machinations.

She stood, gazing up at the magnificence of the Cathedral, wondering what it was that compelled humans to build such a thing; to believe in something that would require it; or, at the other end of things, to be certain that there was no hell – that the taking of a life of another would have no penalty.

Violet was Antonia's child . . .

Martin let this fact move inside her like a marble in a jar, tilting it this way and that; working it around until it settled. Antonia had been made pregnant by Tristan, and Sera had been persuaded to adopt Violet as her own for the sake of the one thing that cemented them all together – the church.

And yet . . .

For a woman who professed her faith so strongly, who had devoted her life to its calling, Sera seemed remarkably impervious to its teachings. Where was her guilt? Where was her sorrow at what she had done? Where was her morality?

This couple, Tristan and Sera: they had created a following, they were worshipped near and far. They had ostracized her father; Tristan had had affairs with God knows how many women, had abused children; Sera had killed her own daughter, who was actually her niece. On and on and on it went. Something rose up in Martin, and she retched, vomiting coffee and sandwiches on to the wet grass.

She paused for a moment afterwards, her face down towards the ground. Then she straightened and wiped her mouth, making her way off the Green on to the pathway. She leaned for a moment against the pale, stone walls of the Palace Green Library, taking comfort in its cool longevity. She needed to continue the interview with Sera, unravel this whole tangled thread. They would start from the beginning and work their way through the labyrinth until they got to the clear air at the end. Martin rubbed a hand over her face. The Cathedral clock chimed the half-hour. She should go home, get to bed.

Martin turned away, her shoulders tense and hunched as she crossed the moonlit grass and jogged slowly back to her car.

As she put her key in the lock, a hand reached out and grabbed her elbow. Immediately, Martin spun round, blocking her assailant with her arm, a knee to his groin.

'Shit. Sam! Sorry . . . I didn't know it was you!'

'Fuck!' Sam doubled over, groaning into his thighs.

'Who the fuck comes up from behind like that?' Martin protested. 'I thought I was being mugged. After today . . .'

'It's why I came, you idiot,' Sam said, raising his head to look at her through eyes crunched up in pain. 'I was worried about you.' He straightened slowly. 'I see I needn't have bothered.'

Martin let out a laugh, blind for a moment to the memory that they were fighting, that things were so intractable, so difficult. She reached out her hand before she could stop herself. 'I'm sorry,' she said again, and then she remembered and the weight of it all fell inside of her with a dull thud. Sam took her hand, watching her face, looking for a fracture in the solid shell around her. She found that despite herself, the very act of him searching for it softened her. 'Come in. Here . . .' she held on to his hand and they walked in together, into the dark hallway.

'Wait, I'll get the light,' Martin said.

'Don't,' Sam breathed, kicking the door shut and pushing her up against the wall. He bent his head and kissed her. 'I was really worried about you.'

Martin sank into the kiss, forgetting about the day and Violet and Jones and Sera. She felt Sam's body against hers, hard and warm. She ran her hands over his back. 'Thank you for worrying,' she said and butted her cheek against his.

'I love you,' he said, simply.

Her heart seemed to stop. Something in her tensed, prepared to flee. The feeling solidified inside her for a second and then it relaxed and she felt a heat move through her, an acceptance.

She opened her mouth to speak but merely nodded, taking his hand in hers and leading him up to bed.

57

The sky the following day had a clear, white clarity about it as Martin made her way back to the ward where Antonia lay in a machine-beeping solitude. The morning air still carried the remnants of the downpour the previous day but Martin breathed it in gratefully, clearing her head; steeling her resolve to finish this case. A part of her never wanted to see any member of this fucked-up family ever again, and that part was riddled with anger towards Antonia – that she could have helped Violet. That she could have saved her, if she'd only have told someone what was going on behind the doors of the Deucalion, got Violet away from Sera. But as a restorative breeze whipped Martin's hair from her face on the walk through the hospital car park, she swallowed the feelings down. She would finish this case for Violet.

After further warnings from the ward sister to not be too long, Martin pushed open the door to Antonia's room. She lay prostrate, white bandages covering her face, from which oozed small caterpillar trails of a greenish-yellow substance. A drip pulsed next to her, wires running into her arm; a machine flashed mutely beside her head. Her eyes had been closed when she entered but now opened slowly as she approached the bed.

'Ms Simpson,' Martin said in a low voice. 'I'm very sorry to disturb you, but I really need to talk to you about your accident – about what happened to you.'

Antonia made no reply, but her pupils dilated a little. She appeared to be waiting for more.

'We haven't been able to question you before now. But I'm very anxious to talk to you. To find out what happened and who did this to you.'

Antonia gave a small blink, water pooling in the corners of her eyes.

'I realize this is all very distressing.' Martin swallowed. 'And I'm afraid I have some other bad news.'

Antonia closed her eyes. 'Where's Sera?' she asked limply. 'Why hasn't she come to see me?'

'Well, that's the thing,' Martin answered, choosing her words carefully. 'Something has happened to your niece, Ms Simpson.'

'To Violet?'

'I'm sorry to tell you that Violet died yesterday, Antonia. I'm very sorry.'

Antonia's shoulders twitched violently. 'I don't understand,' she said. 'What do you mean, *she died*?'

'Violet passed away yesterday. I'm sorry,' Martin said again.

'How?' Antonia's voice trembled as she spoke, and her eyes were wide and fearful under the bandages.

'We're still gathering evidence,' Martin replied. 'But . . . it does appear that your sister was involved.'

Antonia tried to wrench herself up on to her elbows but grimaced with pain before sinking back down on to the pillows. 'Sera was involved? Oh, the bitch!' Antonia spat out with effort, before shutting her eyes tight. The exertion had exhausted her and silence fell across the room. 'Oh, poor Violet. My poor girl. What she suffered . . . That's why she did it, you know. That's why . . .' Antonia's voice was so faint, Martin almost thought she might have imagined it.

'That's why who did what, Antonia? I'm sorry, I can't hear you.'

'She didn't mean it, what happened. She's been twisted all these years. Made to hate me, to despise me,' Antonia swallowed and said with supreme effort. 'But I don't blame her for what she did. I don't blame Violet.'

'You mean . . .?' Martin was tentative, processing what she had heard as she spoke. 'Violet was responsible for the attack on you? Did you see her?'

Antonia gave a painful nod. 'But I would never have said.' Her eyes bored into Martin's. 'But now she's dead, you must see . . .' She fell into silence again, then managed to take another breath. 'She takes all the children. All the children.'

Martin inhaled softly. 'What do you mean, Antonia? Who does? Sera?'

'Evil, evil, evil . . .' Antonia began to cry, the tears dropping noiselessly on to the bandages on her face.

'Sera takes all the children? The twins, too?' Martin persisted.

'She takes everything.'

The door opened with a gust of hospital aroma, of antiseptic and burnt toast, as the ward sister bustled into the room. 'That's enough now, Inspector. She's had enough.'

'What do you mean, Antonia? What did you mean about the children?' Martin persevered, her gaze fixed on Antonia.

'That's it now. Let Ms Simpson rest.'

'Please . . . just two more minutes . . . Antonia.'

Antonia turned her face away from Martin and stared resolutely out of the window, the expression in her eyes the only evidence that the conversation had ever taken place.

58

'We've found her, but she doesn't want to talk to us,' Tennant said glumly, staring into his coffee at the large table in the briefing room. 'Mercy Fletcher, that is. Although, as we know, that's not what she calls herself now.'

Back from her visit to Antonia, Martin sat opposite him at the large table in the middle of the briefing room, next to Fielding – still a little green around the gills, just out of hospital himself. 'Jonah was right then?' she asked.

'Yep. Vicky Sneddon she is these days.' Tennant shrugged. 'She does live in that house you went to, Fielding. She was out when you visited. Was working the day of Snow's murder, and her best friend says she was round at her place the night he was killed. Lancashire MIT door-stopped her yesterday. But she doesn't want to talk.'

'Did she say why?'

'Just got married. Got a brand new nipper. Wants to put it all behind her, she says.'

'So she acknowledges that something happened?'

Tennant shrugged. 'Said she didn't want to hear his name ever again. Tristan Snow's.'

Martin fiddled with her identification lanyard on the table, spinning it round into a circle one way, and then in the opposite direction. 'Can't force her to talk to us,' she acknowledged. 'She's got an alibi for the murder, and there's not much we can do in relation to the abuse allegations if she won't speak.'

'Subpoena her to give evidence against Sera?' Tennant said.

'Evidence for what? She's not a witness to Violet's murder. Or Snow's for that matter,' Martin replied. 'Does she know about Violet's death?'

'Wouldn't have thought so,' Tennant answered. 'I can check.'

Martin nodded, pushing her lanyard away with a tired air. 'How's Jones?'

'Doing better. Think she'll be discharged tomorrow.'

'That's good at least. And have we got any further in working out why Eileen Quinn was doing the poisoning? Why she stole Tristan Snow's cross?' Martin directed the question to Fielding.

'The SOCOs got the teapot from her house and we sent it off for testing,' Fielding explained, with a vague shudder. 'It was crawling with solanine. She's been chopping up potato tubers and shoving them in the pot for weeks. It's a miracle more people weren't sick. I must have a sensitive stomach,' Fielding said, abashed, 'given I got ill so quickly.' He sat up straighter in his seat. 'She gave different answers to why she stole the cross as opposed to the photo . . .'

Martin inclined her head.

'Said she loved him at the time. Stole the photo off his dressing room mirror to remind her of him. When he came to Riverview, though, she stole the cross because by then she hated him. Was going to sell it on eBay . . .' Fielding shook his head. 'She came to the hospital, like. I thought she was going to attack me. But she wasn't. She just wanted to check I was all right. Weird old bat . . .'

'She gave the tea to everyone though, didn't she? Was that just her peculiar insane thing? I mean, was she actually trying to kill Snow?' Martin said. 'Or just make him sick? Wanting to punish him for dumping her? Because that adds her back into the mix, doesn't it? If she was doing that? Tried to poison him and then, when it wasn't working quickly enough, she sneaks in his room and bashes him over the head.'

'She'll be interviewed again tomorrow,' Tennant said. 'She's saying it wasn't intent to kill. And, as you say, it wasn't like she was just poisoning Snow, was it? She was giving it to everyone who drank the stuff. Look at Fielding . . . I reckon she was just doing it to entertain herself. Punishing the Reverend was just an added bonus.' He shifted down in his seat. 'Reckon she's just an old bat with a few fries short of a Happy Meal, like.'

Martin flung him a look. 'Does everything always need to be about food with you?'

Tennant coughed, moving on. 'What was the result of the inquest, Boss?' he asked. 'Of the twins' deaths? Sera Snow's boys?'

'It was open, but a narrative verdict of misadventure,' Martin replied, standing up and moving to the window, missing Jones as she talked, missing her take on things. 'But Mackenzie clearly wanted to bring it to our attention, so I wonder why . . . If Sera was the one to harm them, it's evidence of Sera's instability, of her being unhinged, right?'

'Pretty harsh, if you accept it's true. That you'd kill your kids to have revenge on your husband for playing away . . .' Tennant said with a rare display of caution. 'Who'd honestly think that was a good move? I mean . . .' his voice trailed away, emphasizing what they all thought. That to murder your own children was beyond the pale.

Martin looked at him. 'Notice how Sera changed the spelling of her name? Sarah to Seraphina? Jonah Simpson mentioned it, too. I think her life changed irrevocably after the twins' death. I think she became a different person.' She turned round from her spot at the window and gazed fiercely out on to the tree-lined road that bordered the MCT office. 'What are we dealing with here, then?' she asked. 'A serial killer? Three counts of filicide . . .' She shook her head, her face in an expression of bewilderment. 'What kind of woman does this?'

'And let's not forget her husband,' Fielding spoke up. 'Surely she's firmly in the frame for that after all of this. Especially after what we know about Violet not being her daughter, about what he was doing to Mercy and whoever else?'

'Yep,' Martin replied softly. 'If she could murder her children, I can't see it being much of a leap to move on to her husband. Jesus Christ. What a bunch of Jeremy Kyle rejects.' She cleared her throat, pulling her seat out and taking it, turning a biro between her fingers. 'So the years roll by, Snow's getting his rocks off in the church and God knows where else with the kids who come to see him. And then his whole crew end up here. Under the roof of the Riverview boarding house.' Martin placed the pen carefully on the desk. 'Why there? Who booked them in?'

'Sera,' Tennant answered.

'No, it was Mackenzie,' Fielding said. 'Mrs Quinn told me. He made the booking.'

'We know they were struggling financially, which is why they were staying in a shithole. But why that one? Coincidence? Or did Mackenzie know that Quinn and Snow had history? He must have known, he was around then,' Martin said, pinching her nose and grimacing where it still hurt – an image of Violet coming into her head as she remembered the girl hitting her.

'He's having money troubles, yeah? So he thinks he'll put Sera face to face with one of Tristan's girlfriends and she'll snap and do him in. Problem solved,' Tennant said.

'Except Sera's been traipsing all over God knows where with Tristan's bit on the side, Antonia, for the last twenty years and hasn't snapped before,' Martin observed. 'And we still don't know why that bloody pigeon was under the bed.'

'And what about Antonia?' A voice came from behind them. They turned to find Jones, pale in the face, her left arm in a sling but standing strong, rooted in the doorway. Martin smiled at her sergeant, relief washing over her at the sight.

'All right, Jones?' Tennant asked, with a quietly pleased expression. 'What do you mean, Antonia? Did Antonia do it, do you mean?'

'No,' Jones said, shaking her head and coming to sit at a desk, resting her arm carefully on the arm of the chair. 'I mean, who was it that painted the acid on to Antonia's face?'

'Ah,' Tennant said.

'Ah, indeed,' Martin replied, continuing to look warmly at Jones. 'Violet, right, Jones?'

Jones nodded, surprised. 'Yes. How did you know?'

'I suspected it after I read the transcript of the wire we put in Sera and Violet's hotel room. They allude to it. But I've also just been to see Antonia, who confirmed it. Sera wouldn't have done it to her sister. Whatever else, she was her blood. All these years, she's never done anything to hurt her. Everything she's done has been to hurt either Tristan or herself. I think Violet hated Antonia, hated her for how she had betrayed her mum. Because, of course,' Martin remarked, 'Violet didn't know that Sera wasn't actually her mother.'

'It's true. I remembered in the hospital. I should have said something but things were . . . they were hazy. But in the car,' Jones continued, 'Sera told Violet she knew what she'd done to Antonia, what she'd done to her face. She said she was proud of her.'

Martin raised her eyebrows. 'Well that's another thing to add to the list to put to her in interview,' she said. 'Nice to have you back, Jones.'

'We got you a present actually,' Tennant chipped in, passing Jones a multi-coloured bag, with a grin.

Jones, looking down at the bag, said, 'Juggling balls . . .' She looked up and punched Tennant lightly on the shoulder with her good arm.

Martin shook her head at Tennant as if indulging a child. 'We'd better get back in the interview room with Sera, Tennant. You'll watch on the CCTV, Jones?'

'Wouldn't miss it,' Jones replied.

59

Antonia steadied herself as she finally managed to sit upright. She brought a hand gingerly to her face, feeling the bandages swaddling her cheeks. Her eyes were still half-closed, puffy and swollen. She swallowed as she moved, mustering the courage to keep going despite the throbbing in her head.

She brought her feet to the floor with what seemed like a huge explosion of noise. She moved her head carefully to one side, the movement of an owl, searching through the glass pane in the door for any stirring at the nurses' station. No one was there, for once. Antonia breathed again and put her hands to the side of her hips, pushing gently so that she made it up to standing. She crept forward towards the slim cupboard beside her bed in which her clothes were stored. Inside was the dress that the nice orderly had brought her this morning.

He was sweet. Done exactly as she'd asked; accepted her explanation that she was sick of wearing the hospital gown. It was more than anyone else had done for her in a long, long time. She had been left here alone, suffering these injuries, suffering her grief, all by herself. When her face had been flayed. And now, this news about Violet.

Antonia's eyes swam with tears. She wouldn't cry. No, not this time. She took another breath and slipped off her gown. The lights in the hospital corridors were soft at this time of night. The nurses carried on with their rounds, but at allotted times. It had been just a few minutes earlier when the sister had checked in on Antonia, so she calculated she had at least another forty minutes. Luckily they'd removed the drip that afternoon, so she was free to move around.

It was a wrap dress. That orderly was considerate, Antonia thought; he realized that getting clothes over her head would be difficult. He was odd-looking – bug-black eyes and scraggly white hair. But he had a big heart. *Bless*, Antonia thought with a smile that drained away as she remembered that no matter what the orderly looked like, she would no longer be of interest to the opposite sex. Not with this face.

She pushed that shard of truth out of her mind, turning her thoughts back to what that policewoman had told her. She wished she'd asked more questions, but it had been too shocking.

Sera had killed Violet.

That had to be what she'd meant when she said that Sera was *implicated* in Violet's death. Had she been arrested, though? She must have been. What had she done to Violet? What had happened?

After the policewoman had gone, Antonia had stared into nothing for an hour. Then, she had put the news into the vault where she kept things she didn't want to consider again. And then she had had two thoughts: first, that she needed – and quite frankly deserved – a drink; and, second, that the time had finally come to put an end to this.

She poked her head stiffly outside the door to her room but pulled it back in as quickly as she could muster, as a nurse rounded the corner at the end of the corridor. Antonia swallowed. Any sudden movements made her head seem three times its proper size. Eventually, the squeak of the nurse's rubber-soled shoes faded and Antonia looked once again outside her room.

The corridor was empty. Taking her chance, she sidled out of her door and padded away from the room towards the emergency exit.

Sera sat in the cell at the bottom of Durham police station, with its white walls and its blocked-up window. The door was propped open with her own shoes. She gazed at them for a long while. They had no laces. The policewoman who had put her in here had been pleased with that. Presumably they were worried she would kill herself.

She remembered buying those shoes at some little shop away from the seafront. It wasn't so long ago that she'd done it. A few months before they'd come here? Things were unravelling even then. Violet was older. She was asking too many questions.

Violet . . .

The death of Violet still seemed suspended, unresolved in the universe. The fact of it existed outside Sera; it hadn't penetrated inside. What people didn't understand was – people who had never killed – was how *easy* it was, killing.

It only resulted from actions, after all. A swipe of the hand, a push of a shoulder, a minute too late, too early. Life spun on these seconds and nobody ever realized it. Death was everywhere. You just had to invite it in.

It was funny how nobody ever got it. The force with which you could decide something irrevocable. The secret was that the decisions you *thought* were the big ones, the ones that would alter everything – those generally had the least impact. It was the insidious choices that were the dangerous ones, the ones you hardly gave a thought to: a turn of the wheel this way or that; a flip of a coin; a punt. Those were the times when you should be very, very careful.

Stop yourself and wait a breath.

Like, after her father had left the church, Sera had gone at once to Tristan. He had taken her into his arms; that familiar comfort, the smell of him, his strength. This was the old house, with the polished floors and the mahogany bed; wide window sills squaring off partitioned sash windows; fresh blue light; the yellow comfort of daffodils. He laid her on white sheets upstairs, held himself over her with a look of such tenderness that she was undone.

Then he pushed her over on to her stomach and entered her from behind, fast and hard, causing her to gasp. As if from above, she watched him move inside of her. She didn't resist the violence; the pushing of him, whole and rigid, into her, jabbing at her core. He was searching for her: she could feel him probing, pushing her to the brink of herself. For a moment, it enabled her to forget, just to be. But then, as always, she retreated at the last, as if the truth were too hot to touch. Once again, at the closing up of her, he withdrew and released himself upon her indifferently.

She watched this from above, quiet, unmoving. She watched him fall off her, on to his back, his hair flopping down over his forehead. She saw her wet thighs as she rolled over herself, to lie star-shaped next to him. She gave him everything she had, especially then, in the moments of violence. But afterwards, it was always palpable that actually, she had given him nothing of herself. She remained intact.

'I feel sad,' she had said at last, her eyes sliding over to him, pulling the sheet up to hide her naked chest.

Tristan lit a cigarette, leaning back on the pillows, exhaling the loud sigh of the world-weary wise. 'About Jonah? Don't. He's gone, the stupid prick. It's better this way.'

'Still . . . because it was me. It would have hurt him.' Sera prodded.

'He couldn't have cared less about you,' he said. 'Just liked the sound of his own voice.'

Sera moved her head towards the half-open window. The sweet chirrup of some bird skipped through it, accompanied by a soft breeze of a budding, green spring. She shivered a little. Perhaps she was afraid of him after all, she thought. Despite her deliberate goading.

Tristan turned on his side to face her. 'Look at me.' He took her firmly by the chin and pulled her face towards him. 'Look.'

She moved her eyes to his, her pupils dilating at the closeness of him, the raw quality of his latent anger. To tempt him was to have him. 'You know why you did it,' he said, a menacing roughness in his throat. 'Don't you?'

The banishment of their father.

Yes, she knew. It was his punishment for failing their mother.

'I know that you do,' Tristan said. 'So now, you have everything you need here,' he said. 'Me. The boys. Your sister.'

At the mention of Antonia, Sera stiffened involuntarily under the sheet.

'All you need is right here.' Tristan took his hand from her chin and swept it firmly and carefully across her cheekbone. 'Say it.'

'Everything I need is right here.'

'That's right,' he said. He had swung again, the uncontrolled pendulum of his temper leading him from peace to rage and back again. Now he was quiet, watching her for a change.

Their eyes were locked. And that was it. One of those easy decisions.

Sera would give Tristan everything.

She would make him into the man he was destined to become. And then he would see her, the real her. Then she would be able to see it herself. He would peel her disguise from her like shedding skin until the real person was finally revealed.

Sera shuddered, coming back to the present as a bell clanged somewhere in the police station. Distant voices, raised in a struggle, an alarm blaring. Someone was fighting against being put in their cage. Sera leaned back on to the cold, white wall, and stared again at her moccasins at the door.

Fighting was futile.

60

'I want to talk to you about Michael and Peter, Sera,' Martin said.

Tennant stared at Sera darkly from the opposite side of the table, thinking of Jones upstairs in her sling.

Sera turned to Martin, setting her shoulders as if to meet a task. 'They were my boys,' she replied calmly.

'What happened to them?'

'They died.'

'How? How did they die?'

Sera's eyes rolled upwards in disinterest. Her shoulders were square but her face was blank. She was heavy in her chair, lumpish.

'Would you like some water, Mrs Snow?' Tennant asked, unable to hide the acid in his voice.

Sera didn't respond.

'How did Michael and Peter die, Sera?' Martin repeated. 'I want to hear you tell me. How old were they when they died? Tell me.'

Sera's eyelids drooped.

'Sorry, am I keeping you up?' Martin snapped. 'The boys. Twins. Two years old. Hit by a truck on a dual carriageway leading out of Blackpool. Ringing any bells? I know, Sera. I know what happened. But I want to hear you say it. I want you to tell me.'

Sera shook her head in distaste.

'No?' Martin said, leaning forward. 'Tell me. Was the killing of your sons an accident?' she whispered.

The room hummed in the silence, the tick of Martin's watch the only tiny sound.

'Do you remember, Detective Inspector?' Sera said at last, the tips of her fingers feeling along her forehead in a steady rhythm as she bent her head to the table. 'You said once, that there was no greater crime than murder.' She looked up, unabashed, at Martin. 'Do you remember?'

'Yes, I do,' Martin answered.

'I disagree with you, though,' Sera said. 'I think there are worse things. Evil tentacles which reach around you, shrivel a person and reduce them to something unrecognizable.'

'What things?' Martin asked, swallowing a little, her mouth dry.

Sera stared at her, grey curls stuck to her forehead. 'The destruction of love freely given. The abandonment of a person. When you are given love,' she said, looking with demanding eyes at Martin, 'you have a responsibility. You have to nurture it and keep it safe. You can't just *throw it away*,' she chided. 'If you do, then you deserve to be punished.'

'Tell me about Michael and Peter,' Martin said again.

'What happened to them meant that they would *never* be rejected,' Sera said, at once looking exhausted and haggard, as if this were a position she had defended many thousands of times. 'They would be with me always. They could never be hurt again. Death was the only thing to wash it away. And at the same time . . . I took them from him.'

'From Tristan?'

'Yes,' she nodded. 'I had come to him from my family. I had given him everything. I even abandoned my father for him!' She laughed, the sound like the clang of metal digging into rock.

'Why was that?' Martin asked, taking her lead. 'Why did you subject your father to that humiliation?'

Sera thought for a moment. She seemed to take on a brittle anger, but it was steeped in self-righteousness, Martin thought, soaked in a horrible self-pity. It was the coat of anger worn by mob-rule, when crowds hurl stones at paediatricians' windows, believing them to be child abusers. 'Have you ever known absence, Inspector Martin?' Sera asked, her mouth pursed. 'Have you ever known *abandonment*? My mother abandoned us. I was seven years old. Seven! They say that your emotional life is determined by your mother's behaviour up until you are seven. So I was unfortunate, wasn't I?' She lowered her chin with displeasure. 'In that. Do you know *why* she left?'

Martin knew he wasn't supposed to answer.

'She went because my father couldn't have given a toss about her.' The rage was rearing stronger now, it covered her face, pulling it into a shape of disgust. 'He bullied her and he bullied us and when she'd had enough, she walked out of that house and she never saw us again. Can you imagine? Can you imagine leaving your children in that way, Inspector? Just leaving them to their own devices like that? I was *heartbroken*.' Sera glared at Martin. 'I could hardly breathe, I was so distraught. I was *just a child*.' She lifted her eyes then, as if to apologize for the blasphemy.

Sera shook herself a little. 'So,' she continued, her voice prim with virtue, 'our father needed to learn a little humility. He needed to be taught a lesson. And – thank God! – my husband offered me that opportunity. I would be nothing without Tristan. Nothing!' She sat back, breathing heavily.

The room was a pressure cooker. The fluorescent lights burnt down on the three of them, bleaching them of colour. They seemed as shadows in that room: a space that had become less a place for an interview, more an arena for a personal quest. Martin had never felt so present, her nerve-endings sparking, desperate to try to reason with this woman; tear apart the noxious peculiarity of her . . . philosophy . . . for want of a better word.

'Things did change,' Sera went on, her head to one side, considering. 'Fraser came along and Tristan became well known. People were interested in him, in us all as a family. We had no privacy. We never had any time together. They were always around. Fraser. Antonia. Hangers on. Tarts and whores.' Sera's face suddenly changed, snarling the words, spittle hanging from her lips. A grey lock of hair hung across her forehead, her blue eyes like stars, staring at Martin. 'After everything I'd done for him and the church. I shut my eyes to everything. I knew what he was doing with them. I allowed it all to happen *in my empire*. I was the consort, I was his queen. I allowed it!

'And then Antonia called him and my boys her *family* . . . I mean, how could I accept that? Those boys weren't hers. *He* wasn't hers – Tristan. What would happen? I asked myself, what would happen if the world found out? Who he really was? I would be *fucking belittled*.'

The words shot ice through Martin's veins. Somehow the baseness of the curse opened her eyes to the madness of this woman. And more than that, it was what Antonia had said about Tristan, back in the hotel room. Only four days ago. It felt like years. 'And so . . .' she said softly. 'You took the boys . . .'

'You're absolutely right I took those boys. I took them from him. And I don't regret a minute of it,' Sera frowned at Martin. 'Don't accuse me of heartlessness, Inspector. I missed them. Of course I did. And then I regretted being banished from my own home. *From my life*. But,' she said, giving a quick shrug, moving her thick plait off her shoulders, 'he let me back in. He had to. So, it worked, didn't it?'

'You had your revenge?'

'It wasn't revenge, Inspector Martin.' Sera tutted as if Martin were a child before looking up at her in earnest. 'It was *survival*.'

I know you'll realize this is hard for me. You have some sympathy, don't you? But . . . if I am to be true to myself, I have to go through it.

   Don't pity me though.

   I know you won't anyway. Your hatred for me is almost as profound as mine is for you, I would think.

   Think back on that day.

   I left the church, taking the hand of each of my boys. I pressed the wait button at the traffic lights. The boys' hands were hot in mine, I could feel their pulses pressing insistently into my skin. My own hand was throbbing but I pushed the pain away. Like I always did.

338

The lights beeped and we crossed the road, walking away from Tristan and you and the dirt and the evil and the shit that you were all covered in.

The boys were silent. They could tell I was hurt. Their legs ran alongside mine, trying to keep up; panting quick little breaths as I moved faster and faster.

I headed towards the city centre, pulling the boys along behind, passing over another set of lights and then another. The wind was up and the leaves swirled in the streets. Bushels of grey clouds gathered above, they peered down on me, frowning. It was only lunchtime, but the afternoon had turned dark in that way it does, as if rain beckoned. But the clouds weren't full; they were wisps of air, sodden only in judgment.

'Mummy, stop!' my Michael burst out at last. 'Tired, Mummy Stop . . . !'

But I hunched my shoulders and carried on, pushing on through the streets, past the shop windows and the pier and the lights now flickering into life in the gloom. I spoke words of comfort to myself, words the boys couldn't hear on the rising wind. 'To reach his heart, to break his heart. To transform stone. How?'

'Mummy, what are you saying?' Peter asked, a sob in his voice. 'Please stop, Mummy. We want to go home.'

'I don't like it here, Mummy. Please take us home.'

Home.

I pulled up short. Where had I ever been able to call home? Not Sunny Blunts, that's for damn sure. I'd thought my home was with Tristan. But then there I was today, pouring boiling water on my hand as my sister told me that we were a family. All of us! Suddenly I realized how it would come to pass. You would try to take them. My own children. You had wheedled your way in with Tristan and you would want them for your own.

339

I give him something. You give him something else, you'd said.

No.

They are not yours to take. They are not yours.

Supposing he wanted that? He would like this idea. The idea of polygamy; a fucking harem in his house, stinking out the bedroom with the whoring. When I had given up everything for him! I had betrayed myself. And now he would take everything from me, leaving me with nothing.

No.

A lorry thundered by, jolting me into the present. We had walked out of the city, beyond the lights. We were on the side of a dual carriageway. The boys cowered behind me as cars and trucks rattled by.

Oh, but there was a scrunching inside me, a soupy mix of yearning, self-pity, a need for a point of change, to get relief from what was happening now. And then the terrible, terrible sadness.

He will not be the one to take them. They are mine. They are mine.

I looked up at the road and felt for the hands of my boys, still inside my grasp, sweaty and warm. They seemed more than whole just then, attached to me completely, part of me, as they had been once, each the mirror image of the other, wet, downy heads bobbing at my breast. Now, their bodies were pushed into my legs; a stifled cry came from one of them. They were afraid. He had made them afraid. This was his doing.

But I would protect them. I was their mother.

I would choose for them. I knew best. I am a good mum, I thought. Unlike my own mother, leaving us in the dark, all alone, with no one to hold us, no one to rock us to sleep.

I don't remember much. Horns blaring. Tiny hands reaching for me, reaching inside the tunnels of wind whipping past them. Headlights raining down from all heights; white lights, red lights, green. I stopped pulling. Started pushing; pushing those small, hot bodies into the stream of metal and noise and light. Then it was all upside down; the screams of the boys mixed with my own cries of failure.

Judge me if you want.

But it was done now. They would be safe.

61

Martin stared at her, blood pounding in her head, throbbing rage at every word uttered by the woman before her. She had to control herself, keep the spotlight on Sera. She thought back to the grave, to the posy of violets, and swallowed. She forced herself to detach, to soar upwards so as to look down on the scene from the ceiling above. From there, she could pull her focus solely on to Sera, ignoring what she felt inside, putting in a box somewhere else the hatred that she felt towards this woman.

'Why are they buried in Peterlee? The boys? Why not in Blackpool, where they died?'

'I wanted them *home with me*,' Sera answered in a tight voice, her eyes glassy. 'Always. I wanted them home.'

'But you went there recently, didn't you? To the cemetery?'

Sera's expression was capacious. It could have encompassed anything.

'You left flowers. You left violets. What did you mean by that?' Martin leaned forward. 'Tell me! Did you feel guilt, finally? Did you want to make amends – for all of it? Or . . .' An awful expression flashed across Martin's face.

'Or what, Inspector Martin?' Sera said, her voice light, dripping through the room like liquid through muslin.

'Or was it just a foreshadowing of what you'd already planned to do?' Martin's voice was hoarse with feeling. 'A warning of what was to happen to Violet?'

Sera bowed her head, her lashes resting on her cheeks. She said nothing.

Martin slammed her hands on the desk. 'I think this is bullshit. All this supposed logic you're trying to feed us. There *is* no logic. To any of it! You planned it all – every last bit of it. Because it doesn't work, Sera, this, this *argument!*' she exclaimed, losing control, frustration fizzing through her. 'I get it now,' she said, skewering Sera with a stare. 'I understand who you are.'

Sera's breathing was shallow as she avoided Martin's gaze.

'There's no sense to it – Seraphina, Sarah, whatever you want to call yourself. You told us you'd been abandoned, how dreadful it had been – how it had affected you. But look what you've done to your own children! You pretend it was about wanting to keep the children with you, but it's all a lie. You just wanted to hurt the man you could never leave. Your husband, Tristan Snow. Who, twenty years later, you finally killed.'

'Not true,' Sera said.

'What about the lives of your children? All of the opportunities they had? You took them all away. You robbed them of it all. And you did it knowingly. How could you possibly think that that was better than being alive, having choices, having possibilities? Who are you to make that decision?'

Sera looked at Martin for a long moment.

'Who are you to do that?' Martin repeated, her voice strong and clear in the washed-out room.

'I am their mother,' Sera replied, her fists clenching into tight balls.

'If that's what being a mother is . . .' Martin began, her face dark with anger. 'Then God help us all. They're *dead* Sera. All of them. Michael, Peter, that lorry driver. Tristan. Violet.' Martin stopped. To her shame, she found her eyes pricking with tears. Her voice dropped. 'Look at this damage. Look at what you've caused. All those lives.'

The room lapsed into silence again.

'They were blonde, my boys,' Sera went on, as if Martin hadn't spoken. 'Their hair used to stick up at the back in little tufts.' She moved her hand to illustrate. 'I went to their cremation, you know. I watched two little boxes go on that ridiculous conveyor belt, behind those velvet curtains. And I thought about those tufts. Flattened down with water by the morticians at the crematorium. About to be scorched by flame. And do you know what I felt, Inspector Martin, when I watched that, as I thought about that?'

Martin waited, not breathing.

'Nothing. I felt nothing.' Sera briefly closed her eyes. 'Can you imagine? What it's like? Those warm and tiny bodies, that you pushed out of yourself into the world? To watch them spin and smash before your eyes? They were broken that day. Into a million pieces. And I watched it. I wasn't afraid.

'Do you think Antonia would have done that? Of course she wouldn't. Stupid little rat-faced baby, Antonia. When she was born, she never stopped crying, kept us up all night. Took Mummy's love like she took everything.

344

Like she tried to take my family, later. But when I met Tristan, I could break free of her. I was absolved of all that.'

'Absolved? For what?' Martin asked.

'For not being good enough,' Sera's voice cracked, making Martin feel sick. She was only acting, the emotion was false. 'Not good enough for Mummy. When Tristan loved me, all that went away. I knew I was worthy of love, because he loved me. Don't you see?'

'So when you found out about his affair with Antonia . . .' Martin said, hating as she did so that she appeared to be understanding this woman in front of her, giving her some kind of rational motive.

'Oh, I knew about that the day I married him. I knew he wanted her. I saw him staring at her at the reception. She always took everything from me. My mother. My husband. But she couldn't have my children. No, no, no,' Sera shook her head, emphatic. 'I would not let her have my children.'

'I see. And Violet? Why did she have to die?'

Sera's eyes swam with tears. 'She may not have come from me, but she was my daughter. She was. She wanted to leave, too. I couldn't let her leave me.'

'But she *has* left you, hasn't she?' Martin said. 'She's not with anyone now. She's soon to be lying cold in the ground, Sera. You made sure of that.'

Sera gave a little laugh. 'You don't understand, Inspector Martin.'

'No, thankfully I don't,' Martin agreed.

Sera looked at her, seeming genuinely puzzled. 'Oh, it's easy. Once they're dead, you can keep them for ever.

They'll always be yours. No one can take them away from you. Not ever, ever, ever.'

After she'd explained, she sat back in silence, a smile playing on her lips. Satisfied, she had the plump, feline look of the cat that has eaten up the cream.

62

After getting off the train from Durham, Jonah shuffled along the street where he lived, head down, eyes half-closed against the daylight. He was nearly at his house. He felt so tired, so weary from it all. The death of Tristan had taken something from him. At first, he'd thought it was a weight that had been lifted. But now . . . now, he couldn't place it. He was suddenly hungry. Hungry like he hadn't been for years. He was ravenous.

Mentally, he went through the cupboards in the kitchen, visualizing their contents. Some rice. Some beans. But he needed more than that. He needed something to fill the cavernous hole that yawned inside him all of a sudden.

He had asked to see Sera before he left. Perhaps there was a chance that she would see him. Explain her hatred to him. Why she had done what she'd done to them all. But she had refused. No letter or note or message, the custody officer had said. She had merely turned her face to the wall.

Jonah lifted his head and saw the corner shop at the end of the street. He hurried along, the sun warm on his back. He felt the pinch of the studs in his waist but he ignored them. Let them bleed.

He was in the shop before he could think about it any more. He filled a basket with bread and jam and digestive biscuits. And then he turned to the back of the shop and picked up a six-pack of Tennent's Super. He took the basket to the counter, without meeting the eyes of the elderly man serving him. As it was all rung through on the cash register, Jonah made a sudden turn back to the shelves; the impulse searing through him like rocket fuel.

Nothing he'd done had ever been right. That policewoman hadn't understood. Hadn't got why he'd had to try to humiliate Tristan, show him up for the liar that he was. Now they all knew, now they saw what he was like. He was no man of God.

Jonah's fingers whispered over the top of the bottle of whisky; moved down, stroking the thick glass filled with amber. From outside the shop, a shaft of sunlight poured in and on to his shoulders. He had been betrayed by them all. All of them except God. And now it seemed as though God were approving his choice. *Take it*, He was saying with his golden light. *Take the bottle and drink. This is my blood and my body.*

Jonah put three bottles of whisky into his basket and shambled back to the till. He watched through his lashes as his things were put into a thin blue plastic bag and he grabbed the handles of it as if he were grabbing at salvation.

And then he walked out into the sunlight. Alone.

The wind blew Antonia's hair into a halo around her head. She could barely see ten feet in front of her, the rain was so heavy. The sky was dark, forbidding, but it seemed right that it should be so; it suited her. She took a sip from the Evian bottle, filled to the brim with neat vodka. She stumbled a little, causing her to grab hold of the concrete balustrade to right herself. It wouldn't do to go too early. She had to think things through first.

Antonia felt her face with the tips of her fingers. It was wet from the rain but also swollen and puffy. She drank more vodka, swallowing deeply. The wind had begun to howl; inscrutable moans. It was only after a moment that Antonia realized that some cries were coming from inside her. It brought her back to childbirth, to that guttural keening that was so much a part of her but also something entirely separate. Where did you end and the pain begin? Or was it all part of the same thing? Pain and happiness; often they seemed to come from the same core, deep inside you, where the truth of everything was hidden.

She had held Violet for only a few moments before she had been taken from her. How was that fair? she thought. She'd had to watch Violet grow up from the sidelines. Watched her child run to her sister when she was happy or in pain, watched her throw her arms around someone else, give Sera the secret smile that only connects those so close it's impossible to divide. As she grew, Violet even seemed to despise her. She resented her for the relationship with Tristan – as if Antonia had any choice in that, after a while. She would have done anything to have ended it after Violet was born. She would have given anything, said anything, paid anything . . . just to hold her daughter close to her chest and know that she would remain there.

But the church had to be protected at all costs. Antonia had forced herself to observe the convenience of the lie with the detachment of a stranger. Tristan wanted to protect himself, not the church. Everything was done for Tristan – for him and because of him. And so, when he took her roughly into the room at the back of the hall; and held the back of her head against a wall and pushed into her, knocking her again and again against the cool concrete, until he moaned and jerked himself inside of her: she would say to herself over and over that if he was happy, she could stay near Violet; if he was happy, she could stay near Violet. Once he had finished, wiped himself clean and zipped himself up, Antonia would pull down her skirt and lean for a moment longer against the wall, planning how to get out of there without her sister seeing.

After all of that, who could blame her for a little drink now and again? Antonia dribbled some vodka as she laughed out loud. Yes, the affair with Tristan had begun as far back as his wedding to Sera . . . but after the twins, Antonia thought, wiping her chin, if it hadn't been for her begging, Tristan would never have had Sera back in the house. Sera always had to control things. She always told the story of their mother leaving them as if it had only happened to her. It made Antonia sick. What about her? What about Antonia?

So fuck you, Sera! Antonia cried into the wind. *Get your ghosts out of me! Leave me alone!*

She bent her head to the balustrade, her body trembling with sobs.

It was nearly time.

Violet was gone. It was time to go and join her. Together at last.

Antonia drained the bottle and grimaced slightly before tossing it on to the ground. She smoothed back her wet hair and tried to dry her eyes as best as she could in the pouring rain.

She heard the sound of a faraway click and took a breath, gazing down at herself. Apart from her face, she was looking all right. Still skinny, despite the booze, and her hair was good. She would look okay in the morgue, she thought with some satisfaction.

She took a photo out of her jeans pocket and looked down at Violet as a baby. She had been such a pretty child.

As the train rounded the bend, Antonia pushed herself off the balustrade and let herself run freely down the bank. And for that last moment she was free, thinking only of her daughter, as she stepped on to the track and turned to face the hissing, squealing cacophony of the train as the driver tried to brake, before smacking into Antonia and sending her into dark and blissful peace.

63

They had been inside the interview room now for nearly two hours.

For a moment, nothing was said. The only sound was their breathing against the mechanical hum of the recording equipment.

'Tell me why you came to Durham, Sera? Why did you want to come here with Tristan?' Martin said at last. 'Tell me what happened to him. Please Sera. Please . . . just talk to me.'

Sera met Martin's eyes with her own. Something passed between them: a darkening or a lightening, it wavered on the edge of the room and then seemed to settle inwards, a feather dancing down to the flat of the table.

'They closed the Durham branch of the church about a year ago,' Sera said quietly. 'I deal with a lot of the emails, the admin. I saw it was closing. They hadn't been getting any funds from headquarters for some time. It wasn't financially viable any more. Thinking about this place, here. So near to home. It brought back memories. I . . . I don't know why I didn't tell anyone.'

'You didn't tell Tristan or Fraser that the Durham branch had closed?'

'No. Then, not long after that, Tristan and I had a fight. He took me into a church near where we live – where we don't know anyone else. He wanted me alone, you see. He wanted me vulnerable.

'He said horrendous things. I'd been getting upset about the affairs, the constant . . . it was just so constant. Never any respite. But he wouldn't accept what I said. We had a terrible row. He threatened me with taking Violet away. Brought up what had happened to the twins. For the first time, I thought then that . . .' Sera looked up at the ceiling. 'That life would be better without him.'

Martin held her breath, feeling Tennant stiffen beside her.

'We were arranging the tour. I suggested Durham. Made out like I was in touch with the coordinator up there . . . I didn't really know what I was going to do, but I thought sometimes that it might be right. It was a game I played with myself. A fantasy. That maybe, by God's grace, he should be removed here. Where I had grown up.'

'When you say removed, you mean . . .?'

'Killed. Sent back to the Lord.'

Martin breathed in, her pulse quickening. Was this the confession? She felt, rather than saw, Tennant's scrawling of that reply on his notepad. 'Did you choose the bed and breakfast? The Riverview?'

Sera shook her head. 'Fraser found it. Normally we'd stay in better places, but . . .' She fell silent again for a moment, considering the space in front of her as if she were watching a film playing in the particles of air. 'Later — when Violet and I were in that hotel you put us in, she said she'd had enough. That she wanted to leave. I couldn't bear it.' Sera began to cry, tears streaming down her cheeks. 'I couldn't let her go. My baby. I wanted her with me for ever,' she sobbed. 'That's why I took her. That's why. And then, when *you* turned up,' Sera snarled at Martin, 'we had to run. I didn't know where to go . . . I could only think of one place. The place where everything had started. Where all the unhappiness began . . .'

'Peterlee,' Martin finished for her.

Sera's head dropped to her chest. Her shoulders shook with the sobs that racked her small frame. 'I loved her. My Violet. I really loved her.'

Martin watched her, wondering how things had grown so twisted in Sera's mind. How she could perceive the world in such a dangerous and hate-filled way. Sera might not believe it to be true but, like many victims of bullying, she, too, had become a bully. She didn't love Violet: she only loved herself.

Martin shook her head, passing an empty polystyrene cup between her hands for a moment. 'I think we've said all we can say about Violet's death, Sera. You've been charged with her murder and you will have to answer that charge in court. As I said before, I want to speak to you about Tristan. But perhaps you'd like to take a break now?'

Sera looked confused. 'I don't understand . . . What more is there to talk about?'

'The murder of your husband, Mrs Snow,' Tennant said patiently, as if to a child.

'But . . .' Sera frowned, pursing her lips. 'I didn't do that . . . I didn't kill Tristan. I thought about it, yes. But I didn't *do it*. When he died, everything changed. Don't you see? That's why I needed to do something. To keep her *with me*.'

Something rankled with Martin – something Sera had just said. She glanced at Tennant but his head was back down, focused on his notes. 'Perhaps,' Martin carried on. 'But it seems fairly straightforward that you had good reason to want Tristan dead, Sera. Like I said at the beginning of the interview, who cares, right? The man was a violent bully. Just like your father. I don't blame you for wanting to smash his head in.'

'No, no,' Sera answered, alarmed. 'You've got it wrong. I didn't kill him.' She shuddered in her seat, sinking into herself, her eyelids lowered. She had fastened herself up inside again. 'I don't know,' she said, putting her hand over her mouth as if to stop herself screaming. 'I don't know anything. Please let me go now. I don't want to talk any more.'

PART FOUR

Not too little, not too much: there safety lies . . .

Euripides, 'Medea'

64

Martin was at her desk, staring into space and sipping at a peppermint tea, when Jones hustled into the room, her arm free of the sling. 'I've had a call, Boss – on the Snow case – from Operation Awaken in Blackpool – their dedicated task force for looking into child sexual exploitation. They've been given the brief to investigate the Deucalion Church.' Jones grimaced at the idea of being landed with this assignment. 'I spoke to a good lad across there, Dave Crowther. Talking to him, I think it would be worth going over, seeing what they're doing. Seeing if we can help with anything . . . Share some intel about Tristan Snow.'

Martin continued to look at the screen, saying nothing.

'Boss? What d'you think? Worth a trip or not?'

Martin shook her head a little, bringing herself out of the trance. 'Sera Snow's on remand for the murders, under psychiatric watch until her trial. If anything transpires from a trip to Blackpool, we can re-interview her.' She pushed her chair back and stood up, a dogged expression on her face. 'Tennant checked with Lancashire CID. Mercy Fletcher – or Vicky Sneddon – hasn't been told about Violet's death. Least not by them. Maybe if we talk to her, tell her about her friend, what's been going on, it might change her mind about speaking to us. We can drive across to Blackpool tomorrow if the team there are agreeable.'

'Well if Mercy will talk, it will help. They're between a rock and a hard place, frankly. Only one other girl has come forward after Nina.' Jones glanced ruefully towards Martin. 'Crowther says he's sure there are more, but they're nervous about coming forward. At least the press have shut up about it a bit for now. But that's put a lot of them off talking to anyone.'

'It's not good enough,' Martin said fiercely, glowering at the sky. 'People must have known about Tristan. They're just not saying. Nobody ever bloody says anything about him. But it must go deeper than that. Fraser Mackenzie pimped Nina Forster to Snow. He must know something, I'm sure of it.'

'Difficult though, isn't it? If no one will talk . . .'

'Mercy has to talk. I need to try with her anyway.' Martin scooped her hair up away from her neck and exhaled loudly. 'Shall we get lunch, Jones?' She turned to exit the office, talking as she went. 'When I think about it. Teaching all those children those untruths,' Martin glared down the corridor as if at some invisible manifestation of all that was wrong with the world. 'Some of the YouTube videos I've seen: creationism, calling abortion murder, having them hold ten-day-old plastic foetuses in their hands. They talk to them about going into politics, curing the country of its diseases,' she continued in disgust, as they walked towards the lifts. 'If that isn't abuse – brainwashing small kids, kids as young as four or five – I don't know what is.'

Jones was silent, turning her engagement ring around on her finger. 'Yep. But that's freedom of speech for you,' she said at last.

Martin exhaled loudly. 'That it is, Jones. That it is.'

They reached Blackpool after a Burger King on the way, in a drizzly early autumn rain. They decided to try to see Mercy before going to speak to Operation Awaken in the hope they would then have some information to impart once they met the team. Jones had put Mercy's address into the GPS and they were guided through the Blackpool suburbs by the grating American accent of the satnav's disembodied voice.

Martin pulled up shortly afterwards in front of a meanly proportioned terraced house, lace curtains concealing its interior. The women stared at the frontage, where the front door sat squarely on the pavement, unprotected by any boundary or garden.

'Not much money,' Martin observed, getting out of the car. She rapped on the door and waited. Inside the house a baby screamed, followed by some yelling. After a moment, the door was flung open to reveal a red-faced woman wearing pink velour jogging bottoms and a Fruit of the Loom T-shirt. She had a muslin square over her shoulder and dark circles under her eyes.

'What d'you want?' Mercy asked, in an exasperated voice. 'I'm trying to get the baby down and she's just sicked her milk up all over the carpet.'

'Vicky Sneddon?' Martin said. The girl nodded. 'We'd really like to talk to you, if you've got just a couple of minutes.' Martin and Jones showed her their identification and Mercy looked daggers at them. 'I know you don't want to speak,' Martin cut in, before the girl could tell them to piss off. 'But it's really important. It's about Violet,' she said, her eyes calm, wide in their appeal. 'You remember Violet Snow, don't you Vicky? She was your friend, wasn't she? Your best friend.'

'What about her?' Mercy said, her body half-turned back inside the house. Martin could smell laundry detergent and boiled vegetables. The front door led directly on to the minuscule front room where Martin could see that the television was on, some daytime soap in which a blonde woman was dying dramatically in a hospital bed. Upstairs, the baby continued to cry aggrieved and hiccupping sobs.

'Violet is dead, Vicky. I'm sorry,' Martin said gently.

The girl's face turned pale and she swayed a little on her feet.

'Come on love,' Jones said, stepping forward and steering Mercy by the elbow. She led her into the house and sat her down on the sofa.

'Dead?' Mercy asked over the racket. 'How?'

Martin sat on the armchair next to her and leaned forward in earnest. 'We need to have a chat, Vicky. About everything. How about we make you a cuppa, eh? While you see to the little one. And then we can have a chat.'

Mercy nodded and gave a little sniff. She moved her head in the direction of the ceiling, where the baby's cries had now turned into a noise Martin couldn't even place, a visceral and wild bellowing. Mercy looked bone tired, exhausted beyond anything Martin could imagine. She pulled herself up and stomped up the stairs slowly. Gradually the howling diminished and eventually stilled.

The women looked around the room. A sofa and chair faced a television in the corner. Every available space was covered in soft toys, empty baby bottles, white muslins, mugs of half-drunk tea and baby wipes – some used, some still in their packets. 'Is this . . .' Martin started, waving her hand around, '. . . is this . . .?'

'What having a newborn's like?' Jones said, with a grin. 'Well, I'm no expert but me mam had three. Can be pretty chaotic.'

Martin saw Jones glance down at her engagement ring, which glinted in the dismal light of the cottage. She shook herself internally, annoyed at her awkwardness in this scene of domesticity. 'Better get the kettle on, Jones. She could do with one, it looks like.'

'Right you are,' Jones said cheerily.

After a while, Mercy came down the stairs, a baby monitor in her hand. She still looked shocked by the news and seemed to sleepwalk to the sofa, where she sat down on a discarded dressing gown. She put the monitor on the coffee table; the heavy, sleepy breaths of a baby making the green lights flicker a little on the screen. She roused herself, saying, 'She's an angel, really. Just got a bit of reflux. Drive you crazy, they do, little buggers. But I wouldn't send back my Paige for all the world.'

'Is your husband at work, Vicky?' Martin asked. 'We heard you'd got married recently.'

She nodded. 'Yeah, Colm works at the motorbike place down the road. A real petrolhead, he is.' She managed a small smile before remembering what she'd heard. 'I can't believe it. About Violet. How did she die?'

Jones walked in, precariously holding three mugs of tea. 'Here you go, love. I put a couple of sugars in it. Good for the shock.'

'I'm sorry to say that Violet was murdered, Vicky,' Martin said as she put her mug of tea down on the carpet.

Mercy stared at her, uncomprehending.

'She was killed by her mother,' Martin went on gently. 'You remember her mother, Sera Snow? She's not a well woman,' she said.

'I can't believe it,' Mercy said again. 'I mean, I hadn't seen her in years. Haven't seen anyone from that place in years. Well, apart from Father Jonah once, but that was just for a moment.' She shivered. 'She was my friend,' she said, looking wide-eyed at Martin. 'She didn't deserve that.'

'No, she didn't,' Martin replied. 'And that's why we're here, Vicky. We want you to help us find out what was going on in that place. In the Deucalion Church. We need to understand so we can get justice for Violet. For the children that were there. For you,' she said, holding Mercy's gaze.

Mercy lowered her head immediately, her shoulders stiff and hunched. The breathing of the sleeping baby came warm and calm into the room.

'What happened, Vicky?' Jones asked. 'Can't you tell us?'

Mercy was quiet, gnawing on her index fingernail, staring at the baby monitor. She closed her eyes for a brief moment before forcing herself to look at Martin. 'I was very young when I first went to Deucalion,' she said. 'Mum took me at the start – I must have been about five. They were lovely there. Steve – that's my dad – left us about then,' she said without rancour. 'Mum was lonely, I think. Wanted some help and support.' She gave a small, bitter laugh then, jerking her chin upstairs to where the baby slept. 'I can empathize now, right?'

She was bright, Martin thought. She observed things well, was sensitive.

'We used to go quite regularly,' Mercy continued in a nervous voice, but it had strength to it. She was going to face her demons until they were gone. 'Then Mum got a job and didn't have as much time. So she'd drop me off. I'd go to the Bible classes a lot. They had Kids School on a Sunday – all day it used to run.'

'What would happen at Kids School?' Martin asked.

'It was fun. Most of the time.' Mercy stared into space as if she were back there, watching herself at the church in an old home movie. 'We'd play games in the loft. Listen to music.'

Something burned in Martin's brain as Mercy talked. What had she just said that had caused it? She tried to think back, but Mercy was continuing, running a hand over her face.

'It's sad, when I think about it. How desperate we all were.'

'Desperate for what?' Martin queried, still trying to get what it was that was nagging at her.

Mercy looked openly back at Martin, her voice level. 'Desperate for their love, for their attention.' She coughed. 'I think – looking back – that I wanted a father figure of sorts. You know?'

Martin nodded.

'I needed someone in my life, someone who would love me.'

She paused then, as the baby gave a small cry. The women waited, listening hard, waiting for more. After a while, when no further sound came, Mercy carried on. 'Violet and I were inseparable. And Sera . . . she was like a mother to me. They looked after me. Took me into their home, their family.'

Mercy stopped again, but this time her eyes were filled with tears.

Martin waited, her nails digging into her palms, out of sight of the girl. What was coming? It was like standing at the top of floodgates, waiting for them to burst.

'Just before we went to Margate; that was when it started.' She stared at them in misery. 'The abuse.'

'How old were you?' Jones asked.

'Ten,' Mercy replied. 'At first, I was confused. I didn't know what to think. I liked him, looked up to him. Everyone did. He told me that I was special. That I was his special chosen one.' Mercy spat out the words with vitriol.

'How long did it go on for?' Martin asked.

'Until I left the church. When I was twelve, I changed schools. Went to a different one from Violet. I told my mum I didn't want to go back to the church. She didn't care by then. She'd got remarried. I went to a new school and when I left, I changed my name. Got married. Made sure I never saw any of them, ever again.' Mercy sat back in her chair, grey with exhaustion.

'You never went to the police?' Jones questioned.

Mercy laughed as if tasting something sour, biting again at her fingernails. She didn't answer.

'Did you ever talk to Violet about it?' Martin said.

'No. How could I? I told a friend of mine at our school once. Caroline, I think it was. But I made her swear not to tell anyone. I was frightened. I thought no one would believe me. And I was right. They didn't.'

Martin tensed at that. 'They didn't? Meaning you *did* tell someone? Someone who didn't believe you?'

Mercy began to look about the room like a caged animal.

'It's all right, Mercy. Vicky, I mean,' Martin said quickly, her palms facing down, trying to appease her. 'Just take your time.'

'I need a fag,' Mercy said, with a grimace. 'Gave up, didn't I? When Paige came along. I'm gagging for one now, though.'

Martin and Jones looked helplessly at her, neither having any cigarettes.

'Doesn't matter,' Mercy said with a sigh.

'Who did you tell?' Martin asked quietly. 'Who was it that didn't believe you?'

Mercy looked at her, seeming to weigh it up. 'He told me I had asked for it. That it was my fault. And then at Margate, he showed me. Showed me how unclean I was.'

'Who showed you?' Martin said, confused. 'This was a different person from your abuser?'

Mercy nodded, her fingers red raw from where she had been biting. 'The person I told? He started doing it as well. They were in on it together. *Bastards.*' She began to cry openly, tears streaming down her cheeks.

'Who was it?' Martin repeated, stubborn. She wanted to hug the girl but she wanted the information more.

Mercy raised her head, wide-eyed. 'Tristan Snow.'

367

Martin ran a hand through her hair, bewildered. 'He was the one you *told*?'

'Yes,' Mercy said patiently, sniffing. She hugged her arms around herself as the baby began to mewl through the monitor again. 'At Margate,' she said, standing up to fetch her child.

'But then who was it who first started the abuse?' Martin asked desperately, wanting to get it before the girl went upstairs.

Mercy stopped midway across the carpet. She flung the name at Martin like a spear.

'It was that fucker that worked for him.' She spat the name out with loathing, skewering his name with her tongue. 'Fucking Fraser Mackenzie.'

65

They arrived at the church at dusk. The building was or-
dinary: a brown, prefabricated block with only the golden,
up-lit glow of a cross above the front door to advertise
its purpose. To one side of the door was a large poster
displaying a smiling middle-aged man with white hair and
broad shoulders. 'The new big cheese. The King is dead,
long live the King,' Martin observed. 'Are the Lancashire
boys on their way?'

'Yep,' Jones said checking her phone.

'Where to start, Jones? Eh?' Martin said dismally, shuffling from foot to foot as they waited. This case could be
the death of her, she felt. Physically she felt exhausted,
and the whorls of this family and the people they had
damaged seemed to swirl endlessly around her, pushing
her down, down, to the bottom of a well.

'We'll get him, Boss. We've got Mercy's testimony.
Nina's . . .' Jones said brightly, trying to imbue Martin with
enthusiasm.

'Her word against his,' Martin's voice was flat.

'Operation Awaken can interview every single member
of the congregation. Someone will have seen something.
He won't get away with it.'

Martin shook her head, staring at the poster of the new
Reverend. 'And Tristan?'

Jones looked confused. 'What about him?'

'Where's the justice for him?'

'What do you mean? We've charged Sera.'

Martin frowned as a gust of damp wind rattled at their shoulders. 'Think about it, Jones. What we've heard just now with Mercy. It's always stuck in my throat that Sera was guilty of killing him. Why *then*, after all that time? Even after what she said, about taking them to Durham, it doesn't make sense to me. I think she made a decision a long time ago to stick with Tristan, through good and bad.' She shrugged, shoving her hands in her pockets. 'Mainly bad, true. But she planted her flag when she denounced her dad, didn't she? Everything she's done, the terrible things she's done . . . they've all been for Tristan in a messed up kind of way. For the love of him. And the children.'

'What are you saying?' Jones asked. 'That she didn't kill him?' She waited, but Martin didn't respond. 'But what she said – about sending him back to the Lord? In the interview transcripts. That's why they came to Durham in the first place.'

'I've always said it. If Sera had killed Tristan, why would she want to plant the nightdress which effectively framed Violet for it? Why would she want to do that to the girl she loved, considered to be her daughter? It's not logical. And,' Martin pointed her finger at Jones as a few rogue drops of rain began to spit. 'Whether Sera wanted them to come to Durham or not, she didn't choose the B&B, did she? Why did the Snows end up there with Eileen Quinn? It was like inviting Tristan to a party where all the people who hated him were gathered.' Martin jumped a little on her feet, impatient. 'Come on Jones, let's go in. They're taking for ever with the back-up,' she said, crossing over the road towards the church.

'And remember what Mercy told us?' she continued as Jones scuttled alongside her to keep up, worriedly looking down the road, hoping for the MIT team to arrive. 'Something was bothering me when she was talking in her house and it just came into my head now,' Martin said. 'She told us that the kids were desperate for love. That they'd come to the kids' Sunday School and play games and have fun in the loft . . . Jonah Simpson mentioned the loft, too.' Martin halted in front of the church entrance and turned to Jones. 'What lives in lofts, Jones?'

Jones looked at Martin in silence, comprehension spreading across her features. 'Pigeons,' she said eventually.

'Pigeons,' Martin replied, turning her face to the cross glinting above them in the blackening skies.

Martin pushed open the door and carried on into the body of the church, up the aisle where a small stained-glass window of Jesus smiled beatifically down on them both in the gloomy light.

'Can I help you?' a voice came from behind them.

'We're looking for Fraser Mackenzie,' Martin said, as she and Jones held out their identification cards.

'He's out at a meeting,' said an elderly woman with some papers in hand as she approached. 'I've just been tidying up the orders of service for Sunday,' she commented on seeing their photo ID, as if she'd been asked to account for herself. 'He won't be long. Why don't you wait here? It's cold outside.'

'Thank you,' Martin answered. 'No chance of a cup of tea, is there?'

'Yes! Of course, I'm sorry. I should have asked.' The woman fumbled with her papers. 'Milk and sugar?'

'Please.' Martin smiled.

Their host exited in the opposite direction and, after a moment, they could hear the rattle of china in the kitchen to the side of the church entrance.

'Shouldn't we wait for the MIT? And you don't take sugar . . .' Jones said, as Martin turned back towards the altar.

'I know I don't. But I do want to have a look around before Mackenzie gets back.' Martin walked briskly along the benches that served as pews and looked in a door positioned next to the lectern. 'Choir changing rooms,' she muttered, sniffing disagreeably at the aroma of socks and teenage hormones that emerged. As she carried on, around the church, she had a flash of what the space would be like filled with people. People with golden shining faces, their hands in the air, singing loudly to their God. Martin could picture Tristan, who once strode among them, placing his hand on their heads, giving them hope.

But it was false, she thought as she walked beside the pictures of the saints and the scrolls of the prayers. The hope that he gave came with a price: that he – Tristan – would be adored. Why wasn't it possible to love God without a middle man? Martin wondered. Why did that message get so skewed? What made those very men subsume their faith for the desire of nothing more base than power?

She crossed past the pulpit and opened the other door. 'Bingo,' she said to Jones, and they entered a dark, enclosed space. Jones pulled the door closed behind and a hush enveloped them. Martin felt that prickle of adrenalin she always got when she went into a place where she shouldn't be. It reminded her of childhood games, of hide-and-seek and playing sardines, creeping under beds and lying down on quiet carpets next to balls of dust.

They were in a small footwell at the bottom of some stairs; Martin moved quickly to climb them.

'What is this?' Jones asked, following. 'What are you looking for?'

Martin didn't answer but continued to climb and, within seconds, they had reached the top where a closed trapdoor lay above them in the ceiling.

'I'm sure it's not the time to mention that we don't have a warrant,' Jones said.

'You're right, it's not,' Martin said, pushing against the wooden door. She lifted it easily and carried on up, opening it on to twilight, a soft sound pulsating around them as they emerged into a chilly, damp dusk.

'What is this place?' Jones asked. 'What's that noise?'

They were standing underneath a wooden roof in the shape of an upturned boat. On the ground were big patches of old carpets covered in beanbags and behind them, a rickety wall made of bamboo. To one side of them was a makeshift wall made of MDF covered in posters and pictures drawn by children. Opposite was another unsecured wall, part of which leaned wide open, exposed to the cityscape. The final section of this lean-to structure consisted of rows of shelves and along each one, roosting and ruffling, were twenty or so zinc-coloured pigeons.

Martin and Jones stared at them in silence.

Martin saw it at once – where the beanbags were, Mercy and Violet, all the children scrabbling around, playing Monopoly up here: their own secret den. All under the gaze of the nesting pigeons. 'The loft,' she said, finally.

She went over to look at one: a fat bird, the colour of smoke. Around its wrinkled and gnarly ankle was a tiny white tag. 'Well, that answers one question,' she said. 'Carrier pigeons. That's how he got the pigeon to Durham before he broke its neck.'

'But why would Mackenzie want to put one at the crime scene?'

'Deucalion,' Martin said. 'He's rubbing it in Tristan's face. 'It wasn't Deucalion – Noah – who found the land, was it? That bit of the story always gets forgotten. It was actually the pigeon, the dove.

'Tristan's been lording it over them all for years. Mackenzie is shaming him with that pigeon. Belittling *him* for once.'

'Risky move. It brings us right back to the church.'

'Mackenzie *is* a risk taker. Look at the chances he's taken with the church finances. Plus he couldn't have known that Mercy – or Nina – would come forward.'

'That's always been a possibility, though.'

'Enough time has passed when nobody's said anything. And there's no evidence of Mackenzie himself being involved. Everything leads to Tristan. Without Mercy's evidence, we'd have nothing. Violet never spoke up, neither did Sera. And who told us Sera was dangerous in the first place?'

'Mackenzie,' Jones said.

'He set us up. He wanted us to find out about the twins so that we'd focus on Sera as the obvious killer.'

'So why plant Violet's nightdress?' Jones asked, the wind lifting her fringe off her face.

'Same reason as he booked them all in to the Riverview B&B,' Martin said. 'He presented us with a whole raft of potential killers. So many, for a while, we couldn't see the wood for the trees,' she said, grimly.

The loft was silent apart from the sound of their breathing in the dim light of the dying day. But then a shaft of yellow light slammed into the space like a gun-shot from below.

They heard the sound of footsteps.

'Can I help you, Inspector Martin?' Fraser Mackenzie climbed carefully up into the middle of where the two women stood. He stood in shadow from where he'd mounted through the trapdoor, his back against the lights which now burned brightly from the stairwell. He was wearing his ubiquitous well-cut suit, a tie hanging loosely from his neck. He smelt of whisky and a pungent aftershave.

'Mr Mackenzie,' Martin brazened, 'glad you're back. We wanted to talk.'

'And to look, from what I can see,' Mackenzie said with a cock-eyed smile, taking in the pigeons and the loft. 'Got a warrant, have you?'

Martin shifted on her feet with a proprietary air. 'Oh no, we don't need a warrant in this case,' she said, folding her arms.

'What case is that?' Mackenzie walked over to a bean-bag and budged it a little with his foot.

Martin could barely see him, it had turned so dark. She could just see the outline of his face in the square of light coming from the open trapdoor. 'We've just been in town, catching up with someone. Thought we'd stop in and see you while we're here. I've just got a couple more questions to run past you, if I can?'

Mackenzie inclined his head with a smirk.

'Just a small point,' Martin said, 'but why did you book Tristan Snow into the Riverview boarding house?'

He shrugged. 'Picked a name out of a hat.' Pigeons cooed as he talked, as if welcoming a friend.

Martin nodded, that familiar roil of excitement bubbling up in her. 'I see. Just picked somewhere nice and cheap? Wasn't to do with planting Snow in a place with an old girlfriend? Make him feel a little insecure, on the back foot?'

Mackenzie laughed as his shadow moved about the loft. 'No. How would I know that? Who was the old girlfriend?'

'Eileen Quinn.'

Martin could sense Mackenzie's studied repulsion even with the lack of light. 'Not your type?' she asked.

'Not really.'

'I expect you like them a little bit younger, don't you?'

Mackenzie turned his face and, for a moment, it caught the light. Like a hawk on a hunt, Martin noticed his cheek twitch, and she smiled.

She'd got him.

'And there's one other thing I don't know,' Martin said.

Mackenzie transferred his weight to his other foot as Jones moved imperceptibly around to flank Martin.

'What did you do with whatever it was you wore when you killed him? Or did you wear something over yourself, you know, to protect your clothes?'

'I don't know what you're talking about, Inspector Martin,' Mackenzie said wearily. 'Please. Unless you have anything useful to impart, can we go downstairs? It's cold and I've got work to do.'

Martin reached for her torch in her jacket pocket. 'Do you mind? Can't see a thing up here.' She flicked it on, sweeping the beam over Mackenzie's face. 'I'm sure you have got work to do: settling in the new pastor. Making sure things run on as before. Wouldn't want anyone to ruin this little set-up you've got, would you? Need to sort out that little Winterbourne fiasco for a start, right?'

Martin leaned in closer to Mackenzie as he held a hand up to block the glare of the torch. 'I reckon you dumped your clothes in some other bin, far away from Riverview. Just as you did with the exorcism cross which you'd help-fully wrapped in Violet Snow's nightdress to try and pin the blame on her. An eighteen-year-old.' Martin's voice dripped with scorn.

'The thing is,' she continued, turning round and running her hand along the shelves where the pigeons sat, flicking the light from one to another; they stirred with unease at the approach of a stranger. 'You might be a nasty pae-dophile. All these years, helping your mate Tristan get a little action from the kids that come here. From the young fans that trusted him. But you're not only that, are you? You're a *greedy*, nasty paedophile. Tristan found out about your financial fuck-up and that was it for you. You were out. So you threatened him with a little show-and-tell. Let's tell the world what Tristan Snow is *really* like. Not the clever, charismatic entertainer he comes across as on TV. But a grubby little pervert.

'But he throws it right back at you. You were both in that sordid little mess together. If one of you told the public about what you'd been up to, the other was in the same amount of trouble. And it would have been a great deal of trouble.

'You were stuck. So you planned it all very carefully. You knew Sera would be the obvious suspect. Wounded, embittered wife that she was. We'd all probably have some sympathy for her. But, just in case that didn't work, you thought you'd drag in a few other options. Violet. Eileen. Even Antonia.'

'What do you mean, Antonia? I didn't pour acid on her face,' Mackenzie exclaimed. 'This whole barrage is farcical. All of it.'

'No,' Martin said quietly. 'Violet put acid on Antonia's face. Because when you opened this little can of worms, snakes came out instead. Fat, writhing, hot and angry snakes with years and years of unhappiness and fear and nastiness. All the time, you've been there in the background, whispering in ears, playing with them all. All of those poor, messed-up people. All fucked up because of you.'

'What else, Martin? Anything else you'd like to throw in with the kitchen sink? Lord Lucan perhaps? JFK? Surely you can come up with a few more *salubrious* crimes to put to my name?'

'No. Just Reverend Snow's murder. And the years of child abuse you'll also be charged with.'

'Oh please, I haven't abused anybody,' Mackenzie sneered. 'What about Tristan? What about what *he* did? Why don't you look into that instead of pointing your finger at innocent people?'

'We have looked into that. We're investigating all the current allegations of abuse. And we'll look into any more of them that are made in the future. All of them, every single one.'

'He's dead, Martin,' Mackenzie said. 'Who cares any more? He got what he deserved.'

'I care,' Martin said. 'I care very much.'

'I don't believe it, Martin. You don't care about Tristan – another paedo off the streets. And nobody cares about those kids either. They were left here. No one wanted them. People couldn't have been bothered less. We *looked after them*.' Mackenzie's eyes dipped to beyond where Martin stood, and the scream of the torch light, to the edge of the loft where the city gleamed. The pigeons rustled again, their wings chafing against each other. They seemed to be gathering in closer, coagulating as one blackened ball of feathers.

'We've spoken to Mercy, Mr Mackenzie,' Martin said. 'She's told us about the abuse. What you and Tristan did to children here, right here in this place.'

'It's not true,' Mackenzie said in a suddenly strangled voice, his face sweaty and flushed in the harsh white glare. He continued to look past Martin, to the skyline where the wind whipped and rolled.

'With vulnerable children,' Martin carried on, relentless. 'Kids whose parents weren't around, kids who came here, *to a church*, looking for love, for comfort. And instead . . . they got you and Tristan subjecting them to horrific acts. All in the name of God . . . You make me sick, Mackenzie. You're the vile little boy who never grew up. Even your dog didn't like you. And that's why you like little girls isn't it? Easy to reel them in. Better to do the deceiving than to ever be the one betrayed.'

'You can never prove it,' he said. 'It's her word against mine.'

'There are others, Fraser,' she answered. 'It's over. It's time to face it.' She edged in closer, her hand in the air, reaching for Mackenzie. Her fingers seemed ghostly in the light of the torch, searching, trying to grapple with what lay beneath the man.

He wouldn't do it, she realized. He wouldn't allow it to end like this.

Mackenzie seemed to freeze, as if the decision were made. Martin saw where his eyes led, saw his intake of breath, the energy coil up in him.

'Don't do it,' she warned. 'Don't do something you'll regret.'

His head rocked from side to side, his pupils dilated, his knuckles white as his hands curled into fists.

'It's over,' Martin repeated. 'It's time to come with us.'

He gave a violent cry, pushing past her, hurtling towards the edge of the roof. Jones stepped out to grab him, his shirtsleeves tearing through her fingers as he shoved her too, out of the way.

Martin, though, stayed rooted as she watched him run out towards the city and throw himself off the edge, spinning forwards in the air as he fell. She moved at last to kneel at the side, bending over, seeing his face as he tumbled for the last time, down to the hard, cold ground, his eyes shut tight for the whole of the journey.

She let him go.

66

Three Months Later

The restaurant was filled with chattering and the clank and bustle of cutlery and glasses chinking. Martin opened the door and walked in past the Christmas tree, the warmth of the room enveloping her as she entered. She saw Jones at the head table, dressed in a long white dress, cream silk roses in her hair above her blow-dried fringe. Her brand new husband sat next to her looking like he'd won the lottery.

Martin moved to where Sam sat at one of the tables with Tennant and his wife, and Fielding next to his partner, Dom. 'Sorry, I had to duck out. The solicitor's about to go on maternity leave so she had to see me today,' she said sitting down. 'The ceremony was lovely though, wasn't it?' She caught the eye of Jones across the room, sparkling and flushed from too much champagne. Martin gave her a grin, which Jones returned, and she felt a rush of affection for her sergeant.

'How did it go?' Sam asked lightly, as he poured her some champagne.

'I'm a free woman,' Martin answered, letting the bubbles fizz over her tongue, letting her shoulders relax. The papers had been signed and, as of an hour ago, she and Jim were no longer married.

'How do you feel?'

'Starving,' Martin said, holding his gaze. 'Have I missed the lunch?'

'Don't worry, Boss,' Tennant said, from the opposite side of the table. 'Only the starter. Smoked salmon. Was all right,' he sniffed. 'Fillet steak and Yorkshires for main, though,' he beamed.

Martin shook her head with a smile, sitting back in her chair as Rob stood to toast his bride. She thought about Sera Snow for a moment, who now sat in the high-security wing of Rampton psychiatric hospital having been found unfit to stand trial. As Christmas songs played through the speakers in the restaurant, she thought about Sera's loyalty to her husband, despite his evil, despite his maltreatment of her. Thank God she wasn't her, Martin thought. Thank God that she was a million miles away from where Sera Snow was.

Despite being surrounded by work colleagues, Martin suddenly didn't care if people knew she was with Sam. She picked up his hand and held it in her own. 'It's going to be a good Christmas, isn't it?' she said.

'Peace and joy to all mankind I expect,' Sam replied, putting her hand to his lips.

Martin nodded, drinking some more champagne, the image of Violet Snow floating into her head for a millisecond before it vanished, leaving only the babble and bonhomie of the wedding around her.

'It's going to be perfect,' she said.

Epilogue

I had a dream last night, Antonia. I've often had it. The dream has sat on my shoulder for many years, tormenting me with fear.

I was in the room at the top of Rapunzel's tower. High walls, cream-rendered cement, stretching up to a curved ceiling, ridged with time. The window was barred.

Rapunzel, Rapunzel, let down your hair.

He sometimes whispered that as he pushed into me from behind. He'd wrap my hair around his wrist, the ends of it split and rough like horsehair. As he rode me.

I sat up in my room, sharp, awake. Butting my head against the glass pane of memories, splintering it until the images exploded into shards raining down on to the bed. My right hand clawed at the woollen blanket.

Today, the porter is coming to take me for a walk in the garden. He brings me my paper. He lets me sharpen my own pencils.

They have told me that you are dead.

I watch the leaves turn and fall, summer into autumn. So many people gone. I am the only one who lives. The only one that matters.

Now I know that you cease to live, Antonia, I wonder if I will continue writing to you? I like writing to you. You understand me beyond anyone else. You understood it all really, didn't you? You pretended not to, but I know you did.

I think I will carry on writing to you, beyond your death. My thoughts. The way I think about the world. There should be a record of it. It's important.

I like the porter. He talks to me about his life. He has a step-daughter. She is the same age as Violet would have been. He promised me he would bring her to visit me. He has other children, too.

Children are so important, aren't they, Antonia? They are the future.

Last Thursday, when he came, he kissed me all the way up my arm.

Nobody saw.

I think there are opportunities to take here.

There always are.

THE END

He just wanted a decent book to read ...

Not too much to ask, is it? It was in 1935 when Allen Lane, Managing Director of Bodley Head Publishers, stood on a platform at Exeter railway station looking for something good to read on his journey back to London. His choice was limited to popular magazines and poor-quality paperbacks – the same choice faced every day by the vast majority of readers, few of whom could afford hardbacks. Lane's disappointment and subsequent anger at the range of books generally available led him to found a company – and change the world.

'We believed in the existence in this country of a vast reading public for intelligent books at a low price, and staked everything on it'
Sir Allen Lane, 1902–1970, founder of Penguin Books

The quality paperback had arrived – and not just in bookshops. Lane was adamant that his Penguins should appear in chain stores and tobacconists, and should cost no more than a packet of cigarettes.

Reading habits (and cigarette prices) have changed since 1935, but Penguin still believes in publishing the best books for everybody to enjoy. We still believe that good design costs no more than bad design, and we still believe that quality books published passionately and responsibly make the world a better place.

So wherever you see the little bird – whether it's on a piece of prize-winning literary fiction or a celebrity autobiography, political tour de force or historical masterpiece, a serial-killer thriller, reference book, world classic or a piece of pure escapism – you can bet that it represents the very best that the genre has to offer.

Whatever you like to read – trust Penguin.